Venus in India

Venus in India

Charles Devereaux

MINT EDITIONS

Venus in India was first published in 1889.

This edition published by Mint Editions 2021.

ISBN 9781513291338 | E-ISBN 9781513294186

Published by Mint Editions®

 MINT
EDITIONS

minteditionbooks.com

Publishing Director: Jennifer Newens
Design & Production: Rachel Lopez Metzger
Project Manager: Micaela Clark
Typesetting: Westchester Publishing Services

Contents

VOLUME I

The war in Afghanistan appeared to be coming to a close when I received sudden orders to proceed, at once, from England to join the First Battalion of my regiment, which was then serving there. I had just been promoted Captain and had been married about eighteen months. It pained me more than I care to express to part with my wife and baby girl, but it was agreed that it would be better for all of us, if their coming to India were deferred until it were certain where my regiment would be quartered, on its return to the fertile plains of Hindustan, from the stones and rocks of barren Afghanistan. Besides, it was very hot, being the height of the hot weather, when only those who were absolutely forced to do so went to India, and it was a time of year particularly unsuitable for a delicate woman and a babe to travel in so burning a climate. It was also not quite certain whether my wife would join me in India, as I had the promise of a staff appointment at home, but before I could enter upon that I had of necessity to join my own battalion, because it was at the seat of war. Thus it was annoying to have to go, all the same, as it was clear that the war was over, and that I should be much too late to participate in any of its rewards or glories, though it was quite possible I might come in for much of the hardship and experience of the sojourn, for a wild, and not to say rough and inhospitable country is Afghanistan; besides which it was quite possible for an Afghan knife to put an end to me, and that I might fall a victim to a common murder instead of dying a glorious death on the battlefield.

Altogether my prospects seemed by no means of a rosy color, but there was nothing for it but to submit and go, which I did with the best grace possible but with a very heavy heart.

I will spare the readers the sad details of parting with my wife. I made no promise of fidelity, the idea seemed never to occur to her or to myself of there being any need for it, for although I had always been of that temperament so dear to Venus, and had enjoyed the pleasure of love with great good fortune before I married, yet I had, as I thought, quite steadied down into a proper married man, whose desires never wandered outside his own bed; for my passionate and loving spouse was ever ready to respond to my ardent caresses with caresses as ardent; and her charms, in their youthful beauty and freshness, had not only not palled upon me, but seemed to grow more and more powerfully attractive the more I reveled in their possession. For my dearest wife, gentle reader, was the life of passion; she was not one of those who coldly submit to their husbands' caresses because it is their duty to do so, a duty however not to be done with pleasure or joyfully, but more as a species of penance! No! With her it was not, "Ah! no! let me sleep tonight, dear. I did it twice last night, and I really don't think you can want it again. You should be more chaste, and not try me as if I were your toy and plaything. No! take your hand away! Do leave my nightdress alone! I declare it is quite indecent the way you are behaving!" and so forth, until, worn out with her husband's pertinacity, she thinks the shortest way, after all, will be to let him have his way, and so grudgingly allows her cold slit to be uncovered, unwillingly opens her ungracious thighs, and lies a passionless log, insensible to her husband's endeavors to strike a spark of pleasure from her icy charms. Ah! no! With my sweet Louie it was far different; caress replied to caress, embrace to embrace. Each sweet sacrifice became sweeter than the one before, because she fully appreciated all the joy and delight of it! It is almost impossible to have too much of such a woman, and Louie seemed to think it quite impossible to have too much of me! It was, "Once more my darling! Just one little more! I am sure it will do you good! and I should like it!" and it would be strange if the manly charm which filled her loving hand, were not once more raised in response to her caresses, and once again carrying rapturous delight to the deepest, richest depths of the trembling voluptuous charm, for the special benefit of which it was formed, a charm which was indeed the very temple of love.

Ah! My beloved Louie! Little did I think the last time I withdrew from thy tender passionate embrace, that between thy throbbing sheath and my sword there were waiting for me, in glowing India, all unknown and unsuspected, other voluptuous women, whose beautiful naked charms were to form my couch, and whose lovely limbs were to bind me in ecstatic embrace, before I should once more find myself again between thy tender, loving thighs! It is best too that thou should'st not know that so it was, for who is there that does not know the dire effects of green-eyed jealousy? Thanks be to tender Venus for having raised an imperious cloud, and hidden my sportings with my nymphs, as in olden days Great Jupiter was hidden from the sight of the Gods and men, when he reveled on the green mountain sides, with the lovely maidens, human or divine, whose beauteous charms formed the object of his passion.

But it is time to descend to earth again and to tell my tale in a manner more befitting this common-place world. Already, dear reader, I have, I fear, trespassed in so far that I have perhaps shocked your modest eyes with the name of that sweetest of feminine charms, which neither sculptor or painter will produce in their works, and which is seldom mentioned in public, except by the low and vulgar; yet I must crave your pardon, and beg you to permit me to offer it here of my pen, else I shall feel it difficult to describe, as I hope to all the full joys I so happily reveled in during the five happy years I spent in Hindustan. If you are wise, if you love to have your senses sweetly tickled, if the usually hidden scenes and secrets of delicious combats of love, of the fulfillment of hot desire, of the happy lovers, have any delight for you then simply imagine that your moist eyes see the charm, but not the name or action, and not the words by which I find it necessary to describe it.

It was in the middle of August when I landed in Bombay, that queenly capital of Western India. The voyage had been unimportant. Our passengers had been few and stupid, chiefly old Indian Civilians and officers returning unwillingly to the scenes of their labors in the hot country, after a short spell of life in England. It was not the season of the year when sprightly young ladies go out to India, each one with the fine hope in her heart that her rounded, youthful charms, her cheeks glowing with health, and her freshness might captivate a husband. We were a staid party; some like myself had left young wives at home, others were accompanied by theirs; all were of an age when time had softened down the burning ardors of passion, and when perhaps the last thought to enter their heads, on retiring at night to rest, was to take advantage of the ruined remains of beauty which reposed by their sides. Presently I landed feeling that all love, passion, desire and affection were left behind me, with my darling little wife in England, and that the all but naked, graceful charms of native girls carrying their water pots, could not but strike my eye when I first landed, no spark of desire for a moment made my blood run quicker, nor caused me for a moment to think that I could ever seek enjoyment in the embraces of any woman much less of a dusky maiden! And yet within only ten short days! Verily, the spirit is willing but the flesh is weak! But let us put it thus, the spirit may be willing, but when the flesh rises in all its vigorous power its strength is indomitable! or, so I found it to be! And now, gentle reader, I am sure you are curious and anxious to know who it was who raised my flesh, and whether I made that resistance of its impervious demands which a husband of such a Louie as mine, should, by right have made.

Having ascertained from the Adjutant General, that my destination was Cherat, a small camping ground, as I heard, on the top of a range of mountains forming the Southern Limit of the Valley of the Peshawar, and having received railroad warrants, via Allahabad, for the temporary station of Jhelum, and dak warrants from the spot to Cherat itself. I made my preparations for the long journey which still lay before me, and amongst other necessaries for mind and body I purchased some French novels. One of these was that masterpiece of drawing-room erotic literature, Mademoiselle de Maupin, by Theophile Gautier. But for the burning pictures of love and passion, drawn in the wonderful prose poem, perhaps I might have escaped from the nets in which love entangled me, for of a surety Mademoiselle de Maupin was a tempting bait which summoned my passions from the lethargy into which they had fallen since I had parted with my beloved, yet virtuous little wife, my adored Louie! I declare, dear reader, that I thought I had sown my wild oats, that I had become what the French call "range" and that it lay not in the power of women to seduce me from the path of virtue, along which it seemed to me, and I believed firmly, that I was treading with certain steps, to the road to sanctity and heaven! So long as I had the protecting aegis of the beautiful and lovely charms of my darling little wife, I was, no doubt, quite safe, for frankly, now that I come to look over the past, I quite see why the tempter's darts fell all unheeded by me. Where could I find another girl, clothed or naked, who could compare with my Louie? She simply eclipsed all others. Like the full moon, shining on a cloudless night, she put out the light of the stars! Alas! when she was absent, the stars began to shine again to find places in my heart for admiration and adoration. I had not thought of this! Had my Louie? And oh! how tender, how passionately voluptuous had the last few weeks of my sojourn at home been! How many times had the fervent protestations of love and faith in one another's unspottable purity of affection been sealed by the rapturous blissful sacrifice, when clasped in one another's arms our bodies became as one, and the fountains of inexpressible bliss, set gushing by our voluptuous enlacements, we inundated one another with seas of enjoyment. These sacrifices, so exquisite, so full of fire and action, had undoubtedly, their aftereffects on me, for some few weeks Louie had, by the power of her never-dying charms, exhausted me of my present stock of that manly strength, that essence of my heart's blood, that marrow of my body, without which physical love is impossible, and it seemed to me that on leaving her I had left that power behind me; that all my desires, together with my manly vigor, were deposited for safe keeping in her exquisite grotto, and that I should not find them again until, once more with her I might seek them between her beloved thighs.

So I bought Mademoiselle de Maupin not caring whether it treated of passion or not, and all alone in my railway carriage I read Mlle. de Maupin, but alas! of human frailty! Desire, hot and burning desire, the power, and floods of hot, hot feeling came back to me! I drank the delicious poison of that matchless book, and as I drank I burnt! and yet I would not own to myself that in my deepest heart it was "woman" I felt a raging thirst for. At present desire simply assumed the shadowy form, a kind of image of a woman the nearest approach to which was to be found in far off England, in the body of my own adored and beautiful little wife!

The route from Bombay via Allahabad to Peshawar runs almost entirely through a country as flat as a table. At the season of year, August, when I traversed it, the land dry, parching weather had apparently not been tempered by the rains, which usually fall between June and September. Here and there green waving crops, contrasted with the otherwise generally brown, burnt up soil, and there were few stretches of country which formed such attraction for the eyes as to call for mental appreciation, in comparison with the charms of the beautiful Mlle. De Maupin, especially as painted by Theophile Gautier, in that glowing chapter where she appears in all her glowing beauty, naked, and burning with tormenting desire, before the eyes of her enraptured lover! oh! Theophile! Why did you not allow your pen to describe, with a little more freedom, those undraped beauties? Why did you not permit us to do more than fancy the exquisite pleasures which the panting lovers experienced on their voluptuous couch? I felt that such minute painting was what was wanted to complete the rapturous sensations raised by that marvelous romance, and, gentle reader, I pray you not to exclaim and cry out, for in these pages I endeavor to avoid the one fault I find with Gautier. May Venus guide my pen and Eros hold the inkstand, and mayest thou, shade of the illustrious French poet and author, assist in these compilations of my reminiscences of the happy five years I spent in India.

Only once on this journey, about which I fear I may become so tedious did the tempter accost me, and then so clumsily as quite to prostrate his well-meant intentions. I had to make a few hours stay in Allahabad and to pass that away pleasantly I wandered about, examining the tombs of the kings and princes, who reigned in past times over the banks of the Ganges and the Jumna, and in seeing such sights as I could find to amuse and interest me.

As I was returning to my hotel a native accosted me in very good English.

"Like to have woman, Sahib? I got one very pretty little half-caste in my house, if master like to come and see!"

Oh! dear Mademoiselle de Maupin! I felt no desire to see the pretty little half-caste! I put this self-abnegation down to virtue, and actually laughed, in my folly, at the idea that there existed, or could exist, a woman in India, who could raise even a ghost of desire in me!

The station beyond Jhelum is reached, I having but one mighty river to pass before I leave the bounds of India proper and tread the outskirts of Central Asia, in the valley of the Peshawar. But it took some two or three days and nights of continuous travel, in a dak gharry, before I reached Attock. The dak gharry is a fairly comfortable mode of conveyance, but one becomes tired of the eternal horizontal position which is the only one which gives any comfort to the weary traveler. Crossing the Indus in a boat rowed over a frightful torrent with the roar of the waters breaking on the rocks below the ferry, was a very exciting incident, especially as it happened at night, and the dark gloom added to its magnifying effect, to the roar of the suspected danger. Then again another dak gharry into which I got, lay down and went to sleep, not to waken until I reached Nowshera.

Ah! Mademoiselle de Maupin! What a lovely girl! Who can she be! She must I fancy, be the daughter of the Colonel commanding here, out for her morning walk, and perhaps, judging from the keen expectant glance shot in at me through the half-open sliding door of the gharry, she's expecting somebody, perhaps her fiancé; perhaps that is why she looked so eager and yet so disappointed!

Oh, dear reader! just as I opened my eyes I saw, through the half-open door a perfect figure of feminine beauty! A girl clothed in close fitting grey colored dress with a Teria hat archly sloped on her lovely and well-shaped head! That beautiful face! How perfect the oval of it! Truly she must have aristocratic blood in her veins to be so daintily formed! What a rosebud of a mouth! What cherry lips! God! Jupiter! Venus! What a form! See those exquisite rounded shoulders, those full and beautiful arms, the shape of each can be so plainly seen so close does her dress fit her: and how pure, how virgin like is that undulating bosom! See how proudly each swelling breast fills out her modest but still desire-provoking bodice! Ah! The little shell-like ears, fitting so close to the head! How I would like to have the privilege of gently pressing those tiny lobes! What a lovely creature she looks! How refined! How pure! How virginal! Ah! My Louie, like you this girl is not to be tempted, and long and arduous would be the chase before she could be compelled to own that her failing strength must yield her charms to the hands and lips of her panting pursuer! No! That girl, of all girls I have seen, struck me as one not to be seduced from the path of purity and honor.

And all these impressions flashed through my mind from a glimpse, a very vivid glimpse it is true, that I had of this lovely girl which I caught of her as my gharryman was urging his jaded steeds to a smart gallop, so that the Sahib might enter Nowshera in proper grand style!

The vision so short and so rapid, appeared to make but little impression on me, or rather, I should say, my sensations did not go beyond the sensations I have given above. Hot desire did not set my blood boiling or my heart and sense afire. I think it was rather the other way. I admired, indeed, as I might also admire a perfect Venus in marble. Shape and form pleased my eyes, and although the idea, that this lovely girl might be possessed some day by someone, did enter my head, it only entered in the same way as that the marble Venus might become flesh and blood and form the happy delight of some fortunate mortal. In other words, she seemed absolutely and completely removed from ordinary mankind, and I never dreamt that I should ever see her mound, as, according to my ideas, I was going to change horses at Nowshera, and proceed immediately to Cherat.

But on arriving at the post office, which was also the place for changing horses, the post master, a civil spoken Baboo, told me that he could give me horses only as far as Publi, a village about halfway between Nowshera and Peshawar, and that from that place I must make the best of my way to Cherat, for there was no road along which dak gharries could be driven, and my good Baboo added that the said interval between Publi and Cherat was dangerous for travelers, there being many lawless robbers. Moreover, he added, that the distance was a good fifteen miles. He advised me to put up at the Public Bungalow at Nowshera, until the Brigade Major could put me in the way of completing my journey.

This information was a great surprise and a great damper to me! How on earth was I to get to Cherat with my baggage if there was no road? How could I do fifteen miles under such circumstances? To think I had gone so many thousand miles, since I had left England, to be balked by a miserable little fifteen. However, for the present there seemed nothing to be done but to take the excellent Baboo's advice, put up at the Public Bungalow and see the Brigade Major.

The Public Bungalow stood in its own compound, a little distance from the high road, and to get back to it I had to drive back part of the road I had traveled. I dismissed my driver, and called the Khansamah, who informed me that the bungalow was full, and that there was no room for me! Here was a pretty state of affairs! but whilst I was speaking to the Khansamah, a pleasant looking young officer, lifting the chick which hung over the entrance to his room, came out into the verandah, and told me that he had heard what I was saying, that he was only waiting for a gharry to proceed on his journey down country, and that my coming was as opportune for him, as his going would be for me. He had, he said, sent at once to secure my dak gharry, and if he could get it, he would give up his room to me, but anyhow, I should, if I did not dislike the idea, share his room which contained two bedsteads. Needless to say I was delighted to accept his kind offer, and I soon had my goods inside the room, and was enjoying that most essential and refreshing thing in India, a nice cool bath. My new friend had taken upon himself to order breakfast for me, and when I had completed my ablutions and toilet, we sat down together. Officers meeting in this manner, very quickly become like old friends. My new acquaintance told me all about himself, where he had been, where he was going to, and I reciprocated. Needless to say the war, which was now practically over, formed the great topic of our general conversation. Getting more intimate, we of course fell, as young men, or old too do, for the matter of that, to discussing about love and women, and my young friend told me that the entire British Army was just simply raging for women! That none were to be got in Afghanistan, and that, taking it as a general rule, neither officers nor men had a woman for at least two years.

"By George!" he cried as he laughed, "the Peshawar Polls are reaping a rich harvest! As fast as a regiment arrives from Afghanistan, the whole, boiling, rush off to bazaars, and you can see the Tommy Atkins waiting outside the knocking shops, holding their staffs in their hands, and roaring out to those having women to look sharp!"

This was of course an exaggeration, but not to so great an extent as my gentle reader may suppose.

We had just finished our cheroots after breakfast, when the young officer's servant drove up in the same dak gharry which had brought me in from Attock, and in a few minutes my cheerful host was shaking hands with me.

"There's somebody in there," he said, pointing to the next room, "to whom I must say goodbye, and then I'm off."

He was not long absent, again shook my hands, and in another minute a sea of dust hid him and the gharry from my sight.

I felt quite lonely and sad, when he was gone, for, although the bungalow was full, I was left in a small portion of it walled off from the rest, so that I didn't see any of its other occupants, though I might occasionally hear them. I had forgotten to ask who my next door neighbor was, and indeed I did not much care. I was so bothered, wondering how I should get up to Cherat. It was now nearly ten o'clock, the sun was pouring sheets of killing rays of light on the parched plain in which Nowshera is situated, and the hot wind was beginning to blow, parching one up, and making lips and eyes quite sore as well as dry. I did not know what to do with myself. It was much too hot to think of going to the Brigade Major's, so I got another cheroot, and taking my delightful Mademoiselle de Maupin out of my bag, I went and sat behind a pillar on the verandah, to shelter myself from the full force of the blast and try to read; but even this most charming damsel failed to charm, and I sank back in my chair and smoked listlessly whilst my eyes wandered over the range of lofty mountains which I could just distinguish quivering through hot yellow-looking air. I did not know at the moment that I was looking at Cherat, and had I had a prescience of what was waiting for me there, I should certainly have gazed upon these hills with far greater interest than I did.

Reader dear, do you know what it is to feel that somebody is looking at you, though you may not be able to see him, nor are aware for a fact that somebody is looking at you? I am extremely susceptible to this influence. Whilst sitting thus idly looking at the most distant thing my eyes could find to rest upon, I began to feel that someone was near, and looking intently at me. At first I resisted the temptation to look round to see who it was. What with the hot wind, and what with the circumstances of the sudden halt I was compelled to make, I felt so irritable, that I resented, as an insult, the looking at me which I felt certain was going on; but at last this strange sensation added to my unrest and I half-turned my head to see whether it was reality or feverish fancy.

My surprise was unbounded when I saw the same lovely face, which I had caught a glimpse of that morning, looking at me from behind the slightly opened chick of the room next to mine, I was so startled that instead of taking a good look at the lady I instantly gazed on the hills again, as if turning my head to look in her direction had been a breach of good manners on my part; but I felt she was still keeping her eyes fixed on me, and it amazed me that anyone of the position which I imagined she held, for I was firmly convinced that I was right as to my surmise that my unknown beauty was a lady, and a Colonel's daughter, she should be guilty of such bad manners as to stare at a perfect stranger in this manner. I turned my head once more, and this time I looked at this lovely but strange girl a little more fixedly. Her eyes, large, lustrous, most beautiful, seemed to pierce mine, as though trying to read my thoughts. For a moment I fancied she must be a little off her head, when, apparently satisfied, with her reconnaissance, the fair creature let the chick fall once more against the side of the door and so was lost to my sight. From that moment my curiosity was greatly aroused. Who was she? Was she alone? Or was she with the unknown Colonel in that room? Why was she staring at me so hard? By Jove! There she is at it again! I could stand it no longer. I jumped up and went into my own room and called the Khansamah.

"Khansamah: who is in the room next to mine?" and I pointed to the door which communicated with the room the lady was in, and which was closed.

A Mem Sahib! Now I had been in India before, this was my second tour of service in the country, and I knew that a Mem Sahib meant a married lady. I was surprised, for had anyone asked me, I should have said that this lovely girl had never known a man, had never been had, and never would be had, unless she met the man of men who pleased her. It was extraordinary how this idea had taken root in my mind.

"Is the Sahib with her?"

"No, Sahib!"

"Where is he?"

"I don't know, Sahib."

"When did the Mem Sahib come here, Khan?"

"A week or ten days ago, Sahib!"

"Is she going away soon?"

"I don't know, Sahib!"

It was plain I could get no information from this man, only one more question and I was done.

"Is the Mem Sahib quite alone, Khan?"

"Yes, Sahib: she has no one with her, not even an Ayah."

Well! this is wonderful! How well did my young friend, who had only gone away this morning, know her? You, gentle reader, with experience, have no doubt your suspicions are that all was not right, but for the life of me I could not shake off the firm notion that this woman was not only a lady, but one exceptionally pure and highly connected.

I went back to my seat on the verandah, waiting to be looked at again, and I did not wait long. A slight rustle caught my ear, I looked around and there was my lovely girl showing more of herself. She still looked with the same eager gaze without the sign of a smile on her face. She appeared to be in her petticoats only, and her legs and feet, such lovely, tiny, beautiful feet, and such exquisitely turned ankles, were bare; she had not even a pair of slippers on. A light shawl covered her shoulders and bosom, but did not hide either her full well-shaped, white arms, her taper waist or her splendid and broad hips. These naked feet and legs inspired me with a sudden flow of desire, as much as her lovely face and its wonderful calm, yet her severe expression, had driven all such thoughts from my mind. Jacques Casanova, who certainly is a perfect authority on all that concerns women, declares that curiosity is the foundation on which desire is built, that, but for that, a man would be perfectly contented with one woman, since in the main all women are alike; yet from mere curiosity a man is impelled to approach a woman, and to wish for her possession. Something akin to this certainly influenced me. A devouring curiosity took possession of me. This exquisite girl's face inspired me to know how she could possibly be all alone here at Nowshera, in a public bungalow, and her lovely naked feet and legs, made me wonder whether her knees and thighs corresponded with them in perfect beauty, and my imagination painted to my mind a voluptuous motte and delicious slit, shaded by dark locks corresponding to the color of the lovely eyebrows, which arched over those expressive orbs. I rose from my chair and moved towards her. She instantly withdrew and as instantly again opened the chick. For the first time I saw a smile wreathe her face. What a wonderfully different expression that smile gave it! Two lovely dimples appeared in her rounded cheeks, her rosy lips parted and displayed two rows of small perfectly even teeth, and those eyes which had looked so stern and almost forbidding, now looked all tenderness and softness.

"You must find it very hot out there in the verandah!" said she, in a low, musical voice, but with a rather vulgar, common accent which at first grated on my ear, "and I know you are all alone! Won't you come into my room and sit down and chat? You will if you are a good fellow!"

"Thank you!" said I smiling and bowing, as I threw away my cheroot and entered whilst she held the chick so as to make room for me to pass. I caught the chick in my hand, but she still kept her arm raised, and extended; her shawl fell a little off her bosom which was almost entirely bare, and I saw not only two most exquisitely round, full and polished globes of ivory, but even the rosy coral marble which adorned the peak of one of them. I could see that she caught the direction of my glance, but she was in no hurry to lower her arm, and I judged, and rightly, that this liberal display of her charms was by no means unintentional.

"I have got two chairs in here," said she, laughing such a sweet sounding laugh, "but we can sit together on my bed, if you don't mind!"

"I shall be delighted," said I, "if sitting without a back to support you won't tire you!"

"Oh!" said she, in the most innocent manner, "you just put your arm round my waist, and then I won't feel tired."

Had it not been for the extraordinary innocent tone with which she said this, I think I should at once have lain her back and got on top of her, but a new idea struck me; could she be quite sane? And would not such an action be the very height of blackguardism?

However, I sat down, as she bade me do, and I slipped my left arm around her slender waist and gave her a little hug towards me.

"Ah!" she said, "that's right! Hold me tight! I love being held tight!"

I found that she had no stays on at all. There was nothing between my hand and her smooth skin but a petticoat body, and a chemise of very light muslin. She felt so awfully nice! There's something so thrilling in feeling the warm, palpitating body of a lovely woman in one's arms, that it was only natural, that not only did my blood run more quickly, but I began to feel what the French call the "pricking of the flesh." There she was, this really beautiful creature, half-naked and palpitating, her cheeks glowing with health, though paler than one is accustomed to see in our more temperate Europe, her lovely shining shoulders and bosom almost perfectly naked, and so exquisite! The nearer I got my eyes to the skin the better did I see how fine was its texture. The bloom of youth was on it. There were no ugly hollows to show where the flesh had receded and the bones projected. Her beautiful breasts were round, plump and firm looking. I longed to take possession of those lovely, lovely bubbies! To press them in my hand, to devour them and their rosy tips with my mouth! Her petticoats fell between her slightly parted thighs and showed their roundness and beautiful form perfectly as though to provoke my desire the more, desire she must have known was burning me, for she could feel the palpitating of my agitated heart, even if a glance of her eyes in another and lower direction did not betray to her the effect her touch and her beauty had on me, she held out one and then the other of her fairy feet, so white and perfect, as though to display them to my eager eyes. The soft and delicious perfume which only emanates from woman in her youth, stole in fragrant clouds over my face, and her abundant wavy hair felt like silk against my cheek. Was she mad? That was the tormenting thought which would spring up between my hand and the glowing charms it longed to seize! For some few moments we sat in silence. Then I felt her hand creep up under my white jacket and toy with the buttons to which my braces were fastened behind. She undid one side of my brace and as she did so said.

"I saw you this morning! You were in a dak gharry and I just caught a glimpse of you."

Her hand began to work at the other button. What the deuce was she up to?

"Oh yes!" I said, looking into her small eyes and returning the sharp glances which shot from them, "and I saw you too! I had been fast asleep, and just as I opened my eyes my sight fell upon you! and I. . ."

She had unbuttoned my braces behind, and now stole her hand round and laid it, back up, on the top of my thigh.

"And you what?" said she, gently sliding her extended fingers down over the inside of my thigh: she was within a nail's breadth of the side of my rod which was now standing furiously!

"Oh!" I exclaimed, "I thought I had never seen such a lovely face and figure in the world!"

The fingertips actually touched Johnnie! She slightly pressed them against him, and looking at me again with the sweetest smile, said:

"Did you really! Well! I'm glad you did, for do you know what I thought, when I saw you lying inside the gharry?"

"No, dear!"

"Well! I thought that I would not mind if I had been traveling with such a fine looking, handsome young man! "

Then after a short pause she continued, " So you think me well made?" And she glanced down proudly on her swelling breast.

"Indeed then I do!" I exclaimed, quite unable to restrain myself any longer. "I don't know when I ever saw such a lovely bosom as this, and such tempting, luscious bubbies!" and I slipped my hand into her bosom and seized a glowing globe and as I pressed it gently and squeezed the hard little nipples between my fingers, I kissed the lovely upturned mouth which was presented to me.

"Ah!" she cried, "who gave you leave to do that? Well! Exchange is no robbery and I will have something nice of yours to feel for myself too!"

Her nimble fingers had my trousers unbuttoned, my braces undone in front too, and with a whisk of her hand she had my shirt out, and with it my burning, maddened stallion, of which she took immediate and instant possession.

"Ah!" she cried, "Ah! oh! what a beauty! How handsome! bell topped! and so big! Isn't he just about stiff! He's like a bar of iron! and what fine big eggs you've got! My beautiful man! Oh! How I would like to empty them for you! Oh! you'll have me now! Won't you? do! do! oh! I feel that I could come so nicely if you only would!"

Would I have her? Why! Gods in Heaven! how could mortal man brimful of health, strength, youth and energy like myself, resist such an appeal to his ears and senses, and not comply, even if the fair petitioner were not half nor a quarter as beautiful as this lascivious and exquisite creature, whose hands were manipulating the most tenderly sensitive parts which man possesses! For all reply I gently pulled her on her back, she still kept a firm but voluptuous hold on her possessions, and I turned up her petticoat and chemise, and gliding my burning hand over the smooth surface of her ivory thigh, up to, I think, the most voluptuous bush I had ever seen or felt in my life! Never had my hand reposed on so voluptuous and full a motte! Never had my fingers probed a charm so full of life and so soft outside, so smooth and velvety inside as it did now, that this most perfect place, and the domain around and above it, were in my possession! I was eager to get between her lovely thighs, and to snatch my almost painfully strained organ from her hands, and bury it up to its hilt, and further, in this melting charm, but she stopped me. With her face and bosom flushed, her eyes dancing in her head, and a voice choked with the greatest excitement she cried:

"Let us put on our skins first!"

I was standing before her, my sword at an angle of at least seventy degrees, my sack and groin arching, for the most vigorous action had set

CHARLES DEVEREAUX

in, and my reservoirs had already been filled to the utmost they could hold. I felt, I must either have this beautiful wild girl or burst!

"What do you mean?" I gasped.

"I'll show you! See!"

And in a moment she had, as it were, jumped out of her clothes, and stood, all naked and glowing, and radiant with beauty, real by all that is voluptuous and erotic before me.

In a moment or perhaps a little longer, for I had boots and socks as well as coat, shirt and trousers to take off, but at all events, in a brace of shakes, I was as naked as she! I can shut my eyes now and there before me I see this exquisitely formed creature, surely, quite the equal of the beautiful Mademoiselle de Maupin, standing in all her radiant nudity before me. That form so purely perfect, so inimitably graceful, those matchless limbs! That bosom with its hills of living snow topped with rosy fire and that more than voluptuous motte, a perfect "hill of Venus," clothed with the richest dark bushes of curly hair, sloping rapidly down, like a triangle standing on its point, until its two sides, folding in, form the deep soft-looking and inside line, which proclaimed the very perfection of a Goddess. The only thing which slightly marred this perfect galaxy of beauty was the occurrence of some slight wrinkles, which like fine lines crossed the otherwise perfect plain of her fair belly, that exquisite belly with its dimpling navel!

Gods! I rushed at this lovely creature, and in another moment I was on top of her, between her wide-opened thighs and resting on her beautiful bosom. How elastic did her beautiful bubbies feel against my chest! and how soft, how inexpressibly delicious, did her cavern feel, as inch by inch I buried Johnnie in it, until my motte jammed against hers, and my eggs hanging, or rather squeezed, against her lovely white bottom. I could get in no further. And what a woman to have! Every movement of mine brought forth an exclamation of delight from her! To hear her you would have imagined it was the very first time her senses had been powerfully excited from their very foundation! Her hands were never still, they promenaded over me, from the back of my head to the intimate limits of my body to which they could reach. She was simply perfect in the art of giving and receiving pleasure. Every transport of mine was returned with interest, every mad thrust met with a corresponding buck which had the effect of taking my engine into its extreme root! And she seemed to do nothing but "come" or "spend"! I had heard of a woman "coming" thirteen or fourteen times during one session, but this woman seemed to do nothing else from beginning to end. But, it was not until I had arrived at the exciting, furious, ardent, almost violent short digs, that I knew to what an intense degree my Venus enjoyed pleasure! I thought she was in a fit! She almost screamed! She gurgled in her throat! She half-crushed me in her arms, and putting her feet on my behind, she pressed me to her motte, at the end, with a power I should never have thought she possessed. Oh! the relief! the exquisite delight of the spend on my part! I inundated her, and she felt the spouting torrents of my love darting in hot, quick jets, and striking against the deepest part of her almost maddened cleft! She seized my mouth with hers, and shot her tongue into it as far as she could, touching my palate, and pouring her hot, delicious breath down my throat whilst her whole body from head to heel literally quivered with the tremendous excitement she was in! Never in my life had I such a fling! Oh! why are there no better words to express what is really heaven upon earth?

The tempest past, we lay in one another's arms; tenderly gazing into one another's eyes. We were too breathless to speak at first. I could feel her belly heaving against mine, and her throbbing cunnie clasped my tool as though it had been another hand, whilst her motte leaped and bounded! I looked into that angelic-looking face, and drank in the intense beauty of it, nor could I believe it could be an abandoned woman, but rather Venus herself, whom I held thus clasped in my arms, and whose tender and voluptuous thighs encircled mine! I could have wished that she held her peace and let me dream that I was the much desired Adonis, and she my persistent, longing Venus, and that I had at length won her amorous wishes, and found the heaven in her arms of which, before I entered her matchless cleft, I had no notion. But my airy fancies were dispelled by her saying :

"You are a good poke and no mistake! Oh! You know how to do it! No fellow ever rams like that without he has been taught!"

"Yes!" I said, pressing her in my arms and kissing the ruby lips which had just spoken so coarsely but truly, and pointedly, "I have been well trained! I had good lessons in my boyhood, and I have always tried to practice them as often as possible!"

"Ah! " she said. "I thought so! You do the heel-and-toe better than any man I've ever had, and I've had, I dare say, many more men than you've had women!"

Frank and how!

"What do you mean by heel-and-toe, my pet!"

"Oh! Don't you know? You do it at any rate! And splendid! Heel-and-toe is to begin each stroke at the very beginning and end it at the very end. Just give me one long stroke now!"

I did so. I withdrew until I was all but out of her panting orifice, and then gently but firmly drove it home; as far and as deep as I could, and then I rested again on her belly.

"There," she cried, "that's it! You almost pull it out, but not quite, and never stop short in your thrusts, but send it home, with a sharp rap of your cods against my bottom! and that's what's good!"

And she appeared to smack her lips involuntarily. At length I withdrew, and my fairest nymph at once commenced a most minute examination of that part of me and its appendages which had pleased her so much. Everything was, according to her, absolutely perfect, and if I were to believe her there had not passed under her observation so noble and handsome an organ, and such beautiful, well balanced stones as I had and she was the mistress of! My stones especially pleased her! She said they were so big! She was sure they must be full of spend, and she intended, she told me, to empty them before she would consent to my leaving Nowshera!

This first sacrifice simply whetted our appetites, and still more inflamed with the minute examination of one another's charms, we fell to again, and writhed in the delicious agonies of another amorous combat! It was about two o'clock before I left her, and we had not been at anyone time more than ten minutes "out of action." The more I had of this exquisite creature, the more I longed to have her. I was fresh, young, strong, vigorous, and it was nearly two months (a long time for me) since I had last indulged in the delights of Cyprian pleasures. No wonder my Venus was pleased with me, and called my performances a perfect feast.

They say that love destroys appetite for food. Perhaps it does when it is love unrequited, but I give you my word, dear reader, that I was ravenous for my tiffin after my morning's work. I was really glad to get something to eat, for what with the heat of the combats I had been through, and the parching effect of the terrible hot wind blowing, I was dried up, as far as my mouth was concerned, though far from being so as regards the proceeds of my sack. I never felt so fit for woman as I did that day, and I never probably have had so much joy with so little loss of physical force. Doubtless my steady married life with its regular hours, regular meals, and regular, never-excessive sacrifices on the altar of Venus had much to do with the steady power I felt so strong in me, but over and above that, was the fact of my new lady love being extraordinarily beautiful, and voluptuously lascivious, and the erotic excitement raised in me, was, of course, great in proportion to the cause which gave birth to it. In spite of my hunger for food, I would certainly have remained with her on that most genial of beds, and have reveled on in her joyous arms, and filled her with quintessence of my manly vigor, but she told me she always slept in the afternoon, was hungry herself, and, doubting my power, she wished me to reserve some good portions of my force to be expended between her lovely thighs that night and for the solace of her liveliest of crannies.

Whilst the Khansamah was laying the table I saw a note addressed to me, leaning against the wall, on the mantelpiece, (for in Northern India the winters are sharp enough to render a fire not only pleasant but sometimes quite necessary), and taking it and opening it, wondering who the writer could be, as I was perfectly unknown in this part of the world, I found it to be from my young officer friend who had quitted Nowshera this morning, it ran thus:

Dear Devereaux

"In the room next to yours is one of the loveliest of women and best of pokes!

Yours,
J.C.

P.S.—Don't offer her any rupees or you will offend her mortally, but if you are inclined to have her, and I think you will on seeing her, just tell her so and you won't have to ask twice."

Ah! Dear young chap, now I understand why you were so reticent this morning and did not like to tell me that I had a lady for my next door neighbor! Well! Poor girl! I am afraid that you must be put down as one of the "irregulars," although it is a shame to think ill of one who has given me the first few hours of real delight since I left home!

These thoughts naturally brought my beloved little wife into my recollection and I was somewhat staggered to feel I should so completely have forgotten her and my marital vows! But I was altogether too full of desire. Desire only just whetted and crying for more! More! I was in fact half mad with what some call lust and others love and, wife or no wife, nothing short of death would, or should, prevent my poking that heavenly girl again, and again, until I really could not raise a stand. I longed for evening. I burnt for night. I ate my tiffin like a ravenous tiger, hungry for food, but thirsting for the sweet savour of the blood of a victim he knew to be within easy reach. Tiffin put away, I lit a cheroot, and began wandering round and round my room, balancing impatiently at the door which closed the communication between it and that of my supposedly now sleeping Venus, and like Wellington wished and prayed for night or—not Blucher—her awakening! Suddenly it struck me as very funny that—supposing some catastrophe were to separate this girl and me, neither would be able to say who the other was! We had not exchanged names. My young friend the officer who signed his initials "J.C." had not told me. I did not even know his name, though he knew mine, probably from seeing it painted on my baggage. Of a surety this lovely Venus must have a history, and I resolved to try and get her to give me her version of it, from which no doubt I could make out what was true and what was invention, for that she would tell me the exact truth I hardly expected. Oh! when would she awake?

Should I go and peep and see? By Jupiter, I would. . . Throwing away the fresh cheroot I had lighted I crept, in my stocking feet, to her chick, and pulled it slightly open, and there on the bed fast asleep, I saw my lovely enslaver. She had simply put on a petticoat and was lying on her back, with her hands clasped under her shapely head, her arms, bent in a charming position opened out, showing the little growth of hair under the arm pit next to me; hair same in tint, but not so rich in color, as that magnificent bush I had moistened so liberally, aided by her own offerings this morning; her bosom bare and naked, with its two priceless breasts, so beautifully placed, so round, polished and firm, and her entire body down to her slender waist, quite nude! One knee, that next to me, was bent, the small graceful foot planted on the bed clothes, each gem of a toe straight and just separated from its neighbor, a foot that would have charmed the most fastidious sculptor that ever lived, whilst the other leg, bare almost from the groin downwards, was extended at full length, the lovely foot, which terminated it, resting against the edge of the bed, so that her thighs, those lovely voluptuous and maddening thighs, were parted! Gods! could I remain outside while so much beauty was freely displayed, on which I could feast my burning eyes whilst its lovely owner slept? I went gently and noiselessly in, and passing round to the other side of the bed, so that my shadow might not fall on that exquisite form, and hide the light, already softened by the chick, from it, and gazed in silence on the beautiful girl who had made me enjoy the bliss of Mahomet's heaven in her voluptuous embraces that forenoon. How lovely was her sleep! Who, looking on that face so pure in all its lines, so innocent in all its expressions, could imagine that in that soul there burnt the fire of an unquenchable Cytherian furnace. Who, looking on those matchless breasts could imagine that lovers innumerable had pressed them with lascivious hand or lip and been supported by them when they trembled in the agonies and the delight of having her?

The fair broad plain of her belly was still hidden by the upper portion of her petticoats, but the fine lines, which I had noticed when she "put on her skin," had told me the tale, that perhaps more than once it had been the breeding place of little beings, who, cast in such a beauteous mold, must needs be as beautiful as their lovely mother! I, who, looking at those virginal breasts which seemed as if they had never been disturbed by pent-up milk, and whose rosebud-like nipples seemed never to have been sucked, by the cherry lips of babies; who gazing in the girlish face, could connect such charms with the pains, the caress, and duties of maternity? No! surely, like the fair Houris of Mahomet's paradise, she must have been created for the fulfillment of the pleasure only, not for the consequences of the kiss of love! But the wrinkles told a different tale, and I should like to examine them more closely. It would be easy to do, if only they were naked, all but a small portion near the groin, and all that I had to do was to lift, gently, so as not to disturb her sleep, the part of her petticoat which still hid her there, and lay the garment back upon her waist.

With a hand trembling with excitement, I did so! lo! my nymph almost as naked as she was born! God of Gods! What a blaze of exciting beauty! I had uncovered the sweet belly to look at the wrinkles, but my eye was captured before it lifted its gaze so high! As the bird is caught in the snare surrounding the luscious bait exposed for it, so were my eyes entangled in the meshes of that glorious hair, which from the forest-like bush growing on that voluptuous motte, and shading the slit, the like of which for freshness, beauty, and all that excites desire, could not have existed in that to anybody but that of the great Mother of love, Venus herself. It seemed to me impossible that this beauteous portal to the realms of bliss, could have been invaded by so many worshippers as her speech of the morning had led me to believe. It looked far from having been hard used. What grand full lips it had. How sweetly it was placed. How pretty did the fine dark hairs, which crossed it look against the whiteness of the skin, whose foldings formed that deep and perfect line. What a perfect forest overshadowed it, and how divine were the slopes of that glorious hill, the perfect little mountain, which led up the sweet descent to the deep vale between her thighs, and ended in that glowing grotto in which love delighted to hide his blushing head, and shed the hot tears of his exulting joy.

But what is that? What is that little ruby tip I see beginning to protrude, near the upper meeting of those exquisite lips? She moves. See! I think she must be dreaming! She slightly closes her bent leg towards that one outstretched! It is her most sensitive clitoris, as I live! See! It grows more and more! And by the Gods! it actually moves in little jerks, just like an excited stem standing stiff, and mad at the thoughts of hot desire!

I gazed at the tranquil face of the sleeping beauty, her lips moved and her mouth opened slightly showing the pearly teeth! Her bosom seemed to expand, her breasts to swell, they rose and fell more rapidly than they had been doing before this evident dream of love fulfilled or about to be, invaded the soft heart of this perfect priestess of Venus! Ah! Her bubbies do move! Their rosebuds swell out, they stand, each like an eager sentinel perched on the snowy tip of his own mountain, watching for the loving foe who is to invade this dreaming girl to the soft, and sharp and hot encounter.

Again those thighs close on one another. Heaven! again they open to show the domain of love, excited, moving, leaping, actually leaping! That glittering ruby clit is evidently striving to feel the manly staff of which my charmer dreams. Why not turn the dream into a sweet and luscious reality?

I do not hesitate. I swiftly strip and in a moment I am as naked as I had been that morning, but I would like to see whether, as when I raped my cousin Emily, my second love, I could actually get into this sleeping girl, before she woke to find me in her glowing orifice. So I gently got over her thigh next me, and with knees between hers I supported myself upon my hands, one on each side of her and stretching out my legs backward, kept my eyes fixed on the sweet and burning cranny I intended to invade. I lowered my body until I brought the head and point of my agitated and jerking tool exactly opposite its lower half, and then I maneuvered it in!

Gods! The voluptuousness of that moment! I could see myself penetrating that seat of love and luxury! I could feel the cap fall back from the tingling head of my member and fold behind its broad purple shoulder! For a moment I glanced at her face to see if she had perceived the gallant theft I was making of her secret jewel! No! She was asleep, but in the excitement of an erotic dream! Little by little I pressed further and further in, only withdrawing, to give her more pleasure. I am nearly all in—her thick and lofty bush hides the last inch or so of my spear from my eyes, our hairs co-mingle, my eggs touch her, and she wakes with a start!

In a moment her eyes met mine with that keen, almost wild glance, which had so impressed me when I saw her out of the gharry, but in a moment they changed and beamed with pleasure and affectionate caresses.

"Ah! Is it you?" she cried, "I was dreaming of you! You darling man to wake me so sweetly!"

Some burning kisses, some close, close hugs, some little exclamations of delight, and then breast to breast, belly to belly, mouth to mouth, we play for the ninth or tenth time. I really don't know which, that same excited tune which had sounded all that morning so melodiously to our ravished senses. Heel-and-toe! as she called it: delicious movements mingling in every part, hot, quick, thrilling short digs, and then the torrents of two volcanoes of love burst forth simultaneously and mingled their lava floods in the hot recesses buried below the sylvan slopes of the Hill of Venus.

The gong on which the non-commissioned officer of the guard sounds the hour of the day in India, rang five o'clock. We had been in intense action nearly a whole hour, and my charming beauty was for the fifteenth time examining what she called, my "wonderful" member and stones, wonderful, because the first showed no symptoms of fatigue, and the second no signs of exhaustion or depletion.

"I don't believe this can be a proper tool at all!" said she feeling it, pressing it, and kissing its impudent looking head, first on one side and then on the other.

"Why?" I asked laughing.

"Because it's always stiff as a poker—always standing!"

"That is because it admires your delicious cranny so much, my darling, that it is always in a hurry to get back into it after it has been taken out!"

"Well! I never saw one like it before! All other men that I have had always grew soft and limp, after the second go at any rate, and generally took a good deal of coaxing to get to stand again, unless one gives them lots of time! But yours! I never, never, met one like it! It will give me a lot of trouble. I can see, to take all the starch out of it!"

"Oh! but I can assure you my most lovely girl, that with ordinary women I am just as you describe the men you have known. I can assure you it must be your extraordinary beauty which has such a powerful effect upon me! Come!" I continued opening my arms and thighs. "Come and lie on top of me and let me kiss you to death!"

Enraptured by the lavish, but not unmerited, praise of her beauty, she threw herself, with a cry of delight, on top of me, and my manhood found a sweet resting place between our respective bellies. She took and gave me the sweetest kisses, murmuring little words of love and passion like a cat purring, until I was just going to propose that she should put her thighs outside mine, and let me have her a la St. George, when a sudden idea seemed to strike her. She raised herself on her hand and asked me:

"I say! Have you reported your arrival to the Station Staff Officer?"

What an idea! Fancy talking of such common-place things just as I was about to propose the most delicious thing a woman can have from man, the very poetry of life and love! I could not but think of Mrs. Shandy asking her husband when he was in the middle of that operation which resulted in Tristram nine months later, whether he had wound up the clock.

"My dear girl!" I cried. "Bother the Station Staff Officer and all his reports. Come! I am hungry for another sweet go! I want this!" and I slipped my hand under her belly and between her thighs, and my middle finger into her palpitating cavern.

"No!" she said, forcibly pushing my invading hand away. "No! Not one more until you have gone and reported yourself! Ah! you don't know the regulations, I see! But I do! I have not been in India all these years without learning what they are, and Major Searles, the Brigade Major here, is a perfect beast and devil! You may depend upon it he knows you are here, and he would be only delighted to get a chance of sitting on you, and he will be able to do so if you don't report yourself before dark—mind! you got here early this morning!"

I tried to convince her that I did not care a fig for Major Searles and all the Bengal regulations to boot! I said I was on duty and the post of honor being between her lovely thighs, and my Johnnie anxious to go his rounds of her, I did not think I could properly quit my duty in her body, to go and perform another which would do quite well enough tomorrow, by which time, in all probability, Johnnie would have come off guard, and would require a rest from his labors! But it was of no use: she declared I did not know my man, she told me a great deal more, from which it was very plain that something unpleasant had occurred between herself and Major Searles, and that it really did matter very much, to herself if not to me, that I should report my arrival, and do so at once.

Never did man more unwillingly do anything than I did when, in obedience to my lovely tyrant's commands, I dressed and walked out to find the house of the Brigade Major. I know men will not believe me, and none give me credit when I say, that I felt as if I had not one single lay since I left England. That my groin ached and I had all the sensations of a man who is soon about to have the joust he has most looked forward to, for which he has lived chastely and in reserve, in order to enjoy it more and for which he burns, I can only state the fact and let others believe or not as they like. Certain it is, that there are times when either from length of time, or the way in which a woman affects him, a man exhibits far greater power in the fields of Venus than at other times. Let me imitate Theophile Gautier, and request my readers, male and female, to remember that especial time, when the former had that splendid night, and the latter when she had the active, strong, big lover, the best of all she ever had, as far as love making goes.

In this state I walked over to the bungalow which was pointed out to me as that of the Brigade Major. I was so fortunate that I met him just as he was going out, with his smooth English terrier, for a walk before dinner.

"May I ask are you Major Searles, the Brigade Major, sir?"

"Yes, I am!"

"I should have come earlier to report my arrival, sir, but I have traveled so far in dak gharries that I have been lying down all day, and it was so very hot when I got up that I have deferred my coming to report myself until now."

"And who may you be sir?"

"I am Capt. Charles Devereaux, of the First East Folk Regiment of Infantry, and I am on my way to Cherat to join my Battalion on promotion."

"Oh! indeed! How do you do, Capt. Devereaux! I am sorry that I did not know you at first! Will you come in or are you inclined for a little stroll? Will you come over to Mess of the 130th and let me introduce you to the officers? I am afraid you won't get to Cherat quite so soon as you may wish; every blessed machine with wheels has been ordered for a week to come, so that if I were offered lakhs of rupees I could not get you a conveyance here—besides which the road from Publi to Shakkote, at the foot of the hill is Kacha and bad for anything heavier than an ekkha and you would have to ride up the hill when you get there."

The whole manner of the man was changed when he found I was an officer and what was more a captain, i.e., just one grade below himself in rank. Had I been a subaltern, he might have kept up a higher degree of hauteur.

At first I thought my new acquaintance rather an agreeable man. He spoke affably and pleasantly. Asked me about my voyage, my stay in Bombay, and journey up country. He spoke about the war which would practically come to an end when the Kandahar expedition had blown Ayoob Khan and the conquerors of the ill-fated Maiwand to the four winds of Heaven; then returned to the subject of Nowshera, the Dak Bungalow, its inmates, and turning to the subject of my well-known, as far as her most secret charms were concerned, but perfectly-unknown mistress, and soon he commenced a series of very subtle questions, which, from their very guardedness, showed me that there was one person, and one circumstance, which he was approaching, like a cunning cat stalking a sparrow, taking every cover as a guard as he crept up to it. I remembered the evident repugnance my new love had shown when speaking of Major Searles, and I fenced his questions, until he at last asked me openly:

"Have you seen a woman, a rather lady-like person, in the Bungalow?"

"I have seen one lady," I replied, "but there may be more than that for all that I know, in the house, I have not been over it, so I cannot tell if the one I have seen is the person you refer to."

"Well!" said he, "let me warn you that the woman I refer to is the wife of a non-commissioned officer—she is very pretty, and, I regret to say, about the most abandoned woman in India, if not in the whole world. She must be suffering from nymphomania, for she cannot see a man without she asks him to have her, and as she is really lovely to look at, it is quite in the cards that if she asks a young man, fresh out from England like you, he might accept the proposition, and think that he had fallen in with a very good thing indeed—but—pardon me— let me finish—the penalty for adultery with a European woman, in

India, is two years imprisonment and a fine of two thousand rupees and expulsion from India of the woman herself. Already the woman I speak of has rendered herself liable to expulsion, hundreds of times, but no one has as yet informed against her, but her conduct at Peshawar has been so scandalous, and indecent, that proceedings will most likely be taken against her. A strict watch of which she is not aware is being kept on her, and some unfortunate fellow, say yourself, for you are young and no doubt do not dislike the ladies, ha! ha! ha! might find himself a victim of her lust, for lust it is and nothing else."

"Well! Major Searles," I replied, "I am a married man and so I hope less liable to temptation from the part of duty than the unfortunate bachelor. Many thanks, however, for your timely warning, for of course I know that, married or single, a man may become the victim of his passions especially when taken off his guard by a pretty woman!"

"Ah! You speak truly!" he replied, "and I can tell you that this wretched creature is as lovely as an Houri, and as lustful as the most able whore in Babylon."

I had not lived so long a life of the worship of Venus without having seen a good deal of the hidden springs of men's minds, and I came to the conclusion that this tirade of friend Major Searles was not altogether spoken on the side of virtue, or caution, but that it was a kind of warning—"don't you touch that woman, she is my preserve, and no one hunts in the forest between her thighs but myself!"

The arrival at the Mess brought our conversation to a close. Like most Messes of Regiments, which have been sometime in India, this one was composed of a nice set of generally hospitable officers, but who were more or less languid from a long residence in a hot and unhealthy climate. They were also too much accustomed to seeing new faces, through the men going to or returning from Afghanistan, to be very greatly interested in men, but they were cordial and kind, made me drink a couple of "pegs," asked me to dinner the next night, which happened to be their "guest" night, and begged me to consider myself an honorary member of their Mess so long as I should remain in Nowshera.

I would willingly have been excused from accepting their kind invitation to dinner, because I was so infatuated with my charming girl in the Dak Bungalow, that the thought of being out of reach of her brilliant charms was purgatory to me and my senses, but Major Searles was there, and his eyes were on me and I felt that if my Surmises as to the relations between himself and "my" lovely woman were correct, I

CHARLES DEVEREAUX

had better ward off suspicion on his part, by cordially accepting the invitation, which I accordingly did with all the warmth I could muster. This seemed to relieve the Major, for he turned and chatted with another officer. They asked Searles whether he would come and meet me at dinner but he said he had some work to do tomorrow evening, but if he could find time he would gladly come and rattle the balls about at a game of billiards later in the evening.

After waiting a decent time I said I would go and have a look about whilst daylight lasted, and Searles proposed to accompany me. The man bored and bothered me, and I wished him in hell, for my ideas about him began to become very jealous. I thought it extremely likely that he had had my charmer, indeed, I was certain he had, but I could not suffer him to do so whilst I was in Nowshera. I meant to keep her delicious sex for myself, she had offered it to me and I was its present master and entitled to remain so! I knew of the law and of the fine of which he had spoken and they did not frighten me as like all Draconian laws, it was seldom it was put in force, but I could not hide from myself that a jealous man, if he is at all a brute, would be able to very sadly interfere with such a liaison as I had now on hand, and make it very uncomfortable for the woman too. I had the sense, however, to try and keep my feelings under control, and be as agreeable as possible. Our walk was a very simple and short one, for it was straight from the Mess to the Dak Bungalow, where Searles, as if unconsciously, led the way. I offered him a 'peg,' but he declined, as he said the liquor in the Bungalow was vile, which was true, and they had no ice. Neither had the Mess then. Ice was unknown beyond Jhelum. But the Mess had the simple means, so easily used whilst the hot, dry winds last, of cooling liquids by placing bottles in baskets of wet straw, in a position where the wind blows upon them, the rapid evaporation soon causes the temperature of the bottles to fall very low, and ice is not wanted. I did not know or had forgotten this, but I soon had it put in practice by the Khansamah, and that very night and everyday following I had cool drinks.

We sat in the verandah until it was dark. The gallant Major never referred to my connection, whose brilliant and piercing eyes I felt darting their rays at us from behind the chick, and whose ears I was sure were drinking in every word. Then Searles went, only referring to his important conversation by the warning words: "Don't forget what I told you!"

"All right! Major! Many thanks! Goodnight!"

When it was certain that he was gone, my lady glided into the verandah and occupied the chair that Searles had sat in.

"What has that brute been telling you about me?" asked she, her voice quivering with passion.

I gave her an exact account of all that had passed between us, and when I told her, though in much softened language, of the way he had spoken of her, she strode to her feet and walked up and down the verandah in a towering rage like an infuriated tiger.

"The black livered blackguard!" she exclaimed, "oh! truly a nice man to preach continence and virtue. I should like to know who drove his wife to the hills to become the real whore she is! Yes! she is a whore if you like! She asks money from her men! It's five hundred rupees a night to have her, it is! I never yet asked a man for a piece, and I would not take one, or a million, as payment! If I do play, I play for pleasure, and because I like my lover! But I hate a cad! and if ever there was a cad in this world it's Major Searles," and she spat on the ground in token of her detestation for him!

I used all my arts of gentle persuasion to try to calm her down, and at length succeeded. She told me that Searles had never had her with her permission. He had sent her message after message begging to be allowed to come and pay his "respects" but she had persistently refused all reply. I never got exactly the reason she abhorred him so much, but evidently there had been some circumstance which had raised a wall of hatred and aversion between them. She said that Searles was a man no woman could trust, and that supposing he could get the two thousand rupees for betraying her as a reward, and evade the punishment of the imprisonment, he was just the man who would get her to have him and then report the circumstance! It was evident that she hated him with more than ordinary hate, and I must confess I was glad to hear it, for I feared Searles had some right over her, and I, that I should have the mortification of knowing that he was reaping the indescribable bliss in her arms, whilst I was raging in silent torture in my room and I felt that such a thing would be perfectly unbearable.

Lizzie, for such at last I found was her name, dined with me that night and before we retired to bed she told me part of her history. I propose, but not just at present, to take you, my patient readers into my confidence, and tell you what were the adventures of her amorous love, but before doing so I must explain how the abhorred attentions of Major Searles were put a complete end to, and Lizzie Wilson ridded herself of a man who had been her plague for some years.

CHARLES DEVEREAUX

The fatigue caused by several continuous day and night travels in a dak gharry, the excitement caused by the glorious and wholly unexpected bonne fortune which had thrown me a most willing though surprised victim, into Lizzie's fair arms, and no doubt the excessive ardor with which I had fought the lovely foe, all combined to make me very tired, and after I had manfully resisted the heavy hand of sleep and had come out victorious with flying colors and standard still borne aloft, from two desperate encounters, I could no more, but sank by Lizzie's side into the most complete, and indeed refreshing sleep, which I had since I left Bombay. My readers will not be surprised to hear that when I awoke the next day, I had become what Lizzie called a "common man" i.e. the almost supernatural force which had sustained me the day before, had yielded up its extreme strength and like a second but far sweeter Delilah, she had shorn me of my source of strength, in so far that after the first morning sacrifice my proper weapon assumed the posture of repose and it required the titillations of Lizzie's fair fingers, now toying with and caressing my eggs, now wandering along my groin now running the scale along my staff, and bringing that important charm into the rigid and erect state which enables it to perform its delicious duty. What a day that was! I think the alternate conditions of languor and fiery action were, on the whole, more delightful than the fierce and stormy tempest which had driven us so fiercely the day before. Lizzie too actually confessed that a second day like the first would have killed her. That her back was broken and that she felt she had indeed been grinding and been ground. So in spite of the cruel hot wind, and the savage bitings of the sand flies, terrible little pests so small that they can hardly be seen, and perfect torments to a tender skin, I passed a most delicious day. Lizzie was sand-fly proof, like some people get mosquito proof, but I, fresh from England, afforded those abominable pests the flies a feast, as rich in its way as the voluptuous bower between my Lizzie's thighs had been for me! Every rose has its thorn, my sweet girl readers, and alas! most pleasures have their drawbacks. Happy are those who make the most of the rose and the least of the thorn.

I had hired a native servant as my factotum, when I stayed at Lahore en route for my destination at Cherat, a capable man he was, and one who had an eye to business, for whether he was married or not I do not know, but he brought a very fine young native woman with him, and as the reader will hear her talents were not thrown away at Cherat on others, though I had far finer game to follow than was afforded by

Mrs. Soubratie's brown skin and somewhat mellow charms, for though no more than twenty she had gone the way of almost all Indian women, and her bosom had begun to flow, and her bubbies otherwise fine and plump, hung in a despondent manner, defects however so common that they are little heeded by the British officers or soldiers, who whet their appetites on the fine, juicy slits, rather than on the personal graces of the dames who afforded them pleasure. Soubratie, hearing I was going to Mess, got out my nice, new, clean white mess clothes, and adorned himself also gorgeously, and armed with a lantern, saw me safely across the compound, ankle deep in the dust road, to the Mess of the regiment, where I was going to partake of the generous hospitality of the generous 130th. Is it any use to describe the anteroom, with its swinging punkahs, chairs, tables and pictures, carpets, books, newspapers, trophies of the chase, etc., etc. Shall I tell how the staff and important Adjutant welcomed me in a proper and decent style, the Colonel with an "inspection" looked at me; the other officers whom I had not yet met, with a polite and "glad to see you" from their lips and "I wonder what the devil kind of a fellow you are," glance of their eyes. Most regiments are alike; when you have seen one you have seen all. The English officer is undoubtedly a fearful "stick" and of all weary humdrum lives, Mess life is the most dreary. Along with the air of ennui and boredom there is a more good, naughty, wicked, devil-may-care current, which forms the pit of an officer's life, and I knew well that when a good dinner had been eaten, a good share of fairly good wine drunk, and cigars and "pegs" had become the evening fare, I should hear a good deal more than I was likely to at the dinner table, where propriety and stiffness more or less ruled the roost, accordingly, as I was now. I heard the old stories of the war, tales of savagery, cowardly cruelty on the part of the Afghans, with an occasional growl at the generals and authorities who, it seemed, must have been incompetent to a degree or far greater results would have occurred from the valor of the British troops. I knew how to discount all this; and listened with interest, more or less affected, to my new friends' commiserations and views. But the "cloth off the table" brought a subject which is always congenial to the front. Woman, lovely woman, began to be discussed. My young acquaintance J. C.'s statement as to the complete absence of women from Tommy Atkins' quarters in Afghanistan, and the consequent immense demand for love on his return to civilization and comfort was immediately confirmed. In those days, (it has been very recently altered) the regulations obliged a certain number of native girls to be especially engaged for the services of each regiment, and these ladies of the camp accompanied their regiment wherever they marched in India, just as much a part and parcel of them as the colonel, adjutant, quartermaster. But Tommy likes variety, as well as other people, and in every place where there is a "bazaar" or shops, there are establishments for ladies of pleasure, these latter earn a good many four anna bits which should by rights find their way into the pockets of the proper regimental whores. The recent influx of troops into Peshawar from Afghanistan had created an enormous demand for willing girls and Nowshera, Attock, even Rawal Pindi, Umballa and other places had been denuded of "Polls" who gathered like birds of carrion where the carcass lay. This was the great grievance for the officers of the gallant 130th, who were almost as badly off for women as they had been when they were at Jellabad, and at Lundi Kotal, at which latter place a Goorki soldier, who had got a bad clap from some native woman, was universally spoken of as the "Lucky Goorki!" Not because of the clap, bien entendu, but because, though he suffered afterwards, he had managed to secure for himself a pleasure so uncommon under the circumstances, that it seemed like water a thousand miles distant to a traveler lost in the great Sahara!

Once the subject of love and women was started rolling the tongues of those who had been most reticent during dinner were set wagging, and I found a most entertaining host in the fat, pudgy, double-chinned major, who seemed to take a fancy to me. He proposed that we should adjourn outside where the band of the regiment was performing some operatic airs, and lively dance music, and there we sat, in those voluptuous Madras long arm chairs, enjoying whatever coolness there was in the air, the sounds of the suggestive music and the brilliancy of the myriad of bright stars which glittered over head, literally like "diamonds in the sky."

"Searles, our Brigade Major, said he would come this evening," said the Major, "but I rather think he won't."

"Why?" I asked.

"Because he is struck with a very pretty little woman in the Dak Bungalow."

This I guess was a shot at me.

"Indeed! Well! I hope he will succeed and get his greens! Poor chap!"

"Oh! Do you! Well! We are all saying that it was a damned shame, because we had made up our minds that you were surely in her good graces yourself, and we thought it mean of Searles to try and cut in whilst you were out! ha! ha! ha!"

"Oh!" I said quietly, "but I am a married man, Major! and have just left my wife, and do not go in for that sort of thing! So, as far as I am concerned, Major Searles is welcome to the lady if he can persuade her to grant him her favors."

"Well! But Searles is a married man himself, Devereaux!"

"Oh! I dare say! I don't mean to imply that a married man is impervious to the charms of other women because he is married. I am not strait-laced, and I dare say I should be quite as liable as anybody else to have a woman who was not my wife, but you know I have not been married long enough to be tired of my wife, and I have not been long enough away from her to feel any inclination to commit adultery yet!"

"Well! Searles is a Major—but he's a brute! Yet I somehow pity the poor devil too! I don't know how it is, but he and his wife, a devilish fine woman, a perfect Venus in her way, don't get on altogether well; in fact she has left him!"

"Oh! my! do you say so?"

"Yes! Now mind you Devereaux, you must not give me as your authority, but I can tell you that he treated that poor woman like a brute, half-killing her with a blow from the side of his hair brush; devilish— nearly smashed her skull, you know, and after that she left him, and went and set up on her own account at Ranikhet."

I am sure my dear readers are amused at my assuming the air of a thoroughly moral young husband still contented with the breasts of his spouse, as Solomon, I think it is, tells us we ought to be, but of course I was not going to amuse my new friend or indeed any others, with tales which somehow spread so wonderfully quickly, and in rapidly widening circles, until they reach the ears of those we would least wish to hear them. Really and truly, my heart and conscience pricked me when this conversation brought to mind my beloved little Louie, and I thought of her in her lovely bed, perhaps weeping in sad silence as she prayed for the safety, welfare and quick return home, of him whom she loved so dearly, who made her joyous by day, and gave her rapturous fun at night, her husband, and the darling father of her angel baby girl. But alas! the spirit is willing and the flesh weak, as I have remarked before; and the weakness of the flesh exceeds the strength of the spirit in importance.

But the conversation was bearing directly on a subject which was becoming interesting to me since I had seen Searles and heard Lizzie's indignant remark that his wife was a regular whore, whose price for her charms was, however, uncommonly high. I did not mind what my fat major said about Searles' designs on Lizzie that evening, because Lizzie would have to have been a most unaccountably stupid deceiver, if she had merely expressed abhorrence of him to blind me! No, I felt certain the abhorrence was real and true, and I had no fear that I should find that she had afforded him a retreat, either hospitable or the reverse in her sweetest nook, when I got home to her again.

"How do you mean setting up on her own account, Major?" said I.

"Oh! hum! well! look here; bend your head a little nearer to me! I don't want to talk too loudly! Well! she is—that is any fellow almost, who cares to give her a cool five hundred rupees, can have her."

"Ah! bosh! Major, I can't believe that! Surely you are mistaking some ill-natured gossip for facts!"

"Oh no! I'm not!" replied my pudgy friend, speaking with great gusto. "By God! Sir! If seeing is believing I can swear to it! I can swear to the fact!"

"What!" said I in well effected incredulous tones, "you want to persuade me that an officer's wife, a lady like Mrs. Searles must be, has actually done a monstrous, not to say such an idiotic thing, as not only to leave her husband, a thing I cannot understand, and to set up as a whore, and in such a place as Ranikhet, a thing I cannot understand! Surely, Major, you are mistaken! Remember! we are told to believe nothing we hear and only half what we see!"

"I know! I know!" said he, still as calmly as if he were Moses laying down the law, "but look here Devereaux, you won't tell me I am a liar if I say the proof of the pudding is in the eating, and that my proof of what I say is that I, Jack Stone, have had Mrs. Searles, and paid for my game! Yes sir! Rupees five hundred did Jack Stone pay Mrs. Searles for a night in Mrs. Searles' bed."

"Goodness, and you have actually—"

"I have actually had her, sir! and had her well! and a damned fine poke she is too, I can tell you, and well worth the five hundred she asks for the fun. Such a damned fine poke is she that Jack Stone, who is not a rich man but must lay up for a rainy day, has put three times five hundred rupees away in the bank of Simla, and means to lodge them some day soon in the bank of Ranikhet, Mrs. Searles banker and sole proprietress, which bank is her goloptious slit, between her goloptious thighs. Did you mark that, young man!"

"And does Searles know this?" I asked, still incredulous.

"What? that I have had his wife?"

"No, not that you in particular have had her, but that she is had by other men, and for money paid down on the nail."

"Know it! of course he does! It's her way of paying him off for his brutal conduct to her, to give him nuts by writing and telling him how nicely she is dragging his name through the mud."

"Then why does he not divorce her?" I cried, indignantly, for I felt that it was monstrous that a wife, no matter what her grievance might be, should behave in such an outrageous manner.

"Ah!—but sink your voice a little lower, Devereaux, not that all this is not perfectly well known by our fellows, but about the divorce. Well you see if what I have heard is true, a divorce is the last thing Searles can get, or would care to ask for, no matter how much he might wish it could be managed."

"Certain little things would come out at the trial, and he might find himself not only minus a wife whom he hates, and also minus his liberty and what remains of his honor, and I don't think anyone would care to become a convict even to rid himself of his wife!"

"What was it?" asked I, quite bitten with curiosity.

"Oh! Searles was a long time in Persia before he married, and he got the Persian taste for boys! I wig! sodomy! you know!" And the modest major sank his voice to a whisper. "Sodomy! he tried to get Mrs. Searles to acquire a taste for it herself, but she, like a proper woman, indignantly refused to comply. It might have stopped there, but one night Searles, full of zeal and brandy, actually ravished his poor wife's—hem—hem—well!—bum! and from that day she hated him—quite naturally, I think! Then of course she gave him the nag, nag, rough side of her tongue, until he nearly killed her, as I told you, in his passion. Then she went and set up at Ranikhet."

"But," said I, horrified to hear such a disgusting story, so loathsome on either side, "how is it she can demand such enormous sums for which I expect equally good returns can be got almost anywhere in India!"

"Oh! but you don't know. First of all, Mrs. Searles is in society—she is, I suppose, the most beautiful woman in India, if not in all Asia!"

"In society!"

"Yes! bless you! you don't understand. Now come! You, who have seen the world at home! Have you not heard how Mrs. So-and-So is suspected of poking, and yet you have met her every night at the best houses? Have you not seen common or fast women, who dare to do what your own wife or sister dare not, and nobody says more than that they are fast? Do you suppose you know what women actually do poke, and those who only get the credit for it? It is just the same with Mrs. Searles. She lives in a pretty little bungalow, some three miles deep in the hills of Ranikhet, she calls it Honeysuckle Lodge, but the funny fellows call it Cunnie-Fuckle Lodge; Ha! ha! ha! and she has named the hill it is on Mount Venus; she stays there all the hot weather, in the cold weather she goes to Lucknow or Meerut, or Agra, or Benares, or wherever she likes. No fellow has her without an introduction. The Viceroy is damned spoony on her, and that is sufficient to keep the fashionable people quiet. People suspect, people know, but people only pretend to think it possible for the quiet lady, living in a little bungalow, away from all the world, minding her garden and her flowers, is anything but a poor, persecuted wife whose husband is a brute!"

"Oh! that is it! So to have her you must get an introduction?"

"Yes! Without that you might as well cry for the moon!"

"And how is it to be managed?" I asked out of simple curiosity, for I had no notion of having Mrs. Searles, but I was interested in this curious story, of which I did not know how much to believe or how much to discredit.

"Ha! ha! ha! Devereaux! I fancy you are beginning to think whether you can find five hundred rupees for yourself, eh?"

"Not a bit!" said I indignantly, "I have no idea of such a thing, but simply asked out of curiosity!"

"Well!" said the pudgy little major, puffing his cheroot hard as it had nearly gone out, "no harm to tell you, any how! You can get an introduction from any man who has had her! I could give you one for instance. See! This is how I had her. I had heard of Mrs. Searles and had, like everybody else, heard funny reports about her, which, like I see you do now, you only half believe. Well! I did not then know she lived at Ranikhet, but chance made me pitch upon that place to spend three weeks leave in during the hot weather of '75. The Viceroy and his staff were spending the time there also, and everybody was wondering why he chose Ranikhet instead of Naini Tal. There is reason in everything and Mrs. Searles was his reason, no doubt. However, I must not be too long winded. I met Lord Henry Broadford, the Assistant Military Secretary, you know. Broadford had been at school with me, and is a damned good fellow. One day, soon after I went to Ranikhet, I was standing talking to Broadford, when the finest, handsomest woman I had ever seen walked by, and Broadford took off his hat and smiled, and she bowed. She looked full at me as I took off my hat and by George sir! she made my heart thump in my bosom, she was so lovely. When she was out of earshot I said, 'Harry, who is your friend? By God, she is a clinker and no mistake!'"

"'Don't you know,' says he, 'why, that is the famous Mrs. Searles.'

"'Is it,' says I, and then I asked him if he knew whether it was true she poked, as people said. Broadford looked at me and grinned and said:

"'Would you like to know for certain, Stone?' and I said, 'Yes.'

"'Well,' says he, 'the most certain way is to poke her yourself, for you might not believe me if I told you that I was in bed with her up to five o'clock this morning!'"

"'I don't believe you, you beggar!' said I, 'you are laughing at me.'

"'All right!' says he, 'have you five hundred rupees to lose on a bet?'

"'Well!' I hesitated, five hundred is a large sum and the subject was not worth it. Seeing me hesitate, he said. 'Well, would you give five hundred rupees to have Mrs. Searles yourself, Jack?'

"'Yes,' said I, plump as could be.

"'Then come along with me,' said Broadford.

"Well, we went to my hotel, and there Broadford made me write a cheque, and get five one-hundred rupee notes from the native banker, new and crisp, in exchange. Then he made me write a letter addressed to Mrs. Searles, in which I asked her might I come and take dinner with her on such and such a day, naming the day. I was more than half afraid the fellow was humbugging me, but he pulled out a case from his pocket, and showed me a lovely photo in it of a naked, stark naked lady, bush and all complete, and, says he, Mrs. Searles gives one of these to each of her lovers, and she gave me this this morning, see, her name, date and the number of times I had her last night! Well, I looked at the photo, and sure enough there was no mistaking it was the lady I had just seen, besides which I remembered having seen photos of her taken in the plains.

"By God! sir! the sight of such lovely charm settled my hash. I told Broadford that he would have to bear the brunt if anything went wrong. He swore all would be right, and after I had signed my name to the note to Mrs. Searles, he added his initials and W. T. B. P.

"'What does that mean?' I asked.

"'Will there be pokes? of course!' Well, this done, I put the five good crisp notes in the letter, and we went to the post office, registered it, and then I began to think I had been made a fool of. But it was all right. The day afterwards I got a registered letter. It was from Mrs. Searles. In it were my five notes. She said she was very sorry, but that she did not think she could have the pleasure of my company at dinner for another ten days, would I write again in about a week's time, if that would suit me, and she would be sure not to disappoint me. I rushed off, found Broadford, and nearly had a fit of apoplexy from excitement. By his advice I waited some eight days, then sent another letter, and again enclosed the notes, and I added on my own hook, W. T. B. P. Next came a letter by hand. It said 'my dear Jack' this time. It invited me to dine the next evening at eight, and ended with Matilda Searles. W.T.B.P."

"And did you go?"

"Oh! What a question! Of course I did. By God, Sir! I was simply bursting. Even now I can hardly tell my story with any degree of quiet! Well, I went; I was received by her in an awfully pretty little drawing room, most beautifully furnished, and bristling with knick-knacks, mirrors, pictures and everything that can make a room handsome and elegant. The floor was covered with carpet into which one's feet sank as one walked on it. Mrs. Searles was sitting reading when I arrived, and as soon as the bearer had gone out of the room she came and took my hand, shook it, and then kissed me! I was so excited, I felt such a sense of false shame, that at first I was like a stuck pig! But she quickly put me at my ease, sat on the sofa, made me sit next her, jammed her knee against mine, and whilst asking me where, how and when I had known Lord Henry Broadford, she showed off her splendid shoulders and magnificent bosom. I was awfully randy in my way, I had been randy all the days I had been waiting for her, but I was so knocked over by the elegance I saw, on my first arrival, that I declare, if the truth were told, I felt inclined to run away. But little by little, as I got to see the woman I was going to have, as I began to hear her talk as if we were quite old chums, and as she talked, her hand playing with mine, to say nothing of some kisses from time to time which she gave me, I began to pluck up courage. So by the way of showing her I was no fool, but expected something, I just made the offer to put my hand on her bosom, and take hold of one of the glorious bubbies, of which I saw nearly half over her dress. But she laughed and said it was not time for that yet, that when we had dined, and I had had my smoke, we would go to bed, where I should find her all I could wish for, and where I should have the fullest liberty, so long as I did not exceed the bounds which every honest man observed who had a woman. Well! I kissed her and begged her pardon. I had a rosebud in my button hole, and she took it out and said, see, I place your rose where you shall be! and she put it between her bubbies and said, there it is, a rose among the lilies, but that is all of you I can allow at present to be there. Well, sir! we had a splendid dinner. In spite of my love I did wire into a rattling good feed, and afterwards she made me smoke a cigar, and when it was nearly done she said she would go and undress, and that, when I heard a little bell ring, I was to go to her bedroom which she had already pointed out. Soon I heard the bell and I went. Oh! I was delighted! By God, sir! I had had many fine women, but I never saw one who was a patch to Mrs. Searles when undressed. She had on a quite transparent kind of nightgown, which covered her from neck to heels. It had no sleeves, and her arms were something splendid. Her bubbies looked more enticing covered with this transparent stuff, than when I saw them bare. Her nipples looked like strawberries, red and luscious. I would have been able to see her mound, but all the whole of the way, from her chin to her feet, there was a broad rose-colored ribbon, which fell exactly over it, so that I could only see the fringe of hair on either side, where it passed over her bush. I declare, Devereaux, I cannot describe the night I had with her, for it would drive you wild and you would be trying to slip into that woman at the Dak Bungalow, and it would never do, you being as you say, a married man, but I never—never—never had such a glorious poking in my life. It is true I was five years younger than I am now, and as I keep a pretty little piece of brown meat, and have my regular greens twice a week, I might not be able to do as good a turn now, as I did then, but I had that woman eight solid times, sir, seven times before I went to sleep, and once in the morning. She said herself that she did not expect it of me at first sight, as she said I was too fat, and fat men were bad pokes as a rule. When I went away after breakfast she gave me a case like the one Broadford showed me, and told me not to open it until I got home, and she told me she relied on me not to show it to anyone, unless I thought him a fit fellow for her to have. I'll show it to you now! Ha! Bearer! Khitmatgar! koi, hai!" and the excited major shouted to the servants, one of whom came. By his orders the major's bearer brought a little writing dispatch box, and from this he took a small case, some

CHARLES DEVEREAUX

six inches by four in size, and then, giving me a nudge, he walked to the anti-room of the Mess, which was deserted, showed me a very well-executed photo of a perfectly naked woman. On the back of the photo was written—from M. Searles to Jack Stone—15 June 1875,—8.

"Now!" said the Major, "anytime you would like to have that woman you drop me a line and I will give you the necessary introduction." I thanked him heartily, but I must say I did not feel tempted to give five hundred rupees for the favors of any woman, just then, and mentally I made comparisons between my Lizzie and Mrs. Searles, which were not favorable to the latter, though according to the photo, she was certainly a fine woman.

Then, after smoking another cigar, and drinking a couple of more pegs and talking Mrs. Searles and poking generally, I left to go home, and I looked forward to finding Lizzie, and getting rid of some of the hot blood which was running in a desperately excited manner through my throbbing veins, for the little major's conversation had been the reverse of cooling.

It was very nearly midnight when I reached the bungalow and there was not a light in the place. The stars had shown in the road fairly well, but the verandah and rooms, on my side at least, were pitch dark. I imagined that Lizzie must have grown tired of waiting up for me and had taken the opportunity of getting a good sleep before I came home, as it would not be wonderful, if, after a good mess dinner and full of generous wine, I were rather lively and put her in that condition too.

Full of this idea, and determined if possible to give her second sweet awakening, by getting into her whilst she slept, I stole on tip toe towards my room, to undress there and then join her in her "naked bed." But as I crossed the verandah something white gleamed on one side, and on looking, I saw it was Lizzie, sitting in my easy chair, apparently, from her position, asleep. I stole up behind her and bending over her I kissed her soft cheek, at the same time stealing my hand into her glorious bosom, and caressing her firm, swelling, elastic bubbies, which always gave me such delight to feel. Oh! What nice things good bubbies are to feel!

"Ah! is that you, Charlie, dear! I must have been half asleep," she said.

"Yes! darling!" I said softly, still pressing the delightful globes in my hand, one after the other, and kissing the sweet mouth turned up towards me.

Lizzie seemed to enjoy my caresses, for she returned my kisses and patted my face lightly with her hand. I found that although still dressed, her clothes were loose on her, and that I could pass my hand between the band and her waist, and her beautiful skin felt so soft, so satiny, so smooth, it delighted me as though I had never felt it before; and from her bosom I descended until I reached the pretty plain of her lovely belly. Here I let my roving hand wander from side to side as it gradually crept lower and lower, until I reached the upper fringe of the glorious bush which so splendidly adorned her dome-like motte, and then I threaded my way through this pathless forest until I reached the spot where the infold formed the precious and voluptuous deep line of her delicious nectar pot. I passed my middle finger in the groove, just tipping the awakened and slippery little clitoris, until I reached the entrance to the rich depths I sought for. Lizzie said nothing; my left hand, which was over the bosom, felt the breast rise a little more tumultuously, and my arm bore a slightly increased strain, as she leaned her head back upon it, but that was all. It was so dreamy, so exquisite, that I sat in that position, caressing the warm, moist bower, kissing the cherry lips with little caresses of mine, as if I were a dove billing its mate.

Suddenly a change seemed to come over me. I was no longer in India; it was no longer Lizzie whose charms I was master of, but my own beloved little beautiful wife. I remembered how, on the third night of our blissful and heavenly honeymoon, she had preceded me to bed, how it was the month of July, and the night was warm and balmy, the scent of the blossoming lime trees filling the air with its sweet aroma. I had given my Louie ten minutes to undress and perform those necessary little acts, to make her comfortable for the night, which no young married woman likes to do in the presence of her husband, and then I had gone up to follow her into the bed, my beautiful heaven, in which I expected to find her a luscious feast for my still ardent and excited and rather uncloyed desire. But when I went to the room she was still dressed. She was seated at the open window, reclining back into her chair. There were no candles. The stars were shining brightly but softly; the heavy masses of foliage on the trees loomed dark against the skies, and there was silence outside, except the occasional rustling of the leaves as the amorous zephyr kissed the heads of the trees it loved, and the poetry of the moment filled me with a degree of tenderness and love I had not experienced in a similar manner since Louie and I had been made one at God's holy altar. Like Lizzie she had only half-turned to accept my kisses, with a little question as to whether it was myself, as though it could be anyone else, as I had glided my happy hand into her so lately virgin bosom, and caressed the swelling globes, which it had so delighted me on my wedding night to find did exist in truth and reality, beautiful, round, firm, polished, elastic and rosebud crowned; for Louie had been so jealous of those exquisite beauties, that even when I had seen her dressed for the evening, in her low-necked gown, not one line of the lovely hemispheres did she show and I had to imagine beauties to exist where my fancy painted them; and I prayed I might find she really had sweet bubbies; for alas! how often is man deceived in his expectations as to the physique of his beloved bride. Neither of us spoke; we were too happy: and over her beautiful bosom my wanton hand had descended, until, finding her waistband loosened, it had explored the sweet pastures of her silvery belly, and crossing the rough surface of the mount of Venus, and as my fingers pressed in Cupid's furrow, the lovely little clitoris, ever on the watch, had sprung up to salute it with a moist and eager kiss; a thrill, which I could feel, passed over my Louie's form, and as she felt the strong middle finger bury itself in the hot depths of her, she had pressed my face to her burning cheeks, and murmured, "My man! Oh! my beloved man!"

Full of overflowing sentiment, which this entrancing quiet and this voluptuous scene of love and passion had inspired me with, I quite forgot where I was, who it was I was caressing. I kissed Lizzie rapturously and I murmured in a voice which must have quivered with deep emotion.

"Oh! my darling! my own, own, darling."

Lizzie started. She disengaged my hands and standing up, she exclaimed, in a voice which sounded strange to me, so different was it from her ordinary tone.

"Charlie! Charlie! Don't speak to me like that! Don't! like a good fellow!"

"Oh! Lizzie! what have I done?" I said in alarm.

"Oh! you must not speak to me like that! You know you don't love me, Charlie dear. You don't love me like you do your wife, and if you did it would only make me unhappy. Oh! Charlie! the one thing which would take away the only pleasure I have in life, would be to know that some man really and truly loved me. I could not leave my husband and live with him, and I must have a man as often as I can. You don't understand. When a woman has led the life I have she can't steady down unless some illness puts an end to all feeling of desire in her. She must go on as she is till death or decay, at least, of all her bodily powers. Confess now it was not Lizzie Wilson you were speaking to but your wife!"

"Well, Lizzie, dearest!" I said, quite thunderstruck with her vehemence and her outcry against love, "I won't tell you a lie. I did for the moment forget where I was. It was this way, but sit down darling, and I will tell you truly."

She did so, and still standing over her, and again possessing myself of the sweet charms between her thighs, to which she admitted my full right as a true friend, but not as an earnest and passionate lover, I told her about the scene of which I have given and can give my tender girl readers only a faint notion, as regards its delicious commingling of the adoration of the heart and the worship of the senses. When I had finished Lizzie heaved a prodigious sigh and said:

"Charlie! Take my advice and don't be too long sending home for that true wife of yours! She will keep you from harm out here, and it is not right, it would be a cruel shame to condemn her to pass the life of a nun, whilst you are amusing yourself in India, poking to your heart's content, women who do not deserve such delight. For, mark my words, you are not the kind of man to go without women, nor will you find a station where there are no women, pretty and fine, who will not leave you alone—they will be as eager to have you as you will to have them. Yes! believe me, if ever a man was formed to strike a woman's fancy it is you. Send for your wife, or between you and the woman you will have, some mischief will be brewed, and you may be made to repent that you left her at home."

These words, spoken with great earnestness, struck me very forcibly. It seemed also so like Satan rebuking sin that I could hardly help feeling amused. After a pause of a second or two, during which I gently stroked the sweet moss under my hand, I said:

"All right, Lizzie! I believe you are quite right! I will send for my wife as soon as you advise, but come in, there's a darling, and let us enjoy the fleeting hour. It seems like ages since I last had my manhood in this sweetest, softest, juiciest little place of yours!"

To this she replied, "Searles has been here tonight."

My goodness! All my blood ran cold. I felt now as if my Louie, in answer to my prayer to come to bed, so that I might enjoy her loveliness, told me, "Too late, my dear, So-and-So has just been having me and I'm not inclined for anymore!"

"Searles!" I exclaimed, snatching my hand away from under her clothes. "Searles, Oh! Lizzie! and did you let him have you?"

"I did not say that he had me, Charlie, so you need not get into a fit of jealousy, you silly boy! No! If there is one man in the world to whom I would forever say no, it is Searles, but he was here all the same."

I breathed. Somehow Lizzie had grown dear to me, she had been so nice, such a splendid love partner, and so tender towards me in spite of her disclaimer of love.

"What did he want, Lizzie?"

"What you say you do now, Charlie! But oh! we had such a row! I declare it has given me quite a headache! Oh Scarles! you. . . cursed beast!"

"And what did he do or say Lizzie? Tell me!"

"Well, you had hardly got across the road before Searles, who had apparently been watching for you to go, sneaked into the verandah around the corner, and asked if I had got his note. Now I had received a note from him which I had kept to myself, and which I had not shown you, dear, for I did not want to make you jealous, a fine production it is, too, and a very useful one for me, too, I can tell you. I think he must have been either drunk or mad when he wrote it, for he could not have written a more damning piece of evidence against himself if he had tried to do it in his sober senses. Oh! Mrs. Searles would give a cart full of her rupees to have it, for she could then get the divorce she longs for. Plenty of good fellows are ready to marry her if she could get divorced, and I know she has often said she would be glad to give up her present life, but Searles knows this, and his only revenge against her is to behave so prudently as not to give her any chance. If ever he has a woman it is so on the sly that no one knows it. Well, he has written down in black and white that he has had me and since Mrs. Searles left him, too. Let's light a candle and I'll show you the letter!"

Full of curiosity and rather astonished to find how the truth comes out, for I had certainly understood Lizzie to say that Searles had never had her, nor even should have her by her permission, I went for my candle and lit it. Lizzie then took the precious letter out of her pocket and gave it to me to read.

It commenced with prayers and entreaties to let him come and have her whilst I was at Mess. It said that he knew well that I did nothing all day and night but tumble her, that by this time she must be tired of me and at least that a little change of her accustomed diet would be agreeable. From prayers, it went to using threats. Her husband's regiment was at Peshawar, now with a newly-appointed colonel who was death on adultery and fornication, and he had given out that the first time he found any of it going on amongst the married women of his regiment, he would set the penal laws on the subject in force and that he (Searles), had plenty of evidence which would put me (Devereaux), into prison and send her out of the country branded as an unchaste woman, a whore and an adulteress, and that unless she admitted him to her embraces he would help the colonel to make good his word. Then came more prayer and more earnest entreaties—then offers of a thousand rupees (twice what his own wife charged)—jewelry, anything, if she would but consent, and then in a postscript, he boasted that he had already had her, at Agra, on an occasion when, stunned by a fall from an overthrown gharry she had been carried into his bungalow, and seeing who she was, and determined not to lose the precious opportunity, he had raped her in her unconscious state, and enjoyed the "wealth of her voluptuous grotto," he actually used these last words.

"The intense Blackguard," I exclaimed, moved to great wrath by the reading of this precious epistle.

"You may say so, Charlie! But now hear what the brute did. At first he asked had I got his letter. I said yes. Then he asked me in a wheedling tone would I consent and let him have me. I said not for all the rupees in India, that he was too loathsome a brute for me to touch with the end of a barge pole, much more so than for me to take in my arms. Then he began to threaten me with our new colonel, saying that I could not get away from here now unless he, Searles, gave me an order for a gharry, that everything like a cart with wheels was engaged for the next ten days, and that long before that time was over the regiment would be on, the march from Peshawar to Muttra, and that the colonel, finding me here instead of at Muttra, where he had ordered me to go, would be furious, and he, Searles, would take the opportunity then of telling him why I stopped at Nowshera, namely, to have three separate officers who stayed here, two on their way down country, and one on his way to join his Battalion at Cherat, and he would tell who these officers were, and it would go hard on them, each of them would lose two thousand rupees or get two years imprisonment, and then they will have good reason to curse you for being a damned little bitch, for why should you condemn them to these fines and punishment, when by letting me have you for an hour or two you can prevent any harm arising, and I will keep my word if you don't—and he got more and more angry."

"I told him I would see him damned before I would let him touch me, and I dared him to report me, or you or the others, and I told him what he had said in his letter, and how completely I would cover myself, and you, and others by it, and I advised him to go away quietly or I would call the Khansamah. That put him in as complete a passion as ever I saw a man in. He rushed at me and swore he would have me. I put myself like a shot behind a chair. He stopped for a moment, unbuttoned his trousers, pulled out his member, which was in a furious state, and then rushed at me again. I shouted for the Khansamah, but Searles did not mind. He seized me around the waist, and lifted me off the floor, and ran with me into my room, dashing the chick down as he lunged into it. But I was not going to be ravished without making the best defense I could. I got my ten nails well into his cheeks, and scrawned them down as hard as I could. I could see and feel the blood spurting. Searles yelled and cursed, swore and called me the most awful, dreadful names. I gave him as good a clawing as I could, but he got me down on the bed, pulled my petticoats up to his face, and lay on top of me with all his weight, trying to get his knees between mine. But I kept my thighs locked hard, although he pounded with his knees on my thighs, and nearly choked me with his hand on my throat, he could not get between them. I could feel the tip of his spike banging against my motte like a bar of iron, but he never once got it nearer me than that. At last, finding that he could not manage to make me open my legs to him that way, he began to put his hand between my thighs, and to pinch me most frightfully. Oh! he gave me dreadful pinches. I am sure I am all black and blue, but his weight was off me now, I was able to scream; and I yelled. I called out murder! murder! help! help! as loud as I could, and at the same time I tried to get hold of his eggs, so as to smash them if I could, but he managed to keep them out of my reach, whilst he pinched, scratched and beat my thighs as though he would break them to pieces. But before my fast-failing strength left me, help came. Two young civilians came in today from Peshawar, whilst you were dressing for Mess, and got a room on the other side of the Bungalow. They at last heard my screams, and came running to see what was the matter. When Searles saw them he ordered them out of the room, saying that I was his wife, and that he had a right to treat me as he liked; but I tried to get out of his clutches, and I implored the young men to save me; and I said that Searles was not my husband; and was trying to rape me. The young men then ordered him off my bed, and as he did not obey one of them pulled him off. Then Searles went for him, for he was blind mad with rage and passion, but the young man was pretty cool, and he gave Searles a most dreadful blow in the face with his fist—oh! I was so delighted to hear it,—it made him stagger and the blood spurt from his nose. But Searles seemed really like a lunatic. He rushed again at the young man, and hit him several nasty blows, so that the second one came to his friend's assistance. I urged the two on and Searles got a thrashing. I can tell you! Still he would not quit. By this time the Khansamah, the principal coolies, Oheestres, your servant Soubratie, and everyone belonging to the Bungalow had come. I could not help continuing to scream. Everybody went for Searles, and at last he was turned out of the house, yelling and fighting like a wild beast. Some soldiers came running off the road, and at first, seeing who Searles was, wanted to help him, but the young men told them what he had done, and apparently they don't love Searles at the barracks, for these men joined in beating him, and upon my word I began to get frightened. I thought they would kill him between them all. Oh! the row was tremendous. Presently down came the pickets from the barracks; the soldiers seeing them ran away. Searles was lying on the ground; a crowd around him; some men had torches alight, and the Khansamah had got a lantern, and you never saw such a group as they formed. The young men, who had helped to save me from being ravished, explained the whole matter to the non-com of the picket, and as Searles' trousers were open, and his stem showing, though no longer stiff and standing, they understood the whole thing. Searles, though hardly able to breathe, wanted them to take the young men prisoners, but the non-com officer begged them to go away, and persuaded him to let himself be carried home, for he could not walk. Oh! Charlie! it made me so sick and ill! I don't know how I have been able to tell you so much—my head is splitting, and I feel all pounded to death by that brute."

I leave my readers to appreciate the state of anger and disgust toward Searles which this vivid narrative of poor Lizzie produced. Oh! I had come home hoping for such a sweet night of delightful joy, but it was plain that it was out of the question, and indeed, all desire, except that for vengeance on Searles, was out of my head. Lizzie looked very ill, when I came to examine her by the light of the candle, and I begged her to go to bed.

"Yes, dear!" she said. "It is the best place for me, but oh! Charlie dear! I am afraid I cannot have you tonight! Poor boy! I am sure you came home expecting to have some grand poking, and I am so grieved to disappoint you, but I feel too sick!"

"You poor darling girl!" I cried, "I had hoped, as you say, to have some more delicious turns with you tonight, but of course it cannot come off now. Come to bed and let me help you to undress."

She did as I asked her. I undressed her and was shocked to find the state she was in. Her throat was bruised a little, but her poor thighs were one mass of contusions, all scored by the finger nails of the monster who had attacked her. I kissed them, "to make them well," and poor Lizzie smiled faintly and kissed me, and then lay down and begged me to leave her alone. But hardly had she put her head on the pillow than she called out that she was going to be sick.

"Oh! Charlie! Help me to my bathroom!"

But I ran and got her chillum chee, and brought it to her, and she, poor creature, was deadly sick. I held her burning forehead in my hands and did all I could to comfort her, and to assist, and at last, completely exhausted, she sank back and her whole appearance alarmed me. When I came home she was fairly cool, but now she was the color of a peony, and her skin was hot, parched and burning. I guessed she had fever and the suddenness of the attack alarmed me. All that night I tended her, keeping her well covered up to induce perspiration, and from time to time gave her water to drink for which she moaned. Nobody who has not watched a sick bed under circumstances somewhat similar, can tell how tedious, how weary, such a watch is, especially when, as in my case, the watcher is ignorant of what he ought to do, and has to go by instinct, as it were. At length, just as the morning began to break, Lizzie seemed to fall into a sound sleep. Her breathing was more regular and easy, her color was more natural, and—blessed be heaven—her skin was again cool, and moist. It was evident that the strength of the attack had passed.

A solitary crow gave vent to his rolling caw. The shrill cry of the kite sounded in the air. A squirrel began to run about and chirp, and all the sounds of night passing into day struck upon my ear. On looking outside I could see the distant mountain peak lighting up in the rays of the sun, which did not yet shine upon Nowshera. Satisfied that Lizzie was really in a healthful sleep, I got myself a cool peg, and then going back to the bedside I saw down in my chair, leaned my head against her pillow and, wearied out, fell into a sound sleep myself. How long I slept I did not know but I was at length awakened by Soubratie who touched me and murmured that sickening:

"Sa-hib! S-a-a-hib!" in my ear, with which your native servant always rouses you.

"What is it?" said I, raising my heavy head.

"Major Ish-tone, Sahib! Outside in verandah! wanting see master!" replied Soubratie who spoke English like a native.

"Major Stone! Oh! yes! all right! Tell him I will be with him in a moment, Soubratie!"

"Iss Sahib!" and exit Soubratie.

I felt desperately tired and not in a pleasant humor at having my much needed rest broken. However after a yawn or two, and an anxious glance at poor Lizzie, who seemed to have quite regained her ordinary appearance, and to be having a real sound and refreshing sleep, I tightened the strings of my pajamas, and went into the verandah, where I heard the footsteps of my friend the major, as he moved about somewhat impatiently. Seeing me come from Lizzie's room and in sleeping costume, he put up his hands in mock depreciation and said, Sotte voce:

"Oh! Oh-h-h! Captain Devereaux! Oh-h-h!" and he put on such a comical look I could not help smiling.

"Not so fast, major, please! Appearances may be against me, but I think I can give a satisfactory explanation. The lady who lives in that room was most dreadfully ill last night and I, out of pure charity, have been nurse tending her!"

"In your nightshirt and pajamas, exactly! I expect she required a little cordial administered by an enema, only in front instead of behind, and required your services and elixir! Oh! Devereaux! it won't do, my boy, but Jack Stone is not the man to peach, still he would like his friends to be frank with him, so Devereaux you may as well tell the truth and confess, that, full of my description of Mrs. Searles, and the splendid night I had between her plump white thighs, you came home and spent, I hope, as good a night with the fair lady in there! Confess now!"

"Quite wrong, Major, I can assure you! I plead guilty to having been much moved and stirred by your voluptuous narrative, and as human nature is frail. I dare say, might have spent such a night as you believe, only that the lady was, as I said, fearfully ill, and all owing to that blackguardly brute Searles, too!"

"Ah!" said the major, "that is just what I have come to inquire about. Look here, Devereaux, there is a devil of a row on. Searles was brought home last night between seven and eight o'clock whilst we were at Mess, with five or six ribs broken, his right leg broken above the ankle, his nose smashed flat, his front teeth driven down his throat, and battered, cut and bruised all over. In fact, the Doctor hardly expects him to pull through, he is so fearfully weak, and so completely smashed to bits. The corporal of the picket reports that, hearing a disturbance going on in the Dak Bungalow, he doubled his men down and caught sight of two men of the 130th running away, and heard loud voices in the Bungalow compound, he found a crowd of natives, too, two civilians, Europeans, standing round the brigade major, who was lying on the ground, all doubled up, and from what he could gather there was a woman at the bottom of it, but he could give no clear account of what had happened, or how it had happened, or anything. Well, the colonel is, of course, much put about. We none of us love Searles, who is a sulky brute, if a good officer, but a brigade major can't be half killed without a row being made about it, so he has sent me to try and find out all about it; and as I guessed you would very likely have heard something, I came first to you."

I then gave the gallant major a succinct account of the whole business, as told me by Lizzie. I had to undergo some unmerciful chaffing from Stone, about her, and found it impossible to hide from him the truth about my relations with her. But he promised to be mum, and, as he said, there was no need for my name being mentioned at all in the business, at all events at present, and perhaps not at all, as I was not at the Bungalow when Searles was there but at Mess, luckily for me!

Armed with his news, and quite interested how it was that Lizzie should be after having really had such violent ill usage, and having passed through such a terrible scene as she had been through, he returned to make his report to his colonel, and about four o'clock he sent me a note, or chit as it is called in India, to say that the colonel had agreed to hush the whole matter up, and simply report Major Searles on the sick list, and him—Jack Stone—acting station staff officer. He went on by saying that the sooner the parties were out of Nowshera the better, and he advised me to prepare Lizzie for a start, he would order a dak gharry for her as soon as one could be got, and a couple of ekkhas for me, the only wheeled vehicle which could run on such a road as there was from Publi to Shakkote.

Meanwhile, after he had gone away from the Bungalow, I returned to my post by poor Lizzie. I watched her for a short time and presently she woke; seeing me still there, and neither shaven nor dressed, she rightly concluded that I had not been to bed all night.

"Oh! Charlie! how kind! how good of you! How can I ever repay you!"

"By getting well as quick as you can, my Lizzie! And then—"

"Ah! Won't I just! If I was kind before I will be doubly kind now! But I am all right! I had a bad go of fever last night, and my poor legs are stiff and sore, but I am well! If I only had some quinine, now would be the time to take it, just to keep off a second attack of fever."

I had purchased a bottle of this invaluable powder at Bombay, and I ran and got it, and gave her the quantity she said would be right in a glass of water.

"There," she said, having made a wry face as the bitter dose ran down her throat, "now something to eat, for I feel faint for want of food and I am hungry. You see I was bad, my Charlie, but I think it was more fright than anything else."

I had, when I left her to go and get my peg that morning, and before I went to sleep, called Soubratie and ordered him to prepare and have ready whenever it might be called for, some strong beef tea, and this I had brought, hot and refreshing, to Lizzie, who was really moved at this additional proof of my care and devotion to her.

"Oh! Charlie! If all men were only like you!" she exclaimed, and the soft tears of gratitude rolled down her lovely cheeks. I kissed them off and she put my hand on one of her swelling breasts, saying:

"There! my Charlie! I would let you have me this morning if I could, but I feel too weak for that. I dare say when I have had another good sleep I shall be better, and then darling, we will play, won't we!"

I laughed and said we would, but put her hand in my turn, on my bunch of charms, and showed her how greatly fatigue and watching had reduced the strength and vigor of what the most ardent battles between her shapely thighs had not affected. Poor Lizzie! She looked so disappointed!

But as her little hand toyed with my limp dangle and played with my relaxed jewels, fresh life came, and to her joy she succeeded in raising a perfect standard, to be planted as soon as possible in the keeping of her fort. But both of us were wearied and tired out, and I told her she should go to sleep, and that I would go to my own bed and sleep too, for I was dead tired; and with more sweet kisses and caresses she turned on her side and was soon asleep. I then left her and going to my own room threw myself on my much needed couch, in the cool breeze of the swinging punkah, and was soon sound asleep.

Whilst Lizzie and I are thus hors de combat, it will, I think, be a good time to tell my dear readers her early history, and I will endeavor to keep her words as nearly as possible. So, gentle readers, imagine that

Lizzie and I are either seated in the verandah, after our dinner, or are in, or rather, on the bed together, whilst she tells her artless tale, certain portions of which she and I illustrated by very suggestive action, when either her memory added fuel to the amorous passion which made her blood boil, and my wanton fancy stirred all the man in me.

Well, Charlie, I was born and bred in Canterbury, my earliest recollections are all associated with that dear old place, and for the first thirteen years of my life I never left it. My mother is the only parent I can remember. I really don't know if my father was living when I was born, but I know I never saw him, nor even a likeness of him, and my mother hardly ever referred to him. Who was or what he was, I don't know, but my mother wore a wedding ring and no neighbors ever hinted at her ever having been anything but most respectable, and you know neighbors, especially women, don't always agree, and when they quarrel are very apt to pick up dirt and throw it at one another. My mother was a dressmaker by trade and had a very good custom. She never seemed in want of money, whether she had work or not; on the other hand, though we had an honest plenty in our house, there were no luxuries, nothing for mere show, except perhaps in one of the rooms kept for ladies to try their dresses on, where she had some little knick knacks for appearance sake. As a child I used to think that a splendid room, and wonder if anyone else had as fine things as my mother had! So you must understand we had a sunny, warm house, good food, good plain clothes, good beds, in fact, everything which was required for real comfort, but nothing superfluous.

My mother kept no servant, that is, no one actually lived in the house as such; an old charwoman came every morning and did what scrubbing and cleansing was required. My mother and I did light dusting, made our beds, etc., and cooked our simple meals. Until I was twelve years old I went to school, and as I was pretty quick, I learnt perhaps more there than girls usually do. And then, too, I formed acquaintances among the other girls, and as our conversations were not always about lessons, and sums, apples or lollipops, I gathered some information about the relations of the sexes, about lovers and their ways which I did not repeat to my mother. However what I did learn in this way in no respect had any effect upon me or my morals. I knew I had a little cranny, and that I should have babies one of these days, and that hair would grow where none grew at present, and that I should have regular monthly illnesses. I believed that I should marry, and when I did, I believed that my husband would put his "thing" into my "little thing" and that in time I should have a child, as I saw all married women have, but although girls used to talk about these matters, there was never any reference to the vast delight to be found in love making. We were all too young to know more than something vague and undefined. But before I was thirteen my mother withdrew me from school, not only because I was growing very tall for my age, but because my bosom began to form, and two lovely little doves of breasts to push out on either side of my chest. With what pride and pleasure did I see them grow. Even my mother, when she bathed me regularly every Saturday in a tub before I went to bed, remarked on them, and said to me one day, "Lizzie, you will have a perfect bosom. I don't remember ever seeing prettier and better placed breasts, or any which looked to be so quick growing." And I would notice her eye give a quick look down at my spot, and I guessed she was looking to see if my hair there was beginning to sprout. But my bubbies were a good bit grown before any came. However, the hair and my menses came almost together. First there was a profusion of little black looking points all over what you call my motte, Charlie, and it grew very rapidly, so quickly indeed that by the day I was thirteen I had quite a nice bush, which I could twine round my finger. My cleft, too, underwent a marked change. It seemed to grow fatter and become more formed. I can hardly explain, but I am sure you must have noticed similar changes in your engine and sack when your bush began to grow. You may say, then, that as far as outward appearances were concerned, I was quite a woman at thirteen. I had a fair amount of flesh on my bones, a lovely bosom, a nice waist, fine swelling hips, good thighs and very pretty feet and ankles. I was too well formed altogether for short dresses, and my mother made me some long ones, in which I used to admire myself in the tall glass in the trying-on room. Still although I certainly did admire myself, it never entered my head to court the admiration of men. I had not, as yet, felt the least spark of desire, and if, as I dare say she did, my mother watched to see any signs of coquetry or flirting in me, she saw none, for there was none to be seen. However I was much nearer the realization of the hidden stores of pleasure I had within me, than either she or I were aware of.

At the back of our house was a longish bit of garden, say something like fifty or sixty feet long, by thirty or forty feet wide. This garden was my mother's pride, for she raised early potatoes, and all kinds of vegetables in it for our use, besides plenty of pretty and sweet flowers, so that we always had nice vegetables for dinner, and nose-gays for our table and mantelpiece. At the end of the garden was a lane, on the other side of

CHARLES DEVEREAUX

which was a row of stables, where the officers of the cavalry used to keep their private horses. I used to be very fond of leaning against our little wicket, and see those beautiful horses go out for exercise, all bridled and saddled, being taken to their masters. Sometimes the officers themselves came to have a look at the stables, but they paid no attention to me, so I was quite accustomed to looking on without being spoken to. About August, however, when I was a little more than three months older than thirteen, some stables, which had been empty, were taken by an officer who had three beautiful horses. I was curious to see who this officer was, for he was new and so one evening I was watching for him, hoping he would come, when I saw a tall, slight, but a fine and very handsome young officer in undress uniform, stable jacket, breeches, long boots and spurs, and his gold-laced cap well on one side and far back on his head, come walking at a smart pace down the lane, smacking his boot every now and then with his riding whip and looking right and left, as if he were taking a good look at everything and that everything was new to him.

He looked at me, too, and gave me a good stare, and then he looked at the stable beside me, muttered something to himself, looked at me again, and with a little mock salute with his whip he turned into the stable. Then I knew that that was the new officer. There was something about him which took my fancy at once. He seemed so different from the others I had seen. They had always looked so heavy and black about the face, and altogether as if nothing was worth looking at on either side of them; whilst my new officer was so trim and jaunty, so pretty and nice looking, and he had actually smiled at me, and shown me that he had seen me. I felt quite a flutter when he made his little mock salute, and half drew back from the gate I was leaning on, but I did not go away. I wanted to see him again, so I stayed. Presently out he came, talking to the groom, then the groom went back into the stable. The young officer looked up the lane, down the lane whilst he pulled on his glove, then, seeing me, he came playfully towards me, made me a little bow, smiled and saying, "Good evening, Polly. A nice evening this." He turned and walked rapidly away. A new flutter again came into my bosom. I know I looked wistfully after him, and was delighted when, turning his head, he looked back at me from a little distance, and again waved his whip at me. Poor little fool that I was! I had fallen in love and I did not know it! But so it was!

Well, evening after evening this young officer and I met this way. Nothing more than what I have described passed between us. If an evening came and he did not appear, I used to feel so grieved. I missed him dreadfully. I found out that his name was the Hon. Charles Vincent, and that he was a captain in the Hussars. I heard the groom speak and that was how I knew; besides, all his horses had a big C. V. worked in white letters on their clothing.

Did I tell you that at the end of our garden, in the corner and next the road, was a little old shed without any door? No? Well, there was and I had planted honeysuckle and clematis and a climbing rose against it and as a school girl I used to love to learn my lessons there, when it was fine, warm weather. The honeysuckle and rose and other climbing plants had grown very well, and the dirty old shed was transformed by them into quite an elegant bower.

One evening my handsome officer did not come as usual, and I was vexed and sorry, for I did love seeing him, and he always seemed to look for me. I heard his groom talking to the men in the next stable, saying he wondered the captain did not come, and the bay mare was sick, and he had told his master of it. So I knew my hero was coming, and I went into my bower and sat down, and listened and peeped through the chink into the lane. Soon the grooms all went away but one, and that was Captain Vincent's. At last he seemed to be altogether out of patience, and I heard him swear, and talk to himself, saying he would be damned if he would stay any longer, but go and get his glass, and then he would come back. So he locked the stable and put the key into his pocket and went off. Well, I waited and waited! At last I heard the footstep I knew so well, and with a heart beating as if I had really expected and ardently wished for a lover, I went out, and stood as usual at the gate. The sun was setting and all the lane was in shadow. Captain Vincent came walking quickly, saw me, smiled as usual, saying, "Good evening, Polly!" and trying the door of his stable. Finding it locked he kicked at it, so as I knew there was no one in there, I called out, "Sir, the groom waited for you, and after a while said that he must get his glass, but that he would come back."

"Oh! did he, Polly! Thank you my dear!" and then coming near me he went on, "how long ago was it that the groom went?"

"Oh!" said I, guessing, for the time had seemed dreadfully long to me waiting, "about three-quarters of an hour, I should say, sir."

"Three-quarters of an hour," the captain exclaimed, looking at his watch, "well, then he should be along soon now, I should think. And how are you Polly! I see you here everyday. What a pretty hand! What a lovely girl you are, Polly! I declare I must marry you! Will you marry me, Polly, if I ask you?"

Well, of course I was a little fool, but I could not help being pleased beyond measure at his admiration and question, though it was quite plain to me that his question about marriage was only a joke.

"Oh! sir!" said I, "don't be making fun of me! You know I cannot marry you sir!"

"Well," said he, "at any rate you could give me a kiss, child, could you not, Polly?"

I felt my face burning. It was just what I was longing for. Oh! I cannot tell you how I had longed to be taken notice of by him. I looked around carefully, and seeing no one in sight, I said:

"If you are quick, sir, because someone might see and then there would be talk."

The words were hardly out of my mouth before the gallant and eager captain had his lips to mine, and gave me such a kiss as I had never had before in my life; a kiss which seemed to go right through my body down to my very feet!

"Polly!" said he, in a low voice, "could I come into your Summer House after I have seen my horses and chat with you a little while?"

I knew there might be a little chance of mother seeing him, so I said quickly and with a palpitating heart, "Yes sir! I'll go in now and wait, and you can come in when you are ready, and please don't stand there talking to me—for fear—you know!"

"I understand," said he, his eyes blazing as they looked into mine, and he turned away and walked a little down the lane, in the direction the groom had gone. I went into the "Summer House," as he called it, and stood watching at the chink. Oh! how my heart beat! Would he kiss me again! How I wished the groom would come, for if I stayed out too long my mother might call for me to come in. At last the groom came, the captain and he had some little talk, but no quarrel. I think I prevented that, for I am sure Captain Vincent was angry, when he found his man had not waited for him, but now he was certainly glad. He did not stay in the stable. He and the groom came out together, and walked away down the lane. Oh! what a pang I felt! Was he not corning then? How cruel! how cruel! I could not help it, I sat down and began to cry and sob, and all of a sudden there was my lover, inside the little house. He had come back as quick as he could, and had only walked the groom out of the lane to get rid of him. I sprang up as he came in, and he saw I had been crying, and he sat down and pulled me on his knee, and with one arm around my waist and his right hand on my bosom, he gave me, oh! hundreds of kisses! He seemed quite excited, and I was simply beside myself with happiness and joy.

"Oh! Polly!" he said, "do you know I've been longing to kiss you ever since I first saw you; you are the very prettiest, loveliest girl I ever saw."

I could only smile. It was rather dark now in the little house, but I could see him clearly enough. He kissed my face all over, and my neck too, and his hand closed over the bubbie it was nearest. I liked it too much to tell him to take it off, but I knew he ought not to have done that. All the time he was kissing me he called me his pet, his little dove, his lovely little darling, and so forth, and I stroked his hair and gave him sweet kisses too.

At last he said, "How old are you, Polly?"

"My name is not Polly, sir! it's Lizzie!"

"Well! How old are you Lizzie? Sixteen? Seventeen?"

"Sixteen! Seventeen!" I replied.

"No, sir! I am thirteen! I shan't be fourteen until next year!"

"Thirteen!" he exclaimed in surprise. "Only thirteen! Why Poll—that is, Lizzie, you must be more than thirteen! Who ever saw so fine a girl as you only thirteen?"

"Well, sir," I said laughing, "I am really only thirteen!"

He looked at me; he put his hand on my other bubbie and gave it a delightful squeeze, as if feeling it, and then he put it on its old place on the first bubbie.

"Then," said he, "I expect this, these rather, are only padding!"

"What?" said I.

"Why! these bub—these—what do you call them? Your bosom Poll—that is, Lizzie?"

"Indeed sir"; said I indignantly, "there is no padding about me. I do not require padding! Not I indeed!"

"Oh!" said he, laughing, "but Poll—that is, Lizzie!—I wish I could remember your name, my pet! No girl of thirteen has such fine, well-developed bubbies as these!" and he pressed them again and again. "They are much too fine for a girl of thirteen! You must be older than you think!"

"No indeed, sir! I know I am only thirteen!"

"Well! Then I don't believe these are real! They must be padding, Poll—that is, Lizzie!"

I was vexed. Why should he be so persistent? Why should he believe that my breasts were not good flesh and blood but only padding? So I said, "If you think I am only made up, sir, please don't feel them anymore!"

"But," said he, "Polly—Lizzie, I don't say that they are not real, the fact is I don't know what to think. There is a mistake somewhere, but don't be angry, my pet! Come—kiss!"

Those delicious kisses! Those delightful pressures of his hand!

"Lizzie, let me put my hand inside your dress!"

And so saying he began to pull at the front of my body which was fastened by hooks and eyes. They bothered him and he grew so dreadfully impatient that I, who was quite as anxious that he should be certain that I was not padded as he was to feel my bubbies that he found so nice through my clothes, at last pushed his too eager hands away and undid the obstinate front which opposed him.

"There!" said I laughing, "you can get your hand in now, but there is still a petticoat body inside to unbutton."

But the petticoat body gave him little trouble, and as if be were snatching for a prize which would escape him if he was not very quick, he thrust his strong but gentle hand between my shift and stays, and closed it over the firm little globe he found there.

"Oh!" he exclaimed, making a kind of sipping noise with his lips as if he were taking something hot to drink, "Oh! Lizzie Polly! Lizzie! what a splendid little bubbie, and what a smooth little nipple! Let me feel the other one now!"

And he reversed his hand and pushed it on to my right breast, which he went mad over like he had the other. The effect on him was wonderful. I cannot describe my sensations to you, Charlie, because you, being a man, cannot understand what a girl feels when hers are so nicely handled by a man as mine were then, but a kind of all-overish feeling came over me. I felt that I wanted to put my arms around my lover and clasp him to me! I felt that there was something more that I wanted from him; a something which I could only get by pressing my body to him as close, close as possible, but in the position I was with his arm raised up and his hand pushing at my bosom, I could not think of folding him in my embrace. All I could do I did. I put my arm round his neck and pulled his face down to mine, and kissed his mouth with a passionate energy which put him into a still greater ferment.

"Undo your collar, Lizzie! Oh! I must see and must kiss those splendid little gems of bubbies."

O! how his voice thrilled through me! I felt as if I trembled all over and his voice trembled also. It was passion, desire, love which had seized both of us. One knew its meaning well!—the other—myself—was still in a state of ignorance very soon to be cleared away.

I did not hesitate to obey him. I undid my collar, and he, pulling my dress wide open and off my shoulders and bosom, poured a torrent of kisses on my swelling breasts, and I—oh!—I leant back, supported by his strong arm, and gave myself and my thrilling bubbies to him to do with as he liked. It was beyond description. How his mouth flew from mount to mount. How his lips climbed each hill, and his teeth seized each little ticklesome nipple in its turn, and his hot breath descended into the valley between my breasts, and swept down over my body until my waistband stopped its further progress. But oh, whilst his lips were so busy, his right hand, in my lap, pressing between my thighs, was producing ravages in another part of my body. I felt inclined at first to resist, not because I did not like it, but because I felt a feeling of shame rise in me, almost stronger than the intense sensation of pleasure his moving fingers gave me.

"Ah!" said I.

"What, darling!"

How he said that one word, "Darling," as if his soul breathed it from his heart of hearts.

"Oh! don't put your hand there, sir!"

"Oh! yes! yes! yes! oh! my delicious Polly! Lizzie! What is your name? I must Oh! Lizzie I shall not be happy now until I have had you! You know what that means, don't you, darling? Say you will let me have you? Won't you?"

Well, I didn't know exactly, but I began to guess that love, marriage and the "putting of his little thing into my little thing," as the girls said talking of husbands and wives, were all very intimately connected and the pleasure his fingers caused in my melting little mound made me think that the "putting" too must be something heavenly—and I was right!

I don't know whether I said "yes" or "no," to his question, but he acted as if I had said "yes" anyhow! For he suddenly put his hand under my dress, and before I could say "Scissors!" he had it as high as it could go between my thighs, at the same time pressing me to him and kissing my mouth. My drawers, that came up to the waist in front, offered a slight obstacle, but his eager and nimble fingers found their way in! Oh! the delicious sensation of those fingers as they caressed my mossy bower! and the ravishing of one which he pushed in deep between its glad lips, I no longer attempted to prevent his doing what he liked. It was much too delicious. I opened my thighs a little more, and whilst he sucked my mouth with long burning kisses, that finger went in and out, in and out, every movement giving me more and more exquisite pleasure until at last a throb, a thrill a kind of jump seemed to pass through slit, moue, belly and all of me, and my lover exclaimed, "Ah! ah! oh! Lizzie darling! I have made you spend!"

Then for a moment he took his hand from between my thighs and I felt him doing something to himself. In a voice shaking with emotion and excitement he said, "Where is your hand, Lizzie? Give me your hand!"

He took it and put it on what felt like a great big thick stick, thicker than a broom handle, and hot and awfully hard, except for the outside, which felt like velvet, and which was loose and moveable. It was so big that I could hardly get my fingers round it. The very feel of it, however, made my brain whirl round. "What is this?" I gasped.

"It is me! Lizzie! it's me. It is my—my—my manhood! Don't you know darling, darling, Lizzie—that is what fits in here!" He had his finger moving in my cunnie again, setting me wilder still. "Let me put it in, darling Lizzie! It would kill me if you said no!"

"Oh!" I gasped, for I could hardly speak, "you can't do it sir! It is much, much too big!" and as I spoke I felt the curious, soft and elastic head which crowned his powerful weapon.

For all reply my lover put me off his knee on to the seat, jumped up, undid his braces, pulled down his trousers, pulled up his shirt and I had an astonished glimpse of what looked like an enormous white bar, with a red tip, growing out of a perfect forest of black hair.

Before I could either speak or resist my impatient Charles, as he made me call him, pulled up my dress, petticoats and all, and pulled me on his knees, so that I had one leg on either side, then, whilst he drew the lower part of my body towards him, he made me lean back. I had bend my knees to do so, and stand on the tips of my toes, whilst he was seated on the very edge of the seat. Oh! what a shock of delicious pleasure I received, and how astonished I was when I felt that he had pulled me right on what called his manhood, and that with a little kind of pop it had gone right into my cleft.

Except quickly over and over again, "my darling! my darling!" he said nothing, and as for me I was too much in heaven to think of speaking.

To support myself, however, I had to put my arms around his neck, and I hung back so as to give myself to him as nature taught me to do.

Charles did not make any attempt to take my maidenhead then. He wished to allure me by giving me nothing but pleasure, and oh! he succeeded! He pushed his big staff in until my maidenhead prevented further ingress, a then he pulled it back until it was almost out, and each time he did so I felt my grotto open and its lips slip over its vast head, as it had when it closed in front of it. Again I felt that exquisite spasm, and Charlie cried out that he had made me "spend" again, but soon he got powerfully agitated, his movements grew quicker and quicker, his thrusts more energetic, until all of a sudden he crushed me to his bosom, keeping his weapon in me, as deep as he could, and I felt that he was pouring something in hot, quick jets into me! It made me "spend" again, and then I felt something hot running all down my thighs, inside my drawers, and that all my bush and that part of me was inundated with something which had come from him. I felt almost inclined to faint with the inexpressible pleasure I felt, when all of a sudden I heard, "Lizzie! Liz-zzie!"

"Who is calling you?" said Charles, quickly putting me off him and pushing my clothes down whilst at the same time he jumped up, tucked away that thrilling thing of his, and arranged his clothes as best he could.

"Oh!" I cried, feeling dreadfully guilty and frightened. "It's mother!"

"Well," said Charlie, giving me a hurried kiss, "don't be frightened—fasten your dress—call out that you are coming!"

"I'm coming, mother!" I cried.

"Come then child!" was the answer as my mother went indoors. My lover could see through the tangled honeysuckles which hung over the hole I called my "window" and saw her go in. Then he took me in his arms and hugged and kissed me, and taking my left hand he put it on his stiff, big, huge thing, which was standing inside his drawers all up to his belly, under the front buttons of his drawers, and put his right hand between my thighs, and pressing my throbbing mound, he kissed me again and again, and begged me to meet him again the next evening at the same time, but to be careful not to let my mother notice anything strange in my behavior and appearance now. I promised, gave his delightful tool one more tender squeeze, and ran happy, but still nervous, to the house.

Mother only wanted me because she had some sewing for me to do. The candles were lighted but she did not seem to notice if I had more color than usual, nor if I trembled, and I, at first I felt my face burning, my bosom palpitating and my bubbies as though they would burst my dress. I still had the sensation of Charlie's dear hand and thigh, and as for my cleft, it seemed to have gone mad! It beat! It tickled! and my wet bush and my wet thighs stuck to my drawers! How nice it was! Oh! What sweet, sweet pleasure I had had! And tomorrow night I would have more! And fancy this grand, handsome gentleman thinking so much of poor me! A little girl like myself, not fourteen years old, with a real lover a lover with—oh—such a glorious weapon! Such a pleasure-giving poke! and fancy! I had no idea one's nook was so full of sensation as mine had proved to be! Oh! when he began those quick movements! When he began to spend! How he breasted! His "Oh my God!"

"My little darling!" showed what intense pleasure he felt too, my thoughts ran on that way, whilst my fingers mechanically worked the needle.

After I had gone up to undress for the night I made a minute examination of my naked self. So I was beautiful, was I? I had better bubbies than most other girls, and my little cave was a perfect gem! If only Charles could come to me in bed! How perfect it would be! He would do to me all night long what he had in the Summer House! But he was coming again next evening! I would try to get to sleep as fast as I could and dream of him.

But sleep would not come. I was too excited. I found myself putting my finger into myself as deep as I could, and pushing it in and out, as Charlie did his, but his finger was so much bigger than mine, it had given me more pleasure, and as for his manhood, oh! was it possible so huge a thing could by any possible means all fit in my slit? I could not believe it and yet he had told me it could. Why did it not all go in then this evening? Perhaps it was because he was so hurried! It might require more time. It was ever so long before I did sleep, and then, alas, I was disappointed! I did not dream of my lover or anything else.

Well, the next day did seem long! But I took the greatest pains to seem quite myself, though I felt I had undergone a tremendous change. I did not feel like the little girl who only looked for her admired young officer to be happy at the bare sight of him. I now expected, wanted, desired much more! And I got it! For, although when he came and found me seated in the little house, he at first did nothing more than kiss me, and feel my bubbies and cranny through my dress, because as he said my mother was so near it would be dangerous if I were in such a state of undress that I could not run out at once when she called, and meet and divert her from the Summer House, yet, little by little, he grew more and more excited; he did not, indeed, open the bosom of my dress, but he put his hand under my petticoats, and caught hold of my secret place and set it mad with his caressing fingers, and I, in my turn, felt his iron-stiff weapon, until at last he said, "I think Lizzie, we must have just one poke," and he asked me would I like to get his "man" out. Oh! would I not! I at once commenced unbuttoning his trousers and I got my hand in and pulled away his shirt and oh! the delight of getting that splendid big, hot thing in my grasp! and Charlie, delighted too, told me to be careful but to feel his jewels, telling me how to get at them and I did! The darlings! How nice they felt! Like two fine eggs in a bag of velvet! and then he pulled down his drawers and again took me on his knees, and I had the same delight of feeling his tool just popping its big hard head in and out of me and of spending, and the quick thrusts and his almost groans of pleasure, and the hot quick jets of spend he poured into and all over my excited cleft! This time we were not interrupted by my mother, and whilst he held me, still with his manhood in me, he asked me, "Lizzie, will you come and sleep with me? It would be so grand to be both in our skins in a nice warm bed! and then I could have you properly. I can't do it here. All of me ought to go inside you, but I cannot get half nor a quarter of it in."

"Oh! I should like it, but how can I ever sleep with you, my dear Charlie?"

"Oh! you must of course come with me! Come tomorrow! Meet me here and I will take you to Dover. We will spend a week there! Will you come, Lizzie?"

It seemed impossible. The idea of running away from home was so new to me and at first I could hardly bear the thought of it, but Charlie easily persuaded me; but what his persuasive voice said in words, his still more persuasive staff said in eloquent silence to my eager little slit! Oh! my slit was on Charlie's side.

I said I would do whatever he liked, and just what he told me. So, still keeping me in this delicious position, on him, he told me to get what little things I required, and to bring them during the next day, when I could best do so unobserved by my mother, and put them in the Summer House, and to be sure to have my best dress and best hat, and to bring all I had best, because I should travel as his wife, and I must look very nice indeed as his wife should. Then he said he would not come for me before nine o'clock, and I must manage to be quite ready. He wanted to know whether I should find it difficult to get out of the house so late, as if so, we must make another plan. But I knew I could do it easily, and I did so long, long for the time to come. I assured him I would be quite ready, and as nicely dressed as he could wish for, my mother being a dressmaker and I being a good "model" she always had me dressed, saying I was her walking advertisement. Then after many more sweet kisses and caresses, but no more—what might I call it? Well, make-believe poking, I left my adored lover and went into my sewing and my thoughts. Now I might as well say that although I afterwards repented bitterly of this escapade, and my heart reproached me dreadfully for running away from my mother in this cruel manner, especially as I had not the remotest cause or grievance against her but quite the contrary, yet I could not help it. None of those who, like myself, are endowed with passions of overwhelming force, can tell what a resistless power temptation is. I was indeed maddened with unfulfilled desires. I hungered for a blood feast. I had been as a, hungry tigress sniffing the exquisite prey, forgetful of all but the sight of her craving, ravening wants. I knew I was going to do infinite, perhaps irreparable wrong, but I was not mistress of my own will. My hitherto hardly-noticed or thought-of little slit had suddenly emerged from its obscurity, and captured and made me prisoner. In fact I fully think had Charlie been in Hell itself, I would have jumped in, to be in his arms and obtain his love.

So, after what seemed hours of waiting, and after a night of almost complete sleeplessness, the fated hour came. I carried out Charlie's instructions, I took, bit by bit, the things I required, and hid them in the Summer House, and when Charlie came he found me dressed and ready. I had changed my clothes and left those I usually wore everyday on the seat, where my mother found them a few hours later. I was in such a ferment of mind and body that I have a most indistinct recollection of how we left the little Summer House. I left it a virgin, not quite a chaste one it is true, and when I came back I was one no more! Heigh oh!

Well, I remember things more distinctly from the time Charlie put me into a first-class carriage, and followed me when he had seen my portmanteaus into the baggage van. There was only one other occupant, an old gentleman, who had evidently traveled from London. He took off his spectacles to look at me, and seemed so satisfied that I was worth looking at that he hardly once took his eyes off me until we reached Dover. It irritated me more than I can tell, being so stared at, but it amused Charlie immensely, who gave me sly little nudges from time to time and whispered in my ear that I had made a new conquest.

However I kept quiet, though I would have loved to say something pert to the old gentleman. The fact was that my nerves were strung to such a pitch of excitement that I often wonder my brain was not turned. We went to the "Ship Hotel," which, of course, you know is close to the pier at Dover, and Charlie took a private sitting room and a double-bedded sleeping room, and put himself down in the visitors' book as Captain Charles Vincent, and me as his wife with the Honorable before our names.

I felt very nervous indeed. Everyone seemed to look very hard at me. In my heart I said to myself, "They know I am not his wife!" I was so young, so inexperienced, I fancied that others could see into my heart and mind as easily as I could myself! I was—oh—so glad when we at last went upstairs to our sitting room. There Charlie took me in his arms and gave me, as he said, all the kisses and fond caresses and passionate embraces he would have given me in the train had not the horrid old gentleman been there. He took off my hat and cloak and went back a few steps and admire me, as he said, and when he had looked me over for a moment he ran up and again clasped me in his arms, saying, "Oh! Lizzie! I have never seen you so well-dressed before. You look as perfect a lady as could be, and only thirteen, my darling. This swelling bosom, these lovely bubbies and those splendid hips don't belong to a child of thirteen, but to one of nineteen or twenty; and your beautiful, really beautiful face, though delightfully young looking, is by no means that of a child!" and he kissed and petted and fondled me, and put his naughty, delightful hand between my thighs, and I began to lose all the nervousness I had, and leaned against him with a heart brimful of love and affection; and desire made me throb all over.

Charlie insisted on our having some supper, and we had a bottle of champagne. I did not feel in the least hungry and I told him so, but he said he was certain I had eaten nothing all day. He confessed it had been the same with him, and unless we ate and drank we should have no strength to support us during the night, for, said he, "If you think you are going to get a wink of sleep before four o'clock, and perhaps at all tonight, you are vastly mistaken, my Lizzie darling" and his eyes poured forth volumes of dazzling light into mine.

Before we had our supper brought Charlie had given me two rings. I have them both now. Here they are where he first put them. A wedding ring and a keeper with pearls, diamonds and rubies. This was my mock marriage and real honeymoon. I was afterwards really married with the same ring and that marriage was followed by a mock honeymoon. It was well he did this, for we were waited on by a handsome and pert maid, and several times I noticed her eyes fixed on my hands as if to see whether I carried the outward and respectable mark of matrimony. I wonder how many similar rings Charlie had given to other girls? He was a great ravisher of maidens. A great hand at seduction in all its phases—a perfect hunter after women—and I was only one of a great number who had passed from virginity to womanhood through the gates of his arms; for, like my last Charlie, my first Charlie began slit-hunting very young and being like you, handsome, well furnished with the necessary weapons, and rich, he scored far more successes than failures. He always said I was the gem of all he had had, and that he found me by accident. Certainly he had no trouble with me, for, like a ripe peach, I fell the moment his fingers touched me.

Well! after supper the maid wanted to know whether she should assist me to undress when I went to bed, and Charlie answered for me, saying that I was obliged, but I should not require her services that night, and he added that we were not to be disturbed in the morning, as we had come a long journey, and would probably sleep it out. The girl, I could see, struggled to suppress a smile. I was too plainly very recently married, if married at all, and I think she saw well enough that our night would not be passed in sleep! I know I blushed! I could not help it. As she left the room I caught her running her eye over Charlie, and unless I am mistaken, she thought she would willingly change places with me, and take her chances of getting any sleep in Charlie's bed.

And now I am very near the end of the life of my poor little maidenhead which died before I was fourteen. Few perish quite so early, but I am afraid, at least in that class of life in which I was born, few survive fifteen or sixteen. There are too many opportunities for such girls to get rid of these little pests!—but I did not know I had one at all. I was soon to learn it for the first time, but to know I had one only to see, or rather to feel it disappear forever.

Charlie, as soon as the maid was gone, begged me to go to bed! Now it is strange but true, and I think it is natural, that, eager as I was to be had, delighted at the idea of being in bed with him, knowing the pleasure I had already had from his sweet organ, but the "Bed" rather alarmed me. I would willingly have put it off, but Charlie begged and besought me not to delay his happiness and mine too, and feeling a little like a real virgin bride, no doubt, I suffered him to lead me to our room. There was the altar of love on which the sacrifice was to be offered! A fine, big, wide bed such as I had never seen before. The room was large; there were two tables, with basins, etc., a splendid wardrobe with a door made of a mirror at least six feet high, on the walls were nice pictures of landscapes in oils, and on the floor a carpet which deadened every footstep. I had never been in such a magnificent bedroom in my life. I was dumbfounded with admiration and wonder. It all looked so much too splendid for me.

"Now darling! darling!" cried Charlie. "I must go and take half a dozen whiffs of a cigar, and see who are in the house, so as to find out if there is anyone I had better keep you hidden from. I won't be long. You unfasten your clothes but don't take them off. I will be your maid tonight—and—your man too!"

"Oh! Charlie! don't be long! Don't leave me all by myself!"

"No one will come and eat you, my pet! Besides," said he smiling, "you may like to find yourself alone for a few minutes."

I understood. I did require it very much, and I said no more to detain him. I saw the necessary article, and in my mind I thanked my Charlie for his kind thought. It seemed so delicate of him, too, and I felt my heart bound towards him.

Before I followed his instructions and loosened my clothes, I peeped out of the window and saw a lovely sight. You know Dover, I dare say. The view of the Esplanade, with its lamps all lighted, the lights in the castle, and in the houses along the beach glittering like so many stars, was a sight I had never seen anything like before. The murmur of the waves splashing on the shore and against the pier, came softened to my ears, and made me feel a dreamy happiness which I cannot describe. Then suddenly remembering what I had to do, I let the blind fall from my hands and set to work unhooking my dress, and unbuttoning and loosening the strings and whilst doing this my Charlie came in, with quick, eager steps, catching me in his arms, putting his thigh between mine and exclaiming, "All right, my Lizzie! No one here that knows me or who I know. Now! my pet! let me undress you! We will put our skins on and have a lovely—oh, a lovely night in that heavenly bed."

Oh! he was quicker at taking off my clothes than my experience in the Summer House at home would have made me believe possible. In a brace of shakes he had me naked, all but my chemise, stockings and boots. I thought he would leave me my chemise, but you will see. Taking off my boots and stockings, he made me sit down on a chair, and his naughty hands kept on pushing up my chemise, to be out of his way, higher up my thighs than was at all required, and somehow my mound would come (as he said) in his way. It was lovely! He tickled me so, he made me laugh—he excited me so, that to pay him out I put my now naked foot between his thighs. At once he took it, and put the sole of it on to his beautiful stiff weapon and a thrill like electricity shot all through me. My touch made him hurry up too. Both stockings were off now, and I was going to rise off the chair, when he pushed me back and said he must see my shoulders and bosoms and bubbies bare! In a moment he had my chemise off my shoulders, so it lay round my middle, all above that was perfectly naked. With a cry of delight he fell with his mouth on my bosom, kissing, biting, nibbling, whilst he pressed between my thighs and stroked them beneath my chemise with his hands. Then, suddenly rising, he caught me in his arms, pulled me straight up, and my chemise falling to the floor, he lifted me up, kicked it away, and put me down in front of him as naked as I was born.

"Oh! Charlie!" I exclaimed, "how could you! Let me have my chemise!" and I put my hands, naturally, over my motte, for I felt shame glowing all over me, to be so dreadfully naked in the presence of a man!

"Oh! my lovely, my beautiful Lizzie! I cannot let you cover up that lovely form and those exquisite charms! Look girl! Here! Come look at yourself in this glass, and say did you ever see anything prettier in your life!"

And he half pushed, half carried me, a most unwilling victim at that moment, before the high cheval glass in the wardrobe, of which I have spoken.

Oh! I can hardly tell you what an impression my own reflection made on me! The moment before I felt as if I were crimson all over, from shame at being completely naked in the presence of Charlie, but now I was so struck with what I saw before me, that all feelings of shame vanished, and were replaced by a flood of pleasure. I had never seen myself, as a whole, naked in the glass, for I had no such mirror in my own little bedroom at home, and it never struck me to strip myself and see what I was like, when clothed in nothing but my naked charms, by the assistance of the cheval glass in mother's trying-on room. Besides all the surroundings were in favor of my seeing myself to the highest advantage now. The wallpaper of the room was dark, and reflected light badly, so that my figure in the mirror stood out against a dark background and showed up with dazzling whiteness. I could not but admire myself. Mother had often said I was a well-made girl, but she never expatiated much on my figure or my charms. Here I had them all before me, and I was amazed and delighted at the revelation! You, Charlie, have seen me naked, and know what I am like now. Well! I was nearly as rounded in form and full in figure, and shape of my limbs as now. What perhaps struck me first, most of all, was what a nice unblemished skin I had. Next, how lovely my shoulders and bosoms were, how slender my waist, and how beautifully my hips gradually expanded until they were wider than my chest. My pretty little bubbies, well separated, each looking a little away from the other, each perfectly round where it sprang from my bosom, and both tapering in lovely curves until they came to two rosebud-points, next caught my delighted eyes. I had never seen them look so lovely as they did now, as they gleamed and shone, apparently whiter than the body from which they grew, as the light flashed upon them. My belly, smooth, broad and dimpled in the centre with a sweet little navel, like a perfect plain of snow which appeared the more dazzling from the thick growth of hair which curled in dark rich brown locks on the triangle of my moue, gradually growing thinner and less close as it tapered to that point which receding between my rounded thighs, divided at the spot where my pretty, demure little slit commenced to form. I could not see the whole of my grotto, when I stood upright, for it turned in between my thighs too quickly, so to say, as if it felt that it should hide itself until love demanded it to be displayed by the action of opening my legs. My thighs, knees, legs, ankles and feet next came in for their share of inspection, and by the time I had looked myself over from head to feet, I came to the conclusion that Charlie was right, and that a lover should be permitted to gaze with enraptured eyes on charms of no common class of beauty. Don't think me vain, but I have been too often told that I am beautiful to believe that every man who has seen me naked is and has been a liar.

Well, whilst I was thus intoxicating myself with my own reflection Charlie was not idle. He had completely stripped himself, and came eagerly up, as naked as myself. He put his arm round my neck, and stood beside me, adding his masculine beauty to the picture I saw in the glass before me.

"Now Lizzie! is not that a perfect picture? Don't we make a real handsome couple?"

I could only respond by putting my arms around his waist and pressing him to my side. His warm body sent a thrill through me, as I felt it in this delicious close contact, and I saw a little ruby and shining point suddenly protrude between the upper lips of my excitable little mound. Oh! Charlie looked splendid! I took my eyes off myself to gaze at him in wonder and admiration. He looked so powerful, yet so lithe. His shoulders were as broad as mine were narrow, and his hips as narrow as mine were broad. His deep and manly chest contrasted with my more graceful but completely feminine bosom. His arms, long and muscular, seemed perfect models in marble, and every movement on his part showed the firm muscles move under the skin beneath which there was little of that soft fat or flesh which made my limbs and body so pliant and smooth. But naturally, it was his long, stiff, straight, grand-looking tool and the big rough bunch, which formed his handsome jewels underneath, in their velvety wrinkled bag, which chiefly attracted my burning eyes, for there it was, that truly stalwart staff, pointing up at my face! It seemed a formidable weapon indeed, so strong, so conquering, so irresistible. Its head, of a more or less rosy color with a suspicion of violet at the edges, was half uncovered, and its almost impudent look amused me, as it seemed to scan me with its slit-like little eye on its top. I could see that this splendid weapon grew broader and thicker at its base, where it sprang from a forest of hair which clothed my lover's moue, and slightly tapered until it reached its head, where it suddenly widened in again to taper quickly off to a rounded blunt point, here its "eye" was. Charlie took my hands and when he put one on his sack, and the other on his manhood, and he made me feel and press them for a moment. I almost fainted with the thrilling emotion this feeling of him sent through me, and clasping me to him, he pressed me against himself, so that his mighty spear-like weapon was closed in between his belly and mine. I could feel its point high above my navel, and I remember wondering whether supposing he could get it in I should feel it up inside me as far as that! At the same time I felt certain that to get so huge a volume as that into my tight and small cranny would be impossible. I was convinced of that.

After a few more thrilling caresses on the part of each of us Charlie said, "Now Lizzie!" lifted me up in his great strong arms, and carrying me like a baby to the other side of the bed, he laid me down on my back, pulling the sheets down. Oh! I was inclined to have him! My whole body panted for him! My bubbies seemed to be swelling as if they would burst and the little red nipples on them were as hard as peas and tickling me! As for my sheath, it was raging! Such a throbbing as went on in it I had never felt before, not even when he had half had me at Canterbury. I expected him between my thighs, which I opened for him, but instead of taking his own place there at once, my irritating lover commenced kissing me on the mouth, cheeks, eyes, ears, throat and all of that part, whilst his hand wandered over my bosoms from bubbie to bubbie, which he tenderly felt and pressed. He did not seem to be in half the hurry I was. If his intentions were to drive me half frantic with desire, to raise up all that was lascivious in my senses, he certainly succeeded to perfection! But really he was right. I always think a good preliminary engagement of hands and lips makes a poke much more delicious than when one comes to close quarters without any at all. Charlie's lips descended from my lips to my bosom. He laid his head between my breasts, and turning it from side to side kissed either bubbie as his lips encountered its warm, rounded sides, and whilst so doing his naughty hand crept, crept, crept over my belly, down my groin, down my thighs, up again, all round my motte, then skimmed my bush with finger tips, then just touched, but no more, the line of my sweet tunnel until I could hardly endure the almost agonizing pleasure he caused me! Then suddenly he took a firm bite of one breast, and in went his strong finger, right up to the knuckle, with a bang against me, and this he repeated, biting, but not hurting, my other bubbie, and then with repeated kisses his mouth rove over my belly, down the groin, down one thigh, up the other, just like his finger had done, until suddenly he brought it up right to my quivering spot, which he almost burnt with his kisses! I could feel his tongue darting at my agitated, excited lips, and at last, unable to bear it any longer, I almost screamed to him to leave off that, and give me what I craved for. He turned a dreamy look at me, when he suddenly seemed to wake up, as it were.

"Oh! I nearly forgot!" said he as he ran to the mantelpiece and brought from it what looked like a pot of pomatum.

"This is cold cream, my Lizzie! As you have never had all me inside you yet, and your delicious little cave is as tight as can be, some of this will help us both! Hold the pot darling, and let me anoint your sheath, Queen of my sword!"

He took fingerful after fingerful of the cream, and put so much of its cool substance inside me I thought he meant me to have it all. It was so sweet and cool and pleasant, I liked it for its own sake, as much as for the sake of feeling his finger push it as far in as it could.

"Now," said he, "anoint my King of your sweetest sheath, my Lizzie!" and he turned that awful mad looking weapon towards me. I took it, close to the root, by my left hand, and with my right I anointed its head as I stroked the cream down, its hood slipped right off, and gathered behind its spreading shoulders, and here Charlie made me put a great lot of it. Then with both hands I, by his directions, put all that remained in the pot on his shaft, until it shone as though dipped in oil! Oh! the feeling of that organ! I am sure you remember the excitement you must have felt the first time you had a good free and complete "feel" of a girl, Charlie? Well! think of what I experienced, for this grand rod, those glorious eggs, all mine, to press and caress in perfect freedom for the first time.

Charlie made me wipe my hands on his curly hair and then, with a triumphant, "Now Lizzie, open your thighs! Now for heaven and bliss and all that is delicious," he pushed me on to my back, and was between my willingly opened arms and thighs before I could wink! He made me introduce himself into my cunnie, then he put one hand under my head, and the other under my hips and with a slight pressure forced, or rather easily slid his weapon in as far as it had ever gone before. At first, as if careful not to raise any doubts in my mind, he contented himself with toying in and out, as he had done at Canterbury, giving me delicious pleasure, but suddenly he gave a thrust which stopped my breath, and he kept up such a fearful pressure that it began to hurt me not a little, but a good deal, I can tell you.

"Oh! Charlie!" I cried out, "Don't darling, you are hurting me dreadfully."

He said nothing, but gave me a kiss; then laid his cheek to mine, and gathered me more firmly than ever in his arms, and again seemed to violently burst away into my inside!

I almost screamed, but Charlie would not listen to my entreaties! Again and again did he batter, and at last, with a sickening sensation of rending and tearing, I felt that the obstacle, whatever it was, had gone before his dreadful poke, and that each stroke, each thrust, was carrying it deeper and deeper into my inside! I really feared he had burst my poor little nook, and that I should die in consequence; but, before I could express myself in words, I felt that every atom of that awful machine was buried in me, for I could feel Charlie's sack against me distinctly, and as for our bellies, they were completely pressed together, as well as our mottes! Then Charlie relaxed that tremendous grip on me, and raising his face looked eagerly into mine, and smiled and kissed me and said, "Ah! Lizzie darling! I hope I don't hurt you very much! You had such a dreadfully tough little maidenhead, and your little cave is a tight one—so much the better! for you will have the more pleasure! Do I hurt you now darling?" and he kissed me tenderly.

"Not now! but oh, Charlie! you don't know how much you did hurt me! I hope you have not done me any harm!"

"Not a bit," said he laughing. "I am glad it does not hurt you! But now for pleasure, my Lizzie! You lie quite still and let me play with you quietly and you will see whether you won't forget any pain I gave you."

Then commenced those splendid, exciting, thrilling, long strokes. Even that very first time I felt great pleasure from them, and afterwards when all soreness had completely disappeared, I remember, as it were plunging into the new world! My cranny was like a violin, and Charlie's instrument like the bow, and every stroke raised the most ravishing melody on the senses that could be experienced or imagined! Oh! I am sure he was right when he said that never was there a girl so plainly brought into the world for poking and poking only, as myself! I adore it! I can't live without it! And at times I cannot imagine how any man or woman can pass a day without having it at least once or twice.

That was how I lost my maidenhead before I knew I had one! Ah! That week at Dover will always be remembered by me as the most exquisite in my life. Charlie was never done! He was so kind too! He took me out for long drives—showed me the castle—took me out boating; laid perfect fairy plans for our future. I was to be his own pet love! I was to live in a sweet little house in London, to have my carriage and servants and all that I could want, and I should be his darling mistress, almost his wife. Not once did I remember my poor mother, or my duty to her as a child. I declare it seems most terribly selfish—but oh! I was ravished with my lover, and the whole world seemed centered in him! And yet when the test of that burning love came to be applied, you will see how it stood.

Yes! Yes! It was an exquisite dream! Such a dream as I have often wished to have again but never in my happiest moments since have been able to approach!

Well, it was all settled. Charlie's leave would be up now that our six-days honeymoon was spent. We were to have one more blissful night in one another's arms, and oh! how I had learned to love being well poked! How I had come to appreciate its ravishing joys, its indescribable delights! We were, I say, to have one more night at Dover, and then

Charlie was to take me to London, leave me in a hotel for a day, get more leave, and come and hunt up a nice little house for me, etc., etc., as he had planned, and I was to be his kept mistress. The idea of returning to Canterbury to my mother had completely faded from my mind. From her arms I had been snatched away to quite another, and perfectly different life, and like the brilliant fly, I could no longer think of resuming my life as a grub. The thing was impossible, so impossible that I never gave it a single thought.

But, ah! there are a good many "buts" in the world, which like stones in the road are apt to upset the steadiest and most courageous—but, the last evening of our stay in the Ship Hotel, a note was brought to me, just as I was going to take off my things. Charlie and I had been for a long drive over to the camp at Shorncliffe. A glance at the writing showed me it was from my mother! I dropped on to a chair and Charlie, seeing me look as if I should faint, ran up in alarm.

"What is it, my darling? Who is this from?"

"Oh! Charlie," I exclaimed, "it is from my mother!"

"The devil! What does she want? What business is it of hers, I should like to know, to come interfering?" cried poor Charlie, who forgot that she had every possible business to do so.

"What does she say?" he went on impatiently, for I had not the courage to open the note but held it in my shaking hand. "Here, girl! give it to me! Let me see what the old—h'm—old lady says."

"Lizzie, your mother is on the pier and asks you to come out for a moment to see her, or she will come in and see you here! You had better go, darling! It would not do to have her kick up a row in here. Will you go with her if she asks you, Lizzie? Tell me! God damn and blast it all! What an unfortunate thing! Lizzie, Lizzie! You must not leave me! I can't live without you! I must have you! Do you hear?"

I was drowned in tears and my bosom was torn with sobs. I loved Charlie! Oh! I did! What girl would not love a lover who had adored, worshipped and poked her as Charlie had me? But on the other hand I loved my mother too. How dearly I did not know until now. The two affections, the old and the new, wrestled within me. I was at the parting of the ways, and if it had been possible I would have liked to have walked on each of the roads.

"Oh! Charlie!" I cried, as I threw myself in his arms, "I cannot say! I cannot say! Perhaps mother will tell me that after what I have done she won't have me home again!"

"And then!" cried poor Charlie eagerly. "And then of course, I would come with you, Charlie."

"That means if your mother—confound her!—says come home, Lizzie, you will leave me?"

"Can't I go home with her if she will have me and come to you another time, Charlie dearest?" said I.

"Well!" he cried, "now let us get rid of this uncertainty, Lizzie! Though it rests with you, I fancy! If you had any pluck at all you would send her word that you could not see her!"

"Then she would come in here, Charlie. You don't know my mother! She is very kind, but if she says she will do a thing, she does it!"

"By Jove! Yes! I forgot! She would come in here and then there would be a devil of a row! Run! Lizzie! run, and keep her out like a good girl!"

I dried my eyes and quickly went down stairs, and out of the hotel, and on to the pier, along which I walked, straining my eyes in the fast gathering darkness to see where my mother could be. At last I saw a figure standing just in front of the recess, and I recognized my mother and flew to her. She received me with open arms, folding me tightly to her bosom, and there we both stood clasped together, and both sobbing as if our hearts would break.

Charlie, I can't go into the details of that sad meeting. You must spare me and let me only say that my mother did not say one word of upbraiding or scolding; she told me that she had nearly died of fear and sorrow when she found me gone and keeping her wits about her she spread no report, asked nobody about me, but putting two and two together came to the conclusion that if I had gone with anybody it would probably have been an officer of the Hussars. Then she found out that Captain Vincent had his stables behind our house and that he had gone on leave from the very day I had disappeared, and accidentally she saw his name and that of his wife in one of the Dover papers, as being at the "Ship." She had found out that he was not married, had come straight to Dover, on a chance had sent the note, hoping that the Hon. Mrs. Vincent might be myself, as indeed it was! She said that whatever mischief had been done had been done, and that the only thing to do was not to make it worse by raising a scandal. She told me to go back to Charlie, to stay with him for the night, to manage to return home after dark to Canterbury, where she would meet me and have a cab ready outside the station. Our reserved and quiet way of living had prevented our neighbors noticing my absence, and unless some future event happened nobody need know anything about it.

All my dreams of a little house in London came to an end. I loved my Charlie, it is true, but it was slit love more than that of the heart, and my mother easily prevailed on me to give him up. Charlie, poor fellow, was overjoyed when he saw me return. He fancied I was coming back for good, and his disappointment was intense and bitter when he knew that I had firmly resolved to return to my own home, and not to go to London with him; but presently when the first bitter draught was swallowed, he said that of all wonderfully wise women he had ever heard of, my mother beat all in letting me back to him for the night. There was and could be no scandal, and he thought that a girl possessed of such lively senses as myself could never go back to such a humdrum life as mine had been before he taught me what a heaven was to be found in his arms and from his God-like and splendid staff! We made the most of that night! I, because I firmly believed I should never have Charlie again, and he, because he did not know when he should be able to have me again, though he quite believed our separation would be but a short one.

So I returned home. Oh! what a wonderful woman my mother was! Not one word of reproach did she utter! She left that to my own heart, and I can tell you that myself-upbraidings were infinitely more painful to me than anything she could have said! But what she did do was to point out the awful dangers I had run. She told me how easy it was to lose one's good name and reputation, and how infinitely difficult it was to get anything like that back again. She gave me instance after instance of girls who, commencing by being what I was to have been, the petted mistress of a rich and handsome gentleman, ended as common whores in a brothel, dying of disease and drink before many years, if their unhappy lives had not driven them to put an end to themselves by suicide. One thing kept both of us uneasy for a while. There was every prospect that my loves with Charlie might result in a baby, but that terrible event, terrible for a girl like me and a mother like mine, did not come off. I had no child by Charlie that time, though one of those I had afterwards may have been his, and I used to like to think it was.

Ah! well! I had a quiet and not altogether unhappy life with my mother until I was fifteen. The Hussars had left Canterbury and though I naturally often thought of Charlie. I was rather indignant that he never apparently once tried to see me again. He told me afterwards that he had done all he could think of to get letters to me. Perhaps my mother intercepted them. I never got any of them. I hate the next episode in my life. One day I met a sergeant, dressed in the old and beloved Hussar uniform, I got talking to him, and from talking, I got to walking, and from walking to love making, and from love making to poking! I could not help it! I wanted a man most dreadfully, and all my old fires came back at sight of the Hussar uniform. Of course I acted deceitfully, and hid all from my mother, who hoped by trusting me fully, to prevent all such action on my part. My new lover was only on furlough. He had not been gone long before I found I was, this time, let in for a baby. My distraction nearly killed me, and all the more because I feared to tell my mother. But time told her. My figure lost its elegant shape and I had to confess—the awful, awful pain of that confession. But true to herself, my mother lost none of her wits. She found out my second seducer, went and saw him, found him to be the master tailor of the regiment, told him what an excellent dressmaker I was, proposed marriage, held out the promise of a fair dowry, her savings for many years—poor mother!—and I was married to Sergeant Thomas Wilson in time to save the legitimacy of my baby. But we did not live happily.

One day when my husband was out, Charlie came to see me. Oh! I was glad to see him. We had a long explanation and it all ended on his having me on my husband's bed! I was had again—joyful thought—by the darling man who had taught me what a sweet thing it was! But hardly had Charlie gone than in came Tom. Going from room to room he saw his own bed tumbled, and then he grinned! He accused me of having had Charlie whom he had met, and of whom he had heard about, goodness knows how, and there and then he made me an offer which I accepted. It was that to bring him custom, I should let myself be—admired. He would hear nothing, see nothing, know nothing! I was too unhappy with him not to jump at an offer which would give me back Charlie! All that had to be done was that a suit of clothes should be ordered from time to time, and Charlie ordered at least a dozen. Someother suits of clothes were ordered by other officers, and my husband had them all, everyone, from Colonel to Junior Lieutenant, on his books, and I had them all as my lovers. I had several children. I only know the father of one, for certain, and that was my husband. I think the second was Charlie's but I am not sure. None lived.

That is my story, a sad mixture of happiness and misery, folly on my side and wisdom on my mother's. I know I am no better than I ought to be, but I cannot help it! There! Let us say no more about it!

Poor Lizzie! As I would gaze at her beautiful face in which nothing but purity, chastity and great power and self-control could be seen by the eye of one who had not the same means of knowing what her real nature was, I could not but wonder how it could be that such a sweet countenance could be the seat of a Temple in which Venus reigned, not only to the exclusion of all other Gods and Goddesses, but with more than ordinary power. I must leave my gentle readers to form their own conclusions of this lovely wanton, but that there was much good in her I became convinced the more I knew her. At all events it is not for me to throw the stone of condemnation at her. To enjoy a woman and then run her down is not my motto. Lizzie must have had a yearning for a purer and a better life, for she was constantly urging me to send for my beloved Louie, warning me that if I did not I should most certainly constantly wander from the path of virtue, and also saying that it was not fair to any woman, especially one who loved her husband, in every sense of the expansive word, to leave her to pine alone. Well, it was my hope that either I should rejoin my Louie in England, or that she should come out to me in India, but the fates were against it; and Venus herself, who may have considered that one so fit as myself to be her high priest, should not be restricted to only one Temple in which to offer up the sacrifice of incense so dear to her, but should have his delightful duties extended to worship of her in other shrines, of which so many were either already consecrated, or ready to be opened, for that holy and voluptuous rite.

During the remainder of my stay in Nowshera, I enjoyed my tender Lizzie in all tranquility and my tender girl readers may be sure that every opportunity was taken, and none lost, of procuring both for her and for myself the most complete pleasure which our active senses could expect. Her poor thighs were still marked by the violence of the brutal Searles when I last saw them, but the sweet, sweet mound between them lost neither beauty nor attraction on that account. To this day I look back upon that week of ardent love making with regretful delight. I have never yet succeeded in regretting having sinned against heaven and my dearest wife, in having broken the seventh commandment with Lizzie. Stolen waters are sweet, saith Solomon, and I, Charles Devereaux, say to that Amen, Amen, verily that is true.

Our new station staff officer, my good friend Major Stone, got a dak for Lizzie and two ekkhas for me, and we started off on our respective routes on the same day; Lizzie started in the morning and I in the evening, she making for India proper, and I for Shakkote, at the foot of the hills on which Cherat is situated. It was not without a pang on each side that we parted, and we exchanged locks of hair, pulled from our respective bushes. I have hers still and never look at its now somewhat faded curl but that the delicious days and nights I spent in her fair arms at Nowshera, come back to my memory with a force that if she only knew it, adds to the happiness I feel everytime I seek the joys I experience so keenly, between my Louie's delightful and voluptuous thighs, and my Louie does not lose, I can assure you, by my having been unfaithful with Lizzie!

I took Soubratie with me, leaving "Mrs. Soubratie" to look after my luggage for which her husband was to return when he had seen me safe as far as Shakkote. I heard that she formed the delight of the gallant officers at Nowshera during her husband's absence, and that she brought a big bag full of rupees with her to Cherat, where her charms enabled her to add a good many more to the stock earned by her active and diligent grotto.

Of my journey, of my arrival at Cherat, and the two lovely maidens I found there who as yet had not known man, but to whom it was my most happy privilege to communicate the thrilling sensations of soft desire and voluptuous sentiment, I must tell my readers in my second series.

VOLUME II

Never in my life journeyed in such an uncomfortable conveyance as an Ekkha, and I only hope that none of my fair readers may be subjected to such aches and pains as I had to suffer. As for my brave male friends who may peruse these memoirs, I can only hope that, should an evil fate bring discomfort upon them, they may be solaced by remembering that the fact is that briars and flowers both grow in the world, and that their path won't always be through all briars, that it may be that briars and flowers will follow one another in far too quick succession for a life of even comfort. And yet, who is there who has not suffered agony and nights of ecstasy bought by the subsidence of pain! With me, on this occasion, however, it was pain following the acme of voluptuous pleasure, and oh! how different was my seat in the execrable Ekkha to my soft reclinings on my lovely Lizzie Wilson's fair belly, and the cushion between her rounded ivory thighs! Ah! I had been wandering indeed in the field of flowers, and had now reached the desert of briars and thorns.

But what is an Ekkha? some of my fair readers may ask. I will tell you. It is a two-wheeled conveyance much used in Northern India. It has no springs. It has a platform with but three square feet on which you sit as best you can. It is drawn by a small pony. The shafts generally rise so platform on which you sit generally slips back. The driver sits on the shafts, and if, as is very likely, he is highly odoriferous, you get the benefit of his evil smell. But that is not all about the Ekkha. It has its good points. It can go almost anywhere. It is light and strong. Many and many a time I have seen one carrying half a dozen natives, who can squat with ease where one European cannot find half room enough for himself. It is a cheap conveyance, and it is generally a most gorgeous one to behold, for everyone of its four corners rises a pillar of white carved with all the cunning of the India carpenter's art. Over this is a dome generally surmounted by some brass ornament, and the entire Ekkha is painted in most brilliant colors, and ornamented with quaint patterns cut out of brass, hung with little tinkling bells, and in fact, is of the most barbaric appearance which pleases the native eye and fancy so much.

Amongst the European soldiers and their wives the Ekkha is known as a "Jingling Johnnie," a name which perfectly describes the noise it makes when in motion, for it does nothing but jingle, thus adding to the civilized ear as much torment as its uncomfortable shape and motion do to his feelings. Altogether it is not a kind of carriage which I can recommend as forming one of the comforts of Indian travel.

Added to this great discomfort were several others. First, the road had been cut to pieces—by the thousands of men, and carts of all descriptions which included artillery, light and heavy, which for the last two or three years had been constantly pouring along it, over all the road, to and from Afghanistan. It was consequently inches deep in dust as fine as flour. This dust rose during the day and did not settle for hours and formed a perfect fog which choked the driver, dried up his mouth and filled his eyes and ears, besides covering me from head to foot. Again, how many camels died on the march? I believe they numbered tens, even twenty of thousands. Judging from the stench, which hardly without break, filled the air between the outskirts of Nowshera and Publi, there must have been a fair proportion of those deceased camels all along the road. As fast as possible the carcasses were either burnt or buried, but enough were left above ground to sicken even the strongest stomach. Oh! Lizzie! Lizzie! how different from the sweet perfume which always emanated from your, beauteous charms, when you clasped me in your ecstasies of love and voluptuous lascivious passion, and returned me transport for transport on that never to be forgotten bed, on which I so often, so often, fucked you, in the delightful public Bungalow I am now so swiftly leaving behind me! Oh! indeed these were briars, briars after flowers, pricking thorns after smelling the sweet, sweet rose.

It grew dark soon after I had commenced my painful and uncomfortable journey. Every now and then a mounted Native Lancer would pass and by the feeble light of our candle lantern, I could see his glittering spear and sword, and the metal ornaments of his horse's accoutrements, for the road between Attock on the Indus and Peshawar is never quite safe, and is, or was at this time, largely patrolled. More than once Nowshera itself had been sacked, during years when there was no war in Afghanistan, and naturally if it had been unsafe in times of peace, it was less safe now that the war had just closed.

I dare say had the ekkha been less hideously uncomfortable I might have dreamed away the hours it took me to reach Publi by running over in my mind the totally unexpected and rapturously vivid joys which had made my stay in Nowshera so truly delightful, but I must confess that instead of blessing my stars, I cursed them freely, as I felt my back getting more and more broken by the strained position I was forced to maintain, and I longed for the time when I should be able to leave the cursed vehicle in which my evil fate had condemned me to travel.

At last I reached Publi, a small village situated where the road to Cherat turns off. It was full of liveliness, native shops, in which comestibles and sweet meats were exposed for sale, were still open more or less brilliantly lighted up with—oil lamps, consisting of an earthenware cup and a wick dripping in oil. Men, women and children were moving about, as if the idea of sleep never entered their minds, and the sound of native minstrelsy (God save the mark), and the monotonous beat of the favorite tom-tom, rose fitfully on the air. Bullocks, elephants, camels, horses and dogs lined each side of the road, and added their various noises and smells to the general collection.

We waited just long enough for our drivers to obtain a supply of parched corn, and a drink of water, and to stretch our cramped legs, and then Soubratie and I once more mounted on the ekkhas, and we set off at a good pace along the Kaccha road, towards the mountains now hidden from sight by the deep darkness of the night. But overhead the whole heavens were ablaze with stars, and if we had a more uneven road to travel we at all events left the dust and the stench of the main road behind us. The night air, sweeping across the open plain, felt pure and refreshing, and whatever were the discomforts, if any, of which Soubratie might have to complain I had none but those caused by the uncomfortable position I was forced to maintain in my ekkha. Quite bad enough for me, however, to prevent my entertaining any pleasant thoughts, for, if I did happen to think of Lizzie, it was not to wish for her sweetest, most lovely and delicious cunt, but to envy her the comfort of the Dak Gharry in which she was fast rolling home to Muttra.

In spite of the friendly warning which my excellent friend Jack Stone had given me, not only not to shut my eyes between Publi and Shakkoe but to be sure and have my sword drawn, ready for action at a moment's notice in case of attack by robbers and in spite of my cramped position, sleep at last came with her friendly hand overpowered me. I had indeed so far followed honest Jack's suggestion and drawn my sword, and placed it across my lap, but I could not keep awake. I fell fast asleep, nor did I waken until the ekkha stopped and I found myself in a little grove of trees close to which was the last native shanty beside a guard of native infantry, where I was told I had to dismount as I was at Shakkote.

Towering high above me and looking perfectly unclimbable was the lofty range of mountains, whose torn sides testified to the violence with which the rain shed upon them dashed in its hurry to reach the lower level. Cherat, I was told, was on the very summit, and was some 4,500 feet above where I stood, i.e., higher than Snowdon, the highest mountain I had yet ascended, and these mountains seemed twice as steep. A couple of ponies stood at the door of the shanty, one had a saddle on, the other not. I asked whose ponies these were, and hearing that they had been sent down to meet an officer expected with baggage, I asked no more questions, but at once claimed my right to them, which fortunately was not contested. Mounted on my pony and directing Soubratie to be quick to strap my portmanteau as best he could on the other animal, I told the sayce or groom who was in charge of my beast to proceed, and show me the way, which the half naked savage did. The scenery I passed through was wild and savage to a degree. We mounted almost perpendicular walls of rock, over which my strong and clever pony climbed in the most cat-like manner, or descended into deep and sandy bottomed ravines, the beds of which at times were irresistible torrents. We skirted precipices, along paths dangerously narrow and often very broken, until we at last reached the foot of the principal hill, up which we had to climb. I let my pony pick his own steps. All I cared for was not to let myself slip back over his tail for had I done so I should probably not be writing this now, and the sweet and amiable Fannie and Amy Selwym might still have the holy of holies and their darling little cunts protected by the sacred veil of their virginity. Little did they, still some thousands of feet above me, and little did I, parched, hot, panting with exertion and burnt by the blazing rays of the rising sun at my back, think that in accordance with that mysterious law of nature, which brings affinities into mutual contact, there was then climbing up that broken sided, rough surfaced hill, a man, whose potent prick had been carefully conveyed thousands of miles over sea and land, that it might be planted in those delicious little cunts, and sweep away, once and forever the charming little maidenheads within them, the tool of man thus created to finish and perfect the work of the Creator, in rendering those pretty virgins perfect women!

At last! At last! My pony staggering with immense fatigue and the fearful strain the terrible climb had cost him to reach the top of the spur of the hill, which jutted out from the main mountain range, and formed the buttress by which for the last two hours we had been ascending! Oh! The exquisite, cool, almost cold and bracing breath of real mountain air which swept across my face and filled my lungs with its exhilarating strength! My pony seemed to enjoy it as much as I. For a minute or so he stood and drank in the delicious breath of nature, and then he actually tried to trot; as if he knew he was not far from home, and that the sooner he got there the sooner he would get the drink he had earned so well, and the breakfast, of which the poor beast, no doubt, stood so much in need. But the trot soon died down into a quiet walk, and along a very good, well made path some five or six feet broad, along the edge of the valley, across which I saw facing me a pretty cottage, and good heavens! quite a sweet looking English lassie, walking with a child, evidently taking her early morning walk preparatory to going in to eat a good and wholesome breakfast. Their house I could not see, nor could I see whether my path, if followed conscientiously, would meet them; but I saw this sweet picture of comfort and innocence, and resolved that if I should have to ask my way of anybody, it should be of this true looking girl whom I saw across the valley. She was still too distant for me to be able to distinguish her features, but her general appearance and the willing graceful manner in which she moved, made me feel sure that a nearer view would not dispel the first impression she had made upon me. I therefore encouraged my pony to put on his best paces, and almost as soon as I had caught sight of her, my unknown seemed to have seen me, for she stopped in her walk and stood looking towards me. I soon got within twenty or thirty yards of her, for the path rounded the end of the valley, at the head of which was the cottage I had spoken of, and then I dismounted and led my pony up to where the young lady was standing. She had on a solar helmet such as ladies wear in India, and from under its peak I saw two lovely eyes, of a deep violet blue color, gazing at me with curiosity but without fear or rudeness.

The first view I had of her close, showed me that she was a real pretty girl—not exactly beautiful in the sense that Lizzie Wilson was—but more like my own beloved Louie, sweet, feminine, pretty in every sense.

Her cheeks, rounded with health, were colored like the rose, showing that the climate of Cherat certainly agreed with her. Her skin was white, even clear; and her lips. Those dear lips which were in days yet to come to be so often joined to mine in passionate ecstasy, were of the brightest red, that red that only belongs on the lips of the young, and which my experience has shown me is a sign of a nature tender, passionate and voluptuous. Her throat was beautifully formed, round and full, and her figure was that of a maiden passing from the stage of girl to that of womanhood. I could see that although her bosom was not yet fully developed, it was already adorned with two charming little mounts, for it was evident it was not a pair of empty stays which formed the slight hemispheres, on either side, but good, sound, solid flesh. Her waist, though not so tapering as Lizzie's, was sweetly small, and her hips had that generous breadth which announces a fine, beautifully shaped belly, fit couch for any man to repose upon! Repose! Can a man be said to repose when he lies between the thighs of his darling, and fucks her with movements so full of sweetness, of joy, of ardent rapture for both him and her? I know not I—but no matter—my maiden showed two well shaped little feet and ankles beneath her petticoat, as she stood watching my approach, and a smile began making her eyes alive with a kind expression of welcome, and two bewitching dimples to form which gave her lovely face the appearance of great sweetness, just such a look as might well take any man by storm who saw it for the first time.

I took off my hat and bowed, and asked this charming girl, "Can you kindly tell me where I should go to find Col. Selwyn ?"

"Papa is at the room, but he will be home soon. This is our house. I suppose you are Captain Devereaux?"

"Yes! I have only just arrived. I have been traveling all night and I am afraid I am more than dirty, but you must kindly excuse me for venturing to come near you in such a condition. You see I did not know which way to go, but left it to my pony and he brought me to you."

"Well! Won't you let the Sayce take him, and come in and see my mother? But come in and have a cup of tea! Papa won't be long I am sure."

"I am very much obliged to you Miss Selwyn, but I really feel much too grimy and dirty to present myself for the first time to Miss Selwyn! It would make a bad impression I am sure and I should be sorry for that, for it might perhaps have the effect of her taking a dislike for the man, who since he has seen Miss Selwyn, would wish to be on good terms with her father and mother!"

"Don't talk rubbish!" said this downright little maiden, blushing and looking as pleased as punch. "My mother will, I am sure, make every allowance, and I am sure you must want a cup of tea or a peg, which perhaps you would prefer. Do come in!"

At this moment a lady, somewhat taller than Miss Selwyn, accompanied by another girl, much the same height as her sister, came to the door of the bungalow, evidently attracted by the voices they heard.

"Oh! mama!" cried my friendly maiden, "here is Captain Devereaux, just arrived. I have asked him to come in and see you, and have a cup of tea or a peg, but he says he wants to see papa first, and is much too—too—Well, dirty! Do make him come in!"

"Hush! Fanny! you let your tongue run away with you too fast! I am glad to see you, Captain Devereaux. I suppose you have had a terrible time at Nowshera during the last week. We heard you were there and could not move on account of the troops returning from the war wanting all the ekkhas and carts."

H'm! If they heard of me at Nowshera perhaps Mrs. Selwyn might have heard of Lizzie Wilson, too! But although I thought all this I answered, "Yes, indeed I neither love nor money could procure me a vehicle of any kind, Mrs. Selwyn, and much against my will I had to stay there until the Brigade Major at last got me a couple of ekkhas. I have only just arrived."

"But why on earth don't you come in," proceeded the impatient Fanny who seemed bent on getting me indoors, the curious forerunner of that intense desire which afterwards impelled her to yearn to have me inside her own sweet and lively little cunt! "Mama! Mama! I am sure this poor man is dying of thirst. Do ask him in and let us give him something to drink!"

Mrs. Selwyn complied so far with her lovely daughter's wish as to ask me in, but it was not quite with that hearty good will which would have expressed a desire at all equal to that her hospitable daughter evinced. The fact was, as I afterwards heard from herself, that she did not admire the way in which poor Fanny had at once thrown herself at my head. She would have liked Fanny to have been a little less eager and impulsive. I saw it at once, and therefore, though really dying with thirst, and very much disposed to enter the house and inspect the second daughter, who at first sight seemed to be even more lovely than her sister, I made my excuse, saying that I considered it my first duty to report myself to the Colonel, and that then, after I had made my toilet, I would do myself the honor of calling.

Fanny looked at me with reproachful eyes, as much as to say, "You might as well have done what I wanted." The other girl looked at me out of her great lustrous eyes, her mouth smiled slightly, and Mrs. Selwyn gave me directions how to find my way to the orderly room, viz., by going back a part of the way I had come along the path, until I found a road by following, which I should find the barracks in which all the regimental officers were situated, about a mile from where we stood. Making my bow, and thanking Mrs. Selwyn, giving the now pouting

Fanny a bright look, as full of thanks as my dust filled eyes would permit me, and taking another long look at the daughter whose name I had not yet learnt, I handed over my pony to the sayce and walked along in the direction I had been told to go.

Before turning the corner I looked back. Fanny was alone, still standing in front of the house, looking after me. Her attitude was one of wistfulness. Somehow I felt she had been snubbed, and I was sorry for her, but glad to find my lines would be cast amongst people who, at first sight, seemed to be so lady-like and nice as Mrs. Selwyn and her two daughters appeared to me. I had not yet fallen in love with Fanny, but I certainly was inclined to like her. A pretty girl, without airs, or conceit, can hardly fail to make a favorable impression on any man, and though I have detailed the physical charms which I could descry I must beg my fair readers not to think that as yet, any idea or desire for the pretty Fanny's favors had entered my mind. I could not help seeing beauties which I admire, but I can actually look at a peach without at once wanting it to eat. I certainly admired Fanny from the first, but it was sometime before she made my prick stand, and my balls ache with voluptuous desire, nor whilst I knew she must have a most desirable little cunt, did I all at once want to fuck it. Those desires and that delicious fuck were to come, but as yet they were neither formed nor thought of. I continued my walk along the charming and easy path along the mountainside, delighted with the magnificent expanse of scenery which my lofty position afforded me. Below me were the craggy, rugged serpes, diversified with deep ravines and far jutting spurs, all bearing unmistakable evidence of the fury of the rains which swept their rocky sides. All over these slopes grew innumerable dwarf trees, and shrubs of various kinds but the wild olive seemed to predominate. Far in the distance, rapidly becoming obscured by the thick dusty haze added to the intense heat which was burning up the plain and the valley, I saw two rivers, one was apparently the Indus, which I had crossed at Attock, for I could trace its course to where it emerged from far off mountains and the other was the Cabul river of which I had heard at Nowshera and which flowed only a few hundred yards behind the bungalow in which I had spent such a hot (in every sense), and also such a delicious week, thanks to the beauty and sweetly lascivious disposition of the matchless Lizzie Wilson and my own unimpaired youthful vigor and love of fucking.

From the great height I was at, those two mighty streams looked like mere threads of silver meandering through the dark brown plain, meeting almost at right angles. A group of white buildings, microscopic almost in appearance, announced the position of Nowshera, and as I gazed, in fond recollection of the past week, at them I saw, as it were a bright star, as bright as the sun, suddenly burst into view amidst the haze, and twinkle and flash at uncertain intervals. I at once guessed it must be the heliograph, that wonderfully ingenious instrument so useful in flashing signals by reflected sunlight, and so particularly adapted to a country like India. Perhaps I owed my two ponies this morning to my honest Jack Stone sending a message that I had at last started on my final journey. Perhaps the sad tale of the unfortunate Searle's mishap and the cause of it had been equally and relentlessly flashed through the miles of air and read by my brother officers! Did Mrs. Selwyn know of Lizzie Wilson? No wonder she would not be in a hurry to admit me into a house of virgins if she did! And this might account for her not pressing the invitation made to rest and take a cup of tea, an invitation which, under the circumstances, I felt I had almost the right to demand.

This thought gave me a little trouble, not so much that I minded what perfect strangers might think of me, as regards the condition of my morals, for I knew the world too well, but as a matter of military consideration, it would certainly not look well in the eyes of my commanding officer, that I should waste my time at Nowshera, in the arms of a whore, (as he would certainly and most unjustly consider poor Lizzie), instead of doing my utmost to struggle up and join my regiment. And indeed, I had not attempted in the least to make any such struggle. I was altogether too glad to have the excellent excuse I had to remain at Nowshera, and Lizzie's sweetest cunt would have kept me there even now, if it had not departed 'with her lovely self to Muttra. It is rally curious to note how conscience doth make cowards of us all, and no wise man will ever allow that such a thing as repentance would ever come over us but for the fear of consequences. The girl whose belly fills out, the effect of her too ardent love for the handsome youth, repents and repents bitterly for her "sin" because, for her, it is the most evil consequence which could follow upon the heels of the delicious fuck, but not she, who protected from such unlucky results by her lover, careful and tender, enjoys her voluptuous meetings with him. Repentance, in fact, is all twaddle, and certainly will never come up, unless they have the realistic fancy opening a picture of approaching sorrow and misery.

Obey the commandment, "Thou shalt not be found out," and leave repentance and reproach in the background, my dear girl readers. These thoughts rather interfered with my admiration of the wild and savage beauty of the scenery I was passing through, until turning a jutting shoulder of the wall I saw, perched on a slight eminence above me, a long, low wooden barrack of large proportions, having an extensive red tiled roof. Seeing a group of soldiers in their karki, or mud-colored uniforms, standing at the door, I guessed this was the building adjoining the regimental office, and passing through this group I entered what seemed to be like one vast hall having wooden pillows as supports for the roof. The first person I saw proved to be the paymaster, who hearing my name, welcomed me warmly enough and showed me whereabouts I should find Colonel Selwyn whose office, i.e., table, was at the far end of the building. Thither I proceeded. The Colonel was seated at his table dispensing justice. Around him stood in officers' uniforms, some red, some kharkee, some blue, of different officers who had to bring up men. I stared at him. I knew none of them, and not being in uniform myself, and moreover covered with dust and dirt, I dare say I did not present a very favorable appearance. I waited until the last unhappy "Tommy" was weighed off, and then advancing to the table reported myself as Captain Devereaux just arrived to join the battalion. Colonel Selwyn looked at me with interest for a moment, whilst the hitherto glum and stern looking faces of the surrounding officer broke into smiles of welcome.

"Ah!" said the Colonel, rising, "glad to see you, Devereaux! I heard you were stuck at Nowshera. You came at an unlucky time when all the conveyances were engaged. I am afraid you had a wretched time of it down there!"

He shook me warmly by the hand, and introduced me to various officers, who did the same, and they recommending me to go and get a peg before anything else, he asked the others to show me the way to Mess, saying he must himself hurry off home.

Well, at all events my "repentance" so far, seemed uncalled for, and with a mind a good bit relieved I accompanied my new brothers in arms, who led the way, chatting and laughing and making many inquiries of me, until we reached the miserable shanty, called by courtesy "the Mess."

I will not go in for a description of each and every officer. Suffice it to say that they were a very fair sample of the officers who form a proportion of every regiment in Her Majesty's service. The seniors as usual proved to be selfish and greedy. The Captains verging on the same state, and the subalterns, as usual, gay, devil may care, generous and ever ready to share their pittance with a brother, in distress.

First thing I learnt was that as water was very scarce, it was doubtful if I should get a wash that day, as everyone was on an allowance, and my coming was not provided for.

The next, that unless I had brought my tent, I might have to sleep in the open. The next, that until I got a chokeydar, or native watchman, neither my property nor my throat would be safe, since it was impossible to keep robbers out of the camp at night.

Indeed it was a strange and not welcome contrast to the life I had been so lately leading at Nowshera, where hot winds and sand flies were all I had to complain of, and where I had the soft and delicious cunt of a perfect Venus to revel in. But like almost always is the case, my lines eventually turned out to be not cast in altogether so bad a mould as first appearances would lead one to expect.

In a few days I had found a nice little mud bungalow which would hold me. It is true it swarmed with most formidable looking and really dangerous centipedes, but I never got bitten by any, so that they only helped to keep me in a pleasant state of excitement, and I killed many of them. What made up for a great deal of the discomfort at Cherat was the delicious, cool and bracing air. I felt invigorated and strengthened by it. I enjoyed to the fullest inhaling it; and the savage grandeur of the scenery added enjoyment to breathing the pure mountain breezes which played upon it.

Soubratie had returned to Nowshera for his wife and my baggage, and it was nearly a fortnight before he returned. It was so difficult getting a cart, he had, he said, to stay until Stone could get one for him, but I think, now I really do think, that the profit arising from Mrs. Soubratie's facile charms amongst the officers at Nowshera had much to do with his extra long delay. I had not mentioned Mrs. Soubratie to anybody and indeed hardly thought of her, but I got a most unmerciful chaffing about her the first night of her arrival. A married man! Just from his wife's arms! To engage a woman! It was in vain I endeavored to defend myself, until I said that, as far as I was concerned, any fellow might have her, that it was my belief she would not be coy! At first my comrades would not believe me, but when they realized that such was indeed the case, their joy was unbounded. Like elsewhere, all the regiment's whores had deserted when the cry for "cunt," "more cunt," went over the land from Peshawar, on the arrival of the troops from Afghanistan: and for several months neither officers nor men had enjoyed the sweet solace of a good luscious fuck at Cherat unless, as was the case in a few instances, he happened to be married and his wife was with him.

Mrs. Soubratie was allowed no rest. That night she went from tent to tent, from hut to hut, and by morning a dozen officers had once more tasted of that meat of which, until exhausted nature can no more, man never tires.

There was at this time in Cherat several officers of other corps or regiments in charge of "Details" who had been sent up from Peshawar to recruit their health in our cool and salubrious air. With these gentlemen my story has nothing to do, except that perhaps I should do Mrs. Soubratie the justice to tell my gentle readers that her active and much sought for cunt drew the coin it loved from their balls, and the coin she likes from their willingly opened purses. But there were two officers of the army medical department whom I must mention more particularly, because the action of one of them unconsciously pushed and almost forced me into that road which ended in pretty Fanny Selwyn's delicious little cunt, whence it branched off into that equally sweet one between her sister Amy's plump white thighs. Before going any further, I wish to take my readers into my confidence, especially my girl readers, good, dear, gentle creatures, who I wish I knew in every sense of that expressive word and very intimately! I want, to tell you all then, that though I have been an ardent cunt hunter ever since that eventful sixteenth birthday of mine, on which auspicious day my lovely maid Margaret initiated me in the mysteries of women, and taught me how to fuck, so as to please and to be pleased, yet it has never been my intention or wish to betray girl or woman, virgin or matron. All I have done has been to simply observe and take advantage where I saw the opening and the desired interest. If I saw, (and oh, what a common, everyday sight it is!) that a girl who had never known man, was inclined to acquire that delightful knowledge, I did all I could to assist her to obtain that knowledge. If she happened to be a virgin, I necessarily had a good deal more to teach her than if she had already made man a practical study, and naturally I feel proud of the really pretty string of maiden-heads which it has been my good fortune to have captured and pierced with the spear of my manhood. But I never yet did, and never will try to instill into a maiden's heart desires or thought which she has never entertained. In other words, if I ever did "seduce" a girl, it was for her own pleasure as much as for mine, and my care was that in opening her thighs to me she did not open them to danger and to future care and misery. I always took the greatest care that neither in person nor in reputation should she suffer, and I deeply thank Venus for this, that she has never punished me for being careless of these very essential points. In fact, I look upon it as the act of a dastard to seduce a girl under false pretenses of any kind or sort, but I have always considered it an act of the truest kindness to assist the darlings to satisfy their natural cravings of their feminine nature. At Cherat I found two charming girls, almost children, certainly not more than children in my mind, no matter how mature their budding charms might be. I had, as will be seen, the most advantageous position man ever had of willfully seducing and defiling both. I do not say the temptation was not strong enough, but when temptation is quietly put on one side, or meets with no sympathy, it is easily overcome, and neither by word or act did I endeavor to lure from the path of duty these charming maidens. Later on, when events had involved me in the most delicate relations with Fanny, when I discovered that in her heart I was the man of men, who was adored and desired with passion indescribable, when I discovered that an affection which had at first been merely platonic had developed into a flaming and all devouring erotic love, I did yield to the sweet temptress, and spared no pains to bring her to that point which I knew gave her the only solace that would be effective. I took her maiden-head, and neither she nor I have yet reached the day of repentance and never will.

The two doctors were Surgeon Major Jardine and Surgeon Lavie. The former was a huge, coarse Scotchman, of low birth and low mind. Coarse in appearance and conversation, he was equally coarse in manners and soul, and I was amazed, after some months had elapsed, to find that he had not only thought of Fanny as a wife, but had proposed to her that a coarse man should desire Fanny's youthful beauty, and thought that to fuck her would be fine, I could quite understand, but Jardine was that kind of a man who naturally associated with the lowest whores. A very favorite speech of his was that the only good part of a woman was her pelvis, and one would think that a man with such ideas would never desire to saddle himself with a wife. Yet with all his coarseness Jardine had some good points. He kept good natured and that is about all I could say for him. He was by no means handsome, though he was certainly very big; and in the eyes of some women huge proportions and the appearance of a Hercules strongly outweigh beauty of countenance and elegance of figure. Such women should be cows and consort with bulls.

Lavie was very different. He was a gentleman by birth and education. In mind he was as refined as Jardine was coarse. In manner he was decidedly reserved and shy, not given to much self-assertion, an interested listener and one who, when he did open his lips, spoke to the point. I used to take most pleasant walks with him, and soon he and I became real friends. He told me thoughts he would have shrunk from speaking of to others, and opened his heart to me most fully on all but one subject. Like most men he enjoyed a good fuck, and no one was better pleased than himself when he found me willing to take off my imagined embargo to the freest indulgence of Mrs. Soubratie's succulent and very active cunt.

Lavie's great ambition, as he related it to me, was to get home and to set up for himself as a doctor in civil life. He complained bitterly of there being little or no scope for personal energy and exertions in the grooves of military life, and as my own ideas on this subject coincided with his and our sympathies blended, I think he looked upon me as his trusted friend, from who he could keep back nothing. Apparently he did keep back nothing, yet as my dear, and I trust interested readers will see, he kept back the most important secret which, had it been imparted to me at this time, would, I am certain, have prevented my having any reason to write this portion of my memoirs, for events would have taken a quite different course. In fact, Lavie was the quite unconscious instrument by which the road leading to the sweet little cunts of Fanny and Amy Selwyn was made, leveled and smoothed for me and along which I traveled almost unconsciously until near the end of whither I was being conveyed.

Of my other brother officers it is unnecessary to speak more fully. They and I got on very well together, but I never had any very intimate friends among them. They were not altogether what I might call my sort. I may possibly have occasion to mention one or two of them, but it cannot be because of any important influence they had over my career.

However, ravenous a nos moutons! It must not be supposed that I delayed making my first formal call on Mrs. Selwyn and her fair daughters. Indeed, I went to see them the second day of my arrival at Cherat, when I had at last succeeded in having a bath and a shave, neither of which feats I had been able to accomplish the day of my arrival.

The Colonel was at home also and I saw the entire family. I was charmed with Mrs. Selwyn, who was a pretty nice woman, still beautiful, though, alas! rapidly nearing the grave. She was tall and must always have been slender, and judging from the remains of her now faded charms, she must, when young, have been more than ordinarily lovely. Her face had suffered far less ravages than her person, and she still had most beautiful features and glorious eyes, but her poor bosom, alas! had entirely lost its billowy form, and there is hardly a word to describe the condition of her body. Curious to say, though she knew she was delicate, and her husband had only too good reason to know it also, neither one nor the other seemed to have the remotest idea that her ever increasing emaciation must end in an early death; early, for Mrs. Selwyn was not much more than forty years of age. Lavie, when I questioned him about her, would shake his head and say it was of no use hinting anything to the Colonel, and that the only time he had ventured to do more than hint, the Colonel had got quite angry and told him he was much too inexperienced a doctor to presume to give an opinion, and that all her life Mrs. Selwyn had been as she then was, and he was sure she would outlive them all. Naturally the conversation I had with this family, which was to prove so interesting in every sense to me, when I first called, rambled over a great space, for they knew from my darling Louie's letters, which had reached Cherat before I had, that I must be either married or engaged. I confessed to the former condition, which Mrs. Selwyn declared she was delighted to hear. I thought, all the same, that as she had daughters rapidly growing up, she would have been better pleased had she found I had a heart still to be disposed of. Of one matter I was pleased to find that both she and the Colonel were entirely ignorant, viz: that there was such a person in the world as Lizzie Wilson. They had, of course, heard that the Brigade Major at Nowshera had met with some kind of severe accident and was to be sent home as soon as he could be safely removed, and they questioned me about that accident, as it happened, as they knew, during my stay at Nowshera. I told them all I was disposed to allow I might know, stating that the story I heard was that Major Searle, having made himself obnoxious to the soldiers at Nowshera, had been waylaid and badly beaten by some of them.

"Ah!" said the Colonel, "that accounts for the extraordinary reticence on the part of the commanding officer down there! I could get no details of any kind from him, by either heliograph or letter—of course he does not like to publish the fact that his men have been guilty of so gross a breach of discipline as to beat an officer!"

"Fanny! Amy! dears, now run away to your lessons," said Mrs. Selwyn. "My girls have no governess, Captain Devereaux, the poor things have to learn as best they. can: India is a bad country for young children, but I could not leave them at home. We have not money enough to keep two establishments."

I could see by Fanny's face that she quite understood why she was being sent out of the room, viz., that her mother wished to speak "secrets" and although as I afterwards found, she was not always ready to obey an unwelcome order without more or less remonstrance, she on this occasion rose and led the way, followed by Amy and the rest.

When the room was left to the Colonel, Mrs. Selwyn and myself, Mrs. Selwyn said:

"Whilst you were at Nowshera, Captain Devereaux, did you hear any strange reports about Mrs. Searles?"

"Well!" said I hesitatingly, as though not quite willing to enter on any details of scandal, "I did, but I must say I do not entirely believe what I heard!"

"Then you have heard that she is separated from her husband ?"

"Yes!"

"Did you hear anything else?"

"I heard that she was still in India, living at Ranikhet, I think it was."

"Ah! Well, she is as bad a woman as ever stepped! A disgrace to her sex! I think it scandalous that the government should not force her to leave India! If there is a law which could be brought to act! But the Viceroy—" and she made an expressive stop.

"Oh my dear!" interposed the Colonel, "you forget to say that if Mrs. Searles is no better than she should be; it is an her husband the chief blame should fall!"

"Oh! I know! I know!" exclaimed Mrs. Selwyn warmly and with much excitement, "Oh! Captain Devereaux! I wonder whether you heard what led to the separation?"

"I can't say I did," said I, telling a most tremendous lie, of course, but curious to see how Mrs. Selwyn would be. When she told me, as I could see she was dying to do, that Searles had compelled his wife to commit sodomy.

"Well, read the first chapter of Romans and especially that verse alluding to the conduct of certain men towards men! I cannot be more explicit, Captain Devereaux, and as it is my face feels as though it were burning!" and indeed her ordinary pallid features were crimson, whether with shame or anger I could not well determine.

"I understand perfectly, Mrs. Selwyn," said I, "and if Mrs. Searle has disgraced her husband's name, I think it is hardly more than he can have deserved!"

"But she has disgraced her awn, too, Captain Devereaux! Fancy what the natives must think when they see a lady for she is a lady by birth and education and all—sell her charms to anyone who can afford to pay five hundred rupees for the possession of them—there is only one name far such a woman, and it is not prostitute, but one more vigorous and of course Saxon."

Here Colonel Selwyn cut in, and changed the line of conversation, which was growing rather hotter than he thought it should be on the first visit of his Junior Captain. After having recounted my travels and the impressions made on me by Cherat, my future prospects and the possibility that after all my wife might join me in India, and not having told anything of real importance, I left the house in which the memorable event was to happen and which I shall now relate.

I soon became a welcome guest at the Colonel's house. The family was what we would call "homely." The Colonel had married a penniless lass when he was young, and the natural consequences of having a lovely wife was a large family, some of the members of which were at school at home, some in India. He had not been long in India, and although his pay and allowances as Colonel commanding a regiment were large, he had to pay numerous debts contracted in days gone by, and therefore did not benefit much from the bags of rupees he received monthly from the pay master. Hence the Selwyns lived very quietly and soberly and the advent of ail officer whose tastes were decidedly of a domestic turn was a boon of which they availed themselves.

In spite of my determined wish to fuck Lizzie Wilson again, in spite of my fond recollections of her beautiful bosom, her luscious bubbies and her queenly thighs, between which her perfect Venus cunt was situated, I still remembered with fond affection my darling little wife, whose charms I had once thought had quite ravished me away from those of other women. During our married life Louie and I had lived very quietly. It was in bed that we lived a stormy life if anywhere! Fanny Selwyn, though not to be compared in character with my Louie, did in many ways remind me of her, so that I found a charm at the Colonel's house which made an invitation to tea always agreeable. On one of those early occasions on which I dined with them, our conversation fell on the advantages of education, and Fanny said, with an accent of great yearning, "I know I do so wish I had a governess! I shall never be able to teach myself from books without help, and as for teaching a child anything more than their multiplication table and a, b, c, it is the blind leading the blind."

"What is your special difficulty, Miss Selwyn?" asked I. "Oh! Everything! But perhaps nothing harder than arithmetic beyond the rule of three!"

After dinner I asked her to show me what sums there were she found so difficult, and after a little pressure she brought one of simple fractions. I showed her how simple it was, did one after another for her, and finally pressed her to try her hand on one herself. She did, and though being afraid to express her ignorance, as she said, to her infinite delight she got the right answer. One would have thought I was a perfect God to see the delight of Fanny at what she said was all my doing, and I was so pleased at having been able to give her so much real and innocent pleasure, that the spirit moved me to propose that, as I had so much leisure, I could not do better than come for an hour or so every morning to assist at the lessons if Colonel and Mrs. Selwyn had no objections. Mrs. Selwyn jumped at the offer, but the Colonel hung back a little. Whether this was because he might have thought of Fanny's growing bubbies, and consequent approach to an age when desire, easily raised by close and constant communication with a young and lovely mind, might seize upon her youthful cunnie, even though the young man was married, or rather he fancied I was generously rushing in on a task of which I should soon grow uneasy and repent having undertaken it, I don't know. But I, at any rate, stuck to my offer and it was accepted.

There were no general barracks at Cherat, except on Sunday morning after divine service, at which the Colonel read prayers. Officers commanding companies paraded them on weekdays at such hours as were convenient, and inspected the men and their arms. The regiment had seen such harassing service in Afghanistan, and had so many sick and feeble in the ranks, that it had been sent, almost at once, to Cherat, with positive orders that there was to be as little work as possible, so that good long rest in an invigorating climate might recruit its wasted strength. Consequently I had almost complete leisure from morning until night, and pined for someother occupation than walking along the paths over the wild hillsides, watching the innumerable ravens and gazing into what looked like interminable space. So I at once commenced my new duties of tutor, forgetting all about Abelard and Heloise, and becoming almost one of the family of the Colonel. At first I had a tremendous amount of chaffing to undergo from my brother officers, who could not understand my motives, some hardly hid their suspicions that I aimed at seducing Fanny and Amy—others looked upon me as a lunatic, who did not know how to appreciate the charms of perfect idleness, but I did not mind.

But as for Fanny! She afterwards told me that in those Cherat days she looked upon me as the most wonderful man in the whole world, for I knew everything. Poor little Fanny. The truth was she knew nothing, and my acquirements in the educational line were to her prodigious. It was not marvelous, therefore, that I obtained over her a degree of power and mind which although hardly perceptible to her, existed like the steel hand in the velvet glove. My word of praise or commendation made her joyously happy, a tear would spring in her eyes if I forgot myself and hinted that she really should have done better. It was an association of real and true happiness, undisturbed by the flames of passion, but full of affection on either side—the communion, as it were, of the beloved brother and the dearest sister.

The effect on me was very "purifying" Little by little I thought more of Fanny and Amy, and the less of Lizzie Wilson; more of the extraction of the square cube root than of the matchless cunt of that superbly beautiful Venus, although at times one or the other of my charming pupils, leaning over my shoulder, had her rosy cheek, blooming with health and youth on it, touching mine, her fresh sweet breath mingling with mine, and a rising breast making itself felt against my shoulder, yet, as though fast asleep, my prick would remain perfectly quiescent for his master never once thought of the two blooming little cunts, to which he could even then have easily found a way had he been inclined to take advantage of the dear girls' ignorance and inexperience. Soon the most complete trust was imposed in me by Colonel and Mrs. Selwyn, and after hearing "lessons" I often was trusted to take the girls for a ramble down the wild and beautiful Chapin Gaant, or wherever our fancy led us to stray.

One evening Drs. Jardine and Lavie were invited with myself to dinner at the Colonel's. Jardine, at that time, as I afterwards learned, was looking forward to asking Fanny's hand in marriage. I certainly had no idea of it, judging from his demeanor and Fanny's apparent indifference to him that evening as on other occasions. As usual, toward the close of the party, she had come and sat beside me and chatted in her ordinary lively manner. Her mind was fast opening up and receiving new ideas, and a month's tuition had had a great effect upon her. I little knew that Jardine was watching all this with jealous eyes, but on our way home he said:

"You seemed to be all there, Devereaux, this evening."

"How do you mean, Doctor?" said I.

"Why, the little girl seemed to have neither eyes nor ears for anybody but yourself. And you seemed to have her hands comfortably squeezed between your own. Ha! Ha! Ha!" and he gave one of those disagreeable guttural laughs which I so much disliked.

"Look here! Jardine!" said I, rather nettled, "I can as sure you I don't like the way you speak. Miss Selwyn is nothing to me but an amiable little girl, whom I give some lessons which amuses me and I hope instructs her. She is quick and clever and very intent to learn, and it is only natural that she should like to talk about her work to me, when her whole heart is set upon learning."

"Ah! if you don't teach her any other lessons besides, my boy! What had you to do squeezing her hands, eh?"

"I deny it!" answered I hotly, "your eyes must have deceived you!"

"Well!" he said, "perhaps so! But at any rate, Devereaux, you should remember you have a wife of your own, and should not take up too much of the young ladies attention but leave some chance to us poor bachelors."

I did not reply. I felt angry and vexed that my innocent attentions should be found fault with by a man who professed to see nothing desirable in a woman but her pelvis.

We were now approaching a row of huts in which lived a number of married women of other regiments who had been sent up from Peshawur out of harm's way until their husband's regiments had got back from Afghanistan to their fixed quarters. Mrs. Selwyn, who woman-like, had insisted on "these married quarters" being securely guarded by sentries, whose duties were not only to prevent any "unauthorized person" from visiting them, but to prevent any woman leaving her hut after dark. This was a source of great irritation to all concerned. The officers wanted the women to fuck, and the women would have been only too glad to be fucked, they had great times at Peshawar, where they scarcely went a day or a night without experiencing that delight of delights, and where they harvested bags at rupees from their insufferable and ever changing adorers, but here at Cherat they were, as it were, in a nunnery, and they pined for the longed-for prick, and the accompanying rupees.

It was a very dark night, and a kind of drizzle was falling, a most unusual thing. The first sentry challenged, and being answered, we

CHARLES DEVEREAUX

passed. As we went along the front of the low enclosures before each hut, Jardine said, in a fairly loud voice, "To think of all these lovely women here, and not a chance of having one of them! I believe they are all bursting with randiness, and would give rupees, instead of asking for them, to be well fucked!"

"Right you are, sir!" came a feminine voice in decidedly Irish tones. "Right you are, and shall I come with your honor now?"

"By George! Yes! Come along! but we shall have to pass another sentry!"

"Here! Put on my cloak and cap. There! that'll do famously! Now Lavie! Devereaux! Let the girl walk between you and I'll go in front." Saying this Jardine put his cap on what I could see was the head of a fine and buxom young woman, though it was too dark to see her features. She buttoned his cloak around her, and without anymore ado we four proceeded. Lavie and I carried on a conversation with Jardine in order to deceive the alert sentry we had yet to pass, and soon we had our lass safely from all danger of immediate discovery.

"Now to my hut!" said Jardine, "you are my property for tonight and this is the way to my hut!"

"Faith, sir!" said she, laughing, "I'm thinking of taking your all! I could do it easy, one after another, and indeed all you could do to me tonight would hardly make up for three months total abstinence. I've not had a man all that time, and I did not become a married woman for that anyways!" With a laugh we condoled with her, and she continued: "Oh! it's easy. It would be for any of us to come up to you gentlemen any and every night when there's no moon, but you see there's some so jealous and cantankerous! There's women down there," pointing down towards the "married quarters who would love to come out on the prowl for officers, but who hate it falling to anyone but themselves! Only for that and the reports such like make, there would be half a dozen of us in your honor's beds every night!"

"Well! we are wasting time!" said Jardine impatiently. "Devereaux you won't have much chance tonight, so you had better go home and fuck Mrs. Soubratie, if you want a woman."

"Thanks," said I dryly, "but I don't think I want any woman. All the same I wish you every pleasure. Goodnight," and off I went.

Was it virtue? What was it? Jardine had been right. When I came to think of it I had had Fanny's hands between mine, but I had been quite unconscious of the fact. And here was a chance, at all events, to make an arrangement to have this rich Irish lass; and yet neither Fanny's hands nor the riper charms of this woman, charms which if they at all corresponded with the melodious tones of her voice, must be rich and fresh, had raised the least spark of desire in my bosom. I was amazed and asked myself, are you the same Devereaux who was simply beside yourself a month ago, and whose prick was so ravenous and active with Lizzie Wilson?

I have only mentioned this incident to show how, all unconsciously, I had fallen away, apparently, from that worship which Venus insists on from all her votaries, but it was by the Goddess' own decrees, and my course was being shaped for her by unerring hands. Two holy shrines had been erected all hitherto unknown, between the pretty thighs of Fanny and Amy and my prick was the God destined to be set up within them, and Venus would breathe the sweet savor of the sacrifice, when in due time, the shrines should run, first with blood, and then with the cream of the offerings.

Lavie told me next day that Jardine kept Mrs. O'Toole until two o'clock, and then passed her on to him, and that so ravenous was she that he was completely hors de combat by four, and that but for the distance of my bungalow from the "married quarters," and the near approach of day-break, I would have had a visit from the lively woman. I was glad she had not come, for I suppose I should have hardly, when put face to face with a nice fresh cunt, have hesitated to fuck it, and Mrs. Selwyn would have heard of it as she did of Jardine and Lavie. This was not the only visit Mrs. O'Toole paid the doctors, and they kept it a deep secret from the other officers, but the secret oozed out somehow and Mrs. O'Toole was one of the very first women sent down to the plains when Cherat was gradually denuded of all the officers and men of my regiment.

But early in October a telegram came from Peshawar which sent a thrill of joy through the hearts of the Tommies at Cherat, and made the officers feel happy too, but which somewhat displeased Mrs. Soubratie. It ran thus, "Twelve plump, fresh, young whores will leave Peshawar for Cherat today." This was the telegram from the Kotwal at Peshawar to our regimental Kotwal. The moment Colonel Selwyn heard of it he telegraphed back, "Keep the women until I have inspected them." He did not tell Mrs. Selwyn of the nature of his duty, but he told her he had been called for by the General at Peshawar to go down and see him on important business, and he lost no time about it. I only heard of his intended visit to Peshawar after the Colonel had actually departed and it made me uneasy. The house was very much exposed, being at the head of the Chapin Gaant, and the robbers had been particularly active lately. It is true the Selwyns had a chokeydar, which is the way English people in India purchase immunity from the robbers, the chokeydars being always selected from those tribes or villages in the vicinity which furnish the greatest number of robbers, but there had been many instances lately of theft and in some cases of violence and bloodshed at night, so that my faith in chokeydardom was rather shaken. The nights, too, were brilliantly lighted by the moon, of which the splendor can hardly be imagined by those who have never seen that luminary in the East. Somehow I put it down to those whores that the Colonel wished to see. I knew that from her delicate state of health, Mrs. Selwyn could hardly give the Colonel much pleasure of nights if indeed he could ever fuck her at all, and I also knew, from certain little stories the Colonel told me in private, that he was as fond of a good juicy cunt as any man. I guessed, therefore, that the news of the twelve plump, fresh young whores of the telegram had brought upon him a flood of desire and that he had gone to Peshawar not only to inspect them but also to try them, and fuck them, and see whether they came up to the description given of them. My suspicions turned out correct, for when I went to Peshawar myself, some two months later, the Khansamah at the public bungalow, told me that Colonel Selwyn Sahib was the finest man he had ever seen, and that he always had four women every night; and Jumali, one of the twelve, also told her fellows that the Colonel had at Peshawar fucked her every night during his stay, and took three others, turn by turn. Poor Colonel! He had the biggest balls of any man I ever saw, and no wonder if at times his bottled up emotions would burst forth! I believe myself that the sentries over the "married quarters" at Cherat, were put there by Mrs. Selwyn more as a preventative against the Colonel than against the other officers, at—any rate, this visit to Peshawar had very nearly fatal consequences to some of the Colonel's own family.

The first night I could hardly sleep from ill-defined dread of what might be going on at the far end of the camp, a mile away from me, where the Selwyn house was; and towards morning I rose, whilst the lovely landscape was lighted by the moon only, and walked rapidly until I reached the Colonel's house. Everything seemed all right. The Chokeydar was at his post, giving from time to time that horrid cough which all give, a kind of sentry's "all's well" with them. The next two nights succeeding he took the same walk with the same result. But the next night, at the very time the Colonel must have been between the dusky thighs of the last but one of the twelve fresh young whores, who he had gone to "inspect," I was just turning the corner, where the path joined that from which I had first seen pretty Fanny Selwyn, when I heard a sound which made me shiver with apprehension! I thought I could distinguish my name being called upon. I set legs to ground with all my force, and ran as I had never run before! A few minutes brought me to the house, and during that few minutes the fearful shrieks had never ceased. It was for me that someone, some girl, was calling and Oh! God! the shrieks were suddenly stifled just as I got to the verandah! There, on the ground, with his throat cut from ear to ear, his head thrown back and the horrible yawning gap, from which a stream or river of blood was still gushing, separating his chin from his chest, lay the luckless chokeydar, whose cough had given me such comfort when I heard it on the preceding nights. I trod in his slippery gore before I perceived it but I had no time to lose. The window of what I knew to be Fanny's bedroom was wide open. It was a high lattice window, opening like a door, and the sill of it was no more than two and a half or three feet from the ground. I sprang through it at a bound, and there before me I saw a tawny Afghan struggling between a pair of quivering thighs, completely naked and uncovered, and those thighs and feet and legs I knew to be Fanny's.

For a moment I stood paralyzed with apprehension. The position of the accursed Afghan was exactly that of a man who in fucking a woman had completed the exquisite short digs, and was pressing the very last line of his prick way home, whilst he was pouring out his burning spunk! His struggles were exactly those of a man under such circumstances, and his whole weight seemed to be resting on the quivering form of the prostrate girl. I could not see her face, but her poor left hand lying motionless and palm upwards told me that she was insensible, if not dead. It was only a moment I stood thus. Then, with a stifled cry of rage and despair, I rushed at the sacrilegious brute who was thus defiling the temple reared for beings altogether superior to such as him; he had not heard me jump in at the window, the floor was chaman, i.e., extremely hard lime and mortar, and my shoes had India rubber soles, being in fact, my lawn tennis shoes. I seized him by the collar of his coat, and gave one wrench, pulling him up so suddenly that he had no time to let go his hold of poor Fanny, but dropped her as soon as he recovered from his surprise. The half lifeless manner in which the unfortunate girl fell back with a thud on the bed, her head almost disappearing on the other side of it, gave me a further terrible shock. I was convinced she was dead. But the rotten collar, of which the burly brute's coat was made, gave with a shrill sounding tear, and a cloud of stinking dust rushed forth from it almost like the explosion of a musket. Without attempting to attack me in return, and with a stifled cry of alarm, the fiend made for the window. Before he reached it, however, I had hold of his coat again; but could not manage to get close to him, he was so quick, and I could only make a grab at his shoulder as he fled. Again did the rotten cloth give way, this time, however, not quite so quickly, but too quickly to enable me to grasp the man himself. As the garment almost fell off, his blade or long glittering knife, fell on the floor, and wrenching himself away, the filthy brig—and bounded out of the window, dashed across the path and disappeared as he appeared to hurl himself head-foremost down the steep side of the valley. I could hear him crashing and tearing through the bushes, for all was silent as death. Satisfied that not only was the brute gone, but that there were no others hiding near at hand, I turned with a heart full of sickening fear and dread to the bed across which the lifeless form of the unfortunate Fanny was stretched. The verandah outside somewhat darkened the room even in the day time, but the powerful light of the moon reflected from the ground and the rocky slopes still managed to illuminate the bedchamber, and the small oil lamp, which generally burns all night in every person's room in India, added its feeble rays to show me what looked like the desolation of death!

Fanny's foot just touched the ground. Her pretty legs with such beautiful and slender ankles, the calves round, graceful and well developed, were wide apart, as were her full and really splendid thighs, white as snow and polished as marble.

I could not but see the darling little cunt, for it was looking straight at me, and the light of the little lamp shone full on it, showing me that the bush, which topped the rounded, sloping motte above it, was thickest in the centre, and not very rich or abundant. I shivered when I saw that sweet, sweet, cunt, that holy land all smeared with blood, and a thick drop oozing from its lowest point of entrance. My God! My God! She had then been raped, outraged, ravaged. And by a blasted, cursed and never too much damned stinking, filthy, lousy Afghan. The incredible insolence which could have animated a native, in time of peace and in our own borders, to commit such a crime, astounded me, but I had no time to indulge in thoughts or rather to dwell upon them, for these thoughts rushed through my brain like lightning. I bent over the poor lifeless girl and raised her head. Her eyes were closed, her face looked so pure, so peaceful, and though the color had fled from her cheeks I thought I had never seen Fanny Selwyn look so beautiful. Her lips slightly parted showed the rows of pearls which formed her teeth, small, beautiful and perfectly regular. She felt warm. Of course she would be warm, for if life had indeed departed, she could not have been dead even five minutes yet, so rapidly had events passed, though it has, as is usual, taken me many words with which to describe them. Her lovely sylph-like form felt warm to my touch. Oh! how elegant were its lines! How pure, fine and spotless was that satiny skin! How beautiful were those swelling, rising breasts—not yet full grown, but giving promise of one day being more exquisitely beautiful, even, than they were now—the showy breasts of a nymph of sixteen summers. The little coral beads which surmounted them seemed to me to have more color in them than they could have shown had death really taken possession of this elegant form. I put my hand on her heart! Oh! thanks be to God she was not dead! Her heart was beating and firmly too. In an ecstasy of delight, I kissed those mute lips, and could not resist closing my hand, so accustomed to it when I was kissing lovely girls, and the sweet little bubbie was near her heart. It was lovely! so firm! so hard! so sweetly filling to the hand. It was an unwarranted liberty, but I could not resist the temptation! But suddenly I thought about the base effects of the deeds of the monster who had ravished her virginity. My eyes glanced again down over the lovely, smooth, dimpled belly, over the delightfully but slightly forested slopes on the rising hill of Venus till they traveled along the deep line of her soft little cunt. What if within those so lately virgin portals were lodged the accursed spawn of a loathsome Afghan! What if, as might be the case if she lived, that lovely little belly were to swell to become the mother, the mold of a child to be looked upon with horror and dismay! Oh! what should I do! Suddenly the idea struck me to endeavor to prevent such a terrible catastrophe by opening the beauteous gates of the temple, and trying to coax the beastly slime to flow out. No sooner thought of than done. I did not hesitate! I passed my trembling middle finger into that soft little cunt, until my knuckles prevented further ingress. To my inexpressible joy I discovered that Fanny had not been ravished. The close little maiden-head was distinctly there, unbroken, unscathed! I felt

CHARLES DEVEREAUX

it well to make quite sure, and then withdrawing my finger from the hot depths, delighted to find by its moisture that nature was all alive there.

I once more looked to see if I could discover the source of the blood, if blood it was, which covered that lovely cunt. I could not imagine what it could be from, and fearing that perhaps the frightful and agonized shrieks I had heard might have arisen from the torture of some dreadful internal wound, caused by the violence of the ruffian who had assailed her, I parted the hair of her dear little bush to see could there be a wound hidden by it, but feeble though the light was by which I worked, it was too easy, alas! (for I love a fine, thick, curly forest to adorn the sacred Mount of Venus!) to see every particle of skin under it, and there was not a scratch. On moving about my foot suddenly trod on something soft and flabby; I picked up the object it had encountered and found it to be a cloth covered with blood, and I had hardly to glance at it to recognize the source of all my alarm. Poor Fanny, in fact, had her menses and the blood I saw was the harmless result. I almost laughed with joy and amusement. But whatever might be the cause of the blood, there could be no doubt that the girl, in such a serious faint, must be in a bad way and I began to get alarmed on that account. I had laid her in a more commodious position, hoping she would come to quickly, as I had generally seen women do who had fainted, but she lay so dreadfully motionless. Her moving breasts alone told my eye that she was alive. They rose and fell but through a very small space. Poor, dear little breasts! I caressed them. I pressed them. I gently pinched the little rosebuds. But Fanny's eyes remained hard closed. I passed my hand all over her, over her smooth sides, over her dimpled belly, over her precious motte, down her lovely and beautiful thighs. I even slipped my finger again into her luscious cunt, hoping to awaken her from her torpor, and did arouse the active little clitoris, but though I pressed its velvet lips together, and could feel the clitoris swelling under my titillations, Fanny felt it not. At last I spied a tumbler on the table, and I sprinkled her face and undulating bosom with the cold water. She moved! Cold had done what warm caresses had failed to—she opened her glorious eyes, gazed wildly at me for a moment and then shrieked with fear and dreadful alarm. I clasped her in my arms and tenderly pressed her to me, she struggling violently all the while.

"Fanny! Fanny! Miss Selwyn! Fanny dearest!" I cried in imploring and soothing accents, "it is I! Captain Devereaux! Don't be frightened, there is no one to hurt you now! I hunted that fellow and he has run for his life!"

My voice calmed her somewhat. The poor girl turned her face to my bosom and clutched me wildly, whilst she burst into almost an agony of weeping, and cried aloud like a child. Her convulsive sobs and almost hysterical movements forced her hard little breasts against me, and I could feel them distinctly, although I had my coat and waistcoat on and she was naked. I caressed her, tried to soothe her, and she clung all the closer to me. I felt I was a brute, but her nudity, the warmth of her body, her clasped arms, and above all the sympathetic sensations her bubbies caused all over my bosom, made my prick stand with tremendous force. I had no idea of profiting from my situation, but I could not help feeling the delicious excitement of the moment. All the time I kept trying to prevail on Fanny to subdue her emotion of terror. I spoke, I know, in the fondest manner. I was much moved myself, and I found myself calling her my darling! My tender, beloved little pet and similar endearing epithets. Fanny at last seemed to cock her ears and listen. Her sobs grew less violent. She left off crying aloud. She turned her face up to mine, and I kissed the cherry lips and tried to dry the flowing tears on her cheeks with my mouth. Oh! she liked that!

"Oh! dear Captain Devereaux, you have saved me! How can I ever thank you?"

"By being good now, dear Fanny! By trying to recover your courage and tell me how that brutal Afghan got into your room?"

"Was he an Afghan? I could not see well! I was asleep and suddenly I felt a hand between my thigh—on me—somewhere—and when I opened my eyes I saw two natives—"

"Two!" I exclaimed.

"Yes! Two! I am sure of it! There was two, one had his big face close to me—the one who had his hand on mean me—somewhere! The other had a knife in his hand and was; grinning! I could see his teeth! Then I shrieked and tried to jump out of bed, but the man whose hand was who had his hand on—who had his hand on—who—"

"Yes I darling!" I said, seeing she was embarrassed, "the man who was attacking you—"

"Yes! He put his hand on my chest and held me down. I hit him in the face, and must have hurl his eye, for he cried out and put his hand to it, and I jumped up, escaped for a moment, and began to call out as loud as I could. He reached round for me and caught me, and I felt him tear my nightgown, and he dashed me down on the bed and fell upon me with all his might, and seized my throat with his two hands, and I

CHARLES DEVEREAUX

suppose I fainted then, for I remember nothing else. Oh! how did you come here, dear, dear, dear Captain Devereaux?"

All this time the gentle, frightened girl had her arms round me. She did not appear to know, that except the upper parts of her arms, she was as naked as she was born. In fact, although able to talk now, it was plain to me that she had not yet fully realized her exact position. She clung to me with the grasp of the drowning; and this was what was so charming, and yet so dear, as it was like the embrace of a girl who feels the lively and moving prick giving her rapture beyond compare.

"I had been nervous ever since your father went to Peshawar, Miss Selwyn, and every night I have patrolled to satisfy myself that you were safe. I heard your shrieks and that is how I happened to arrive just in the nick of time."

Fanny raised her head and looked at me with eyes from which love and gratitude both darted most speaking rays.

"Kiss me!" she cried, with passion plainly thrilling through her, "you are a good fellow!"

I did not wait to be asked twice. I passed my thirsty lips to hers in one long, deep draught, but whilst doing so an idea struck me, what had become of the second Afghan? Had not this occurred to me, I really don't know what might have happened. I was rapidly losing control over my passions. Fanny was in a glow of more than loving gratitude; a very little pressing and I felt sure she would welcome me between her thighs, and in spite of her "illness" I should have there and then swept away the charming maidenhead I had discovered to be safe and secure. A standing prick has no conscience, saith the proverb, and for that, mine was worse than standing! It was in a terrible state of agonized extension, and fighting to crack the outer skin!

But that second Afghan!

"Fanny! Did you not say you saw two men? One with a knife?"

"Yes, I certainly did!"

"Where is the second?"

"I don't know! I suppose he must have run away when he saw you."

"But where to? Your door is shut! There is only one window and I am certain that he could not get out of that. That man is in the house somewhere."

I released myself from her clinging embrace and I looked under the bed. I found something, but no Afghan! If you want, dear reader, to know what it was I must refer you to Byron's Don Juan, Canto I, when the suspicious husband is searching for Juan, whom he suspects to be not far off, and who indeed was couched between the beauteous Julia's thighs, under the bed clothes. I forget the exact lines, but, like him, that had found something under the bed, but not what they sought. I fear I am trifling, for indeed the matter was serious enough that I have to write about.

It being plain that the second Afghan was not in the room, I insisted on searching the house. It struck me, too, as so odd that no one seemed to have been roused by Fanny's shrieks, and yet I had heard them a hundred yards off, when I was outside the house. Cursing my folly in delaying when each moment might be precious, and for thinking of how sweet it would be to fuck Fanny, when perhaps Amy might be lying ravished or murdered, I sprang to the door though poor Fanny did all she could to try and hold me back. She was alarmed at the idea of seeking danger and her forcing me was selfish. But I persisted.

Between her door and her sister's was a passage. But I must first say I had picked up the knife my Afghan had dropped. This I held sword-like in my hand. I opened Amy's bedroom door suddenly and quickly, and there I saw another sight which made me sick with horror. The Afghan was apparently buggering Amy. Apparently? Alas! no! He was actually doing it! And like the other ruffian who I had so fortunately caught just in time to prevent any real damage being done to the suffering Fanny, this Devil's spawn was so intent on his rich enjoyment that he did not at first notice my entry. All took place so rapidly that I cannot attempt to imitate time in my very true history. I dashed at the villain who withdrew his glistening black prick from poor Amy's bottom so suddenly that it made a "pop" like a cork coming out of a bottle. He reared himself upright, seized a long knife from off the bed where he had placed it ready for use before he had begun buggering the poor girl, and with a shout of triumphant defiance, and the expression of a fiend courting further victory, he rushed to me crying out, "Ah! Ha! Bahin chut! I eri IDa ki chut!" the gentle Hindu and savage Afghan in common, meaning that he who addresses you has defiled and fucked both your (Sister's cunt! thy mother's cunt! Terms of abuse used by sister and your mother.) "I have fucked and buggered your sister—I will now bugger thee also!" In my rage I roared in reply, "I'll be buggered if you do!" quite an unnecessary piece of bad language on my part, because had the ruffian succeeded, I, of course, would have been buggered.

I now found what a mistake I had made in not holding my knife dagger wise instead of as a sword, for before I could make any attempt to stab my huge antagonist he had his knife twice in me, once in my left shoulder, and once in the breast. He was trying to stab me down to the heart through the shoulder, and only that I sprang back his second stab would have succeeded. As it was he cut me terribly all down the left breast. I however caught my knife well into his left side and turned hard. Fanny, screaming at the top of her voice, had fled the moment she saw this second devil, and all the time the combat lasted I could hear the hills and rocky caverns resounding with the shrill shrieks, for she had gone to the open window and was literally yelling. Meanwhile the burly and really immense Afghan was getting the better of me. He was far more accustomed to using the dagger than I was, who had never fought with one in my life. He stabbed me many times, but fortunately, chiefly in the left arm, though I caught some fearful rips in the chest like the first one. I began to fight at random, for I felt bewildered by his extraordinary activity and lightning-like blows which I had to ward off as best I could, or avoid him by jumping from side to side like a cat, but at last a lucky and desperate stab from me laid the red brute lifeless at my feet. I had struck him an upward blow in the stomach, and the keen knife, having penetrated his clothes and outer flesh, passed as through a pat of butter, up to the hilt into his body, and transfixed his heart. He lay on the floor a moment writhing and trampling with his feet, and then he gave a dreadful gasp or two and died! To the last his fierce eyes seemed to bore deadly hatred into mine, and I could not help shuddering even in victory, at the terrible escape I had had.

At first I was overcome with faintness and fatigue. I could hear Fanny yelling, but could not go to her assistance. I sat on the bed next to the motionless Amy and panted. I did not feel my wounds much, but they made me sick. Poor Amy was lying on her face which I could not see. She was stark naked. Her arms were tied behind her back, her elbows being made to meet. The bandages fastened also behind, passed apparently over her face, but confined her rich flowing locks at the back of her head. I had not time, nor spirit to fall to admiring her lovely form, but to this day I see those rich full hips and those beautiful hemispheres, between which was that back entrance so lately defiled by the beastly Afghan's black prick. At last, somewhat recovered, I began with hands trembling with fatigue and excitement to try and undo the bandages. They were knotted too tightly, and I had to carefully use the knife I held to cut them, and wherever I touched her the blood streamed from me on to her fair white skin, until she looked as if she were weltering in her gore, but at last I succeeded, and got the arms over, and the bandage off her face, then putting my hands under her, I turned her on her back. In doing so I unconsciously grasped two full and firm bubbies which adorned her bosom far more richly than Fanny's did hers, for, though some eighteen months younger than her sister, Amy was more "grown up" in body than Fanny. I was in an agony to know if the Afghan's brutal boast was true. Had he fucked as well as he had undoubtedly buggered the unfortunate girl? Hardly noticing the fact then that the bush which curled all over the plump and well shaped motte under my eyes was far thicker and more grown than on Fanny's, I slipped an inquiring finger into the palpitating and sweet little cunt, feeling sick at heart with dread and apprehension! Oh! joy! she had not been fucked! Her dear little maidenhead was intact. Buggered she had been, but not ravished. Full of this good and important discovery, I ran to Fanny, whose voice was hoarse, and implored her to go to her sister's assistance. Already I could hear voices of men running up the steep path, which led from the bazaar in the valley, on the other side of the house, and fearing lest in their zeal to help, a number might break in and discover the two girls naked as they were, I implored Fanny to put on her petticoats and to go and cover Amy. But Fanny had quite lost all self-possession. She indeed went to Amy's room, but on seeing her naked, bleeding and apparently dead, and the gory carcass of the slain Afghan lying on the floor in a lake of blood, she rushed out again, screaming and crying like one demented. I ran to the door in time to prevent the kotwal from letting any of his men climb in through the window, and I begged him to set guards round the house, to remain where he was, and to send at once for Dr. Lavie and the picket of the regiment. Satisfied that my orders were being carried out, and that though bursting with curiosity neither kotwal nor peons would try to get inside the house, I went to Fanny who was crouched in one corner of the room, endeavoring to assuage her fears, telling her that Amy was only in a faint, and that was my blood and not hers which covered her body. The poor girl had received so many shocks to her nerves that at first it was almost impossible to rouse her to her senses, or make her understand that her sister must be attended to. I called her attention to the chattering and hub-bub outside, and I really was anxious to get her out of the room, for I could hear the remarks made to each new-comer and ughs! and oh's! with which each one saluted the dead body of the murdered and unfortunate chokeydar.

I wished this piece of news not to get to Fanny's ears yet awhile, and at last I persuaded her to go and look after Amy. I threw a dark blanket over the bloody corpse of the abominable Afghan, and Fanny, with visible shudders, picked her steps over the blood-spattered floor. She did not seem to appreciate that she was, to all intents and purposes, naked. The Afghan had not, as the one in Amy's case had done, torn her night dress completely off her. He had rent it from top to bottom in front, and Fanny still had her sleeves on her arms, short sleeves which permitted her arms to be almost entirely seen.

Perhaps feeling the fluttering remnants of her night dress made her think that she was covered, but as a matter of fact I saw, and as I saw I admired, and as I admired I desired the whole of her body in front, and she looked bewitching, with her eyes wildly glancing about, her sweet little bubbies rising and falling rapidly, as her bosom expanded and contracted with her quick breathing. Her pretty motte pushing out a little into a perfect cushion, rapidly narrowed to the point whence the plump little gem of a cunt showed its deep and tempting line. Her bush was not thick enough to permit me to yet see that line which is visible when a naked girl stands upright and is not conscious that she is displaying her secret charm of charms to an admiring man, and when she sat down beside her completely naked sister I could compare cunts, and fancy which one would give me the greater pleasure to fuck. Goodness! what strange thoughts do get in a man's mind at inopportune moments! I was perfectly conscious that what I had to do was to relieve Amy, and further search the house, and yet there I was debating those two lovely girls' cunts in my mind, and comparing their bubbies, their forms, their thighs.

I got Fanny the water and bade her sprinkle Amy, and I begged her again to be quick and put something on, for, "You are perfectly naked, my dear girl!"

"Oh! What does it matter! What does it matter!" she said, bursting into tears again. "I feel as if I should die!"

"But look, Fanny darling! You must not give in so! Remember, you are a lady and a soldier's daughter, and be brave! That is right, dry your tears. I have sent for Dr. Lavie and expect him here. Be quick and bring Amy around. She breathes all right," I added, laying my two hands on her lovely bubbies. "Sprinkle her well! That's right! She will soon be all right! Then cover her up in bed and get in with her. You have not been half so badly used as she has!"

"How?" asked Fanny, in a voice of surprise.

"She was gagged by that ruffian," I said, pointing to the dead Afghan in the blanket, "and he had tied her arms behind her, and I don't know what else he, may have done."

Fanny had been long enough in India to have learnt all about the theory of fucking, even if she had not been old enough before leaving England to know it in that happy land.

She burst out, "Oh! poor, poor, Amy! Oh! Captain Devereaux! What shall we do? What shall we do?"

I understood her cry.

"Don't be alarmed, dearest Fanny. I don't think the ruffian did any wicked deed that will leave bad results. But I am sure Amy must have fought, and perhaps got badly bruised and hurt."

I could not tell her that I had actually seen the Afghan's prick in Amy's bottom up to his beastly balls, and Fanny had run away too soon to have seen it herself, and she knew nothing of Sodomy at that time.

Fanny set to work in real earnest, and having something to keep her thoughts on, took them off herself. I persuaded her to be brave whilst I went and visited the rooms, saying that I felt sure no other Afghans were in the house, but I would first make sure. Before going, however, I called in the Kotwal, and posted some men in the passage, shutting Amy's door so that no curious eye could see the naked girls. The first room I visited was the Colonel's bedroom. There was Mrs. Selwyn apparently fast asleep. I tried in vain to rouse her. I opened her eyes and the immensely distended pupils told me what was the reason of her torpor. Opium! Drugged! There had been premeditation, and there must be a traitor, or a traitoress, in the house.

I next went to what was called the nursery. There Mabel, a fine girl, about twelve or thirteen, slept with the younger children, and an Ayah ought to have been there also. But there was no Ayah!

Mabel was awake, crying and sobbing. She gave a little shriek as I came into the room, but the moment she saw me she sprang out of bed in such a hurry and in such disorder that although there was but a feeble little light, burnt as I have said by everybody at night, I not only saw her sweet little cunt to perfection, but could see that already a downy growth was shading the motte, which promised to be beautiful when the season for collecting the ripe fruit from the garden of Venus should have arrived. Mentally I exclaimed to myself, "I seem to be destined to see all the fuckable Selwyn cunts tonight." For Mabel could certainly have taken me then, young as she was. I knew the measure of a cunt which would admit my prick by this time. How ever, let me proceed.

Mabel, delighted to see me, and not, as she feared, an ogre or a robber, flew into my arms and hurt my left one, beside my chest wounds, so much that I could not refrain from calling out. She started back and roared when she saw her nightdress all covered with blood. I had great difficulty in pacifying her, but got her back into bed, where I kissed her and begged her to stay quiet. I told her how the robbers had come, and I had killed one, after being wounded myself, and that everybody was safe and sound, and that I would tell her more in the morning. She was a biddable girl and really was very quiet, lying down and promising to be good. I examined the two other children and found them in the same state of stupor as Mrs. Selwyn. Evidently they had been drugged and the whole thing was a plot. The Ayah's absence assured me of this. Had she run away to give the alarm help would have come long before, but the Kotwal had told me that it was Fanny's unearthly screams that had aroused the Bazaar. It seemed plain to me that the mission of those two Afghans had been to rape, perhaps to bugger also, Fanny, Amy and Mabel, and that Mrs. Selwyn and the two younger children had been drugged to prevent their adding any outcry in case of a squalling match on the part of poor Fanny and her sisters, whilst they were being raped, etc. The man I had killed had done his work better than the fool who took Fanny, for he had commenced by gagging Amy, who could not utter a sound, even whilst she was being buggered, poor child! Else I would have heard her when I was trying to bring Fanny around. But I did not hear a single sound; had I, poor Amy might have escaped. I went back to Amy's room, but dreadfully sick, ill and in pain. No wonder. She expressed her gratitude more by her eyes than by her voice and she put up her sweet face so imploring to be kissed that I bent down, though it hurt me to do so, and gave some warm kisses on her trembling lips. Then bidding Fanny to remain where she was, in bed with Amy, I went to see whether there was any signs of Lavie and the picket.

I had not to wait long. But during the interval the Kotwal told me that three of the Colonel's house servants were lying dead in the go-downs of the outhouses, viz., the cook, the bearer and the sweeper, and that the Chuprassi could not live long, having been repeatedly stabbed, and two children had their throats cut. It was a fearful massacre, and I could hardly believe that two men could have done it. There must have been more, but I only saw two and no one lived to tell the entire story though the enquiry elicited the cause of this ferocious attack.

Soon the regular beat of drilled and disciplined men was heard, as the picket came as quick as they could, up the steep ascent from the bazaar, and jolly little Crean, the wild spring from the Green Isle, and Lavie both appeared. In as few words as possible I put them in possession of the facts. Lavie instantly sent off for his stomach pump, which he had not brought, not expecting he would require that implement. Crean set his sentries and scoured the bushes and rocks, but found nothing new. The bodies of the slain were put in one outhouse by themselves; and as soon as Lavie said the young ladies could bear it, the party entered their room and carried off the huge carcass of the dead Afghan. He was an enormous man, and I shuddered for poor Amy's bottom, when I saw the immense size of his now dead, limp and hideous prick! No wonder it fitted tight and made a "pop" when he had suddenly pulled it out of her unhappy behind! I had determined not to tell Lavie what I had seen that prick doing, but left him to suppose that I had arrived just in time to prevent a rape.

Then, and not till then, did I let him see the state I was in. Dear reader, have you ever been wounded? If you have, you will remember how sickening it was, when the skilful surgeon dressed your wounds. Mine were not dangerous, except one which had just penetrated inside my ribs, but they grew necessarily painful as they got uncovered and the clothes were pulled, no matter how gently away from them. Lavie insisted on my going to bed in Fanny's room.

He said I must remain perfectly quiet and drink nothing but water (for I was dying of thirst and longed for a peg), for fear of inflammation setting in. Luckily I had lost so much blood that unless I did something foolish there was little fear of my getting into a bad state from inflammation, still, it was wisest to take every precaution.

Leaving me there I wondered how my prick could have stood so exorbitantly stiff such a short time since, whilst I was toying with Fanny's cunt, trying to bring her to, for now it felt as if it would never stand again! I felt so deadly weak. The excitement was over and the reaction had set in. I blamed myself, for I thought had I had my wits about me I would have left Fanny's cunt alone and visited the other rooms first, and then in all probability poor Amy would never have been buggered. I wondered did she know she had been? Or did a merciful heaven render her insensible before the brutal Afghan defiled her bottom with his beastly prick? I hoped the latter. I wondered at Fanny. I thought she would have been more heroic, but I made due allowance for her, and oh! she did look so lovely, and so did Amy, when they were both naked! And what a charming little cunt Mabel had too! And so on, and so on, until I fell into a kind of delirious sleep from which I did not waken for several days.

I remember that awakening very vividly. It was bright daylight. The window was open, as well as the door of the room, and the sweet cool air blew gently in upon me in the most refreshing manner, sometimes mingled with a loud laugh, came rolling up from the hillside from the busy bazaar. The twelve fine young whores had arrived, and I dare say I heard the happy laughter of some of the Tommies waiting anxiously for their turn for a jolly good fuck. I heard of this event from my young friend Crean, who told me later that Jumali was really an A-1 poke, and a splendid and very pretty woman. In fact, Jumali was the favorite of all those useful and graceful women. It was she who I afterwards heard at Peshawar had always commenced the night with the Colonel to be followed by three or four of the other fresh and plump ones. Ah! that "inspection" cost the Colonel dear, and might have cost him more than it did. Poor Amy! Poor Amy!

Well, then, I woke up, and at first wondered where I could be but my arm in a sling, and a feeling of painful stiffness all over me, quickly recalled my wandering memory. There was someone in my room. I could hear him or her gently stirring on the chair, but I could not see who it was. I called out in a weak voice, "Is anyone there?"

"Oh! Captain Devereaux! Are you all right then? Do you know me?" cried the sprightly Fanny, who came swiftly and smiling to my bedside, looking as fresh as a rose and as neat as usual, for Fanny was a very tidy girl at all times.

"Know you!" I cried in surprise, "of course I know you, Fanny dear!"

"Mama! Mama! Papa! Come! Captain Devereaux is not silly now! Come! Come!" she cried, running out of the bed room.

Mrs. Selwyn soon came as fast as her weakness would permit her, for the deadly narcotic which had been administered to her had made her exceedingly ill, and this was the first day she had left her bed since the events which I have, I fear, so feebly described, took place. At first she could not speak from emotion. The tears rose to her eyes and sought along the lashes a place to roll forth, which at last they did. She took my unbound hand in both of hers and pressed it, and at length finding her voice, said, with much emotion and very slowly, "Oh! Captain Devereaux! Captain Devereaux! What do we not owe you ?"

"Nothing at all, dear Mrs. Selwyn."

"Nothing! Oh no! We owe you everything, the lives and honor of our girls! We can never repay you!" and without another word she bent down and kissed me, letting her tears fall upon my cheeks.

I could not but feel moved. Fanny stood by looking on with a mixture of amusement and apprehension on her face, very comical. She was evidently amused at her mother kissing me, but why she should be apprehensive I could not tell. At all events she said nervously, "He does not call me Louie now, Mama!"

"Why! Did I call you that?" said I.

"Oh yes! You seemed to think I was your wife! You would insist that I should come to bed! You said you wanted me very badly, and I do not know what other rubbish." Mrs. Selwyn looked at Fanny and then at me.

"Well! Fanny! That shows that Captain Devereaux loves his wife and that his only thoughts were on her when he was delirious!"

"Was I delirious?" I asked in amazement.

"I should think you were," said Fanny, bursting into almost uncontrollable laughter. "The things you said to me! You would have it I was your wife!"

"Ah me!" said Mrs. Selwyn, "I never saw your wife Captain Devereaux, but I never in my life wished a man to be a married man as I wished you were not!"

"Because then he would marry me!" laughed Fanny.

There was a little awkward pause which I ended by saying, "And I should have got a good and very lovely wife in that case, Fanny!"

Fanny blushed and looked more than pleased. Her eyes assumed that look which at times gave them the appearance of speaking love and affection.

"Ah now!" said I, laughing, "if I were only a Mohammedan and you another, Fanny, I could marry you now! But you see we have the misfortune to be Christians."

"Worse luck," said Fanny with a sigh.

"Well!" said Mrs. Selwyn, "I can only say if it could be a pleasure to a mother to give her daughter to a man, it would have indeed been a pleasure to me to give Fanny to you, Captain Devereaux, for you have deserved her."

"And who can tell," said Fanny, innocently and quite unconscious of the sense of her words, "why he may not have me yet!"

I thought of that sweet, little cunt I had seen so much of and a feeble ripple stirred my prick. This latter sensation astonished me, for it suddenly flashed on me that I was desperately weak. Whenever the thought of fucking a girl had got into my mind before, it was always accompanied by a vigorous stand, but though Fanny's sweet naked charms floated before me, strengthened by her presence, clad though it was in the flesh, only a ripple passed along that hitherto noble weapon. I had never known what it was before to doubt of my power, and the shock I sustained was far greater than I can hope to make my readers understand.

Mrs. Selwyn noticed the change in me and said, "Come, Fanny! Get Captain Devereaux's beef tea, I can see he is tired. We have been talking too much to him and Dr. Lavie will be mad with us if he finds it out"

The Colonel here entered the room. He looked the picture of misery and woe. His conscience smote him. He knew that the young man lying prostrate and unable to move before him on his daughter's bed was in that condition owing to his "lust." Poor man! He knew that a number of innocent persons had gone to their doom for the same cause, and that his wife and one daughter were still ill from effects springing from the same cause. I took his grieved appearance to be simply that of sympathy, but as he wrung my hand, he said quietly to me, "Devereaux, I owe all to you, and you owe all to me!"

"How, Colonel?"

"I owe you the honor and lives of my girls—and—I ought never to have gone to Peshawar!" and he drew his hand across his eyes and groaned heavily.

Presently he added, "Lavie tells me it will be some little time before you are strong enough to do duty, and that he would like to see you in your own quarters which are nearer to him, but he allows that you will be better in a house where you can be nursed and looked after, so you will remain here till you are quite well and strong again."

"Thanks very much, Colonel. I hope however I shall soon be all right. How is Amy?" I added, "I have not seen her."

"She is still in bed, poor girl!" said the Colonel. "The attack made on her had a very curious and I am sorry to say a serious effect. She had the recurrence of an ailment which attacked her as a baby."

"There! Never mind," said Mrs. Selwyn, "never mind what is the matter with Amy. Captain Devereaux will be contented with knowing she has received a shock—not to be wondered at—and is still very low and depressed. Come, Fanny! get Captain Devereaux his tiffin!" and mother and daughter both left the room.

"It is a most singular thing," said the Colonel, looking carefully out of the door before he spoke, "but poor Amy as a baby had a relaxed sphincter ani—you understand? And it has come an again. Lavie says it is most unusual, but hopes to get her all right again so long as she is not allowed to pass anything but liquid. You understand?"

I felt inclined to burst with laughter, only I was so weak, and I remembered that my amusement arose from poor Amy having been buggered.

"But Colonel, what could have brought it on now?"

"Lavie says shock, only shock"

My goodness! I had noticed the peculiarity in the Colonel before, viz., a determination not to see, or want of power perhaps to see things as they were, but as he did not like to think of them. He knew as well, perhaps better than I did, how addicted Afghans are to Sodomy. Another man would have at once suspected this relaxation of the sphincter of poor Amy to be due to her having been buggered, but like the Ostrich, the Colonel buried his head in the sand of obstinacy, and thought nothing was apparent. He did not wish to think a daughter of his could be buggered, therefore she had not been buggered. That is all. Lavie, too, questioned me very closely as to what I saw the Afghan do when I caught him with Amy.

"Now, Lavie," said I, "I don't know what you expect to hear, but let me tell you this, the light in her room was very dim, I could not see very well. The moment I saw him, he seemed to see me, and we were hard at it trying to kill one another immediately!"

"You could tell me more, Devereaux, I am certain. I see I must tell you what I fear happened. Poor Amy has the sphincter of her—her—anus ruptured—at least I say it is ruptured. Jardine says it is only unnaturally distended. If it is ruptured, an operation will be necessary. If Jardine is right none may be wanted. I should feel myself on safe ground if I knew for a certainty that she was buggered, for then the state of her anus would be explained. The Colonel says, however, that as a child Amy always had a weak sphincter, even so, some violence must have brought it on bad again."

"Lavie, you are a gentleman, and I can trust you, but don't let it go any further, don't even tell Jardine, for it may be one of the unhappiest things that can happen to poor Amy, to have the truth known. She was buggered, and completely buggered, too! The blasted Afghan's prick was buried in her arse as deep as his balls, but he roared at me that he had buggered her and would bugger me too!"

"I thought so," said Lavie, thoughtfully. "I knew I was right. I am certain it is rupture and not abnormal distention of the sphincter. But I am afraid, Devereaux, that the mischief has been done. Nobody, of course, knew for certain, but everybody in the whole camp believes that Amy was buggered, and the men are ready to kill every Afghan that comes in. You see, too, unfortunately, the lessons you have been giving to the girls came in so handy for a joke. It was young Crean who started it when Jardine said he was not sure but that Amy had been buggered. Says Crean, 'Then she is B. A., buggered Amy! Oh! ho! Now we can chaff Devereaux and congratulate him on one of his pupils having taken her degree B. A.'"

I must leave it to my readers to appreciate the degree of annoyance this unsavory joke gave me. It was lucky far young Crean that he was not near when I heard this—not that I could have laid hands an him, for I was too weak at the time—but I would have given him a piece of my mind. The good feeling of the officers, however, made them, after the first enjoyment of the joke, drop allusion to it, as naturally they did not care to pain or wound.

It took me nearly three weeks to recover sufficient strength to be able to get up and crawl about. I had lost such an enormous quantity of blood. My delirium had resulted entirely from weakness, not so much from fever, though some have it. I ate like a horse. I never was so continuously hungry as during that time. Amy, whether operated upon or not I don't know, also got better slowly, and she and I used to sit out in the evenings surrounded by Colonel and Mrs. Selwyn, Fanny and the others, and chat and admire the exquisite beauty of the sunsets over the snowy peaked mountains of Afghanistan, as seen through the lovely and wild Chapie Ghaut. My blood letting had the most cooling effect upon my amorous disposition, and though I had a perfect recollection of the sweet little cunts I had seen, the thought of them affected me no more than if I had been a eunuch. In fact, I mentioned to Lavie that I feared I was done for all fucking in the future, for instead of finding my prick stiff and standing each morning on awakening, as it always had done, it now was limp and perfectly dead. He encouraged me, however, to look upon this as nothing but fancy, for it was due entirely to my weakness consequent upon the loss of blood I had experienced.

Before I was able to quit the almost home I had at the Selwyns, I received a letter, a most tender, loving letter from my darling Louie, written in the most melancholy strain, describing the terrible loneliness, especially at night, which she experienced now that she had no longer her "adored" husband to fill her arms. And she implored me to say when she might look forward to coming and joining me. I cannot give my readers, tender hearted and passionate as I know they are, any further idea of this letter, but it had a great effect upon me. There could not be a doubt but that Lizzie Wilson's voluptuous cunt had given my fidelity to Louie a tremendous shock, and I felt sure in my mind that quite near me was a little virgin cunt, between sweet Fanny's thighs, which longed for me too. I had begun to think that when I was well I would endeavor to raise the hopes of that dear little cunt, but Louie's letter, without in anyway even hinting that I might possibly meet with temptation to stray from the right path, smote my conscience with great force. I resolved I would not tempt her. The more I looked at it the more did I see how vile it would be for me to tempt the sweet girl to sin with me. Fanny was young and as yet pure minded. She had indeed let me see her heart, and I knew it was all my way, but I had not yet said or done anything to draw it nearer to me than it was. I made up my mind I would little by little draw off. Ah! easier said than done! but still I did manage to keep more from her, for I was well enough to go home, and it became a semi-estrangement which was most painful to me, for I did love the manner in which she told me all her thoughts, as though I had been either her betrothed or her brother. But Venus had marked me out as the intended high priest, and Fanny's maidenhead was foreordained to fall a prize to my stalwart prick.

Of course such a business as it could not be hid under a bushel. When I was well enough an official inquiry was held and briefly, these were the facts which were elicited.

The soldiers were, on arrival at Cherat, warned that if they ever went shooting on the mountain sides, they must never be in parties of less strength than five or six, or more than that in number. If fewer, they might be attacked, if greater, it might alarm the natives who might fear attack. But the whores had deserted, and the only fucking the men could get was such as at the danger of their own lives and those of the obliging women they could from time to time obtain from such females as they found herding goats and cattle. It appeared that two parties of six men each, making a total of twelve, met accidentally at a lonely place in the glen, in which were two fine young Afghan lassies herding some cattle. The offer of a rupee from each man made the maidens joyful and they willingly earned twelve rupees each, for each man had each girl turn about. The girls returned delighted to their village and the Tommies came back to camp much relieved. The promise had been given of more rupees for more fucking, but alas, it never could be fulfilled.

Somehow or other the tribesmen found it out. The inevitable consequence for the poor unfortunate girls was, that after their noses had been cut off, and thus mutilated, they had been paraded before the assembled men, women and children, and then they had been slowly burned to death, and further it was resolved that—these poor girls having been considered to have been virgins—a desperate vengeance should be taken on the English at Cherat. It was a pity that Mrs. Selwyn should have engaged her Ayah at Peshawar, where she had gone to meet her husband on his return from the war. This Ayah had Afghan blood in her veins and Mrs. Selwyn made a mortal enemy of her by boxing her ears for either some impertinence or slackness of duty. This happened just about the time when the irate tribesmen were looking out for English virgins to rape. Fanny, Amy and Mabel were the only fuckable girls in Cherat, and the Ayah, knowing what was happening, plotted with the tribesmen to give these poor innocents into their hands. She also took the opportunity when Colonel Selwyn had gone to inspect the whores, and the consequences were what I have endeavored to narrate. It goes without saying that that Ayah disappeared and was never heard of again. Only for the fortunate circumstance of my having that extreme feeling of uneasiness, the whole three girls would certainly have been raped, buggered and perhaps killed too, as it was, poor Amy was buggered.

It is curious how events hang one upon another; The flight of the Ayah necessitated the hiring of another, and Mrs. Selwyn took, on the recommendation of a lady of Peshawar, a woman whom I felt certain she never would have entertained had she first seen her; for Sugdaya was the most lovely native woman I ever saw. Mrs. Selwyn knew that owing to her own weak health and consequent inability to give the Colonel those satisfying nights of real succulent fucking which keep married men chaste and quiet, a man whose temperament and whose balls must feel desire at times press him immensely. To admit so tempting a piece of flesh as Sugdaya into her house was therefore rash to a degree, but once done it was impossible to undo it. Sugdaya was modest in demeanor, of course avoiding the Colonel, devoting herself to her duty to Mrs. Selwyn and the Misses Baba, and in fact becoming Mrs. Selwyn's right hand. We shall hear a good deal more of Sugdaya, gentle reader, especially in the series after this.

I visited Peshawar several times after my recovery. In fact, as far as I decently could without making it too marked, I avoided the Selwyn's as much as possible. I thought the Colonel was glad. He used to seem uneasy at the fondness poor Fanny evinced for me. The poor girl often chided me for being so much of a stranger now, and I found it difficult to collect myself with her, but I was determined to keep out of her way, and the sweet temptation I once loved so much.

Things therefore wore on and we were getting tired of Cherat, and wondering where we should go, and when, for the Government never left troops there all Winter, and we expected to go to a station on the plains. Mrs. Soubratie's nose had been much out of joint at the superior charms of Jumali and the eleven other fresh young whores, but she had realized a perfect fortune. Certainly she had made an instant use of her fine cunt, and had lost no opportunity of gathering rupees by the free use of it. But since Jumali's arrival Cherat had lost much of its attraction for Mrs. Soubratie, and she very often had "pains in her belly," necessitating whiskey, sugar and water, which during the halcyon days of her fucking she had never asked for.

At last came the longed for orders. We were to start to march in December to Rawal Pindi—take the train there the line having been opened as far as that now, and then proceed to one of the nicest stations in Bengal-Fackabab.

If I had time I should like to describe this march in detail, for marching in India is truly delightful, but I can only tell of two incidents which as the first effected the relations of Colonel Selwyn and myself, and the second raised me to Heaven to immediately push me down into Hell!, I must narrate.

The first night of the march we encamped at Shakkote at the foot of a hill. Lavie and I, who were inseparable, went for a stroll and did not get back to camp until after dark. Going to my tent I met Soubratie outside of it who made me a mysterious sign and told me in a whisper that the Colonel Sahib was asleep on my bed.

Out of curiosity and wondering why he should have chosen my bed instead of his own, I gently and in spite of Soubratie went and peeped. My camp lantern was dimly burning, turned down as low as possible and on the ground, but there was light enough for me to see hat the man was on my bed between the thighs of a woman and fucking her deliciously. I could not see their faces, but I could see their bottoms and I did see such an enormous pair of balls hanging and quite hiding any part of the cunt which might otherwise, perhaps, have been seen when the prick to which they belonged was drawn out of it as far as could be before the next home thrust, that had not Soubratie told me it was the

Colonel, I should have guessed it was he. I could not resist it. I went straight in as though I had expected nothing. The poor Colonel looked up, blurted something, and I roared laughing!

"I really were here! I beg your pardon, Colonel! I did not know you never mind, I won't say a word and I won't disturb you." And before he could say anything I left the tent.

By and by out he came. I made as if I didn't wish to see him, but taking me by the arm he said, "Devereaux, Devereaux, I must offer you a thousand apologies! For God's sake don't tell anybody! My dear boy, if your wife were as delicate as mine, you would understand how impossible I find it to go without a woman. Don't betray me, Devereaux! Don't! It would kill Mrs. Selwyn! I can't help it! But she would not understand! Oh! boy, speak!"

"Of course I won't tell, Colonel. But why on earth do you look at Mrs. Soubratie when you have such a lovely Ayah in Sugdaya?"

"Because, my boy, take my advice. If you ever fuck a woman who is not your wife, don't let her be one of your own household. Now! see! if you would like to fuck Sugdaya yourself, you are welcome. Would you?"

"My dear Colonel, I am really very greatly obliged, very greatly indeed, but I think I lost too much blood up the hill there to expect to feel the want of a woman before my wife joins me."

"Well! If you do—you know Sugdaya or any other—remember," said the Colonel. I am sure he did not intend to include Fanny or Amy in the "any other."

On the third day of our march we arrived at Nowshera. How my heart beat at seeing the familiar Dak Bungalow, once the very temple of Venus, in which I had officiated as her high priest, and had offered so many sacrifices to her with joy and thanksgiving in her favored shrine between the force of the fair Lizzie Wilson's voluptuous and beautiful thighs. I was tired with the march; not that the distance we had taken was at all excessive but I had not yet recovered my strength after the tremendous blood letting at Cherat. Lavie had marched with me. The Colonel and his family, attended by Jardine, had gone ahead, and sat in the very verandah where the struggle between Lizzie and Searles had begun, looking at us—as we marched by with the regiment to the camp ground behind the bungalow, between it and the Cabul river. Fanny had ridden a pony. Amy was not allowed to ride. She and Mrs. Selwyn had each been brought in a Dhooli or palanquin, and Jardine and the Colonel kept Fanny company. In the evening after I had strolled on the banks of the river, from visiting which I had been withheld on my first stay by the superior attractions of Lizzie's delightful cunt, I got back to my tent where I found Soubratie mounting guard, and he told me with a grin that the "Colonel Sahib there speaking to his woman in Master's tent." I went and peeped very quietly and had the felicity of seeing the Colonel without his coat or trousers on, laying beside Mrs. Soubratie, whose fine, fat, brown cunt he was manipulating with his hand, whilst she was grasping those balls of which I have mentioned seeing and their colossal size. Evidently the interested pair were making ready for a second assault, and soon I saw this accomplished.

The Colonel, evidently, enjoyed himself very much, and judging from the little feminine ripple of laughter which from time to time issued from Mrs. Soubratie, she likewise profited by the nice titillation which her admirer's very full sized prick was occasioning her. Soon came the vigorous short digs and then the final hard squeeze home, which told me in eloquent silence that the Colonel was inundating the shrine with the oil of his manhood, and then withdrawing his prick from its hot retreat, he lay down panting for a few minutes and after a little while got up and commenced dressing his nether limbs. Had I seen this good performance some weeks earlier, before I had been so disabled by my wounds, I should have been driven nearly frantic, and have had my own prick in such a state of alarming stiffness and fury, that I should probably have waited to see the Colonel safe out of the tent, and then gone in myself and, in spite of Mrs. Soubratie's big hands, which always spoiled any idea of fucking her that came into my mind at Cherat, where I had at the time no other available cunt, I should have gone in and had a round or two with her, then and there, and worked off the extra effervescence of my feelings. But now! Oh! It was sickening to me! Not a stir came in my prick! Not a ghost of a stand! Not even a ripple!

In deep despair I left the place from which I had been watching the performance and went to Lavie's tent, where after a little I told him I had just seen a Tommy fucking a woman and that it had had no more effect on me than it would have had on a dog or someother animal whose desires did not lie between a woman's thighs. Lavie laughed and assured me that I need not despair, that when I had eaten enough food to replace the blood I had lost, I should perhaps find my prick an intolerable nuisance, because being a married man, I could not do as he would under similar circumstances, send for Jumali or another of the twelve, and reduce the dimensions of the implement with her assistance. In fact, he seemed to think nothing of what plagued me day and night, for I was seriously alarmed. No wonder poor Louie complained that my letters were all couched in such a minor key; for all the time I was writing them I was fearing I should never again hear her soft sighs of delighted gratitude as I made her spend and buck under the impulse of my active fucking. I really thought I had become once and forever impotent!

But ah! during the next day, during the next evening, a delightful and most cheerful change, in this respect, came Over me! If any medical man should happen to read this exact narrative of my feelings and history I depict so he win be able to account for it, but I cannot, at least I cannot give scientific reasons, which no doubt he can and will to any inquiring soul. Well, the next morning I got a nice little note from Fanny:

Dear Captain Devereaux
    Mamma wants to know why you are making yourself such
    a stranger. We have caught hardly even a glimpse of you for
    a long time now. Will you come and dine with us tonight? It
    will be an early dinner, at six, because we have to get up early
    tomorrow morning for the march. Do come! Yours, always
    affectionately,

                                                    Fanny Selwyn

I sent back a little note accepting, feeling a strange beating of my heart, for Fanny had grown much too dear to me, and the reader knows why I did not cultivate her love more ardently than I did.

Meanwhile honest Jack Stone had been to see me, and told me that the unfortunate Searles had died of cholera on his way to Bombay. The wretched man had recovered sufficiently to enable the doctors to recommend his going home to England on sick leave, but before he got to Bombay he was attacked by cholera, and had to be put out of the train in a dying condition, and he lies buried at a lonely little station where not even a headstone records who lies buried in the small cemetery. Many poor travelers die in this manner in India, are buried, forgotten and have nothing but the station-master's book to tell where they sleep their last sleep.

Stone was dreadful anxious that I should not add flame to spreading any reports about Mrs. Searles and her establishment at Honeysuckle Lodge and the reason for this became apparent to me some years later, when I met him and a lady who he introduced to me at Brighton as Mrs. Stone. This lady's features struck me as being somehow familiar to me, and on racking my brains I remembered they were extremely like those of the naked lady in the photograph he had shown me on that eventful night when Searles had tried to ravish Lizzie Wilson. The gallant Jack had made Mrs. Searles an honest woman again in the sight of the world, and had gained an equally honest right for himself to fuck her whenever he liked without having to pay five hundred rupees for that grand pleasure. She seemed a fine voluptuous creature with decidedly large, well formed bubbies, and I dare say old Jack had many voluptuous nights between her voluptuous thighs, fucking her voluptuous cunt, as he had expressed it. Poor old Jack Stone! There are many worse men in the world than he, and I dare say little Mrs. Searles made him as good a wife as many another woman whom he might have married would.

It was not without still further heart stirrings that I found the Selwyn's occupying my hotel room in the bungalow as their sitting room, and using what had been Lizzie Wilson's as a bedroom for the girls and children. The door which communicated between the two rooms was open, and there, as I sat beside Fanny at dinner, I saw the very bedstead on which I had so often fucked the beautiful Lizzie with rapture indescribable. As I looked at it and revolved past scenes in my mind, Fanny caught the direction of my eyes.

"That is my bed," said she, innocently. "Is it?" I replied mechanically. Oh! What had come over me that the sight of that bed stead did not make my prick rage? I am sure I was dull and stupid at dinner. The Colonel, however, was in high glee. I knew why.

The poor man had at last outwitted his careful wife and obtained the much longed for fuckable cunt. So he was beaming and overflowing with anecdote. I let him talk, and behaved as a respectable listener, only occasionally replying to some question Fanny put, from time to time, hoping to bring on one of our old time free and unconstrained conversations. The way she stuck to me all that evening touched me. Instead of being offended at my obstinate silence, she came and sat next to me in the verandah, where I smoked cheroot after cheroot, listening to the Colonel's continual chatter, until at last Mrs. Selwyn with a warning that it was growing late, carried him off to bed, leaving me with Fanny alone.

"What is the matter with you, dear Captain Devereaux?" at last she said, laying her gentle little hand on mind. "You have hardly spoken one word to me since you came. I am afraid the march is too much for you and you feel done up."

"Well! Fanny, I do. But I don't know that it is exactly the march. I can't quite tell you what it is, but I have never been myself since that fierce night of the Afghan."

"Ah! Mama says she is sure that had something to do with you being so gloomy. Why should you be? If I had killed an Afghan under such circumstances, I should be so proud there would be no holding me in."

"Ah! Fanny dear, before that night I was a man. I had power, force, strength, but ever since I have felt that I have none left—no power—do you understand?"

"Power? What do you mean by power?"

"That which makes a man acceptable to his wife, dear!"

"Oh!"

Did Fanny understand? I fancied she did, and after a little silence she said, "Do you know I had such a funny, such a nice dream bout you last night! I dreamt it three times—but I am afraid—that is, I don't believe it can ever come true for all that."

"What was it?"

"I dreamt that you came whilst I was asleep, in that room, and woke me just like the Afghan did-only more gently-you woke me in the same manner as he did, and you asked me to let you warm yourself in my arms, and you did plead so very earnestly that I said you might, and then—"

"And then?" said I, eagerly.

"Well! I don't quite know how to tell you! However, you got into bed and right onto me, and folded me to you so tight—Oh! so tight! and—I don't know what you did exactly—but, Oh!—it was so delightful and you were so happy—but I awoke—all of a sudden—and you were not there. I positively cried for—Oh! Captain Devereaux, you know we all love you!"

If this was not straight talk I don't know what it was. But the effect an me was magical. In a moment my weakness seemed to leave me and my long dead and useless prick sprang up in all his pristine might and stood as it had stood for Lizzie Wilson. The whole atmosphere seemed redolent of fucking, desire as strong as ever had assailed me came. Fanny's bosom I could see was rising and falling rapidly. It seemed to me that she was then and there offering herself to me if I would but have her. Her hand tightened on mine, and I gently drew it forward, intending to lay it on my now rigid prick, and to show her that I understood and was quite ready if she was so willing. A standing prick, dear reader, has no conscience! All my fine resolutions not to take advantage of Fanny had flown to the four winds of heaven! I could remember nothing but the sweet vision I had had of her dear little cunt, spoiled as its beauty was by the unclean blood of the menses, but tempting all the same. Whether she actually felt my prick or not I did not then know, for at that moment Mabel came quickly out of the bedroom and said, "Fanny, Mama says you must not stay up any longer, and that you are to come to bed." Without even saying goodnight but with a firm squeeze of her hand an mine, Fanny jumped up and ran.

Excited as I was with the tumult of joy and passion, desire and the stream of luxurious wine in my heart, I jumped up too, and taking Mabel round the waist I kissed her again and again, pressing her two nice young little bubbies as I did so to her last delight.

"What a regular woman you are growing, Mabel! What a fine bosom you have! What perfect little bubbies! I suppose you have plenty of hair here," and I slipped my hand down to her motte and pressed my itching finger between the thighs tell her little cunt.

"Oh! Captain Devereaux!" she exclaimed in a low tone, "you bad, naughty man!" but she made no defense. I sat down and pulled her to my knee, and had my hand under her petticoats like a shot, and my finger buried in her little virgin and warm cunt before she knew what I was up to!

"Mabel! Mabel! You are a woman!" I exclaimed, quite beside myself with excitement. "Don't you think you want a husband?"

"Yes," she whispered hotly, returning my burning kisses.

"I often feel I should like a man."

God only knows what I should have done but I think I might say that Mabel's maidenhead would have been done for there and then, only for Fanny's voice ringing angrily out of the room, "Mabel! Come to bed!"

With a last feel of the sweet little cunt, which alas! I had not had time to make spend, and with a last kiss fully returned by the gratified girl, who only twelve as she was, was precocious indeed, I let Mabel go, whispering to her "not to tell" and then rejoicing over my fully regained power and "standing" I went home to my tent and quickly undressed and viewed with delight that fine stalwart Johnnie who had so often stood to me so well in my encounters with the lovely foe.

I must leave to my male readers, especially those who have been really ardent and stood vigorously, to try to realize what it was to me to have regained "power." Certainly I had never in all my life been so intensely unhappy as since the day when first I began to think that my prick would never stand again, for I thought I had been weakened almost to death by the loss of my blood, yet by degrees my strength returned more and more from day today as far as my muscles went, but not so far as my prick or balls were concerned. At last this fact had been forced upon me, and from that day I began to get more and more depressed. But now, now wonder in my tremendous excitement, my unutterable delight and frenzy and happiness, for I had seized upon the lucky little Mabel and given her young heart joy and her youthful cunt happiness and pleasure. For everyone of my dear girl readers will allow that it is an awfully pleasant thing to have their own sweet bubbies and delightful cunts felt and caressed by the man whom they admire, and Mabel was surely as delighted as they had been, and will, I hope, often again be. The only wonder is that I had not been much more quick with Fanny, for I could have no doubt whatever of the meaning of her telling me of the dream. Ah! she, like Mabel, had no doubt often felt too that she would like a man! And the man she wanted was myself! The whole thing had happened so suddenly, and she had run away so quickly that I had not fully realized my position and hers before it was too late to talk to her, and I had taken Mabel instead. I went to my bed in a fever of joy and happiness. From this moment I would devote myself to fiercest siege of Fanny's dearest and sweetest cunt, and it would go hard with me if I did not take that tempting little maidenhead within a week or ten days. As for Mabel, I felt a little sorry that I had gone so far with her, not that she was not quite fuckable, and very nice indeed, but I might find her in the way. She was quite as eager for my prick as Fanny could be, and in time, perhaps, I should see my way to entering her little tender cunt also. Strange to say I never contemplated Amy at this juncture.

I had ravishing dreams. I fucked I don't know how many of my former lady loves, but neither Fanny nor Amy came in for their share. In the morning I woke and found not only my dear old prick, to my joy and delight, standing as full as in days of yore, and unmistakable signs of a most prolific wet dream, a sure sign that my balls had recovered their power of secreting the essence of man, so dear to the sweet girls who know its value, and I trust equally well know the terrible danger involved in receiving it into their glowing cunts without the most perfect precautions. For 'tis a powerful poison to happiness if taken wrongly, sweet maids!

Why does malicious fortune so delight in raising the cup of glee and happiness to our lips, just to dash it away as we commence to recognize how sweet are its contents? But is it not too often so? As I went to fall in with my company I met, the regimental postman, who handed me a letter, which I saw at a glance was from my beloved Louie. I had a conviction that there would be bad news in it. Bad news! Oh! what had I become when I deemed it bad news to hear that she was starting by the next mail to come to join me in India! And further that she had waited until now to announce that we had another baby to expect, the fruits of our too prolific fucking, about March next. She had not been sure, so did not like to mention it until she was certain. The usual signs did not show themselves, but now she was certain that a baby was really in existence and had run nearly six months of its natural life! Then—if she did come—and Louie was a woman of her word—I should have before me a time when I should not have that intense pleasure in fucking her which I had when her womb was free from lading.

She said my letters had been written in such increased low spirits, unlike myself, that she was getting more and more alarmed, and that conte que conte, she would come and join me, she did not know where, but she would find out in Bombay on landing. Next mail here—she must be in the Red Sea now! Or perhaps in the Indian Ocean and she would get to Fackabad, almost as soon as we would! Oh! Fanny! Fanny! How could I have you now! Gods! To think that the day had come when I did not want the woman who at one time had persuaded my soul and my senses that I should never care for another, the woman whose darling cunt also made my prick stand and had taken the shine out of all others! I was I tell you dear readers, torn with contending emotions. It was too late to stop Louie. She was as surely on her way as I had felt Mabel's little cunt, dear little cunt! I should never fuck it now! No! nor Fanny's either! And just about as I had at last made up my mind that I could not without dishonor to myself or either of these charming girls stay the craving which we all three felt. No wonder Lavie, who soon join me on the dusty road, found me glum and cast down.

"Look here! Devereaux!" said he, "I know well what it is. You are just killing yourself with the foolish fancy that your prick will never stand again! Now listen to me! Be wise and give up such absurd ideas!

You will find the old gentleman lift himself up again some day soon, if you will leave him alone, and let him wear off his sulks, but if your mind dwells on it you may render yourself permanently impotent, for the mind has great power over the senses. I'll just tell you a little story of myself as an illustration. It happened at Woolrich three years ago. I had been on duty at the Herbert Hospital, and a brother officer came walking home with me in the evening, a fellow I was very fond of. It was about nine o'clock, and on passing the Artillery Barracks I saw a very nice looking girl, evidently a Poll, standing on the pavement. I wished her goodnight and asked her if she was expecting anybody. "Yes, dear," she said, "I was expecting you."

"Oh!" then said I, "come along and I'll go home with you, where do you live?"

"In Wood Street," said she. "That is not your street, Lavie," said my friend, "and it is mine, so you had better let me see the young lady home, and go to your lodging yourself."

"Not I," I replied, laughing, "I want a poke and I am going to fuck this girl, am I not, my dear?"

"Of course," said she, "you asked me first and I'll come with you, but if your friend likes, I'll go to him or he can come to me when you are done."

"Buttered buns!" said my friend, laughing, "No thank you. Tomorrow night, however, if you will meet me at the road to the cemetery at eight, I will take you home and we will have it out then."

"All right," said she. Well, we walked on and soon were at Wood Street, and just as the girl turned in at her gate, and I was following her, my friend called out to her, "You had far better have come with me, for Lavie is good for nothing, and you'll get no change out of his balls tonight." The girl laughed and so did I. Well, we went upstairs to her bedroom and undressed and she was as fine and nicely made a little Poll as you ever saw; good bubbies, nice skin, good arms and legs, and a fine black bush hiding a soft, fat little cunt! But by Jove! I could not get a stand! The words of my friend kept ringing in my ears, and when he first said that I thought to myself, my God! fancy if that came true!— and true it did come. Simply because I doubted my own power. The poor girl was very much put about. Everything she could think of was tried, but in vain, to make my brute of a prick stand. I wanted to pay her and leave her, for I was miserable, but she, like a little darling, would not let me go. You try and sleep, said she. "I won't touch you anymore, and I dare say your prick will be all right by morning, and we can fuck then. I thought I never would sleep, but at last I dozed off and I suppose in an hour's time woke up and found I had a glorious stand. The girl was fast asleep, with her back towards me. Without waking her I got one of my legs between hers, working myself round and along her, until I had the right direction, and when she woke I had my prick buried in her cunt up to my balls. Well, she would not have it that way, but insisted on my doing Adam and Eve and I never enjoyed a night's fucking more. I had her seven or eight times and when I went away, after she had given me some breakfast she asked me if she had not done right to not let me? She said she knew it was only nervous depression, and the effect of fancy, and that she had more than once had experience with it, and so was not surprised that she was disappointed. So you see, Devereaux, how I who had no such cause as you have had to be weak, lost my power from simple imagination. Don't you indulge in fears anymore."

I thanked Lavie heartily for his sympathy, and then told him that I had quite unexpectedly recovered, how I had had a wet dream and how delighted I had been. He was glad to hear what I had told him, as he had begun to get alarmed for me, but he evidently was curious to know why I was so very despondent. So I told him it arose from my having received a letter from my wife announcing her speedy arrival in India with a six month's baby in her belly, and I said I was alarmed for her safety. Lavie was quite taken in, and the rest of our conversation turned on the folly of pregnant women undertaking long and tedious journeys, the terrors of the hot weather, infant mortality in India, and so forth, but my mind lamented the lost chance of dear Fanny's cunt, just as it seemed so well within my reach.

On arrival at Akhora I went direct to the Selwyn tent and found Mrs. Selwyn and the Colonel sitting in the shade of it, for the sun was burning hot, although the air was so cool, it being in the middle of the delicious cool weather of Northern India. Fanny, who was also sitting by her mother's side, blushed. Oh! she blushed a beet root red blush, which fortunately her mother did not see. Mabel, standing in the tent door, leaning against the door pole, grinned at me, and turned red too for a moment, but knowing that she had a dark background, she gave me a perfect contour of her rising bosom, swelling out her fine little bubbies as much as she could, and showing her legs too by occasionally putting her foot up against the opposite door pole as high as she could reach. She had extremely good legs and very pretty feet and ankles. Jardine and

Amy were sitting at the far corner of the tent. The Colonel soon went off to see the camp, and I then told Mrs. Selwyn. about Loutie's letter.

Both she and Fanny called out in surprise at the sudden determination Louie had taken, and looked at one another. Poor Fanny turned as white as death. So white that I thought she was going to faint. Mrs. Selwyn saw it, but fortunately did not put it down to the real cause.

"Fanny! Fanny! God bless the child! Did you ever see a portal turn so white in a second?"

Fanny's faintness, however, only lasted a second. With that wonderful determination which I afterwards found to be so strong a feature of her character, she pulled herself together again and said it was nothing.

"Nothing!" exclaimed her mother, "I'll tell you what it is, you are overdoing yourself. This march and the long rides are wearing you out. You must ride in the Dhooyl like Amy and me."

"Oh! Mother!" cried Fanny, "I really can't! I assure you it is really nothing! I really am as strong as a horse and quite fit to bear—" but here she paused as if seeking for a word.

"A husband and get children!" cried the impudent Mabel. "Mabel!" cried Mrs. Selwyn, "how dare you! How dare you say such things, and before Captain Devereaux too!

Go into the tent, miss and don't presume to come out until I let you! I'll give you a whipping miss! Go in, I tell you!"

Mabel looked at me, and, as she turned to obey, laughing, acted as though she had a baby in her arms which she was giving suck to. Her mother did not see it, but I did and was amused as well as a little, a very little, shocked, of course. "It is all this horrible India!" cried Mrs. Selwyn to me. "Fanny, dear, is not that your Papa coming back? Get up and see, that's a dear girl"

"It is all this horrid India," repeated Mrs. Selwyn. "Children learn about things which girls sixteen and seventeen know nothing of at home."

"Yes," I said, "I believe that's it, Mrs. Selwyn, but I always think it best not to appear to notice that they do; it should be the object of everybody to try and keep impure thoughts out of young persons' minds, but especially out of those of girls."

"Ah! Captain Devereaux! That is why I like you so much. I feel I can trust my girls with you anywhere, and at anytime. When your dear wife comes I shall tell her so too."

Oh! my Venus! My blessed, blessed Venus! And yet all chance of fucking Fanny destroyed just when it was so feasible. Loved by Fanny, trusted by her mother! I should have had every chance but now my Louie coming would send all my lovely castles in the air tumbling to the ground.

"Yes," continued Mrs. Selwyn, "it is wonderful how precocious children become in India, both in mind and body. Now look at that naughty Mabel. She is not much more than twelve years old, and, as you see, I still keep her in short frocks to let her remember that she is not grown up yet. But dear Captain Devereaux, for all that Mabel is grown up, and could marry tomorrow, and get children as fast as could be. You would be surprised if you were to see her in her bath. Of course you are a married man, so I can speak to you about things if you were a bachelor I could not, so I can tell you that Mabel has breasts like a woman, thighs like an unmarried woman, and hair—hem! ahem! what was I saying? Oh! yes, she is fully developed."

I could hardly help laughing at the slip she had so nearly made when she mentioned "hair," but I refrained, for the thought of that hair around the pretty little cunt, which I had now both seen and felt, entered my mind, and I sighed to think that probably my prick would never gain entrance there, nor indeed that darling one, for which my whole body craved, that between lovely Fanny's thighs.

"Well! Mrs. Selwyn," I said, "the only thing for it is to do as I say. Try and not notice anything which is not too openly said and done in the way of precociousness, speaking sexually; and try to lead the youthful mind into another channel. I promise you I will try and do my best to second you."

"Ah! my dear Captain Devereaux, how good, how good you are!" And the good lady let some tears run down her cheeks. Positively I felt an awful beast. For I had not at all intended to lead the girls themselves into any other channel than that which would the most speedily bring my prick slick into their charming cunts.

But something checked me. Perhaps Venus herself made my reach to those delicious charms a little more difficult, in order to by that painful climb I might more safely harbor in the forest shaded grottos when I got them.

At first I got, as it were, a regular fit of obstinacy. My Louie was coming out. Her coming must, according to all rule of law, put an end, a complete end, to any schemes I might have of fucking any girls but I was all the more determined that I would fuck them all the same, and so I fell to work to prove to mine and to Louie herself, in order that I might by profound study of her ways and thoughts find that loophole through which I might escape from her observation, and keep Fanny safe too, when I should (as I swore I would), fuck her. But alas! the more I thought of Louie, the more prominently did all her sweetness of character and her passionate love of me come before me. Although a man of the most intense passions, I am not altogether depraved. And I could not but recognize what a cruel, cruel thing it would be to betray this darling wife of mine. It would kill her, I thought, should she discover it. Doubt was the last thing she had ever had of me. She had become part and parcel of me.

Never yet had I understood her, and so sweet and pleasant was she that, even after the conventional honeymoon, after that conventional glimpse of the Christian and Mohammedan heaven rolled into one, after I had gone back to the daily work and worry, she was just the same to me. By day she was my second self, helping me, cheering me, never in the way, and I never felt happy after she left me until she had come back again. At night she was no longer my wife. Not a bit of it. She was my love! She was Venus and all her company of brilliant nymphs, in one! No woman could have endeavored more than she did to give me the intensest pleasure when I reveled between her thighs, nor do I remember any woman who seemed to enjoy being fucked by me more than my Louie did. Oh! Lizzie Wilson! Lizzie Wilson! What a pity it was I ever had you! But for that I should have been overjoyed at my Louie's coming to me, but alas! Lizzie's delightful cunt had brought before all that old burning love of change which had made me a cunt hunter before I was married.

I must leave my sympathizing readers to realize the contending passions which tore me. There were now dancing before me two sweet, sweet cunts—Louie's and Fanny's. Mabel's did not count. I had the most intense desire to taste Fanny, I felt so sure it would be so superb to fuck the girl on account of her passionate temperament. I had the liveliest recollection of my Louie's and the more I recalled it to mind, the more I loved the thought of it, and the stiffer it made my prick to stand.

At last a thought struck me—should I be a fool, and like the dog in the fable lose both of these sweet cunts, by leaving my firm hold on the one to try a new pleasure. I came to the conclusion that so long as Louie was with me any such act would result in dismal loss and failure, and so, on the lowest ground, I made up my mind to forego the attack upon Fanny.

Man is a funny animal. Like the fox and the grapes he, if he does not actually disparage the results of his labors, likes to give himself a good and high sounding reason for ceasing to strive for what he knows he cannot get. Little by little, in the course of time, I tried at first and succeeded at last, in persuading myself that I had nearly sinned, but that it was my love of Louie, and not the fear of her finding me out, that made me give up the idea of fucking Fanny Selwyn. In fact, I was virtuous! Had been sorely tempted by vice, had nearly succumbed, but had finally been saved by virtue!

What helped me to attain this degree of spiritual excellence was the repetition of a number of false alarms. I had fully expected on arrival at Fackabad, to have found Louie there, or a letter announcing her arrival at Bombay, whereas, what I did find was a letter, written in the greatest despondency, saying that on application to the agents of the P. & O., she was told that there would be no room for her until the third steamer after the one she had intended going by. Sure that she was coming, I behaved according, though I kept as much out of Fanny's way as I could without being downright rude. Even Mrs. Selwyn complained of my making myself such a stranger. The Colonel did not mind, because Mrs. Soubratie satisfied his every want regularly, I having taken a bungalow just at the back of the Selwyn's, so making it very handy for the poor Colonel when he felt cunt hungry, which was very often. But Fanny was awfully offended with me. There was no deceiving her. She knew quite well what it meant, and that I was simply sacrificing her happiness to the exigencies of the case. Yet at times when I was unavoidably thrown into her society more closely than at others, I could not so well preserve the gravity of my demeanor as to prevent her seeing it. I admired her, and what a real pleasure it was for me to be with her. Once indeed she said to me, "Captain Devereaux, once upon a time I thought you the wisest man I ever knew."

"And what do you think me now, Miss Selwyn?"

"A fool!" said she with emphasis. Jumping up, she walked away with her head in the air and in the most disdainful manner.

After that I thought that the sooner Louie came the better. If once a woman despises a man, it is a poor chance he has of ever having her.

But it seemed to me that there would never be a chance of poor Louie's coming. By some extraordinary error on somebody's part she missed the steamer and then came a catastrophe which caused a silence of two mails, and nearly, indeed, ended her life. I think what I felt most was Fanny Selwyn's apparent nonchalance when she heard that Louie's life was in great danger. At one time she would have found it difficult to avoid expressing openly her joy at such a catastrophe, for if Louie died, she would (she was sure of it) marry me, but now she coldly hoped that poor Mrs. Devereaux might recover. The accident which so nearly put an end to poor Louie, very nearly put an end to my offspring also. Our little baby girl playing at the top of the stairs very nearly tumbled down them. Louie, who was watching her sprang to help her, and, in doing so, tripped and not only fell, but precipitated herself and baby down the whole flight. Fortunately the child was not seriously injured, but poor Louie, now being in the family way, was terribly hurt. The result was a premature confinement, and the delivery of a dead boy, and the hovering between life and death for some weeks. My anxiety was fearful. Poor Mrs. Selwyn did all she could to comfort me. All the family, even Mabel, who had developed into a very naughty girl, forever talking double entente since I had tickled her cunnie at Nowshera, showed their sympathy with me, except Fanny, who openly said that I did not deserve a good wife, and so God was taking mine from me. I can tell you that there was much more hate than love between us at that time. Fortunately it was, however, only skin deep. Fanny and I were both deceiving ourselves. She imagined that she detested me as much as she had loved me before, and I tried to think that, after all, she was by no means as desirable as I had first thought, and that if I had the chance now I would not fuck her.

So days and days rolled by. There was an assumed truce between us, and things might have gone on so until, in the course of time, Fanny and I should have been separated in the natural course of events, but all was in the hands of Venus who smiled at our puny efforts to guide our own course. The time for the sacrifice had arrived, the veil of Fanny's maidenhead was doomed to destruction, and in the shrine of her virgin cunt, was to be set up that prick which had once been the God of her ardent devotion. Yes, Fanny Selwyn with joy opened her thighs to me, and I will now tell you how it all came about.

Fackabad is a large station. A European and a native regiment are always quartered there, with a battery of artillery and a squadron of native cavalry, there was plenty of civilians also, so that we had some very good society in the place. In this way it was very different to Cherat, where there were no civilians, and only our regiment, and the details of others. At Fackabad we had a judge, a deputy commissioner, a civil doctor, a civil engineer and a number of others of civilians, besides a Roman Catholic Padre, a Church of England Padre, a Presbyterian Minister and others and above these male exhorters who lived pure and simple and blameless lives, we had a number of very charming youthful ladies known as the Zenana mission, one of the fair female missionaries being so beautifully furnished with those charms of face and person that she raised desire, far more carnal than spiritual, in the minds of those mundane inhabitants of the cantonment, who like myself worshipped the Creator in his creatures.

Lawn tennis, polo and cricket occupied the quiet ones, and all were good, in the beautiful evenings when the cool shades made exercise delightful, and even necessary, for it can be very cool from the end of November to the beginning of March in the northern part of India, and we soldiers had plenty of parades, with drills both morning and evening, except on Thursdays and Sundays, days always devoted to rest and ease in that country. If we had been idle at Cherat we made up for it now at Fackabad, and there were not a few who welcomed the coming hot weather, hot winds, hot nights, hot days, for the sake of the nominal parades and the minimum amount of work, for man is by nature an idle animal, when his pleasures are not concerned.

Hence my patient readers can readily understand that as the houses of the cantonment spread over a very considerable space, and our work lay in very different directions, Lavie and I did not meet as often as we used to at Cherat. We saw one another at Mess in the evenings, and would say a few words to one another, but as I was never much addicted to staying longer than to smoke a cigarette after dinner, I really saw very little of my once constant companion. I was too glad to go home, and to take off my uniform, and, clad in loose clothes, to sit in my long arm chair and smoke and read at my ease, to care to stay late after Mess.— Besides I was sore at heart. I was in great anxiety about poor Louie after her accident and I could not but recognize that, so far as Fanny Selwyn was concerned, the course of true love did not only not run at all smooth, but that to all appearances, the frail bark in which I had sailed down that current had got stranded, if it was not altogether wrecked. I felt defeated, and defeated through my own fears, and I felt somewhat degraded in her eyes, in the eyes of the girl who had almost invited me to fuck her. I felt that she despised me, and my want of that courage which is so grateful to the girl full of desire and passion. But, instead of trying to regain my lost footing in her esteem, I had quite come to the conclusion that I must give up all idea of Fanny, that the enterprise I was once so naturally embarked upon had been providentially nipped in the bud, and that to endeavor to again embark upon it would be to tempt providence to pour down the vials of its wrath upon my foolish head. But I was unhappy all the same. I did not like it.

Venus behind her ambrosial clouds, naked, loving, beautiful, smiled as she read my heart.

I might have kept up my acquaintance more vigorously with the Selwyns but for Mabel. That little girl, ever since I had tickled her cunnie at Nowshera, evidently looked forward to be fucked by me very soon, and she was more than daring whenever I visited her family. She plagued beyond bearing. Her delight was by word, look or gesture, to make my prick stand, no matter whether her mother was standing beside, and my embarrassment was simply enormous. Pretending to consider herself as a mere child, she would, in spite of her mother's too feeble chidings, seat herself on my lap, and, hiding her hand under her, feel for and clutch my infernal fool of a prick, which would stand furiously for her though I wished it cut off at such moments. If I happened to be spending an evening at her father's house, and to be engaged in a game of chess with one of the two girls, Mabel would find her opportunity, slip unnoticed under the table, crawl to my knees, and with her nimble fingers, unbutton my trousers, and putting in her little exciting hand take possession of all she found there. I should have laughed at it only that I was terrified lest this very forward play might be discovered, I had to sit tight up against the table, and do my best to seem unconcerned, whilst Mabel's moving hand was precious nearly making me spend! A catastrophe, I am thankful to say, she never quite succeeded in bringing about. I took my opportunities to beg and implore her to be more careful of herself and me, and her reply would be to toss up her short frocks, and a complete exposure of her lovely thighs, downy motte, and sweet young cunt, which she would insist on my feeling, and which she would insist I on my feeling, and which I was too weak to resist doing. It was the torture of Tantalus I was called upon to endure, and the consequence was as much enforced absence as I could keep from the Colonel's house, and the consequent feeling on Fanny's side that my object was to avoid her. I could not tell Fanny the truth, for she would have been madder than ever, to have heard that I had felt Mabel's cunt, for the first time, immediately after she had told me of the wonderful and delicious dream she had had of my fucking her at Nowshera.

The month of March had arrived, the sun was daily gaining power, which before the end of the month would be tremendous. This is the season when fruit is most abundant in Northern India, and I daily feasted on figs, peaches, grapes, and even strawberries. The letters I had lately deceived had been of a more cheerful character, and you know what it is to be relieved of such killing anxieties.

One morning at the beginning of March I came home from parade, and whilst drinking my tea and eating my chetah, hazir of fruit and bread and butter, the postman came and handed me a letter addressed to me by the darling Louie herself. It brought a joy not to be expressed in spoken or written words to me. That kind of joy which makes one clasp one's hands and look up to try and pierce the clouds for the sight of that God to whom one's heart bursts to offer up praise and thanksgiving. I was lifted out of myself. I walked up and down the verandah in an ecstasy of joy. I even leaped and jumped. Louie was safe, quite safe! Up! Able to be about! Able to sit in her arm chair and do a little needle work and read a book! And write a letter! Here was the very proof of it! In this darling letter written to me by my own darling wife. Ah! but that every cloud has its silver lining, so does every rose have its thorn. For though really convalescent, though her doctor assured her that no permanent injury had been done to her, he had told her that on no account must she go to a hot climate, and on doubly no account was she to sleep with her husband, if he came home, for though fucking, though so sweetly, so gloriously, so entrancingly genial, was the last thing she should do for at least two long years to come! Else he would not be responsible for her complete cure, and immunity from danger. He even warned her that fucking might result, if soon indulged in, in pain and anything but pleasure, and he said that as I was "providentially" in India, it was well to allow me to remain where I was, out of the way of doing her any harm.

Poor Louie! She told me that the tears were rolling down her cheeks as she wrote the sentence of the banishment of my prick from her longing, really longing cunt, but she said, "It is only for a short season, though two years seems a long time to young people like us, my beloved, darling husband Charlie! Still, just fancy what grief and utter desolation it would be, if our coming together too soon would result in what the doctor threatens, the complete death of all that lovely love which made our marriage bed so supremely delightful to both of us! Oh! I love my

Charlie, and I desire the staff of his manhood, that splendid, splendid 'prick' as you have taught me to call it—too, much too well, to like to think of endangering all the happiness and delight I can give him, and all the rapture and heaven he can give me. No! I will stay at home and be a nun, and who can tell but that when I may be, as it were, a new bride for my darling husband to enjoy. Without that fearful shyness which to some degree marred the joy I experienced when he first entered the virgin territory of which he, and he alone, is Lord and Master!"

I was joyful. I was so full of the thought of my Louie that the thought never struck me that part of my joy might arise from the fact that she could no longer stand in my way toward a certain delightful little cunt, that that cunt was between Fanny Selwyn's thighs. I say I did not think consciously of Fanny but as my story will now tell, I had no Louie to raise a warning finger and say, "Not into that cunt, but into mine only, must your prick glide, Charlie!"

Whilst thus walking up and down in the verandah, looking abstractedly at the shrubs and flowers in my garden, I all of a sudden I noticed a butterfly, a large yellow, swallow tailed butterfly, with black and red markings, hovering in a most becoming manner over something which I could not see. I still had my helmet on, and I went to see what could be attracting him. There, on the leaf of a shrub, was a female butterfly of the same species, with wings drooped and sometimes quivering, and tail imploringly lifted, as she courted her admirer to come to closer caresses. But the male seemed delighted to find her so voluptuously inclined, while he, with great self-restraint, could raise her desire to still higher burning point. He would only flutter down, so that she could feel the air from his beating wings, and then just as she expected to feel his sweet weight on her back, he would soar a foot or two higher, above her. In vain did the poor love-sick, burning female shift from leaf to flower, from flower to leaf, as though to find a couch which should prove irresistible to her cruel tormentor. He would not approach her nearer. At last she suddenly flew and hid behind a bush. The male missed her and seemed much put out. He flew here, he flew there, in evidently great anxiety until he found her. But oh! ungrateful insect! Instead of giving her what she evidently begged for so earnestly, so hard, he resumed his teasing, tantalizing maneuvers, until at last, outraged and disgusted, the female took sudden and serious flight and swiftly disappeared around the corner of my bungalow. The male seemed to take it quite hardly this time. He found her once, he would of course find her again. So he did not seem to trouble himself much until, having been very cool in his search without success, he suddenly became intensely agitated. He flew here, there, everywhere, keenly looking, eagerly searching, but he found her not, for she was gone. Gone! It was really remarkably curious to see the expression of real grief and disappointment which the vain butterfly now evinced, but it was to no purpose, his abused love had vanished, and he would never fuck her. After a while he flew off in another direction, well punished for his cruelty.

This little scene of love, passion, desire, cruelty, disappointment, and well merited punishment excited me greatly. I did not there and then take the lesson home to myself, as regards my behaviour towards Fanny Selwyn, but afterwards I remembered it and thought how very apt it was. I did not lose Fanny Selwyn's darling little cunt it was not because I deserved a better fate than the male butterfly, but because my adored Goddess Venus had decreed that my service to her must be performed in that adorable temple. I claim no need of praise for having fucked Fanny.

I went back to my seat and lit a cheroot, and thought of my Louie's letter, and the butterflies, and while thus in a kind of delightful dream, I heard footsteps, and looking up I saw Lavie come down the verandah towards me.

"Ah! Lavie, good morning! How are you old chap? Sit down!"

"No thank you, Devereaux," said he with a half sigh.

"Why, what is the matter with you, Lavie? You sigh like a calf kicked away by its mother. Has Jumali, or any other one, given you the clap?"

"Ah no! Please don't talk that way. I am in bad spirits this morning."

"Why?"

"Oh! I don't know!"

"Bosh! My dear fellow, your liver must be out of order Go home and take a dose of black draught, or better, sit down and have a cigar and a peg, and tell me all the news."

"Ah! Devereaux, you rattle on! You are a happy chap! You never are in bad spirits."

"Except that time when I fancied my prick would never stand again, eh Lavie?"

"I forgot that," said he with a sickly smile.

"So you see I am sometimes in the dumps, Lavie."

Lavie said nothing. He looked real pale and worn out, as if he had not slept all night. He sat down heavily on the chair, and as he did so he groaned and covered his eyes with his hands.

"Now Lavie!" said I, seriously, "there is something the matter with you. Come! out with it! I must be your doctor now. Tell me what it is."

But for some minutes he remained as he was, then slowly raising his head he looked at me with the queerest expression and said, "Devereaux, I can trust you! You swear you won't tell a soul if I tell you what it is?"

"Of course!" I replied, wondering what on earth it could be.

"Well!" said he, speaking extremely slow, "I love Fanny Selwyn!"

"Good God!" cried I, roaring with laughter, "is that all? But, man alive, if you are in love it should make you frisky and not as gloomy as you are, like a sick cat!"

"Ah! but she does not love me," he groaned.

"How do you know?"

"Oh! I know it well, too well!"

"But, my dear fellow, can you tell me why you know it so well? Perhaps I may be able to give you some comfort, if you will treat me as your mental physician, and tell me the truth, the whole truth and nothing but the truth."

Lavie groaned, leant his elbow on his hands, hid his face in his hands, and at last he said, evidently with an effort, "Last Sunday evening she would not walk with me to church."

I roared with laughter! It was so superb! A young lady does not walk to church with a gentleman who admires her, and thereby proves that she does not love him!

Well, I heard the whole of his story, which was, that up at Cherat he had been very much struck with Fanny Selwyn, and in secret he had been fanning the spark of love within him, which had at last burst out into flame. He had indeed never shone Fanny any marked attention, but as she never seemed to avoid him, always spoke kindly and politely to him, he imagined she adopted his quiet way of showing his admiration, and that, in due course, she would give him to understand that she quite understood and that she was quite ready to marry him. But on that unlucky Sunday evening, he was sitting in his verandah without his coat on, expecting he would see Fanny and her sisters pass on their way to church, and if he called out they would wait, as they had done on previous occasions, until he had got his coat on, for it was very hot, and he did not wish to put that garment on a moment sooner than was absolutely necessary. But Oh! grief! dismay! horror! Fanny would not wait, and not only did she not wait, but, when he hurried out after her, he saw her and her sisters running. Yes, actually running away! It killed this poor heart! His hopes were violently dashed to the ground! There was nothing in life worth living for now, it was plain that Fanny did not love him.

I listened with ever increasing amazement. Hitherto I had looked upon Lavie as a particularly sensible fellow.

But the story he told me, and his reasoning, were absolutely childish, and proved him, when in love, at all events, to be an egregious ass and fool. I however liked him a deal too much not to feel sorry for him, and I set to work to comfort him, and succeeded in doing so, by telling him that accepting his story as absolutely true, it only proved that Fanny Selwyn amused herself by giving him a chase after her, and I admitted that she was a fine enough girl for any man to take some little trouble in trying to run after, and I wondered that she had not been snapped up, young as she was, not quite seventeen, a year ago.

But, do what I would, I could not screw Lavie's courage up to going at once, to see her (she lived only just across the road, within seventy yards of. my bungalow), declare himself and find out what her real feelings were towards him. He funked it, I told him, in vain, that faint heart never yet won fair lady. All I could persuade him to do was to go and see Colonel and Mrs. Selwyn, and see whether they would countenance his suit. To this, at last, he assented, and went off leaving me more than astonished at his pusalimity. For Lavie was a man of strong passions, an ardent fucker; he had a reputation among Jumali and her companions, of being one of the very best pokes in all Fackabad; and I should have thought that where his prick led the heart, his courage would have followed. For it was evident to me that he was much more cunt struck with Fanny Selwyn than smitten with what we mean by the honorable term "love."

Whilst I was still thinking over this astounding announcement of his, and inwardly congratulating myself on my being free in the form of responsibility towards Fanny, he returned, his face wearing the appearance of satisfaction. He had seen the Colonel and his wife, and they had been very kind. They said they could, not urge Fanny to marry him, but they had no objection to his doing so himself. That their girls should choose for themselves, and if Fanny chose to be his wife, they would not say no. But when I asked him had he, there and then, asked to see Fanny, he said he had not—another day would do! Gods alive! I did my best to make him go at once, but it was of no use. He was satisfied to a certain degree and would live on what hopes he had extracted from the permission he had been granted by Fanny's Papa and Mama! Well! I knew Fanny better than he did, and I said to myself that Fanny would not thank him for asking Papa and Mama before asking her. Nevertheless I hoped against hope that she would take him.

Why? Why? Ah! a smile comes the more I look back on the past, the more did I think it impossible that I could have even a chance in Fanny's heart. She had deliberately called me a fool. She had, in a hundred of little acid feminine ways, shown me that she despised me and I believed that she would be more than delighted to say something sharply cutting if I ever showed that I sought her love once more again. When a girl offers herself, take her, for she won't be likely to ask you afterwards, my dear male friends! Again, although my faith in Lavie had been rudely shaken by his asinine ideas of conduct, I thought he would make Fanny a good husband. He was essentially a gentleman; he had a good profession at his back; and I knew he would fuck her to her heart's content; and when a woman is well fucked she is always contented and happy.

I have known so many instances of girls marrying against their wills, going to the altar, to the nuptial couch, perfect victims, becoming quite happy women, simply and solely because their husbands turned out to be first-class fuckers. This is absolute gospel and my gentle readers may believe it.

I was sitting reading Louie's delightful, loving, passionate letter for the fiftieth time, my prick standing deliciously all up my belly, under the buttons of my trousers as it thought of the dear cunt it had so often fucked and spent in, when I was suddenly astonished at seeing Mrs. Selwyn and Fanny walking into my room unannounced. It was very hot and I was surprised at seeing Mrs. Selwyn, who was so delicate, expose herself so much to the sun.

"Oh! Mrs. Selwyn! What on earth has made you come over here in this blazing sun? If you wanted me, why did you not send word for me? Here, sit down under the punkah! Here is a chair! There now! Tell me what I can do for you, and you know I will do it."

Mrs. Selwyn looked at Fanny and smiled; Fanny looked at me with the queerest expression of half fun, half earnest, in her glorious violet eyes. She looked extremely pretty. She had not lost any of the fresh color she had brought down in her face from Cherat. Clad in a thin muslin dress her bosom was that of a glorious nymph. Its two little mountains, evidently much grown since I had seen them bare and uncovered some months before, were swelling out in the most voluptuously tempting manner on either side. Her well rounded and beautifully shaped thighs were equally well shown off by the soft folds of her dress, and her lovely little feet and ankles, crossed in front of her, ended a fine pair of well developed legs, which I did not wonder Lavie would like to open and take his pleasure between. Fanny seemed to me altogether more beautiful this day than I had ever seen her before. But I looked upon her as never to be mine, and so schooled was I in this thought, that much as I admired her, my prick grew none the stiffer, and was standing simply and solely for the sweetest cunt between my Louie's thighs, thousands of miles away.

"Now, Mrs. Selwyn, please tell me to what I owe this unexpected and pleasant visit?"

Mrs. Selwyn looked at Fanny and smiled. Fanny returned the look and did not smile; on the contrary she looked rather put out.

"Well! Captain Devereaux, I, that is Fanny and I, have a crow to pluck with you. What made you send Dr. Lavie on a wooing errand to my house?"

"I never sent him at all, Mrs. Selwyn."

"Then he told me an untruth, for he certainly told Colonel Selwyn and me that you had sent him to ask permission to pay his addresses to Fanny."

"Well!" I said, "there is just this much truth in that assertion, Mrs. Selwyn, and I will tell you just what took place between Lavie and me this morning. I was sitting in the verandah outside there, when he came, looking the picture of misery and woe. For sometime he would not tell me what was the matter with him, but he sat and held his head in his hands and sighed and groaned in the most dismal manner. At last he said that he loved Miss Selwyn."

Both Mrs. Selwyn and Fanny here burst out with merry laughter, Fanny's being sweet, silvery and hearty. There was no unkind ring to it, but it was evident that she was greatly amused.

"Yes! and then!"

"I said there was no reason to be so miserable," and he said, "But she wouldn't walk to church with me last Sunday evening."

"The fool!" cried Fanny, again going off into another merry peal.

"That is what I thought too. I had a long talk with him, and asked him did Miss Selwyn know of his feelings towards her. He said he expected she did. I asked him had he spoken to her. He said no. Well, I said, if you have not done that yet, you had better do so as soon as possible, and not go imagining all kinds of things. But he seemed to be frightened at the idea. At last I suggested that at least he might see you, Mrs. Selwyn, and the Colonel, and see if you approved of his proposal. The fact was I did not know what to do with him. He acted on my hint and went, and apparently received a satisfactory reply, for he seemed much relieved when he came back to me."

For a moment or two neither of the two ladies spoke. Fanny looked at me half reproachfully. Mrs. Selwyn was evidently cogitating something. My prick, no longer interested in Fanny's cunt, and the current of its thoughts recalled from Louie's sweet secret charms, had begun to drop a bit, and I waited to hear the next thing.

"Well! Neither Colonel Selwyn nor I would object to Dr. Lavie. He is a nice fellow, a thorough gentleman, and no one could have been more attentive or kinder than he was to poor Amy, when she was so ill after the attack of those horrid Afghans at Cherat, but then both. Colonel Selwyn and I think it only right and fair to let Fanny choose for herself. We cannot bring ourselves to advise her at all. Anybody may come forward as a suitor, so long as he is a gentleman, and, has sufficient means to keep a wife, so far as we parents are concerned. So Fanny must speak for herself in this matter."

I looked inquiringly at Fanny, who colored a little, and then turned pale, whilst the movements of her lovely breasts showed that some thoughts, perhaps not pleasant ones, were agitating her.

"All I can say at present," said she, speaking slowly and deliberately, "is that I find he is not the man I can marry!" She laid some little stress on the word marry.

"Perhaps," said I, "when you have thought of Dr. Lavic you may get to think him eligible, Miss Fanny."

"I don't think so," said she. "I like Dr. Lavie well enough as a friend, but I do not feel as though I could ever love him, and I could never have a man unless I loved him."

"Well! give him a chance," said I. "Hear what he has to say, and perhaps when you examine him from the point of view he desires, you may see more in him than you do now."

"I suppose," said she, a little sharply, "you would be de lighted to see me take him, Captain Devereaux?"

"I would if I were sure you would be happy with him, Miss Selwyn, but not otherwise. Lavie is a great friend of mine, and I know him to be a real good fellow. I think he is a little off his head just now, but when

I look at you I am not surprised. Is not Fanny looking really very pretty, Mrs. Selwyn?"

Both mother and daughter looked as pleased as could be at this compliment, which, however, was not said merely to please, for Fanny did really look uncommonly lovely, and I had spoken the words quite unaffectedly, and spontaneously.

"I often have wondered," I continued, "that Fanny has not been snapped up long ago! Such a pretty girl, a girl so nice, so desirable in every way, should by this time have had a great number of adorers, and several offers of marriage. I cannot make out where the men's eyes are."

"Oh! Fanny can tell you if she likes," responded the mother, "that she has had two or three offers. There was one gentleman in particular who was very much in earnest. Dr. Jardine, who on the march down proposed for her."

"Dr. Jardine!" I exclaimed.

"Yes. He asked Fanny, but she said no, and then he asked the Colonel and me, and tried to persuade her to take him, but we told him we objected to such a course, and if Fanny said no, it meant no as far as we were concerned."

"I am glad Fanny did not say yes," I replied.

"Why?"

"Because Dr. Jardine might be a clever doctor, but he is a bad man, and quite unsuitable for Fanny in anyway. At least that is my opinion."

"I think so too," said Mrs. Selwyn decisively. "Still, if Fanny had said yes, we should not have declined, though we might have been grieved she should wish for such a man as Dr. Jardine."

"What made you marry, Captain Devereaux?" suddenly cried Fanny.

"My dear child! What a question to ask!" exclaimed Mrs. Selwyn.

"I married," said I laughing, "because I had at last found the girl I fancied, the girl in fact, who seemed to me to be altogether superior to any I had seen in my life, and the one I felt really and truly in love with."

"And I suppose," said Fanny, trying to seem cheerful, "that you have never seen anyone since whom you would have married, had you never met your first wife?"

The question was too plain to me, and for the life of me I could not resist giving the answer which I knew she wanted, but which the tone of her voice told me she did not expect.

"I can easily and truly answer your question, Miss Selwyn. It is true I am not easily pleased, but I have seen one lady since I married, who I should have asked to marry me had I not already been married," and my eyes told Fanny who that lady was.

The color again mounted in profusion to her lovely face, her eyes glistened and shown with satisfaction, she looked at me from head to foot, and her entire appearance told me, "and had you asked me I would have said yes; and the sooner the better!"

"Poor Lavie! I saw now only too well that he was right, and whomever it was that Fanny loved, it was not him. A secret satisfaction filled my soul, and a flood of voluptuous desire came over me, as I again ran my eyes over Fanny's graceful form, charming appearance and my slumbering prick once more swelled and swelled, until I thought it would burst the buttons, and spring out to frighten the mother and daughter.

Mrs. Selwyn asked Fanny to go out as she had a word to say to me in private, and Fanny did so, her eyes met mine; Oh! the things they said! The girl seemed elated by what I had last said, and her step was that of one who had at last obtained what she had most wished for in the world. In spite of my feeling how dishonorable it would be now, to try and cut out poor Lavie, I could not but say to myself, "Fanny's cunt is mine, whenever I like to put out my hand for it."

As soon as the delighted girl was in the verandah, Mrs. Selwyn rose, and I did so too, and she said to me in a half whisper, "Dear Captain Devereaux! You know Fanny too well not to know that she will never take Dr. Lavie. Do please advise him to give up the idea of her. He will only make himself unhappy, and I am not strong enough to go through scenes. He thinks you sent him to us. Please undeceive him."

I promised I would do my best, but Oh! How I wished that I did not desire Fanny's sweet little cunt! It seemed to me that I was about to keep Lavie out of it in order that I might fuck it myself.

I saw Fanny and her mother half way home, and the way Fanny pressed the moist palm of her hand in mine sent a thrill through both of us, and I could see that she had quite made up her mind to have me at the earliest opportunity. By God! How my balls and groins did ache all that day. Willingly would I tell my readers the ins and outs of the courtship, as performed by Lavie, which filled up the next fortnight, but I fear to be tedious. Never was there a more terrible lover than he. I did not act upon Mrs. Selwyn's request. I thought it best to let Lavie hang himself, and he did so most effectually. He had one or two interviews with Fanny, and stood like a dumb calf, open-mouthed and gasping, but utterly unable to formulate a word. Both she and her mother were nearly driven distracted by the poor cunt struck fool, and the last scene, in which Lavie having been refused admittance by Fanny, had insisted on seeing Mrs. Selwyn, and in weeping and wailing before her, because she would not order Fanny to marry him, drove both ladies once more to my bungalow.

It was in the middle of March, the sun was simply blazing through the day, the crows, fowls, all birds in fact, went about in the shade with their beaks wide open, and wings lifted from their bodies, so much did they feel the blasting heat at this time. I was seated in my long arm chair, dressed only in the thinnest of jerseys, without sleeves, and the slightest of pajamas, in fact, as naked as I could well be, for the clothes I had on hid only the color of my skin, and even that very imperfectly. The Punkah slowly swinging from side to side, poured down a breeze of cooling air upon me, and wafted away the smoke of my cheroot. It was midday, frightfully hot, and I could hear the leaves of the trees crackling under the sun's rays, when to my in tense astonishment, Mrs. Selwyn and Fanny rushed rather than walked into my room.

Mrs. Selwyn seemed half demented. Fanny looked as if she had been crying and fearfully annoyed. Both looked reproachfully at me. I jumped up, apologized for my state of dishabille, for I had not even slippers on, and was in my bare feet, and I got them chairs under the punkah. But before she attempted to sit down, Mrs. Selwyn cried, "Captain Devereaux, you must, you really must, insist on Dr. Lavie ceasing to annoy us anymore! He is killing me! He is mad! I am certain he is not right in his mind! He is killing Fanny too! Oh!" and down she flopped into her chair.

I looked at Fanny but said nothing. Mrs. Selwyn then told me that Lavie had taken to going at all hours, even at night when everyone had gone to bed, and that he moaned and raved and wept. That Colonel Selwyn had spoken to him kindly, harshly, every way, had ordered him never to come again, and so forth, but it had no effect, and they were at their wits ends, because they feared if they took any other, that is, forcible means, and kept him out of the house, it would only create a scandal, and the people were dying with laughter over Lavie's miserable courtship.

Whilst she was telling me this, and I was wondering what I could do, in came Lavie, his eyes glaring, his face pale, his lips hard set. He went straight up to Mrs. Selwyn and asked her to go into another room which I had and which was empty.

I begged him to sit down where he was, but he smiled inanely at me, and said he would not keep Mrs. Selwyn two seconds, and she weakly rose and followed him. Fanny drew her chair near mine and begged me to do what I could.

"Oh! dear, dear, Captain Devereaux, do rid us of this monster!" was her cry. I took her hand and assured her that I would; that I had a plan, and that was to get him sent to someother station. I knew the P.M.O. very well indeed, and I would represent the case to him. Poor Fanny was delighted. She gave me one of those looks which meant "kiss me!" I hesitated a moment, but at last I could resist no longer. Jumping up I seized the willing girl round the waist, lifted her to her feet, and pressing her to me I kissed her red, red mouth, over and over again.

"Oh! my darling Fanny!" I exclaimed in a low tone, quivering with passion that communicated itself to her. "How I do blame myself for having countenanced that idiot's making love to you!"

"Oh! Charlie! Charlie!" she cried, pressing her swelling bosom to mine, and letting me pull her to me until our bodies seemed to form one, not denying me the thigh I took between mine, nor the motte, the sweet, delicious motte, against which I pressed my own thigh, "I know now that you love me as I love you! Oh I my darling! darling! so I forgive you! But oh! if it were not for that I would hate you!"

"And do you really and truly love me, Fanny? Oh! My sweetest, own girl, and you must be all mine! Every bit of you! heart, soul, body, all!"

"Oh! I do! I do!" cried the excited girl in an ecstasy of passion. "Oh! can you not feel that I do?"

"With your heart, my own love!" and I pressed a delicious and firm, round, hard, elastic bubby in my hand.

"Yes! Yes!"

"On your soul?" and I glided a hand swiftly between her thighs and pressed the equally elastic and soft motte, and delicious cunt with my fingers. For a moment Fanny drew her hips back, but on my again pressing her matte and throbbing cunt with my hands, closing her thighs also on it, and giving me such a kiss as I had never yet had from her. That was, her answer. Gods! Gods! I took my hand away. I put my arms round her yielding waist. My prick furious, mad, raging to get at her, made a perfect tent pole, and stood out my pajamas in front of it. But for the pajamas it would have risen at a bound to an angle much too acute with my body to have enabled me to do what I did, but the pajamas held it's head somewhat down, and I pressed the mighty weapon against Fanny's quivering matte with all my force, whilst I kissed her and felt her tumultuous bubbies, which she was pressing against my bosom as though she was trying to flatten them against it. For a moment we stood thus, only that I kept, as it were unconsciously, thrusting at her astonished matte. Then suddenly putting down her hand she said, "Oh!" what is that pressing against me?"

"It is me, my darling!" I whispered in a voice hardly audible or articulate from the excess of passionate emotions, "it is me!" There, take me in your dear hand "and take possession of the treasure which is yours henceforth and yours only."

(Poor Louie! Had she heard those words spoken in a moment of blinding passion!)

"Oh! my darling! My darling!" exclaimed Fanny absolutely beside herself with ecstasy. "My darling! my darling!" and her little hand nervously and excitedly kept clasping my burning prick, as if she hardly knew what to say or do, but in delight inexpressible.

"Yes! Yes! Darling Fanny! That is for you! For this! It must be admitted to this above! To the temple of love!" I again had my hand once more excitedly caressing her now maddened cunt, between thighs more than willingly opened to admit it!

Fanny could not stand this caressing. She let go of my prick and tried, clothed as she was, to impale herself on it. It slipped beneath her motte. She felt it do so. She pulled up her dress a little and, suddenly opening her thighs, she closed them, equally suddenly, on my prick, and I acted just as though it had been in her cunt! Gods! Gods! I think I should have burst, only nature came to my relief, and I poured forth a torrent of hot, burning spend! This recalled me to my senses.

Gently pushing Fanny away, I begged her to seat herself, whilst I went and changed into trousers. The intelligent and excited girl saw the necessity and reason, as she looked at me in the quite transparent pajamas flooded with spend, and extended in front by my enraged prick, of which the coloring and shape of the head was as clear as if seen in crystal water. But instead of sitting down she came and peeped at me from behind the purdah, as I took off my pajamas and fed her eyes on the galaxy I showed her, with pleasure indescribable. She saw the mighty prick, its ponderous, well shaped balls, and the forest out of which they grew, and knew that they were now all hers, as she gazed, she tried to quiet the throbbing of the hot little cunt by putting her hand between her lovely thighs. But before I had finished putting these treasures away from sight, some stir made her drop the purdah and flee to a chair, and when I came out, in shirt, trousers, socks and shoes, she was seated in it. She looked for her new possessions, and with burning eyes asked me where it had gone. For all answer I took her willing little hand and laid it on my prick which was buttoned back against my belly. Once more did the excited "My darling! my darling!" resound, but in whispered tones, and then feeling frightened lest our disordered minds might betray themselves to Mrs. Selwyn who was still talking to Lavie, who might at any moment come into our room, I got a book of views, and opened it so as to look as if Fanny and I had been examining it during their absence.

"You made the wet come in me, as well as yourself, my darling! my darling!" whispered Fanny.

"Did I? Well! my sweetest, next time such wet comes it must not be outside of us, but inside you. Inside here! Do you understand?"

For all answer Fanny kissed me, whilst she pressed the hand I had slipped between those thighs, which, if ever opened for man, would first be opened to admit me!

Whilst thus engaged in deliciously feeling one another and talking the language, not the less eloquent because it was dumb, Mrs. Selwyn came almost staggering into the room. She was evidently overcome with emotion, and was far too excited herself to notice any appearance of heat in either Fanny or myself. She managed to reach the chair, to drop into it, but for a moment or two could not speak a word. Fanny and I, both in alarm, were at her side at once, and waited for Mrs. Selwyn to speak.

"Oh! Captain Devereaux!" she whispered, and then paused for breath for she was panting with agitation, "Go in! go in to that—that—mad man, and for goodness sake, for God's sake, I implore you, calm him, and tell him he must not persecute me in this manner. He talks of cutting his throat if I do not give him Fanny!"

"I will settle him, Mrs. Selwyn," said I, as quietly as I could, "I will go in now. Fanny, look after your mother, there's a good creature!" and so saying, I made her eyes speak volumes. They said to me, "Get rid of Lavie and then we will fuck, my Charlie!"

I went into the next room and there I found the miserable lover, who had, that very morning, been talking, whilst I had been acting! That very morning! Why, it was not yet five minutes since I had had my prick, not in Fanny's darling little cunt indeed, but between her thighs, and had spent a perfect flood, and had shown her my prick and balls naked, and had had her hand caressing it, and herself calling me "darling," and telling me I had made her spend, as she had made me! I must say I felt a considerable amount of contempt for Lavie, and wondered where all that good sense had gone to, for which I had once given him so much credit.

Poor devil! The fact was, he was quite out of his mind, and his lunacy had taken the form of a passion for Fanny Selwyn. But no one knew or suspected the facts for some days still. No wonder it was no use my speaking to him or advising him to desist from following Fanny, for a time at least. He moaned and groaned, and weeped, and behaved in the most extraordinary manner. At last I persuaded him to go home, promising I would see him again the next day. But when he had gone, and when I had ascertained that Fanny and Mrs. Selwyn had gone too, I put on my helmet and went myself to Dr. Bridges, our P.M.O., and put the whole case to him, and begged him to get Lavie removed to someother station. Bridges hemmed and hawed at first; but at last he said that he had noticed that Lavie was not doing his work as well as he used to, and he would see him and come to a conclusion in a day or two. I had to be content with that, but it was something.

That afternoon I got a little note from Fanny saying that Mama had desired her to write and ask me to dine with them unless I had a prior engagement. That was the propriety part, but in the corner, written very small and hurriedly, was, "Do come, my darling!" I sent reply that I should have much pleasure in accepting the invitation and I went.

As I suspected it was for the sake of a council of war that I was wanted, and I told Colonel and Mrs. Selwyn what I had done, saw old Bridges, and both thought it was an excellent move. The poor Colonel was especially anxious to get rid of Lavie, for that fellow used to come in by the most convenient door of my bungalow which happened to suit him, at anytime of the day he wanted to see me, and as he used to come some nine or ten times a day, the Colonel was twice nearly caught, in one of my spare rooms, fucking Mrs. Soubratie, and for a week or more he had been entirely without his accustomed greens, and as he never knew when Lavie might perhaps find him partaking of them between Mrs. Soubratie's brown thighs, the Colonel, also, naturally, wanted to put an end to the courtship, which was ridiculous and scandalous, so he determined to see Dr. Bridges himself, and insist on Lavie being sent away.

After dinner we all walked up and down the fine avenue, in the cool evening air, and with the sky lit up by a myriad of lovely stars.

We talked of nothing but Lavie, until Mrs. Selwyn, getting tired, took the Colonel in, leaving Fanny, Amy, Mabel and me walking together. Amy got rid of Mabel and I would have been as glad as Fanny if we could have equally got rid of Amy too. Our conversation naturally fell on love and matrimony, and Amy said, "Well! I only hope nobody will ever ask me to marry them. I will surely say no!"

"Why?" said I, laughing.

"Oh! Fancy going to bed with a man! I should die of shame!"

"Your mother goes to bed every night with your father, Amy, and she does not die of shame."

"Oh! that's different!"

"I don't see it."

"Well! anyhow I should die of shame. Would not you, Fanny?"

Fanny hesitated. She had hold of my hand and gently squeezing it, she said, "I think that would depend upon whether I loved the man or not."

"Exactly," said I. "I know my wife was rather ashamed the first night I came to sleep with her, but long before morning she laughed at her foolish fears!"

"Oh! Do tell us all about it!" cried. Amy, who seemed to have an eagerness to know how such a change could ever come over my wife in such a short time.

"Well!" I said, "I will tell you willingly, but mind you, if I do; I shall have to touch on subjects it is not usual to speak of to young virgins."

"Never mind," said Amy, "it is dark and you will not be able to see our blushes."

I was delighted at the prospect of being able to inflame still more, if possible, the already highly raised passions of Fanny, whose little hand trembled in mine, and I commenced.

"Well! I will not tell you all about the marriage ceremony, because you, I dare say, have often seen the open daylight mysteries of marriage. It is of the secret, or real marriage, of the nuptial couch of which I shall speak, and I warn you, if I once begin, I can't leave off. So if I say anything which sounds shocking, you will have to hear it in silence. Do you care?"

"Yes!" cried both girls, and glancing at Amy, I saw her press her hand for a moment between her thighs, for, dark as it was, it was not so dark but what I could see that much. I was satisfied. It was evident that her little cunnie was tickling and I was determined that it should tickle her a good deal more before I was done. Not that I had any designs on Amy's cunt; I aimed at Fanny's rather.

"Well! my bride and I went to Brighton to spend the first night or so of our honeymoon. All the way in the train we had to appear calm, to speak to one another as naturally as could be, but I could see that Louie was not quite the same as she had been before that day. Had we been going to Brighton unmarried, and not as we were, bride and bridegroom, I am sure she would have talked and laughed in a free and open manner, whereas now some thought, which I could easily guess at, was oppressing her. That thought was, of course, that her whole life was going to change now, that I had rights over her body now, which I had never had before, and that, surely, in a very few hours time I should be exercising them. She told me afterwards she had often longed for that time to come, but now, when it had come, she felt nervous."

"No wonder," said Amy, again pressing her cunnie with a trembling hand. I saw the movement, quick as it was, and put my prick more comfortable under the buttons of my trousers, an act which Fanny saw and which she responded to by a hard squeeze of my hand.

"Ah! no wonder! as you say, Amy. And yet, if our courtships were more natural and less conventional than they are, there would be none of this unnatural restraint. Why, I loved my Louie as I had never loved a girl before. There was not a part of her I did not ardently desire to kiss, to devour! The very ground she stood on, the chairs she sat in, were all sacred to me! In fact, I loved her! I had fancied I had loved others before, but I now knew, for the first time, what love was. Ah! it is not all a matter of the heart alone, but of the body also. I wonder if either of you two girls have any notion of what passion is? When all one's being is stirred up by the thought of the presence of the beloved, of the desired one! I suppose, in fact, I know, that girls do perceive much physical excitement when the passion comes on, but in man the change from quiescence to storm and fury is enormously marked. Yet, in our cold way of making love, which is the conventional way, it would appear to be proper to forget all ideas of knowledge of difference of sex, or even the meaning of marriage. A lover may speak of his Mistress' beautiful face, her beautiful figure, or her beautiful arms, feet, but he must not acknowledge to have even thought of her beautiful bust, her beautiful breasts, her beautiful hips, or her beautiful legs, or thighs, and never, under any circumstances, of that most exquisite and beautiful charm of charms, which, made for him and for him alone, lies between those beautiful thighs."

"Oh! Captain Devereaux! For shame!" cried out Amy.

"Do be quiet!" exclaimed Fanny. "Captain Devereaux is quite right Amy, and you know it."

Amy laughed and seemed uneasy and remained silent. "Well! I was thinking, thinking, all the way down to Brighton, of all those charming charms, which were now mine, and which I was literally burning to possess myself of, but, ever and anon, would come the thought, how might I do it. How am I to dare to lay a hand on my Louie, which must startle her modesty, even if she has ever let her thoughts run on the consummation of our marriage, a thing I thought not at all unlikely; for, modest and virtuous as my Louie was I knew, from her general demeanor, that, although innocent, she could not be ignorant.

"Afterwards Louie told me that similar thoughts had been plaguing her. She longed for me and for my marital and lover's embraces on the nuptial couch with great ardor, but she dreaded the first steps. Oh! she longed to give herself to me, she said, but she feared that in doing so, she might lose something of that valued respect for her which I had so constantly shown. She feared to be immodest. Yet how could she give me her naked charms without doing that which from her babyhood she had learnt to look upon as immodest to a degree. No wonder that we felt an unnatural degree of restraint. A kind of fear of one another, for, believe me, although especially when passion drives hard two lovers can be absolutely naked to one another without a particle of immodesty, yet it is only too possible, without such passion, such nakedness, which ought to be so glorious, and so divine, may be degraded to indecency and nastiness."

"I cannot imagine it ever being anything else!" exclaimed Amy, vigorously caressing herself between her thighs. "However—"

"Amy, I wish to goodness you would be quiet, and let Captain Devereaux tell his story!" cried Fanny, petulantly. She had been now walking with her own hand constantly on her thrilling little cunt, quite indifferent whether I noticed it or not. I pretended not to do so, however.

"Well!" I resumed, "at last we arrived at Brighton. Having eaten our dinner, we tried to appear calm to one another. Louie even having ventured to sit on my knees, with her arms round my neck, but careful not to press her bosom against mine; having exhausted every available topic of conversation and, I admit, having behaved like a pair of fools, so terribly afraid were we of one another, I ventured to hint that it was time to go to bed. 'Oh!' said Louie hiding her hot and blushing face in my neck, 'not yet, Charlie darling! It is not half past ten! I never go to bed so early!' Then for the first time did I pluck up a little courage. I kissed her over her lips and I whispered, 'But this is our wedding night, my darling, darling Louie.'"

She gave me one quick little look, then cast down her eyes, gave me a kiss and whispered, "Well, don't come up too soon, there's a good fellow. Oh! Charlie! I wish it was tomorrow!" she jumped up and ran out of the room.

Thus, having ventured to hint at what was to follow, and as it was our wedding night, it inspired me with some degree of courage, and with courage came desire, in floods far greater than I had yet experienced with Louie. I literally burned to have her! How long would it be before I might go up? There was a clock on the mantelpiece; and it seemed to take an hour to mark one minute. At the end of ten minutes I could stand it no longer. I was in real pain, for you must know, if passion means pleasure, it means pain too, until it is indulged."

Here Fanny looked at me and pressed my hand. By God! I wished Amy anywhere but where she was. My voice trembled as I resumed:

"On going upstairs to our bedroom, I saw Louie's pretty little boots outside the door. I hailed this as a good omen. I picked them up and kissed them, and then, giving a little warning knock, and without waiting to be told to come in, I turned the handle and entered. Louie was in her night dress just getting into bed. She gave a little cry. 'Oh! You have come sooner than I expected!' and she huddled herself under the clothes, showing only the upper part of her face. Oh! once she was in bed, I seemed to shake off my most unnatural cowardice. I closed the door and running over to her, I turned the clothes off her face and neck, and I put one arm round her shoulders, and rained the most burning and ardent kisses on her sweet lips, at the same time I slipped my hand into her bosom, and for the first time took possession of the two most beautiful globes which adorned it. Louie did not draw back. She in no way tried to prevent my caressing her there. I was more than tempted to let my hand stray much lower, and to seek for the temple of love of which the closely barred door is to be found at the foot of the forested hill, sacred to the goddess of love!"

"Gracious!" cried Amy, "where and what is that?"

"As if you did not know, Amy!" exclaimed Fanny, indignantly.

"You will soon hear, Amy," said I. "Well! I did not do so. Louie had both her arms around me and held me tight, but I should have liked to have undone the front of her night dress altogether, and to have kissed the beautiful breasts I had found there, but poor Louie, who would have liked me to have done that too, was still a prey to the struggles of her dying modesty. At last I slipped my hand under her armpit and tickled her. With a little shriek she let me go, but she did not cover herself up anymore. She lay looking at me with really longing eyes whilst I rapidly undressed. I put my watch on the table. I managed to get off my clothes, to put on my night shirt, without offending modesty very much, and I was just going round to the other side of the bed to get in, when Louie told me I had not wound my watch, and that she had not wound hers either. 'Oh!' I cried, 'let them go down, my Louie, never mind now!' 'No!' said she, 'Charlie, darling, don't let us begin our married life by leaving undone anything which we ought to do.' 'Oh! bother!' To please her I wound up both watches with a hand trembling with excitement and then jumped into bed."

"Did you not blowout the candle?" asked Amy.

"Amy! if you interrupt anymore," cried Fanny, angrily.

"I will ask Captain Devereaux not to let you know what happened next."

"No," I did not blowout the candle, Amy. Louie said something about it, but I pretended not to hear. I jumped into bed, and put my arms around her, and I hugged her to me. For just a moment she resisted a little stiffly, but the next moment she yielded, she hid her face, which was all on fire, in my neck and whilst I kissed her frantically, I put down my hand and gently drew up the veil, which interposed itself between me and those glorious charms, which could not much longer be kept from me or remain virgin. With as much delicacy as possible I passed my trembling hand over the smooth surface of her exquisite thighs, until I reached the "Bush with Frizzled hair, implicit," as Milton says.

"Captain Devereaux!" shrieked Amy.

"And finding the sweet entrance to the temple, I caressed it with an ardor which Louie could feel pouring in burning flames from my fingers. All she did, or said, was to hug me closer and murmur, 'Oh! Charlie! Oh! Charlie!' Finding her so quiet, I—"

"What?" cried both girls in suffocating tones.

"I begged her to make place for me, and let me worship her with my body, as I promised to do in my marriage vows. Gently she turned on her back, and putting one knee first, and then the other, between hers, I gently, but in the greatest excitement, lowered myself on to her beautiful body, and then awoke every hidden source of pleasure and passion in her as I made the High Priest enter the Holy of Holies. Oh! dear girls, the rapture of that moment! To feel that I really and truly was now the husband of my Louie! That I was, really and truly joined to her, and that the same throb which pulsated in and through her, equally pulsated in and through me! It was a glimpse of heaven! It was love! Love in its very highest fulfillment! Louie gave herself to me without further Restraint—all fear was gone—all ill placed modesty has banished, and before morning light had come, to take the place of that still yielded by the nearly burnt out candles, my Louie lay, perfectly naked, but not red with shame, in my equally perfectly naked embrace. There was not a part of our bodies which he hadn't mutually caressed and gazed upon, and eaten up with kisses, ardent and plentiful! Our sacrifices were without number! We kept no count! But the entire night was spent in revels, which the angels, sexless and passionless, must have envied had they the means of realizing, even in imagination, what they were like!"

Neither Fanny nor Amy had done more than breathe during the last part of this recital, and their steps had grown so short that we hardly moved over the ground. It was evident to me what constrained them moving, was owing to the fact that each of them was trying to control the powerful throbbing of her little cunt, by squeezing her thighs tightly. We were near the front of the bungalow and Amy, without a word, but with her hand still pressed between her thighs, suddenly darted into the house. Fanny remained with me. I took and put her hand on my burning and terribly stiff prick, whilst I at the same time kissed her and caressed her delicious little cunt.

"Come! Oh! come! quickly!" said she.

I felt her draw me quickly towards the lawn on one side of the house, where some thick shrubs grew. I guessed her intention. Arrived at the edge of the grove, I unbuttoned my trousers, and taking her hand, slipped it in. Fanny eagerly seized the tremendous weapon she felt, but alas, my shirt was still in the way, and so excited was she that all she could do was to exclaim, "My darling! My darling!" as her little hand nervously clutched and grasped my burning prick, in alternate tightening and loosening of her fingers. Not apprehending that Amy would return, that she had gone in to solace her little cunt there with the help of a finger or a plantain, or anything which could imitate the "high priest," I had spoken of, I stood, and enjoyed to the fullest Fanny's excitement and the pleasure her hand gave me, yet whilst so standing, I suddenly and luckily saw Amy coming. I whispered to Fanny, "Take care! Here is Amy!"

"Ho! ho! There you are!" she cried, "kissing I do declare!"

"No!" said Fanny in muffled tones, "I have sprained my ankle!"

"Yes!" said I immediately, glad and delighted to find Fanny so quick witted as to invent a reason on the spur of the moment for not moving on. I had my prick right out, sticking out from my trousers, covered still by my shirt indeed, which had interfered with poor Fanny's endeavors to feel it naked in her hand, and it would have been instantly seen by Amy, only that Fanny leant against me, as it were for support, whilst I did my best to push back the most unruly and raging member.

"Yes!" I repeated, "poor Fanny somehow turned her ankle, and I am afraid it is hurting her very much, poor girl!" Then addressing Fanny, I said, "If you will let me apply my Grandmother's remedy, I am sure I can relieve the pain, even if I cannot take it away altogether. But the sooner you let me do so, the more certain the result."

Fanny gave a kind of groan as she said, "Oh! do whatever you like, and quickly, for it is hurting me so!"

I knelt on one hand, keeping myself close to Fanny's petticoat, whilst, with rapid fingers I managed to fasten a couple of the more important buttons, so as to keep my beast of a prick a tight prisoner. Then taking hold of her right ankle with my left hand, I pretended to press it with my other hand, but the temptation to do more was too strong, and Fanny felt, with delight, my wicked, delicious hand rapidly mount her well turned and beautiful leg, pressing her calf most voluptuously and amorously, as it got. Higher and higher. She bent a little more over me, resting her hands on my shoulders, and gave a little groan from time to time.

"It will be better soon, I think," said I, as my hand reached her smooth, warm, polished and plump thigh. Fanny had really beautiful legs and thighs. My prick bounded and throbbed.

"Yes! I think it will!" gasped Fanny, if you continue as you are doing now."

Amy stood by, looking on and sympathizing, but quite unable to see what I was doing I rapidly moved my hand up that glorious virgin thigh, pressing it and feeling it delightedly as I mounted, until I arrived at the spot between the delicious columns of ivory, I turned my hand back down, and gently seizing the two soft full lips of her plump little cunt, I pressed them together by alternate squeezes, so as to tickle and excite the clitoris, until Fanny could hardly stand still. Then slipping my big middle finger in, up to the knuckles, and using my other finger as a fulcrum against her swelling and bushy motte, I imitated what my prick would have done, had it had a fair chance, until almost expiring with pleasure, Fanny deluged my exciting and lascivious hand with a perfect torrent of hot spend, which run down my wrist and arm. I caressed the sweet, responsive cunt, with my most voluptuous touches and then, hardly able to keep a steady face, I asked her, "Well, how does it feel now Fanny?"

"It is all right! Oh! thanks—that was nice! Now that the pain is gone!"

"Did what he did really do you any good?" asked Amy wonderingly.

"Of course it did, you silly girl!" cried Fanny, "or I shouldn't have said so!"

"Well! That is wonderful!" said Amy, "I'll tell Mama!"

"Don't do anything of the sort!" exclaimed Fanny, "you would only frighten her. I dare say it was nothing but a sprain. At any rate, I'm all right now."

"Mama told me to tell you to come in," said Amy.

"Oh! bother!" cried Fanny. "Amy! there's a good girl, go and ask her to let me stay out a little longer."

Amy was not inclined to do so, and, much to Fanny's and my dissatisfaction, we had to go in. Before we did enter the house, however, Fanny managed to throw both her arms round my neck and give me two most ardent kisses, without being seen by Amy. Gods! how my balls and groin did nearly split with aching.

After I got home I had the inevitable visit from poor Lavie. What a terrible plague he was! I did my best, as usual, to try and reconcile him to his fate, and I strongly urged him to do as much fucking as he could.

He said he had been doing this regularly and irregularly every night but could not work off his passion for Fanny, and I resolved to do my best to get him removed. Before going to bed I wrote to Dr. Bridges and I told him that I feared that Miss Selwyn was not safe. That Lavie prowled about all night, round her house, and that he had a perfect lust for her, which might induce him to attempt to rape her. I really believed this, for Lavie was like one mad for Fanny. He had begun a habit of muttering to himself, and I overheard a semi-threat to fuck Fanny whether she like it or not. Calling up Soubratie from his slumbers, I told him to take the letter, first thing in the morning, to Dr. Bridges, and the results will be seen in the results of that never to be forgotten day, the seventeenth of March, the very next day, the day on which Fanny Selwyn attained the double dignity of seventeen years of age and womanhood, the day I, at last, took her most charming maidenhead, fucking her, both to her and my hearts' content, relieving her sweet cunt and my balls and groins of the load which had oppressed them since we had declared our mutual passion. I knew the seventeenth was Fanny's birthday, but I had no idea I should be invited to assist at keeping the feast. However, after breakfast I had two very agreeable visits. As usual I was very much undressed, having nothing on me but my short sleeved jersey and pajamas, for it was much too hot, and there was far too blazing a sun outside, for me to expect visitors. The first who came to see me was old Bridges, our P.M.O., who seemed very anxious about Lavie. He said he had lately noticed a considerable alteration in him, a laxity in the way he carried out his duties, which he could not account for, until he heard of his unfortunate love affairs. He now wanted to know about the subject of my last letter, because it was of a very serious nature, and, if I did think there was any danger, he would telegraph to Simla for permission to send Lavie to Benares, where, he understood, there was room for another doctor. I easily satisfied Bridges on this head. During our conversation I had noticed his eyes constantly directed at the still blue and red looking scars on my left arm, caused by the knife of the brutal Afghan who had buggered poor Amy, and after he had finished speaking about poor Lavie, the good doctor went in for a complete history of the scars.

I showed him the rose looking ones on my chest, and Bridges exclaimed that I ought to consider myself the chosen of Providence, for I had had the most extraordinary escape he had ever heard of. Of course I did not tell him about poor Amy's catastrophe, but he had heard the rumor that she had been buggered. I lied to him, I told him the rumor was false, and I was glad to be able to do so, although I had to tell a lie, because I knew that Bridges would talk, and would look upon anyone who persisted in believing in the buggersy as a slanderer whom he must at once put down.

Hardly had he gone and I resumed my book and cheroot, than in ran Mabel, in real hot haste. She sprang into my arms, and gave me a number of hearty kisses, and then looked over her shoulder, to be sure that no one had come yet, she pulled at the strings of my pajamas before I knew what she was up to, and had my prick in her hands as stiff as a poker. As I have before said, I should never at anytime object to so great a pleasure as having my prick and balls handled by a very pretty girl, whom I knew to be fuckable, but Mabel was so frightfully daring. I guessed she was not coming alone and asked her. To my horror she said that her Mama with Fanny and Amy were on their way over, and she had run ahead to peep at her "pet" if she could manage it before they came into the house. As she spoke I heard Mrs. Selwyn's voice and the footsteps of the three coming along the verandah. Hastily pushing Mabel to one side I ran to my bathroom, where I at once splashed myself with water, as though I had been bathing my face and neck, and then fastening my towel around my waist so as to hang down in front and hide the tent formed by my terribly excited prick, I came into the sitting room and, as if quite surprised, greeted the ladies and begged them to excuse my dishabille.

My jersey, still open, showed the really terrible looking scars, and then Mrs. Selwyn and Amy, who had never seen them since the bandages had been taken off, for Mrs. Selwyn had been too much agitated when she came and found me in the same dress, or undress rather, to notice anything, gave little cries of horror and sympathy, which did me good to hear. All three inspected them, and Mrs. Selwyn laid her finger on one, on my chest, and asked was it still tender. I said not there, and then my darling Fanny (pretending to feel one also), took as much of my left breast as she could gather in her hand, and gave me such a tender little squeeze, as I should have done to one of her own sweet, pretty bubbies had I had the chance. Amy exclaimed at the thick hair between my breasts, and I made her blush by saying, sotte voce, to her and Fanny:

"Ah! Amy, you are as beautiful as could be! You've Jacob's beauty in your face; And Esau's—where it should be! Whereas I am Esau all over!"

"For shame!" said Amy.

Fanny only smiled and reddened, and I knew longed to let me see that she, too, had Esau's beauty covering the mount above her lovely cunt.

Well, the visitors having talked the whole story of the attack on their house at Cherat over again, now declared the object of their visit, which was to invite me to dinner that evening. They were not going to ask anyone else, but Mrs. Selwyn said she had looked upon me so much at one time as quite one of the family, that she hoped I would let myself be prevailed upon to come and see them very much more frequently than I had recently done. Fanny looked at me with imploring eyes, full of passion and desire, and she looked so lovely, so delicious, so voluptuously tempting, that I could not have declined, even had my old virtuous intentions returned again. Ah! no! Those virtuous intentions had altogether died away, and my prick stood upon them, stiff and erect, and swollen with pride, as a perfect conqueror naturally feels when he has overcome his foe. I therefore accepted, with every manifestation of real and unmistakable pleasure, and as I escorted Fanny out of the house, following her mother and sisters, I took the opportunity of letting her judge of the sincerity and strength of my passion by the relative force and intense stiffness of my prick. But for the friendly towel I could have given another view, that is sure, and I felt thankful to Mabel after all, though at first I was vexed at her insane liberties taken with me under such dangerous circumstances.

Now, dearest reader, I hope you are interested in Fanny's sweet, thrilling little cunt, as I was. As interested in hearing about the fucking of it as I was also. Girls, darling, who may read these dear but naughty pages, I hope your delectable little cunnies are moistening and tickling with sympathy, and Oh! ye, my male readers, may those pricks, which I trust are stiffly standing, have sweet cunts to cool their ardor not far off!

Fanny, seventeen years old, was this day promoted to the dignity of low dress, and when she welcomed me that evening I found her as proud as a peacock, in all the glory, not of extended tail, but of a very lovely exposed bosom. The two darling little breasts were indeed more hidden than I could approve of, but I could see some small portion of their smooth and polished globes, and my delighted eye gazed on the sweet path between them which followed lower, would end in her exquisite little cunt. Alas! the presence of her father, mother, sisters and little brother Harry, prevented me taking my privileges, as her lover, and once more feeling those beautiful bubbies, but I gave my eyes such a feasting that I found it necessary to be very careful how I moved, for fear of displacing my terrible prick, which had, as usual, become unmanageable. I sat next to Fanny at dinner, and whenever occasion offered gently pressed her thigh, a compliment she returned as often as she could. Oh! if chance was but a little favorable, it was in the hands of that most revered and beloved Goddess Venus, was most favorable.

After dinner, we all walked up and down the avenue, where in the semi-darkness, caused by a sky only lighted by the stars, I was enabled to let Fanny judge of my feelings by the never failing stiffness of my prick. I could, however, take no freedom with her. Mabel, whether suspicious or not, was too attentive an observer, but though she could not see what I did with Fanny's hand when we turned in our walk, any movement of mine towards Fanny's cunt would certainly have been detected by her. I was on thorns, and also in real pain, for my balls were really on fire, and my groins paining me from the overstocked fullness of the reservoirs, the magazines of spend which had been storing up, waiting for an opportunity to be unloaded.

At length Mrs. Selwyn proposed that we should all go in and play a round game of cards and, once it was set going, Fanny and I very quickly managed to lose all our cards, and pretended to watch the game very eagerly. In reality I had one of her legs on my knee, her foot hanging between my calves, where I pressed it. I whispered to her to come out, but she seemed afraid to attract attention and did not stir. We were near the corner of the table, which was a long rectangular one.

Everybody else was deep in the game going on. I became desperate. We were losing an opportunity which might not recur that evening. I unbuttoned my trousers and getting my prick out, free from my shirt, I took Fanny's hand and put it on it. She gave a perfect jump! Her hand tightened on the subject of her delightful thoughts and wishes, and her bosom rose and fell to such a degree that, together with her intense color, made me fear she would burst! But in a moment or two she got up and said she would go out for a moment, it was so hot.

"Do, darling," said her mother, "I dare say Captain Devereaux will go with you."

Fanny went at once, and I, rising quickly and turning my back on the company, walked with rapid strides after her, my prick completely out and pointing like a bowsprit at the ceiling. Oh! that walk across the room! How I dreaded anyone calling me back! But Venus, dear Venus, protected her servants, and I joined Fanny in the verandah safe and unsuspected. Neither of us spoke a word to the other; our feelings were too intense, and her's altogether too agitated.

Quietly and swiftly we made for the friendly shrubs, of which I have spoken before. Arrived on the grass between them, I put my cracking prick again into Fanny's trembling hand, whilst I rapidly undid my braces and unbuttoned the rest of my trousers; for though poor Fanny tried her utmost to manage these, she was in such a state of nervous excitement that her strength seemed to fail her. However, man can make! I could not restrain the lava torrents very long, and amidst a chorus, or rather a duet of sighs, voluptuous groans and little cries, and at the rushing end of the maddening short digs, at last carne that burst of spend which makes a man drive in his prick as though he would send it through his lovely comrade, and press his motte to hers as though to flatten it forever. Certainly Fanny was well anointed with the holy oil that first time. I had only spent once, or at least twice, since I had last fucked Lizzie Wilson. The first time was when I had the wet dream at Nowshera, and the last time was when I had sham fucked Fanny yesterday in my bungalow, and I was boiling over. But all things come to an end, and after enjoying for awhile the leaps of Fanny's motte and the compressions of her lovely little cunt, I withdrew my still iron stiff prick and wiped the sweet girl between the thighs with my handkerchief. Fanny lay still on the ground, her eyes turned up to the stars, and her thighs open, in the most voluptuous attitude, whilst I was rapidly restoring the disorder of my attire. She seemed like one in an ecstasy. At length I roused her, and assisted her to rise to her feet. For a moment she seemed hardly able to stand without support, and then she threw her lovely arms around me, and pressing me to her, she gave me a shower of kisses which I returned with interest.

"Oh! my darling!" she cried, "at last you have loved me as I have so longed, longed to be loved! But, oh! I am all wet down my legs!"

Of course. Her overfilled cunt was overflowing and that reminded me that I must take care of Fanny. Kneeling down and telling her to let me do what I liked, I passed my hand up her thighs, and introduced two fingers, as far as they would go into her hot, soft little cunt. I used them like glove stretchers and succeeded in bringing another flow of imprisoned spend down my hand and wrist, and so relieved Fanny of what might otherwise have proved a dangerous burden.

She asked me why I did that.

"I will tell you another time, darling. But come, let me wipe you once more, and then we will take a turn of the avenue and see whether anyone is corning out."

Fanny submitted to the further wiping with a voluptuous surrender of herself, which was exquisitely delicious to me. Oh what a jewel she was, if I could but wear her properly! What an immense pleasure did I see before me in training this ardently voluptuous girl to enjoy in its fullness the pleasure she could give! She loved me, I knew, and she even now loved my prick, but it should, if possible, be my care to make her adore my prick, without loving me the less.

We walked slowly together, arm in arm, for we feared anymore lover-like attitude, lest eyes might see what none must even suspect.

Twice we walked up and down before the house and looked in to see whether any move suggested an exit of anybody, but as far as we could see all were busily engaged. Then Fanny did one of those bold things which made me respect her so much. She went in, spoke to her mother and asked when someone would be corning out and was told to go and enjoy the walk with me as the game was not likely to end very soon. She carne to me all radiant and joyful.

"Come! darling Charlie!"

I knew what she meant. We hurried to our temporary nuptial couch between the shrubs. Here Fanny performed my toilet and I performed hers, and when we were, both of us, as naked as could possibly be without actually taking off our clothes, we joined in another one of those particularly rapturous fucks which neither man nor woman forgets all the days of their lives. Oh! dear readers, my pen fails me when I try to write down the burning reminiscences of those burning moments, but all my soul, my heart and my life seemed to be centered in Fanny, and the seat and acme of pleasure to be in her cunt, between her beautiful thighs!

"Oh! Fanny!" I said, as we walked up and down, "to have you properly we should both be in a comfortable bed, and naked as we were born! How can we manage it? Can I come to you darling? Could I not come in by the far bathroom door, across your room, and so get into yours?"

"Oh! no! It is impossible" she replied. "Amy sleeps in my room, and my bed creaks—and—but—Leave it to me darling Charlie and I will find a way! In the meanwhile let us enjoy one another as much as we can as we have done. Oh! Charlie! I never, never, never could have enough of you, or as much of you as I should like!"

If the never quiet Mabel had not come out just then, she would have seen me fucking Fanny for the third time that half hour, but, fortunately for us, that licentious little maiden came out just in time to prevent our proceeding to the shrubs. It was very disappointing, but, after all, had we not been lucky? Fanny seemed in the very heavens! She spoke very little, her intense excitement was past, and she seemed like on quiescent from the very intensity of our happiness. This was most fortunate for, had our success led to any exhibition of demonstrativeness, some suspicion might have been aroused.

The remainder of the evening passed quietly and I went home about eleven o'clock. Arrived there, and carefully spreading out my handkerchief to dry, for it had on it the precious bloom, mixed with our offerings, of the sacrifice of Fanny's maidenhead.

Before going to bed I, as usual, sat in my chair and tried to view calmly all the immense happiness I had attained. But I was still in quite a state of excitement. I had indeed fucked Fanny twice, but here were my balls and groins aching. Was it really so impossible to get at her in her house? Should I risk going over presently and having a try? I knew I could make her hear me from the verandah, for I could whisper her name through the lattice of her window. I must fuck her again and very soon! I was rapidly coming to the conclusion that I could not really wait any longer, but must go to look for Fanny, when to my great surprise and intense joy, as well, however, as alarm, in came Fanny herself.

"Oh! Fanny, darling, how did you come here?"

"I walked over, of course," said she. "Oh! my own love! Oh, my own darling Charlie, I could not sleep after I went to bed, I lay and tossed about. I longed for you, my darling! my darling! and at last I made up my mind that no matter what would happen, I would risk all and come to you, and now, see! I am come to give myself, wholly and entirely to you! Naked as I am by nature to you I give myself all naked, there!" she exclaimed, as she tossed aside the grey cloak and the night dress she was clothed in, and took her feet out of her slippers, "there! see! do you like me so Charlie? Am I pretty enough to please you, my own, own darling?"

Was she pretty enough? There standing before me, lit up by the light of the reading lamp, shining white against the darkness beyond, stood a perfect nymph. A perfect incarnation of youth and freshness, and beauty! Lizzie Wilson, indeed, might have won the palm, had she compared her exquisite form, in all its glorious nudity and beauty, with Fanny before a jury of cold and unimpassive artists but, at the moment, it seemed to me, that never had I seen a more exquisite girl than Fanny!

Fanny had one of those fresh, clean looking skins, so desirable in women. Her arms were full, (round, and beautifully shaped. Her shoulders sloped exquisitely, and her bosom, like that of a young nymph, was adorned with a pair of well separated, boldly self-sustained breasts, so often seen in sculpture, and yet so really rare in nature. The little coral beads of them shown clear and red, a lovely brilliant red, like that of her lips, and each sweet bubbie looked a little away from the other. Her form was, even the perfection of elegance, that of a really well made girl, and her ivory belly, dimpled by a lovely navel, was a couch fit for Jupiter himself. Below that fairest belly was the swelling mount of Venus, and with pleasure I saw that her bush was considerably grown, as indeed were her breasts, since I had last looked on them at Cherat. But below that mount, receding between her really beautiful thighs, was that most tempting deep line, which formed a cunt to be desired by the very Gods themselves! A cunt all mine now! A cunt no man had ever caressed or fucked before. I had done so today! A cunt which longed for me, and which was brought over by Fanny, for me to fuck, to love now! A cunt which I had indeed tasted, but had not yet fully savored, but of which the first rapid, incomplete taste had made me eager to devour it more and more!

Fanny had, as I have said before, really beautiful thighs. Indeed her arms, thighs, legs and feet were her strongest points, and were fit for models for any artist. They struck me as particularly beautiful in the light I now saw them; and the sweetness, the glowing sweetness of really healthy youth shone from them, much enhanced near the groins by the dark curls of her fairly grown, dark brown bush. The more I gazed at all these exquisite charms, the stiffer did my prick grow, and the more did I realize what a prize I had so fortunately obtained. Fanny, as though conscious of the power her beauty had over me, stood smiling, with lips slightly parted, as though waiting for that burst of praise, admiration and passion to which she felt she was entitled. Had she been conscious of not being well made, of her skin not being really pleasant to look upon, she would never have given herself, all naked in this manner to me, for woman's modesty too often is the quality under which they hide their blemishes. I have never yet fucked a really pretty and well made woman who, from the first, objected to appearing naked before me. On the contrary the better were the forms, the easier did the fair and beautiful owners of them find it to exhibit them to me without disguise.

"Oh! Fanny! you are lovely! My darling girl! you are the very perfection of beauty! Come, come, until I eat you up!"

Fanny's eyes blazed with pleasure, happiness and passion! She came with a little cry of joy and threw herself onto me as I reclined in my long chair. My prick opposed her belly and she pushed it to one side to enable her to lie on me and press me in her energetic arms, whilst she rained the hot, burning, happy kisses in my equally responsive mouth. All the while she was murmuring little passionate love sentences into my ears, and she moved her breasts from side to side over my bosom, so that I could feel the hard little coral nipples, as it were, scoring it, and the firm elastic bubbies passing like waves across it. I gently pressed her lovely haunches in my two hands, and tried to reach her warm little cunt from behind, but she laughingly kept it from me, until as though a fresh burst of passion seized her. She lay along my left thigh and side, with her arm round my neck, her left hand moving up and down my excited prick, occasionally grasping and feeling my balls most tenderly, whilst she said in tones of greatest excitement and the deepest feeling, "Oh! Charlie! Charlie! You don't know how I love and adore you, my own darling! I thought I knew what love was, but I did not. There was a time when I thought I never could give myself to you, unless I was sure that I could call myself your wife, and make you marry me. But now! now! I feel that I do not want to marry you. What I should like to be would be your own beloved concubine. Yes! to have you I would willingly be a servant in your house, and wait upon your wife if I might, from time to time, sleep with you and have you as I had you this evening on the grass! I wish concubines were allowed now.

They had them in the old days—why should not a man have more than one wife now? Why should he not have concubines too? Let me speak. When I went to bed I felt so happy. I had had you—twice! Think of that! Twice had this darling thing of yours been buried deep in me! Twice had I felt it pour the splashing and essence of my Charlie in me! Oh! I could feel it so well, so distinctly, and each time it seemed to kill me with pleasure. The more I thought of it and remembered all you did, the more did I long to have it again, the more did I want to feel this." (she gently handled my balls.) "Pressed against me, for they told me when my Charlie was inside of me! And I remembered what you offered to do, to come to me, and have me in my own bed; how you said you could so easily come to me, by the far bathroom door, and I was almost sorry I had said no, for after all, we might have gone into the next room and lain on the floor, and there would have been no creaking bed to waken Amy. I tried to sleep, I could not—my—I don't know what you call it, Charlie, but in Hindustani it is called Choot."

"Cunt, darling!"

"Cunt? Cunt! is that the English name for it? A nice, soft name. I won't forget it! Cunt! Well, my cunt troubled me terribly and called for this—what do you call it, Charlie, dearest?"

"Prick, darling!"

"Prick? What a funny name! Prick! well! never mind! My cunt then called for its darling prick, and at last I could not stay in my bed any longer. I jumped up. I went and looked at Amy. She was fast asleep. I went and looked into the nursery. Sugdaya was asleep on the floor. I listened at Papa's and Mama's room but could hear them both snoring. So I took my grey cloak and slippers and ran out of the house, by the bathroom door, and here I am with my own Charlie. Are you glad, darling? Are you glad that Fanny has come and is in your arms now?"

"Oh! my Fanny! My Fanny! How could I be anything but glad, darling, darling, girl! Yet I feel a little nervous on your account. Fanny, if you should happen to be missed! What a row there would be if you were found here! Now, if I were found in your room, it would not be half so bad, because no one could say that you had invited me there, but it would be different if you were found in my house!"

"Oh! I am not at all afraid of that, Charlie! I feel sure in my heart that no one will miss or find me out."

"But, darling, Lavie is such a night bird, he often comes much later than this to see me, and—by Jove! I hear him coming now!"

Fanny started up into a sitting posture. She still held my prick in her hand, and we both listened for a moment. The footsteps came rapidly towards the door. We could hear them crushing the gravel on the avenue and it was plain that in another moment Lavie would be in the room. I recognized his footsteps and knew it was he. Fanny was about to jump up but I held her tight. The footsteps paused beside the door, then paused a little longer, then passed on! Lavie appeared to me to hesitate and it was clear to me that he was changing his mind, and that, as he so often did, he would go first and walk around the Selwyn's house and then return to bore me. The moment he had commenced his walk again I told Fanny to pick up her chemise, cloak and slippers and run into my bedroom and lie down, and cover herself with the cloak, whilst, if possible, I would stop Lavie and send him home.

Fanny darted with her goods into the bedroom, and I went out into the verandah. My fright was so real and sincere that my prick had at once lost all its stiffness, and hung with very abashed head, whilst I again tied the strings of my pajamas. I got its hood on to its poor shriveled head again, and set off to catch Lavie, but when I got round the corner of the verandah he was nowhere to be seen or heard.

Uneasy, I hurried back to my sitting room, meaning to visit Fanny, and see that no light entered my bedroom in case Lavie happened to return that way, for each of my rooms had four doors by which it could be entered on all four sides, as is common in Indian houses, where every provision is made for the most thorough circulation of air, and as I entered my sitting room I met Lavie coming out of my bedroom.

I am sure my anxious and generous minded readers will not accuse me of cowardice, for I confess that my hair naturally stood on end with fright when I saw the unhappy doctor coming out of the room where I believed Fanny to be lying naked on my bed! But I trust they will anyhow give me credit for not losing my presence of mind under great peril. It was not for myself I feared; Fanny! Had Lavie seen her? Then goodbye to her reputation and future happiness. One glance at his absent-minded, moody face, told me that that misfortune, or rather piece of evil fortune, had not taken place. I steadied my face as much as I could, for I was indeed intensely agitated and said, "Why, Lavie! where have you come from? I thought I heard your footsteps outside, and went to call you in, but I could not see you. I fancied I was a victim of imagination."

"I did pass your door. I meant to have come in, and changed my mind and went on. Then I thought I must come in and tell you what I think. So I came in by the other side of the house."

"Well; sit down old fellow. What do you want to tell me ?"

"No! Devereaux! I will not down in your house again!"

"Goodness! Why not?"

"Look here? Devereaux!" said he in most menacing tones. "I believed you were my friend. I told you that I loved Fanny Selwyn and you promised to help me get her. But it is my belief, I am sure of it, that, instead of speaking up for me, you said and did everything to make the Selwyns and Fanny in particular think me a fool and a bad match! You can't deny it!"

"Now, in reality, nothing" could be more untrue and unjust than this stupid accusation. I had, at first, done all I could to help Lavie with Fanny. I had spoken to her, told her what an excellent fellow I knew him to be, and in every way I had urged his suit on, as though he had been my own brother. I had so entirely given up all idea of having Fanny that I was absolutely glad to do all this, and it was only when it became altogether too clear that Fanny abhorred him, and the idea of being Lavie's wife, that I slackened my efforts. It was, I saw, of no use to try to fan the flame which did not exist, even in the embryo of a spark. Then it was that I discovered, that, although Fanny had treated me most unkindly for a long time, had called me a fool, and never spared me with her biting sarcasm, she really loved me with passionate eagerness. Was I going to throwaway my chance of happiness, was I going to refuse a proffered cunt, which I had once so much desired, and which I fancied was gone forever from my grasp, because I had promised to help a man who I could not help? I indeed take no credit to myself for having fucked Fanny. It was not I who sought her, in the end, but she who sought me. But at the same time I did not consider I in anyway harmed Lavie, because I took possession of a delicious little cunt which would never have been his. Lavie's words offended me. Nevertheless, I am sure I should have forgiven him, if I had not already fucked Fanny. I seized the opportunity therefore of banishing him from my house forever, and all the more eagerly, because I knew that my naked darling was waiting for me on my bed, in the next room.

"Lavie!" I exclaimed in determined tones, "if this is what you have come to tell me, let me show you the door. Do you see it, Sir! Out you go, and never come into my house again! I consider you the most ungrateful wretch I ever had to deal with!"

Lavie glared at me, hesitated, then slowly walked to the door, where he once more paused and turning, said, "Yes! I will go! I will never call you friend again! You won't succeed in keeping Fanny Selwyn from me, for as sure as God is in heaven I will fuck that girl!"

I thought it prudent not to answer him. He glared again at me for a moment, and then slowly walked down the avenue, out to the road, and departed in the darkness.

I stood watching him for a moment or so, and was just going to bolt and shut the door, when I saw a light approaching. Cursing in my heart whoever it was, who came to interrupt my solitude on such an evening, I waited to see who it was. It was Dr. Bridges' Chuprasse with a note:

"Dear Captain Devereaux, make your mind easy," I read,
about Doctor Lavie, I have permission, by telegraph from
Simla, to send him to Benares and he shall go tomorrow.
                                        Yours very truly, J. Bridges

"Give the Doctor Sahib bahut, bahut salaam!" cried I, in delight, and the Chuprasse, with a lordly salute, turned and departed. I shut the door and bolted it, took my lamp and swiftly went into my bedroom.

Fanny was lying on my bed covered with the grey cloak. She raised herself on her elbow, holding the cloak ready to cover herself with in case of need, but displaying to my delighted eyes almost all the glories of her lovely nudity. I saw her bosom to perfection, and her body, foreshortened, offered itself to my eyes in a passion new to me in her. Oh! how I can see even now, the delicious bush of her motte making a sharp pointed triangle towards her thighs, for she had them close shut, and was leaning on her left elbow. My prick had been about dead from the alarm it had received, but at this exquisite sight he raised again in all his glory and, running to Fanny, I clasped her in my arms and told her all was safe so far, Lavie was gone, and I gave her Bridges' note to read. Fanny was delighted. She threw her arms around me, and called me all the loving names she could think of. Then throwing her cloak completely off her, on to the floor, she opened her arms and parted her knees, and with eyes darting the most voluptuous desire, and in a voice thrilling with passion, she said, "Oh! Charlie, darling, don't let us lose anymore time!" and although the scenes I had gone through were enough to make me forget everything, but the delicious pleasure I expected to take between those lovely thighs, I did not forget myself. Foreseeing that I should, now that I had once fucked Fanny, fuck her many times, I had prepared that saviour sponge which should render inonious those otherwise pleasant but dangerous streams of spend, which would naturally gush from me, and inundate the shrine of love. I did not expect Fanny in my house indeed, but I had the sponge in a little glass wide necked bottle, with a weak solution of phrenyle and water, ready to be carried in my pocket for use in her house, where I hoped next to have the joy of fucking her. This I now got and placed handy on the floor. Then I stripped. I stood completely naked before the admiring and panting girl. She gave a cry of joy and admiration, and put forth both her hands to grasp my big, swollen and immensely strong prick, and the potent balls beneath it, and, with delicious rapture I felt her lissome fingers twining round the objects, which by their touch alone filled her with still more delightful voluptuous and deliciously lascivious longings.

"Oh! let me kiss it! let me kiss it, Charlie!" she cried, and smiling I brought the head of my excited prick to her ruby lips; With unmistakable rapture she pressed her mouth to the rounded tip, and with her tongue to the little orifice in it. I took my part, bending over her, I parted her willingly opened thighs with my hands, and covering her glowing little cunt with my mouth, I shot my tongue as deep into it as I could. Fanny, who had never been so caressed before, uttered a little cry of pleasure. I could feel her hands, both hands, grasp my prick with renewed force and ardor, and, as though to repay the compliment she felt I was paying her cunt with my tongue, she took the head of my prick right into her mouth, passing her tongue all over it, and making me thrill through and through with the rapturous sensation!

But such caresses serve only to excite to madness almost. Turning to her I caught her arms and pushed her on her back. I took the sponge and squeezing the superabundant moisture out of it, I pressed it into her little cunt, her tight little cunt, and, getting between her thighs, I quickly followed it with my prick, and then mouth to mouth, and bosom to bosom, belly to belly, we had our first really luscious, fully voluptuous, deliciously delightful and rapturous fuck.

Fanny, voluptuous by nature, was truly formed for fucking. Not even Lizzie Wilson could have better or more fully evinced the pleasure, the rapture she felt, than did Fanny. Although she had never been taught the refinements of fucking, she seemed, instinctively, to drop into them, and nothing could have been more graciously superb than the way in which she gave a firm little buck each time she felt my balls come against her. Had I not known that it was I who had taken her maiden-head that very day, I should have concluded that Fanny had often been fucked before that night, but my heart was easy on that score. With some girls it seems natural, others can be taught, but most require to be trained.

When the hot, quick, rapturous short digs came, Fanny almost lost her senses, so much was all that sensuous in her touched. Her voice rattled, or rather gurgled in her throat, her eyes opened their widest and seemed more gloriously beautiful than ever. In her agonies of pleasure she nipped my shoulder with her teeth, whilst I thrust my tongue into her ear, and she met my torrents of hot spend with foaming floods of her own.

Then came that exquisite period, when as though exhausted, our grasp on one another relaxed, and we lay quite still. Her bosom heaving under mine, making me feel the full elasticity of her lovely bubbies, her belly rising and sinking, her motte leaping and giving mine little blows, whilst her cunt squeezed my prick with a force which made me fully conscious of how powerfully pleasure had effected her.

Then came all those sweet, sweet little expressions of love, devotion, passion, those kisses over such parts of the body as we could reach, and then finally the withdrawal from one another's arms and the immediate and satisfactory inspection of the charms which had been the chief extremes of our mutual pleasure.

"Oh! Charlie! How grand! How big! Who ever would have thought so small a thing as I have could take in such a lovely monster?"

"Ah! darling Fanny! But your sweetest little cunt is really very tight! But not too tight all the same!"

"Oh no! It can take it, Charlie! But why did you put the sponge in?"

I was glad to explain. I gently drew it out by the thin silken thread I had fastened to it, to the outer end of which I had also fastened a little cross-bar of silver, to prevent its being entirely sucked up into her cunt, by the backwards and forward strokes of my prick, and I showed her the great quantities of spend which I had poured into her, and I explained to her the formation of her womb, and how necessary it was for her safety to prevent a possible baby, that the mouth of the womb should be prevented from being watered by the prolific produce of my balls, and that, to still further deaden the vitality of that spend, I had used phrenyle. She quite understood me as I proceeded, and kissed me again and again, thanking me for the great care I took of her and saying that she had never thought of any danger. I told her I had written to Cawnpore for a powerful enema, and sent a receipt to be made up which would be more effective and pleasant than the phrenyle, as it would have rose water as one of its ingredients, and would have a more pleasant aroma; and then I proposed that she should get up, and let me wash her pretty cunt, so that I might pay it again the homage of my kisses. To this she joyfully assented. I got a basin of water and a towel and bathed her hot little cunt. She enjoyed the freshness of the water, and when I had dried her bush and cunt and thighs she insisted on washing my prick in her turn, laughing and happy.

"Now!" said I, "my darling, lay across the bed, and put one leg over each of my shoulders. That is right!"

I hid my face between her thighs, my mouth on her sweet, sweet cunt, and up stretched hands grasping each a polished globe of her bosom. Fanny lay still for half a minute, while I searched the depths of that voluptuous little cunt with my tongue and pressed my nose on to her excited little clitoris, but at last she snatched those charms away from me and said, "Oh! at least let us lie so that I can do the same to you, as you do to me, my Charlie!"

Delighted to find her so ready to play every air on the sonata of voluptuousness, I stretched her on the bed, and again took my position over her, leaning on my elbows, embracing each of her thighs with an arm, and again searching her cunt with my tongue, whilst my chin tickled her clitoris, and gave her my prick for her mobile lips and sweeping tongue, and my balls to her agitated and excited fingers! And then once more placing the sponge of safety within the rosy portals of the temple, I reversed my position and again thrilled the deliciously lascivious and voluptuous girl with my impassioned fucking.

Oh! those mad delights of love and passion! When man and maid do in hot blood things which, if thought of coldly, are seemingly repulsive! Yet I ask any ardent lover what can be sweeter to his lips than those of his beloved and adored mistress' cunt? And so I found was my case with Fanny. I do not think I should, even in my maddest moments of lascivious passion with Lizzie Wilson, have cared to go the lengths I did with Fanny. But Fanny was my own virgin, a girl I was really fond of, for more reason than that furnished by the sweet charm between her snowy thighs, and Fanny was in that state of passionate adoration of me, that nothing that she could do could satisfy the craving of her soul.

A passion, even when backed up by a prick whose vigor apparently never slackens, and balls which, like the widow's cruse, fill as fast as they empty, will moderate its force. If men and women were simply animals they would fuck until they could fuck no more, and then they would separate, and take but little interest in one another; but human beings have hearts, and souls, and after the immediate desires and most pressing wants of the senses have been contented, they find a new pleasure in the communion of thoughts, which is so exquisite when love stirs the depths of the heart.

When Fanny and I had fucked almost continuously for a couple of hours, our senses had seeming need of rest, and then it was that we began to speak to one another, more like rational beings than the mad faun and nymph we had been. How pretty she did look as she lay all naked in my arms, her cheeks flushed, but not too much, her lovely violet eyes beaming with satisfied love and affection and pleasure, and how delightful was the litheness of her supple body, the prominence of her charms, the satin smoothness of her thighs so closely interlocked with mine!

I asked her when it was that she first thought she would like me to fuck her.

"From almost the very first day I saw you, darling!" she answered. "That very first morning, when I met you as you rode up on your pony, I said to myself, that is the kind of a man I should like to be mine, and after that each time I saw you made me wish more and more that you were not married, for then I might have had the chance of being your wife. I was always thinking of you and marriage. Of course I knew well that husbands and wives did not go to bed only to sleep and, little by little, I began to think how nice it would be to have you in bed with me, to hug you to my bosom, hold you in my arms, and then my cunt would begin to tickle. Each day I got to longing for you until there were times when I felt it was hard I could not even ask you to kiss me. And then came that dreadful night. And do you know, when the Afghan woke me I thought it was you! I thought it was your hand that pulled up my chemise and your finger that I felt in my cunt, and I was Oh! so glad! But Oh! so frightened to open my eyes!"

"And did that brute actually slip his finger up this lovely cunt, Fanny?"

"He did! It was his voice that first wakened me to the fact that it was not you, darling, and then I screamed. And you! you know the rest. Oh! Charlie! how glad I am it was you should save me, and not another! For that reason I am glad to give myself to you. I feel I can reward you a little for all your courage and bravery. My darling; my darling!"

Here there occurred a very natural interlude, in which the savior sponge, my prick and balls and Fanny's cunt had their innings. After the ablution I asked Fanny, "Tell me! Did you really dream that I forced you at Nowshera, darling ?"

"I did, really and truly, and most vividly too! There was something in that room that set me half mad with desire, and I never knew my cunt so troublesome before, as it was that day. It tickled, it throbbed. I can't tell you how it plagued me. Why was it, I wonder?"

"I can't tell you, darling! But tell me this, do you re member my taking your hand and putting it—"

"Oh! yes! you dear, naughty Charlie! Oh! I felt it. I did! I felt it edging by me on my hand, and it made me jump."

"Then why did you run away, Fanny darling, if you wanted me so much?"

"I did not mean to run away. But just at that moment Mabel came to call me to bed, and I was so vexed that I felt I should burst out crying if I did not run that minute. I suppose you thought I was offended, and that made you timid to speak to me afterwards. Oh! how angry I did feel with you for being, as I thought, such a fool!"

I thought this a good opportunity to explain to Fanny the real reasons of all my hopes and fears. I told her one of my principal reasons was that I did not know what the effects of her morally and mentally might be if I fucked her, and I told her that, when I heard that Louie was coming out, I made up my mind that the result seemed to me to be inevitably this, that two girls whom I loved to distraction would be rendered unhappy. Louie, because she would find me unfaithful, and herself, because she would naturally think me a brute to leave her, and that I saw no alternative than to haul off and try and forget that she had a cunt that I longed for.

And so the night wore away. We laid no plans for the future. Here in the happiness of one another we never thought how needful it would be to so manage that we could meet and fuck without fear of detection. We were just like a bride and bridegroom and this, the first night of our marriage.

Towards four o'clock Fanny, tired and exhausted from the strain on her nerves and senses, sank off to sleep in my arms, after the last ablution, and I found I had done the same too. For suddenly I felt a hand on my nose, gently pressing my nostrils, and opening my eyes I saw Sugdaya!

"Hush!" she said, "Sahib! Miss Fanny Baba must come home now, before the day breaks!"

"How did you know she was here, Sugdaya?"

"Oh!" she said, laughing softly, "I have known a long time that Miss Fanny Baba meant to be fucked by master. I kept my eyes open and I saw you in the shrubs last evening. I saw you go twice and I saw everything! Miss Fanny Baba did not tell me, but I said to myself, when the honey does not come to the bear, the bear goes to the honey. I went to see if Miss Fanny Baba was in her bed at midnight, and I found it empty. I came over here, and have been watching your pretty pranks through that door, and now you must wake her up, Sahib, and let her go with me!"

"Wait a moment, Sugdaya!" said I gently withdrawing my arm from under Fanny's neck, and got out of bed. "Go into the next room."

Sugdaya followed me. I unlocked my dispatch box and took a roll of twenty-five rupees out, and laid them on the table. Then taking Sugdaya's right hand I put it on my balls. She smiled and gently grasped them, with a voluptuous folding of her hands and fingers which made me know that she was not at all unwilling to feel them on her own account, and knew why I had put them into her hand. Then slipping my right hand under and between the folds of her robe, I found her cunt, and covering it with my palm, I dictated to her and she repeated:

"May my cunt wither and burn and shrivel, if I betray the girl against whose bottom these balls have pressed. May Vishnu, Ram, Sita and Lachman curse me, if I break my oath!"

Sugdaya laughed on the completion of this very necessary ceremony and said, "Oh! Sahib! no oath was required to bind me not to betray Missy Baba or you! I am more than glad Miss Fanny Baba has had the pleasure of being fucked. No girl needed it more. She will eat and drink and sleep all the better for it, and I know that the Sahib will not proclaim his conquest on the byways, but hold his tongue!"

"You may be sure of that, Sugdaya!" said I, kissing her, "and when Miss Fanny Baba goes away from Fackabad, will you let me fuck this nice cunt of yours?"

"Before then, if the Sahib wishes!" laughed Sugdaya.

I had been caressing her well formed, elastic and prominent and perfectly smooth motte, for Sugdaya, like all Indian women, either plucked out or shaved off every vestige of hair from that region. She had, in her turn, been caressing and feeling with hands evidently not strange to the act, my prick! which was in that vigorous condition women love to find.

"Now, Sahib!" said Sugdaya, pressing her swelling breasts against my bosom, "there is time for one more. Come! and wake Miss Fanny Baba as a lover should rouse his beloved!"

Nothing lost, I accompanied her to my bedroom, quite ready to do as Sugdaya had suggested, but Fanny, tired out with the long and exciting night's arduous and always ardent combats, was lying on her side, fast asleep, with one hand between her knees. She looked lovely as she lay slightly curled up, and her dear little face looked the picture of sweet Innocence. Sugdaya read my thoughts, for she said, "Her cunt is asleep, Sahib, but when I waken it up you will see another expression on her face!"

Looking round for something she evidently wanted, Sugdaya saw some peacock feathers and selecting one which suited, she approached Fanny, and deftly commenced drawing the soft feather along the line of her cunt, which gathered up as she was, I could hardly see anything at all of. At first there seemed to be no effect, but Sugdaya, with the utmost patience, continued those soft cares sings with the feather, and Fanny presently murmured something in her sleep, and turned a little more over forwards, as though she felt too tired for anymore fucking and depreciated the invitation. I glanced at Sugdaya who smiled and seemed in no way discouraged. She however, withdrew the feather and passed it several times over my prick, up and down, before she recommenced acting on Fanny. Whether the feather conveyed any subtle influence with it from my prick or whether, what seemed more likely, the continued soft rubbings of the down along her soft cunt slips caused a sweet excitement with desire, Fanny murmured again, and slowly turning on her back, opened her lovely thighs a little, so that the rays of the lamp distinctly it up the whole of those domains of which, in the name of love and Venus, I had taken possession. Sugdaya changed the end of the feather, and with a quill stroked Fanny's bush, occasionally touching the tip of her lovely cunt also. Presently out peeped the little ruby point, glittering with generous moisture, and the slight tremor of her motte, with the almost imperceptible, but still marked parting of the rounded lips of her cunt, told us that desire had laid his wanton hand on the charm which we wished to arouse from its state of torpor. Still Fanny remained fast asleep. Her bosom indeed rose and fell more rapidly. Her lips moved and here eyelids quivered. A smile wreathed her lovely mouth, and she parted her lips as though to speak, but, except those of her delicious little cunt, all her senses were still locked in the embrace of sleep. Sugdaya again reversed the feather, and slightly smote Fanny's cunt and bush. The sweet girl's thighs opened wider and wider, and her feet separated. She drew up her knees; it was evident, from her quick breathing and the rapid quiverings of her motte that the voluptuousness had fastened itself on her. Sugdaya gave me a nod, and I, very gently and with as much quiet as possible, got between my darling's knees. Bending forward I rested on both knees, as I had done with Lizzie Wilson, and Sugdaya, seizing my prick, directed it so as to strike the doors of the temple at that very spot where they opened with the least pressure. I glided in. Still keeping my belly from touching that of Fanny, and it was not till my balls touched her that she awoke.

"It is true, then! Not a dream!" she exclaimed, "Oh! my Charlie! I forgot for a moment that you were my real lover, and I thought that I was only dreaming my Nowshera dream again! I was afraid to open my eyes till I felt your dear balls against me!"

I stopped her further speech with my ardent kisses, and Sugdaya, who had discreetly moved a little to one side, out of the reach of Fanny's eyes, witnessed the voluptuous combat, which judging by the vigorous way she crossed her thighs, and the occasional passing of her hand between them, must have moved her very much. What a grand, grand poke that was! I enjoyed it more than any I had hitherto had, and when I withdrew my proud and delighted prick from the overflowing cunt of my darling, she exclaimed, "That is the best one we have had yet, Charlie!"

Sugdaya came forward. Fanny seemed no way put out by her presence, and I afterwards found out that for months Sugdaya had been inculcating the joys of love in all three girls, and that she had urged Fanny in particular, to do all she could to seduce me. It accounted for the extraordinary bold conduct of Mabel who, before Sugdaya entered the Selwyn house, had, like her sisters, been very modest and—reserved. It accounted too, to a great degree, for the free conduct, if I may so call it, of Fanny, in telling me of her dream when at Nowshera, for when I first knew the Selwyns there were not three purer minded girls in all India than these three young maidens, and I certainly did no more than foster the plant of desire when I saw it was growing.

It was still dark when the two girls left my bungalow, and having seen them depart in safety, I returned to my room, put out my lamp and lay down, certain of a grand sleep, for there would be no parade that morning, and I need not get up early. I remembered that in our last fuck I had not used the savior sponge, but it gave me no cause for alarm, it being a well attested fact that the last few spends of a man who has fucked all night, are not at all prolific.

The next day all Fackabad was electrified by hearing that Doctor Lavie had been ordered off at once to Benares. Everybody gave Colonel Selwyn the credit of having got this done, but the Colonel and Mrs. Selwyn, whilst not unwilling to be considered as the authors of his banishment, gave me the real credit. Old Bridges held his tongue. Nothing could have been kinder or more grateful than the conduct of the Selwyns in this business. They insisted on my renewing my old former intimacy, and in order to be near one another, Fanny and I agreed to recommence our studies. Oh! those happy days! Those still more blissful nights! No one but Sugdaya knew it, and Fanny came and slept with me almost every night, and we lived by night perfect husband and wife. There was just enough danger to make our intimacy spicy and piquant, but Sugdaya was so clever, so watchful, that we were never once incommoded. Yes! at first no one knew it but Sugdaya, and the only one who discovered it afterwards kept the secret locked up for use in her bosom, until the moment came when she could profit by it.

The Colonel continued fucking Mrs. Soubratie very comfortably in my house, where in the spare room next to my bedroom I had a special bedstead for him and his dusky concubine. So papa and daughter got their greens regularly, and all went on as tranquilly and as happily as could be. But alas! a terrible crisis overhung this happy family. I have spoken of Mrs. Selwyn's delicate health. About July she began to fade rapidly. The close, hot atmosphere of the rains, with its accompanying relaxing efforts, pulled her down, hand over hand. To the terrible grief of her husband and children, she breathed her last. That night, by the most extraordinary good fortune, Fanny was not with me. The only night that she had not come over for weeks. Thus did Venus watch over the safety of her tender adorers.

I will pass over that sad time during which I was for a period deprived of my Fanny's company, but it did not last long and once more we were united.

But the poor Colonel, I grieve to say, took to driving away his cares, as so many do, by the aid of the bottle. For some weeks even he did not come over to fuck Mrs. Soubratie. The loss of his wife brought to his memory the many years of sweetest happiness he had had with her and he used to speak to me of the grief it gave him to think that he should have committed adultery, and with a black woman too, during Mrs. Selwyn's last year of life. This stung his conscience. But I knew that a man with such balls as he had could not long remain a monk and little by little I cheered him up, until desire returned, he once more made Mrs. Soubratie happy, and drew upon his storehouse of happiness between her luscious thighs.

Of Mabel's pranks I have hardly time to speak. She used to implore me to fuck her. She would use every possible inducement, but I was too fond of Fanny to wish to give her a rival, especially as her affectionate passion for me seemed to increase with our intercourse. I had what I loved, a charming girl, all mine, to be my companion by day and by night. Mabel could make my prick stand indeed, and I would willingly, gladly, have fucked her but for Fanny. Little by little Fanny was taking Louie's place in my heart, and she wisely hid all signs of jealousy of Louie, if indeed she felt any. We both lived in the present hour, it was so happy, so genial and neither of us looked ahead. If we regretted anything, it was having lost so many months, and weeks and days, when we might have enjoyed one another as we did now, but, if such thoughts entered our minds they simply served to make us all the more determined to lose time no more.

About the time that the Colonel recommenced fucking the, to him, delightful cunt of Mrs. Soubratie, another death at Fackabad caused a change in his world affairs. Our "Brigadier" Colonel Wilson, suddenly left this for the next world, and Colonel Selwyn, from temporary commandant of the station, was appointed, not long afterwards, "Brigadier" vice Wilson, deceased. This was a capital stroke of luck for me, for Major Mortimer, the station staff officer, son-in-law to Colonel Wilson, had to go home to attend to his late father-in-Law's property, to look after his wife's interests, and I was, through Colonel Selwyn's means, and by his recommendations, appointed acting staff officer. But for my darling Fanny's sweet cunt, I do not think I should have got this appointment, not that the Colonel thought me in the least unfit for the office, but Fanny turned his thoughts to me and gently but persistently urged that I was the one who should get the post, though, by rights, someother officer who had been longer in India than I should have had it. But you see, dear reader, that the sweet delights I gave Fanny, through her charming little cunt, made her very solicitous about me and "Amor vicit omnia" in this instance. So, my soldier readers, if you want to get good appointments through your Colonel, fuck his daughter well, as I fucked my darling Fanny. Really and truly, all joking apart, this appointment was very pleasant. I had no longer to command my company. I had nothing to do with my regiment as an officer of it in the way of duty. I had therefore no morning parades, no drills, nothing to lug me out of bed at ungodly hours in the morning. I only attended general parades when the Colonel did. I had a good deal of signing my name to letters, etc., prepared by my clerks, but as everything was in good order the work was light. The emolument of my office did not matter much, as I had no need of money, having plenty of my own; for all that the extra rupees were not by any means a nuisance to receive. Darling Fanny profited by my not having to go to parade. Some mornings when we had slept later than usual it had happened that she had had to run home without her daybreak fuck; now she always had one and sometimes two, and she was just as ardent and eager for them as ever my sweet Louie had been. Oh! I was really very happy and contented.

But, although no real harm was done, yet a circumstance occurred which might have brought all this happiness to a disastrous end.

Colonel Selwyn's command comprised all the army, not only at Fackabad but also several other stations where there were detachments of troops. Amongst these was Rampur, some seventy miles off, and to be reached only by Dak Gharry.

One evening early in October, that is just a year since I had first seen my darling's cunt for the first time, and since Amy had been buggered, the Colonel electrified Fanny and rather astonished me, who had no notion of his intentions, by saying that he thought he would go, in a couple of days time, and commence his inspection of the troops at Rampur and that he would take Fanny with him.

"Oh! Papa! but I would much rather not go!" cried poor Fanny, looking at me with an aggrieved and startled face, "could you not take Amy?"

The Colonel, who had not yet drank enough brandy and soda to be fuddled, looked rather angrily at Fanny.

"No! I said you were to accompany me, Fanny! And I shall not take Amy! I don't like to be dictated to by my daughters!"

"I did not mean to dictate, Papa," urged poor Fanny, who struggled visibly to restrain an outburst of temper, "but I should really be obliged if you would let me remain here and if you would take Amy or Mabel instead. Come, there's a dear, good, kind papa. Do!"

Now the Colonel was a weak man, and therefore obstinate. He was offended at Fanny's outburst, and he had got into a sudden rage.

He looked black as thunder and roared at Fanny, "Miss Fanny! I have said that you will go with me! Let me hear no more about it!"

He turned his eyes to me, and for a moment I wondered had he any suspicions as to the very intimate terms Fanny and I were one. Yet how could he have discovered them so suddenly? I was mistaken however.

"Miss Selwyn," said I, seeing Fanny ready to cry with vexafon, "Do you know I rather envy you? I hear that Rampur is a very pretty place, and that the road there takes you through some very lovely scenery though it is all plains. I only wish the Colonel would take me too, as his staff officers. "

"Well, Devereaux, so I would, but for that—confounded new order which requires special application to be made for permission to take a staff officer with one when on these irregular inspections. I am afraid you must wait a little longer. But I will take Fanny."

His voice had lost its angry tone and if by chance Fanny's reluctance had brought his angry mind within a measurable distance of suspicion my little speech had turned the current of his thoughts in another direction. Fanny looked at me with expressions of dismay, but wisely held her tongue.

Two hours afterwards, when she had assisted me in offering up that incense so sweet to our revered Goddess Venus, and so delicious to the Priest and Priestess, she poured forth her griefs in my bosom. She would be a week away from her adored Charlie, perhaps ten days. Fancy ten days, ten nights without even one solitary fuck! And her usual monthly "illness" would be due about the time she got back to Fackabad, and there would be a further put off of the sweetest pleasure she knew in the world. What would she do with herself at Rampur? Oh! no matter who was there, or how nice they might be, no one could make up for the absence of her Charlie, her own, own love, and lover! Poor little Fanny! She did indeed love me, and I did indeed love her. There was more than mere animal affection between us, though in truth her cunt and my prick and balls were extremely strong links in the sweet chain which bound us together. Well, had we been married, people would have said, "Oh! how they love!" But not being married, I expect good people who read this will say, "What disgusting animals!"

There was living in the compound next to mine the Protestant Padre of Fackabad, one Mr. Corbett, a married man with a very amiable and young not too strait laced wife. These people were great friends of the Selwyn's and Mrs. Corbett, who knew I was fond of Fanny, often joked me about her. I had even "confessed" to her that I admired Fanny so much that if there was no Mrs. Devereaux, I should be very much inclined to ask Fanny to become that lady. But long practice had made me a consummate actor, and Mrs. Corbett, without thinking me a saint, never suspected that the cunt she knew I must fuck (she was a woman of the world), whilst Louie's was not available, lay between Fanny's thighs of snow. No, she fancied that I relieved my necessities between some brown thighs, and more than hinted that Sugdaya owned them. I rather encouraged the idea, and if ever I had cause to mention Sugdaya, I spoke of her with that apparent consciousness that made Mrs. Corbett more certain than ever that I did fuck Sugdaya regularly. So we were both contented.

With the Corbetts then Colonel Selwyn arranged to leave his children during his absence with Fanny at Rampur. Their house was large enough to accommodate them easily, and no country in the world makes such temporary movements more easy to be performed than India. All that was—required was that a few bedsteads should be carried over, and the thing was done.

The last night had to be a very short one for Fanny and me. Her father intended starting at four in the morning, and Fanny had to leave me at half past two. She was ravenous. In the few hours she still had to enjoy my prick she lost not a moment, and the interludes between act and act only lasted just so long as it took the pretty hands to operate the resurrection of my prick, a thing extremely easily performed, I am glad to say. I may tell my fair readers here that as a little boy, when I first began to understand why I bad a little prick and girls had little cunts, I had marveled at the story of Hercules and wondered how he had taken fifty maidenheads and put fifty virgins in the family way in one night, could be considered labor. Well, I had had no practical experience then, but later I learnt from women of all classes whom I fucked, that I was more abundantly blessed than any man they had ever met in having an unconquerable prick, and a pair of balls which never ran completely dry. I do not mention this to boast, but only to say how thankful I am that such has been my lot. So poor Fanny left me with her sweet cunt throbbing with pleasure, and her heart grieved to think that it would be perhaps nearly a fortnight before it would throb again from being well fucked by me.

For my part I was as grieved as Fanny. I loved that girl.

She was a second edition of Louie. I never could have enough of her, by day or night. I was certain that her absence would be as grievous to me as my parting with Louie was. It took me a long time to feel desire again after I had left Louie, as the readers of my first series will remember, and I felt very nearly the same now that Fanny was gone. There was this difference, however, when I left my Louie I had an idea it might be years before I should again know the glorious pleasure of fucking her, and fucking her meant in my mind, then, fucking at all. I really and truly thought that I had done with women, i.e., all other women than my Louie. My readers may remember the soft influence of Mademoiselle de Maupin, and the realization of that beauteous power in the person of the lovely and delicious and really lascivious Lizzie Wilson. Her cunt proved its power, and the far distant one, between poor Louie's thighs, no longer traumatized over my, till then, moral prick and modest balls. Well, then, I did look forward this time to some more luscious fucking, at no very remote day, for Fanny's dearest little cunt would surely again be mine within a fortnight, to caress, to kiss, to fuck to my heart's content. Still it was a grievous annoyance to lose it, even for that short time.

The day passed wearily, far more so than I anticipated it would. My thoughts were all with Fanny. I knew she went away grieving, and all my sympathies were with her. I went to bed early, hoping to get some sleep, and so pass away as many hours in an unconscious state as possible.

I don't know how long I had been thus sleeping, when I woke, feeling my nose gently pinched, and—there was Sugdaya!

The first idea that came into my mind was that Sugdaya, mindful of my little speech to her on the first night that I fucked Fanny, had taken advantage of my words literally and that Fanny having left Fackabad, though only temporarily, she had come to be fucked herself. The dear reader will remember that I had proposed to Sugdaya to fuck her whenever Fanny went away. I meant for good, and now I imagined that Sugdaya wanted to take my words literally.

"Well, Sugdaya, what is it?"

"Sahib I Miss Fanny Baba wants me to ask you to come over to her. She is in bed and wants master!"

"Good God! Has any accident then happened, Sugdaya? What made the Colonel come back? I hope no one is hurt I How is Miss Fanny Baba?"

"There has been no accident, Sahib!" said Sugdaya laughing, "no one has been hurt. Miss Fanny Baba is quite well but her cunt is hungry for this," and she took possession of my prick. I did not repel her. I never repel a pretty woman when she takes hold of me there.

"I'll come at once, Sugdaya! But tell me, why did the Colonel come back?"

"He has only come back for the night, Sahib!" said Sugdaya, sitting on the edge of the bed and gently moving her hand, in the most delicious manner, up and down my prick; I lay on my back and let her. It was so pleasant and I wanted to hear particulars. "They got as far as Dharra, that is the first stage, you know, Sahib!—Ah! What a handsome, grand prick you have, Sahib!—No wonder Miss Fanny Baba loves it I And grand balls too! Some day, you know, Sahib, you must fuck me, you know you promised!"

"So I will, surely, Sugdaya. But take care. Don't make me spend."

"No, Sahib!" said poor Sugdaya with a sigh, "Miss Fanny Baba's cunt must make it do that! I'll play with your balls only," and she began those caresses with the finger tips, so exquisitely delicious.

"All right, Sugdaya. That is very nice. Now tell me, what did they do at Dharra?"

"Oh! Sahib! There were no fresh horses ready. The Colonel Sahib wanted to go on with those which had come with him from Fackabad, but the hairy man would not.

Then they found it would not be possible for them to leave Dharra that day, and the Colonel Sahib waited, and when the horses were rested came back slowly to Fackabad. He and Miss Fanny Baba will try again tomorrow morning now! Come Sahib. Poor Miss Fanny Baba wants you badly."

I jumped up, fastened my pajamas, felt Sugdaya's nice little brown cunt and bubbies, kissed her, sham fucked her a little, and saw plainly that I had only to say, "I'll fuck you instead, Sugdaya!" and she would gladly have taken Fanny's place in my bed; but although all this sporting was dangerous, I had no idea of being unfaithful to Fanny, and with steps as noiseless and swift as possible, Sugdaya and I went, hand in hand, over to the Colonel's bungalow.

Before Sugdaya let me in by the bath room door she said, in a low tone, "Don't speak to Miss Fanny Baba, Sahib. The Colonel Sahib is not sleeping well, and he might hear you. For that reason, too, Miss Fanny Baba has only a small light in her room. Just go in—get right into bed with her, and fuck her quietly and nicely."

This was the very first time I had ever been in the Colonel's bungalow to fuck Fanny in her own bed. I had fucked her in the compound and, on one or two occasions which I have not mentioned, I had fucked her in the drawing room, taking her on my knees, but I had never fucked her in her own bed, and the idea seemed delicious to me. Though no longer a virgin herself, her bed was virgin, and she seemed to me like taking her maidenhead a second time. I went into her room then, palpitating with desire, and with my prick as vigorous as if the long week or ten days had passed during which I had expected to be a widower.

The room was all but pitch dark. There was a light indeed, but so covered that not even its miserable feeble rays could fall on the bed which I dimly saw, and on which I could just discern the figure of a girl, who looked naked. I could not distinguish any features, only general forms, but Fanny's bush struck me as looking much darker in this darkness than usual. Sugdaya led me still by the hand, and when at the bedside whispered in lowest tones:

"Don't make any noise, Sahib. I will go and lie at the Colonel Sahib's door."

And she left me and glided out into the pitch darkness of the other room.

Delighted to be with Fanny again, so much sooner than I expected, I gently got into her bed, fearing to make it creak, but it was firm, now at any rate, for it made no sound. A gentle but nervously hurried hand took possession of my prick, whilst I drew honey from her warm lips and pressed the lively bubbies I found one after the other. I longed to speak, but the first attempt I made was met with a warning "hush!" from her, whilst a gentle little pull at my burning prick told me what the darling girl wanted it to block, in silence, to the equally burning little cunt, of which the soft lips were already moistened in anticipation of the delight it expected. Carefully making no creak occur from the bedstead, I gently turned over on to the dear girl, whom I could feel panting with hot desire, and taking my place between her exquisite thighs I drew my quivering prick against that throbbing and excited cunt, enraptured at the idea that I was now at last fucking her in her bed. Fanny kissed me as though in an ecstasy, my prick glided in, doffing his cap as he did so, and then to my complete surprise was met by a complete denial of further ingress.

At first I imagined that Fanny was practicing on me. I had taught her how to imitate a virgin bride, and by straightening her legs stiffly, raising her belly as high as possible, and withdrawing her cunt from the invading prick, as well as by taking a slightly crooked position sideways, she could make it difficult for her husband, when she had one, to get into her. But on putting my hand to feel how her thighs were placed, I found her knees were bent. I could not detect any willful upraising of the belly, nor any refusal of her darling cunt. I tried again. No go. There was a real obstruction. What could it be from? I tried again. There was the same result. I began to feel hot with shame, and wondered could my prick possibly be failing me. Oh! no! It was as stiff as when I first had Fanny. As stiff as it always had been when between the delicious thighs of a girl! I quietly and suddenly slipped away, and off of Fanny, and put an enquiring finger up her cunt. I imagined that she might have manufactured a savior sponge, for Sugdaya had not asked me to bring mine, and I had forgotten entirely to do so, and that this caused the obstruction. Fanny let me feel her without making the least objection and—I felt—a maiden-head! Oh! There was no doubt about it. In a moment the idea flashed upon me that it was not Fanny, but Mabel. I strained my eyes, but could not make out the face, so close to me, but yet so hidden by the darkness.

"It is not Fanny!" I said in my lowest tones. "Is it you—Mabel?"

My question was answered by a peal of loud, merry laughter, which considering that I still believed the Colonel to be in the house, and just across the drawing room, astonished me for two reasons—first, it was not Fanny's laughter, nor Mabel's—but Amy's—and secondly it was so noisy!

Sugdaya came running in. When she saw me with my finger in Amy's cunt, which she easily saw by the lamp she carried, and my look of astonishment, and Amy writhing in uncontrollable laughter, she joined in and rolled about in excessive merriment!

"Ah! Sahib! Sahib! What a lucky man you are, that all the Misses Baba think that there is only one Sahib that can fuck, and that one Captain Devereaux Sahib. Well, Miss Amy Baba. Did he fuck you nicely?"

"No," cried Amy, "he can't do it."

"Can't do it," cried I in anger, for I felt I had been most cruelly deceived, "can't do it, Miss Amy. I'll show you that I can do it and well, too!"

And so saying, I again plumped on top of her, inserted my indignant prick, and stretching Amy in such a manner that she could not possibly escape me, I forced my excited weapon as hard as I could against the rash maidenhead, which had by the voice of its owner sneered at me.

"Oh-h-h-h! Captain Dev-er-eaux! Oh-h-h-h, for God's sake! Oh! You are killing me—you—are—killing me! Ah-h-h-h! Oh! Oh! Oh! Oh-h-h!"

It was a tough job. Amy's maidenhead was thrice as strong as Fanny's, and much more unyielding than the majority of those it has been my excellent good fortune to take. And I did not feel tender minded toward her. I am afraid I was more rough than I should have been but oh! Had she not deceived me and robbed her sister? So without mercy I went on plunging and plunging, ruthlessly grinding and tearing my way up, until that really sweet little cunt was filled, and stretched, to the uttermost, and my balls rattled against her bottom, just at the exact spot where the Afghan's had first had that pre-eminent happiness.

But Amy, though she said I hurt her dreadfully forcing my prick in so roughly, was by nature voluptuous like Fanny. Her "Ah! Now that's nice. Ah! Do that again. Oh my! Oh! Captain Devereaux! How you tickle!" told me that fuck, and, my temper having been satisfied by my first burst of anger, I fucked her as sweetly as I could, and was rewarded by her spending copiously, and ravishingly, at the exact moment that I inundated her cunt with the first boiling torrent which had ever been poured by man into it.

Sugdaya stood by, holding the lamp, and watching, with keen and voluptuous interest, the real combat' between my prick and Amy's cunt, and when she perceived by the cessation of my movements, and the way in which Amy was holding her breath, that I was inundating the shrine, she gave vent to the prolonged "oh-h-h-h!" as though she envied the girl who was getting such delight.

"Now! Miss Amy Baba! Now! You have been well fucked!" cried she.

"Yes. I suppose I have," said Amy, in a kind of dreamy manner, usual with her when her thoughts were much occupied; then waking up as if from a trance, she clasped me tight, and gave me kiss after kiss.

"Ah! that is all very well, Amy," I said, "but I have a bone to pick with Sugdaya and you. A very nice pair you are. Do you know what you have done?"

"Yes, dear," said Amy, laughing, and closing her legs over me, for I had commenced to withdraw my prick from her strongly palpitating cunt, "I do. I laid a very neat trap and caught a very splendid bird, and I have him now in my cage."

"It's all very well, Amy. You have won this round—but oh!" and I felt my voice quiver with the anguish I really felt, "you do not know what you have done! Here! Let me go!"

"No, indeed," said Amy, folding me tighter and tighter, and forcing her cunt about my prick, which had been half pulled out of it. "No! I won't let you go. You are my property now, Captain Devereaux. I have fairly caught you—to think of letting you go yet! Oh dear no! You will have to fuck me now as often as you have fucked Fanny. And as she has had you ever since last March, you will have to pay me a good deal of attention, before I shall be even with Fanny."

"Oh Amy!" I cried, bitterly, for I assure you, dear reader, much as I love fucking, and well worth fucking as Amy was, and still is, I felt that I had been betrayed, quite and perfectly innocent indeed, doing what I now had done, would come nigh to breaking Fanny's heart. Now I loved Fanny. I was passionately devoted to her, and not for all the cunts in the world did I feel inclined to outrage her by fucking her sister, before her own sweet cunt could be said to have ceased throbbing from the very recent fucking it had had from my prick. I did not desire Amy. The stand I had, when I got into bed with her, was not for her cunt, nice as it was, but for Fanny. But oh! Amy! I'll tell you what you have done! You have broken poor Fanny's heart!"

"Pooh! ha! ha! ha!" laughed Amy. "What do I care? Broken her heart indeed. Oh ! Poor Fanny! Much I pity her! What more right has she to you, I should like to know, than I have, or Mabel? She is not your wife. But to hear her talk, and to hear you, too, Captain Devereaux, one would think there was no Lome in the world. I tell you I have every bit as much right to you as Fanny has, and mind, if you refuse to fuck me, you will never fuck her again. I can tell you!"

This thrust I felt was no empty one. Amy had once said she could not imagine herself going to bed with a man, and that for herself to be stark naked in the presence of a stark naked man would be something too horrible to contemplate! Here she was, however, stark naked in my stark naked arms, and the will to fuck was all on her side, not mine. It was plain all her former ideas had become completely changed; and her whole tone and manner was that of a strong-minded woman, who knew what she was about, and that she could compel, if she could not gain her ends by anymore gentle way. Unfortunately it lay in her power to put an end to the delicious liaison between Fanny and me. I lay quietly in her arms, thinking how I should escape this terrible dilemma.

"How do you know that I fuck Fanny, Amy?"

"How do I know? Now, Captain Devereaux! Do you take me for a complete fool? Do you think that Fanny could leave this room, with me sleeping in it, night after night, without my knowing it sooner or later? Do you think I cannot put two and two together as well as yourself? Why! I have known it these five months at least. I taxed Fanny with it, and she could not deny it, and she told me herself, too, about how you fucked her twice, that evening of her birthday, when she and you left us playing cards. Well! I don't care! I thought her a fool for her pains, but by degrees I began to think it must be as nice as Sugdaya has always told me it was to be fucked, and the moment I heard that Fanny was to go to Rampur with Papa, I laid a plan with Sugdaya to catch you! Ah! now, my boy! You wanted me to go to Rampur, but here I am. You wanted Fanny's cunt, did you? Well! Now you are in mine, and I think mine must be every bit as nice as Fanny's. I have better and bigger breasts, too, and more hair than she has, and J don't think you have any reason to complain of Fanny either."

I saw it was no use trying to urge a higher tone with Amy. It was of no use talking to her of love. Fucking was all she could see in my intimacy with Fanny, nothing nobler.

"So you see, my dear Captain Devereaux, you will now have two wives in India, and one at home, perhaps three wives in India, because Mabel, I know, wants to be fucked too and you will have to do it."

"I will not!" I cried passionately and angrily.

"Oh I dear, yes you will. The thing is in a nutshell.

Do you really love Fanny? Are you really so fond of her as you say?"

"Oh, Amy! You don't know how fond."

"Very well! Then I suppose you would be awfully sorry if anything happened to prevent you fucking her again."

"Don't speak of it!"

"Oh! but I will. I have only some night to pretend to be ill, call Papa and let him see Fanny's bed empty, and Sugdaya not to be found in the house, and I think Fanny will never see your prick again, Captain Devereaux."

I groaned.

"What an ass a man is!" cried Amy, half angrily, half laughingly. "I should like to know who has such a grand chance of having three pretty girls all to himself, all ladies of his harem. And the idea shocks him. Now! see, Captain Devereaux, and do be careful what you say. Is it a bargain? Do you promise to fuck Mabel and me whenever we like? For if you don't you may say goodbye to Fanny."

Now I had had a good deal of experience with girls and women, and have often been helped into a nice little cunt by the owner of another, but I never was treated in this way before. The idea that if I did not fuck Amy or Mabel I should lose Fanny was paradoxical! I felt a child in Amy's arms, and that I had learned my lesson wrong. I thought I should lose Fanny if I fucked her sisters, not if I did not do so. It seemed I was all wrong. Yet a little reflection told me that the laws of ordinary life did not obtain in this instance, and, that to keep possession of Fanny's dearest cunt, I must fuck those of her sisters also!

"I think you very hard hearted, Amy. I see I have nothing better to do than surrender, but, when the Devil drives, needs must"

"Thank you for the compliment," laughed Amy. "Well, the devil in this instance flatters herself that she has a very nice cunt, and desires her slave to amuse her for the rest of this night!"

All this conversation having taken place in English was unintelligible to Sugdaya, who looked on with surprised and perplexed eyes, but when Amy told her what the result of the conversation had been, that not only had I consented to go on fucking her, but that I would fuck Mabel, too, she was delighted, and said:

"Oh! sahib! Now I am very glad indeed. Won't Miss Mabel Baba be glad to hear it, too!"

I begged her to go over to my bungalow and bring my enema and savior sponge, and I asked Amy to get up and let me assist her to wash her cunt, which required it sadly. Sugdaya left and Amy rose. Of course the sheet was a sea of blood. Amy was rather frightened when she saw it, but I comforted he by saying that any girl, who has really lost her maidenhood, ever did so without losing a lot of blood also. Whether the tone of my voice was more gentle than it had been, or whether my comforting words struck a chord of gratitude in her heart, I don't know, but she put her arms around my waist and lifted her face up and kissed me affectionately.

"Ah! Captain Devereaux, now let us be real good friends, we need not quarrel because we fuck, need we?"

The absurdity of such a question struck me with all its force, and I could not help laughing heartily. I looked at Amy. Naked, as she was, I could see all her form, and person, perfectly, and she was a really splendid girl. Her hair, both of her head and bush, was darker in color than Fanny's, and very much more abundant. Her arms, thighs and legs, as full, as white, and as well formed. Her waist was more slender, her hips wider than those of her sister; and her bubbies, beautiful round, full and coral tipped, were fully one-third larger. Her hands and feet were small and well shaped, and as her face was very pretty, with a fine oval form, and with large, dark, lustrous eyes, she was altogether very desirable, and formed a fine addition to my "Harem." The regret I so sincerely felt for having been made to be unfaithful to Fanny began to die away at the sight of all these beauties, and Amy received caresses from my hands, and kisses from my lips, which made her as proud as could be, for she rightly judged, that had not her beauty been very real, she would hardly have got off so soon for her cruel treatment of me.

"Come!" said she. "Come, Captain Devereaux, Help me to wash myself, and let Sugdaya find us fucking when she comes back."

The ablution was quickly performed. Amy had never seen my prick and balls before, nor indeed those of any man, though she had had a very big one up her bottom once! She therefore delayed a little whilst washing me, and thoroughly enjoyed the sight and feeling of those treasures.

Sugdaya returned just in time to see me getting "home" well, for the first time, and consequently was an excited spectator of the first good will fuck I gave Amy. Like the voluptuous minded creature she was, she greatly added to my pleasure by manipulating my balls, which she took possession of from between my thighs, behind. Amy seemed frantic with pleasure, Every stroke I gave her threw her into ecstasies. I think Mrs. Selwyn must have had a voluptuous nature, and I know that the Colonel dearly loved fucking. Certainly Fanny and Amy had inherited their parent's disposition of sensuousness, and it was my extreme good fortune to have been the first to inspire their loving cunts with desire, and make them throb and over flow with pleasure.

Once more, good friends, Amy and I passed the rest of that night in the most delicious manner possible. Long before the hour, four o'clock, at which she had to leave to go to the Corbett's bungalow, whence she had come, we had become very confidential, and I had managed to extract a promise from her, that she would not insist upon my fucking Mabel yet awhile. I pleaded hard. I said that poor Fanny might forgive me having fucked her, Amy, but that it would be almost too much to expect her to sit down contented and her thinking that two more cunts were to share my prick with hers. But Amy was determined that nothing should be done outside the strict bargain and she only agreed to this arrangement on the understanding that I was to fuck her every night until Fanny returned. I willingly agreed to this. It was agreed that I should meet her where we then were, every night at ten o'clock, for the Corbett's being early people, and going to bed at nine regularly, Amy could easily keep that appointed hour. Sugdaya was sorry for Mabel, but agreed not to tell her yet of my having agreed to fuck her; she only hoped I would not delay doing so too long.

And now I have to relate an incident which even now, several years since it occurred, makes me shiver to think of it. I had nothing on but my thin jersey, pajamas and light slippers, and Sugdaya and Amy walked as far as the entrance to my compound with me, and after some caresses and kisses hot and strong on either side, Amy, in happy, good natured contempt for the proprieties, even requesting me to stroke Sugdaya's nice brown cunt, before kissing her for the last time! With my fingers still throbbing from these exquisite contacts with two such blooming cunts, I walked rapidly up my avenue, not thinking of anything but what I now considered my extreme good luck, for I had had a really delicious night between Amy's fairest thighs, and had enjoyed so much undeniable pleasure, both from her cunt and from her curiously improper mind, that for the present, at all events, my sorrow on Fanny's account was considerably deadened.

But all of a sudden I felt something hard under my feet and, as if instantaneously, my leg tide round and round up to the knee, by a rope which tightened and tightened, until it caused me considerable pain. The thing was instantaneous. I had no time for reflection, yet Providence made me halt as though shot, and prevented my raising my foot. Had I done so, Amy would never have been fucked by me, nor Fanny, nor would Mabel, Sugdaya, or Mrs. Paul—but halt! I must not tell all my secrets out at once. Well, I never would have fucked again in the world. For I had trodden, as good luck would have it, on the head of a very large cobra. I say by good luck, for had I trodden on it on any other part I should have been inevitably bitten, and in a couple of hours, or three at most, I should have been a dead man. With intense fright and that ungovernable rage which ensues, I ground that unlucky serpent's head until it was nothing but pulp, and then, and not till then, did I attempt to remove it from my leg, which, even in death, it grasped as though it were a vise. Covered with a cold perspiration and trembling with excitement due to shock, and not denying the fright I had received, I ran to my bungalow and right glad was I when I got well within its safe walls, and there I examined the reptile which had so miserably perished, because it had so foolishly crossed my path, but which might have put an end to me as easily as I had done to it but for the upholding hand of a merciful providence.

Sleep was out of the question for a long time, and it was broad daylight before its refreshing hand touched me. My thoughts ran on Fanny and the awful risks she had run twice almost every night, since she had been in the habit of coming over to my bungalow to be fucked by me. She must never do so again. How lucky it really was that Amy had entrapped me. There would be no reason why I should not go myself now every night to the Colonel's bungalow, Amy would not be in the way! I should fuck Fanny and her, turn and turn about, and there would be no danger to either of them from snakes. It is true I should have to make my peace with Fanny, but I had no doubt, at that moment, of being able to do so. Meanwhile I must warn Amy, who would run risks just as great, going to her father's bungalow from the Corbetts to be fucked.

It was late, about five o'clock in the afternoon, before I went over to the Corbetts to see Amy, and Mrs. Corbett after a cordial reception of me, told me in the presence of Amy that I must really scold that young lady, as she had been extraordinarily lazy, not having got out of bed until nearly four o'clock. Amy, who blushed a little, excused herself on the ground that she never could sleep for the first few nights in a strange bed, upon which, Mrs. Corbett, looking significantly at me, said that her husband would be delighted to find that this was the case, as men loved to talk a good deal to their wives in bed, especially when they were first married. We all laughed. Amy took the chaff very well and rather astonished Mrs. Corbett by her aplomb. After some more conversation, I proposed a stroll around the garden to see Mrs. Corbett's vines, and as that lady wished to continue a novel she was reading, she did not volunteer to go herself.

"Oh! Captain Devereaux!" said Amy when we were alone, "I can hardly walk. You stretched the joints of my thighs last night to such an extent and I feel so stiff and regularly ground about the lower part of my body."

"Does your cunt feel sore today, dear?"

"No! not at all! Oh! how you did hurt me the first time!

And how delicious it was everytime after that! I do so wish it was ten o'clock. Mind, don't keep me waiting. You won't do that, now, will you, Captain Devereaux"

I told Amy that I was not in the least attempting to evade my promise, but that I really thought that this walk in the night extremely dangerous on account of snakes. At first she indignantly refused to believe that I had trodden on one, saying it was very curious that Fanny should have never even seen or heard of one, and that she believed it was a trumped up story, and that the truth was I wanted to get out of fucking her.

"But if I have to come to you, I will, Captain Devereaux!

You don't know how angry I am with you for never having offered to fuck me, all these months. What do you see finer in Fanny than in me, I should like to know! I know I consider myself better than she is in every way. Now tell me, you have fucked me, am I not as nice as Fanny? Has she a sweeter or nicer cunt than I have? I have better bubbies I know."

Ah! Amy dear, don't talk that way! If I could come and fuck you in Mrs. Corbett's house, I would. But I really am alarmed at your having to walk at night to your own house to meet me."

"Then I'll come to yours if you prefer it."

"That is just as dangerous—more so, in fact. My compound has a bad name for snakes, as you know."

"A very proper place for you, Captain Devereaux! I call you nothing more or less than a deceitful serpent."

No, she would risk everything. She did not believe in the cobra, and she was determined that I should fuck her every night. She threatened to send Mabel to me as soon as I got home, if I did not stop at once all reference to danger.

"Amy, do you think I have an objection to fucking you? Do you think I would rather not—or that I don't think you worth it?"

"Something like that idea comes into my head I must say!"

There was a stable in which was a lot of grass freshly cut for the Padre's horses. I took Amy in and looking around that there was no one watching us, laid her on the grass. She laughed and clapped her hands and then, undoing my braces and trousers, I turned up her petticoats and had a truly delicious fuck. Amy went almost mad with pleasure, and when it was all over, she let me do the glove stretcher to her cunt, to let out the dangerous spend, and when I had wiped her between the thighs with my pocket handkerchief, she kissed me most sweetly, saying she saw now I had no personal objection to her and that I was really not a bad fellow.

"A personal objection, Amy," said I, buttoning my prick and balls away out of sight, "why you know I think you a splendid girl, and well worth going thousands of miles for to get at, but you must remember that Fanny is almost a wife to me, and I never had the slightest intention of being unfaithful to her."

"Then the sooner you see things in the proper light the better for you, Captain Devereaux! Fanny is not your wife. You have no business to love her. For the matter of that you have no more business to fuck her than to fuck me, but as you have chosen to do that, and Fanny thinks it nice, I choose that you should fuck me also, for; to tell you the truth, I think it something more than nice. It's simply rapturous! Oh! don't be a stupid man! Now, are not two cunts better than one?"

I laughed. I could not help it.

"Well, Amy, only help me to defend myself against Fanny and get her to see things with your eyes and I will prove to you that I do think two cunts better than one."

"All right. I'll easily do that. Now come, let us go back to Mrs. Corbett's, and mind you are not a minute later than ten o'clock over there."

All this part of my history is still painful for me to remember. I do not deny the sweetness of Amy's really delicious little cunt. It was of the very finest sort, and I had the most real pleasure fucking it. It had the advantage of being a new one for me. It had been deflowered by me. It belonged to as pretty a girl as there was in India. It was extremely sensitive to pleasure and was a perfect fountain under my vigorous treatment of it, but, alas for the buts, Oh! how much more delightful to me it would have been had I not been so entrapped into it. I could now understand what a woman feels like, who has been fucked against her will and without her consent. Over and above these latter feelings was the absolute certainty of the pain, the mental and heartfelt agony Fanny would surely experience, when she came to hear, that within twenty-four hours of my being between her thighs, I had passed between those of her sister, and that, night after night, I had fucked Amy.

Evidently from Amy's account, Fanny had confided in her, and months had passed since that confidence had first been given. Once it may have been enforced confidence, but at any rate Fanny had the right to expect that Amy would not take advantage of it now, at this late period, when she might have profited by it months ago. Poor Fanny had gone away to Rampur, sure of two things, the fidelity of her Charlie and the faithfulness of her sister. I trust therefore that my gentle readers will excuse me from dwelling on the events of the next six nights, during which I fucked Amy regularly, and really well, in Fanny's bed. I had pleasure—a great deal—but it was mingled with pain, the pain of the heart. No more cobras invited destruction under my feet, or threatened me, and Amy utterly disbelieved my story. I, however, had the cobra carefully bottled up in spirits, to show Fanny, and Amy, too, if she cared to come by day light to my bungalow.

Amy certainly gave me no rest. I don't think she could know it was possible to exhaust a man. Feeling herself always ready to be fucked, she regarded the stand of a prick as quite voluntary on the part of the lover. Thanks to the splendid constitution I had been born with, and the powers which, from what women have told me, I fancy very few men are endowed with, I was quite "able" for Amy, and never disappointed her a single time. In fact, I believe, she would have been the first to say, "I've had enough," had we continued this night after night fucking. Hence it was that she did not mind sharing me with Fanny, and wished, really wished, me to fuck Mabel too.

She knows different now. She is married now and has discovered that there are men and men. In her last letter to me, received not a week ago, she speaks very penitently of the way she treated me at Fackabad, and says she had no idea then of what a treasure she had in me. It is very nice to be told this now but I did not admire being by her as a complete tool at Fackabad.

The Colonel had only written once from Rampur, and Fanny not at all. I was glad and sorry she had not done so.

She told me, when she came back, that she was burning to write, but feared her father's asking questions and perhaps seeing her letter, and she said if once she began to write, she could not have kept her pen from speaking some burning words, which she was so accustomed to use, when we were in our skins together.

So she thought it best not to write except one short little note.

On the morning of the day we expected them back from Rampur, just as I was putting on my pajamas and jersey, and looking at the naked Amy, who had so cruelly robbed me of my peace, of Fanny, and her full share in future of my prick and balls, Amy said, "Oh, by the bye, Captain Devereaux! I've got something for you here."

"What is it Amy?"

"Oh! a letter from Fanny."

And she put her hand under her pillow and drew forth a little note she had put there over night and had "forgotten to give me before."

"Oh! Amy, why did you not give me this before?"

"I forgot."

"You know I love Fanny. It is cruel of you Amy."

"Pooh! What do I care. Lord, what a rage Fanny will be in when she hears the news!"

"It will break her heart."

"Fiddle-de-dee! She will roar and cry, and call me names and you too, Captain Devereaux! Oh! she will tear your eyes out!"

"I will tell her the truth, Amy, and then if she can forgive me I shall be happy—but—will she?"

"Of course she will. Bless you, I know Fanny better than you do, Captain Devereaux. She will try it on. Yes, she will try it on. She will rave, and storm, and threaten, but if you take her coolly and let her know that it is of no use crying over spilt milk, but there is more milk for her if she chooses to take it, she will quiet down fast enough. Fanny is not quite such a fool as not to know that half a loaf is better than no bread. But she is greedy. She never offered to share you with me, and now she must. It serves her right. And I am rather glad you don't like fucking me, because it serves you right too!"

"But Amy, I do like fucking you! As far as mere fucking goes you are quite as good as Fanny."

"Thank you for nothing! Mere fucking! You won't persuade me you see anything more in Fanny than a nice little cunt! I don't believe in it. No, no, Captain Devereaux! You are sore because you have to fuck me whether you like it or not. Only for that you would not be sorry to have both me and Fanny, aye, and Mabel too, and Sugdaya and every other woman in Fackabad also!"

It was no use trying to make: Amy sensible that granting all cunts to be equally delicious from a physical point of view, and all girls equally young, nice and beautiful, yet love distinguished one above all others, and her cunt is, after all, the most delicious of all. I left her in disgust, mad with myself, because I could not master my prick and because I could not help confessing that she was a perfect and exquisite poke.

On going back to my bungalow I read the precious letter from Fanny. It was full of love and happiness at the prospect of being once more in my arms. Poor, dear girl! She appeared not to have the least doubt as to Amy or anyone else occupying my thoughts during her absence. So far from imagining that I should take advantage of her being at Rampur, and endeavor to get into Amy, or Mabel, she said, in her letter, that she hoped on her return to hear that I had not forgotten that they were her sisters, and to find that I had, for her sake, been kind to them, and had been to visit them at Mrs. Corbett's, where she imagined they must have been very lonely without her and papa.

This letter gave me the greatest possible pain. What would Fanny say, when she discovered the truth? It would nearly kill her! She trusted me so much and so completely. She did not dream of a rival, and she could have had no notion that she would find a most formidable rival and oppressor in Amy, her own sister. What a deep and designing game Amy had played! And how patiently had she waited until she could put her scheme into action. Herein I saw Sugdaya's hand. No one but a native, or one governed by a native, could have possessed their souls and senses in such a state of entire patience as Amy had done. For she was everything but cool and composed while I fucked her. She was such flame and fury that it was impossible to suppose that she did not enjoy to the fullest the glorious pleasures my prick and balls procured her. She must consequently have endured the most real pains of unsatisfied desire, and, Eke the Spartan boy, have suffered agonies which were eating her living flesh whilst she smiled in apparent calmness on all. I dare say it was the recollection of these poignant sufferings which made all her words and actions towards me so cruel and spiteful. However, she had been well fucked and perhaps, when I had smoothed down Fanny and calmed the storm which threatened a catastrophe, we might so manage as to all events render Amy amiable. For if Fanny, as I fully expected she would, declared she would no longer be fucked by me, I determined I would not fuck Amy anymore, and as Amy liked being well fucked so much, so very much, she might discover that any ill advised attempt to drive a man might result in a revolt, whereby her newly acquired kingdom over my prick might be lost.

Full of these thoughts tearing me I lay down, but could not sleep. Hour after hour passed away. Full daylight came after dawn, and with it, one by one, the numerous signs of life, the birds, insects, animals and men. But I heeded them little, all my thoughts were concentrated on "what will Fanny say?"

"And how shall I ever recover my position in her love and admiration?"

"The Devil take Amy and damn Sugdaya for her infamous plotting and scheming!"

A good swear relieves a man when the cause for irritation is passed and gone, but alas! no amount of cursing will soften the expected pains of approaching doom. Else mine would have obviated the misery I expected, for I swore enough to blow all misery to the winds, had the misery been tangible and not yet for to come. Fanny and the Colonel were not expected to arrive until seven in the evening and Amy and the children were not to leave the Corbett's until a little before that hour. I passed that most wretched day in writing letter after letter to Fanny trying to explain what had happened, in such a way as not to inculpate Amy anymore than possible, but yet to exculpate myself.

Needless to say all my efforts were in vain, and each letter I wrote seemed worse than the former, and all were destroyed by me. Oh! dear readers, may you never, not one of you, have reason to suffer such torture as I endured. It would not have been so bad had I deliberately and of afore thought been unfaithful to Fanny. But to have been so trapped and betrayed into doing what I really had not meant to do, was a cause of the greatest mental anguish to me. Suppose I told Fanny the exact truth, was it likely she would believe me? Would she not also say and with a great show of justice, that I need not have gone on fucking Amy? Ah! she had no prick and balls to drive her as I had It would be difficult to understand, too, that in order to keep Amy in good humor, I had to go on fucking her: and yet I felt I really had no better card to play. I could not help it if I found fucking Amy truly delicious. I dare say a girl who is raped, rather enjoys the sensation, although in her heart she may feel the deadliest enmity against the man who rapes her, because it is done without her consent. I really could not prevent my prick standing and stiffly raging when it was near Amy's cunt. A prick is like a gun. The enemy can take it and use it against its proper owner. It shoats just as straight and as hard for the one as for the other, and has no will in the matter at all. All that my prick saw in Fanny was a delicious and sweet cunt between her thighs—it saw exactly the same thing between the thighs of Amy and its one desire was to get into that one which was nearest. This is certainly not the case with most cunts. It was in Lizzie Wilson, but hers was by no means the one to give the rule. Look at Amy. Amy wanted to be tucked. Well, she had plenty of friends who would have been delighted to have fucked her, but she never hinted her desire to one of them. Look at Mabel. If anything she was worse and hotter than Amy. The reader will see in time what she did. My prick was always ready for Mabel's cunt and, but for the most determined opposition, it would have got into it. Oh! let a woman understand this: "A standing prick has no conscience!"

Everything comes to an end and that horrible day came to an end too, but not until I had at last written a little note to Fanny, in which I begged her not to come over to see me, for a very particular reason, which I could tell her as soon as I could find an opportunity on the morrow. This note I took with me to Amy, at the Corbett's, and went out into the garden together, Amy refusing to let Mabel accompany us.

"Well! you do look bad, Captain Devereaux. Are you so awfully afraid of Fanny then? You are as white as a ghost. "

"I am not afraid of Fanny, Amy. Nothing she could say to me could be half so painful as what my conscience tells me. But the fact is, I could not sleep a wink when I got home this morning."

"Ha! ha; ha! ha!" laughed Amy, as merrily and cheerfully as if I had told her something more than ordinarily pleasant and delightful. "Oh! I do like to hear that! What a fool you are, Captain Devereaux! I wonder you don't put more value on yourself. Now if I were you I should say to Fanny, if she is at all cross, look here, Fanny! You can take me or leave me—it is all one to me. I can't fuck any the more because I have two cunts instead of one to fuck. Only Amy will get all the more if you leave me."

"That would be adding insult to injury, Amy."

"Well! what of it? Is it not the truth?"

"You don't consider the pain such speaking would give poor Fanny."

"Pain! And pray did she consider what pain I suffered from her not even asking me would I like to be fucked by you when she was. Sisters should share. I only ask for my share. I don't want to take you altogether away from Fanny, but I must be fucked as well as she."

"Well, I should not be surprised if it all came to an end now."

"Why?"

"Because I expect, when Fanny hears the news, she will go into one of her dreadful states of excitement and do or say something rash before your father; and, if he hears of what has happened he will certainly take steps to prevent anymore of my fucking his daughters. He could, for instance, as easily get me sent to another station as I could get Lavie sent to Benares. Nobody need know why, but you and Fanny would have to find another beau, if fucking is all either of you wish for."

This speech made Amy thoughtful. She had entirely lost sight of the possible effects a too brilliant triumph over Fanny might have.

"That is worth thinking about, Captain Devereaux."

"It is, Amy, in all solemn earnest. Now will you do me a favor?"

"What is it?"

"Will you give this note to Fanny for me?"

"What have you said in it?"

"All I have said is to ask her not to come over to me tonight."

"Have you told her what has happened?"

"No!"

Amy walked in silence, evidently thinking what she should do. I imagine she had intended to crow vigorously over Fanny, but my warning had made her begin to reconsider this. As we walked we approached the stable, and Amy, who had been twisting my note to Fanny between her fingers suddenly looked up.

"Oh! Here we are at the stable," said she.

"Yes," said I, reading her thoughts, "but, Amy, dear, I really could not do it now!"

"What nonsense!" she cried, reddening, "I never asked you either, but now, for saying that you shall."

"I really can't, Amy."

"Bosh! come, Captain Devereaux, I wish to be fucked now, this instant. It may be my last chance, if so much depends upon Fanny, as you seem to think. I will not throwaway a chance. Come into the stable at once and do what you are bid."

"I will go into the stable, Amy, but you will see I speak nothing but the truth when I tell you that I am not able to fuck you now."

I went in.

"Now," said Amy, "explain yourself."

"Here is the best explanation possible," said I, undoing my braces and letting down my trousers, "look, and see if you can get that into your cunt, Amy."

Amy raised my shirt and saw me in a state that she had never contemplated as possible. My prick hung dead and nerveless, my balls were loose in an elongated and relaxed bag, everything denoted the most marked fatigue.

"You are, foxing!" cried Amy angrily, stamping her foot. "Make it stiff at once! Do you hear me! Ah! Do! Captain Devereaux!" she continued in an imploring tone of voice. "Don't be so unkind to me."

I heard her with a mixed sentiment of amusement and pain.

I was amused at her thinking I was my prick's master and able to make it stand or not, at my pleasure, and pained that I was really unable to comply with her wishes and fuck her, for I felt if I could gratify her now she would be in good humor, and more inclined to spare Fanny, and so soften down the announcement of her triumph.

"Amy dear! I would if I could. But the want or sleep and the painful anxiety about Fanny that I have been under all day, have killed me; but try if you can make it stiff yourself! I really am not foxing. I should very much like to fuck you, if I could. Here. Let us lie down in this grass, and while you try what you can do with your hands, I will feel your nice, soft cunt."

We lay down. Amy cuddled up to me, looking at times into my face with a keen glance as if to see whether I was deceiving her or not, whilst she handled my prick and my balls, in the most voluptuously exciting manner possible. It was of no use whatever I was in a state of mental and bodily prostration, and my prick remained as limp as ever, though my balls gradually grew up in a tighter bunch than they had been in before Amy's gentle fingers titillated them.

After about ten minutes of these mutual caresses I with drew my hand, wet with her frequent spendings, from between Amy's lovely thighs, and said:

"I am afraid we must give up the idea of it, Amy. My prick is too dead. Too tired."

"Too obstinate and too abominably selfish, you mean," said Amy in great anger, "take that for the sulky beast you are," and with these words addressed to my prick, she suddenly gave it a stinging slap with her hand, not only hurting it considerably, but making my poor balls throb with pain.

"Oh, Amy! Oh, my! You have hurt me."

Now if a woman has a tender place in her heart for anything in this world, she has for a man's prick and balls. Let my readers think for a second, and I think nearly all must recollect instances where women of their acquaintances have heard with apparent indifference of men being mutilated in any particular, but have shown the very greatest sympathy and have shuddered when they have been told of the mutilation of prick or bans, or both. Amy was no exception.

"Oh! Captain Devereaux! I really did not mean to hurt it so much. Oh, poor thing, poor thing. She hung over me, as I had turned on to my face, for I had some extremely sharp pains in my groin, and a dull heavy pain at the lower part of my belly. I felt Amy's hand groping along my right groin, and at first I resisted a little, but a sharp bit of grass happening to run into my prick, I made a sudden movement, which enabled her to get at what she wished to caress and soothe, but to my astonishment, for I had no sensation to ten me the fact, she cried out:

"Oh, Captain Devereaux! It's stiff. It's stiff. It's standing beautifully."

The pain I had endured had been sharp enough, but it passed like a sudden twinge of toothache. Amy's exclamation seemed to drive it away and I could now feel that I had indeed a glorious stand. I felt so grateful to Amy that I turned and caught her in my arms and kissed her before I pushed her on her back, and got between those beautiful rounded, snowy thighs, which she uncovered for me with immense haste and speed as though she feared the stiffness of my prick might go as suddenly as it had come.

It was a lovely fuck! A completely glorious luck! and at the end, whilst I was still lying with my motte hard pressed to her which leaped and jumped, and whilst I still enjoying the throbbing and squeezing, and cuking of her deliciously excited and melting little cunt, I could not help saying:

"Oh, Amy, try and reconcile Fanny and we will have many another like this."

The episode did me considerable good. It broke the current of my thoughts. It raised the tone of my body. It gave me more hope towards Fanny, for I left Amy in a much more amiable mood than I had found her in, and my limp prick, and the idea of what might happen should Colonel Selwyn discover that I fucked Fanny, were things both new to her, and I was sure were going to do their work on her mind. Fanny would be angry, grieved, and more or less destroyed by hearing the news, but bad as that would be it was not so bad, as if added to all this, was the stinging and triumphant insults which I felt certain Amy, in true sisterly fashion, had prepared for her.

Since I had become Station Staff Officer, I had been relieved from the necessity of dining at the mess of my regiment, so that I used my freedom in this respect pretty largely, and seldom dined here two nights running. The truth is, I disliked Mess dinners more than I can express, and I do not think anybody can like them as a continuance. This night, however, I was glad to go and sit at dinner with my brother officers, for their chat helped me to pass away some of those hours which I felt to be purgatorial, between the house of last fucking Amy and that when I was to meet Fanny.

On my way home I looked in at the Colonel's Bungalow. I knew I had better take the bull by the horns, and I rather expected to find Fanny ill or unable to see me. But no, there the sweet girl was, glad and happy—she was all too evidently still unaware of my terrible infidelity. It was clear, too, that Amy had not given her my note, for poor Fanny took the opportunity of whispering to me that she was quite "well" and that she had a lot to tell me when she came over. Amy was a perfect study. She acted her part to perfection. She was just exactly the same Amy she had been, to all appearances, before Fanny went to Rampur, and before there had been any question of my fucking her. I warn Amy's husband, should he read these pages, that he might as well not attempt to keep her under watch and guard. If Amy ever takes a fancy for some young fellow, she will have him and her way, and that right under her husband's nose, and he won't know it. Her manner to me was astounding. Since the moment she had got me in the trap between her thighs, she had been so unlike the old Amy, that the sudden assumption of a driving, domineering, hard hearted, willful woman's manner had stunned me, as much as her extraordinary behaviour. She had had me quite under a spell in consequence. She had jumped upon and crushed me by the suddenness of the blow. But tonight she had so completely resumed her old manner, appearance and tone, that, but for the too, too sweet reminiscences of her ofttimes visited cunt, I should have imagined I must have dreamt I had fucked her, and not that I had really had her something like fifty different times during the past week. Alas! My prick which had refused to stand that afternoon for her until she had beaten it, did what it had never done in the old days before Fanny went to Rampur, those old days, which though only separated from these new times by a week, seemed so long, long ago, for it stood stiffly the moment Amy came near me. In the old days that irrepressible organ would have remained quiescent until Fanny's approach would have aroused him to assume his grand proportions, but tonight it grew stiff the moment it perceived the nearness of Amy's cunt.

I went home then, knowing that the storm had yet to burst, for I imagined that when she and Amy retired for the night, Amy would surely tell her all, and the first effect of her grief and indignation would be to make her take a vow never to see me again.

But instead of going to bed I sat up. My head buzzed with fatigue and excitement, but tired as I was, I knew that if I did go to bed I should not sleep. Whilst I was thus seated in a half dreamy and truly painful state of mind, I got a shock which woke me to life and action in a moment, for I heard the swift, light steps of Fanny coming down the verandah. Before I could rise she was in my room, into which she burst, as if life, or all that was worth having, depended upon the swiftness of her movements. On seeing me she stopped dead. A glance at her face told me she was in possession of the news. Poor Fanny! Ah! Gentle reader! Tell me, do you know anything in this world as hideously painful, so agonizing to the mind and heart, as the discovery that the person in whom your confidence is placed, on whom all your love, devotion, heart and soul are raised, is false, a traitor! Fanny had never loved before she loved me. With the whole heartedness of youth she had given herself to me, heart, soul, body, unreservedly, and she trusted in me as in her God.

For a moment she stood looking at me, her lovely eyes expressing all the pain she felt, but at the same time a kind of hesitancy to believe that what she now knew was real and not a dreadful dream. Her lips were parted as though to speak, but no words came. Her bosom heaved tumultuously, and her lovely firm breasts seemed as though the struggle going on within her would make them burst their points through the bodice. I had seen Fanny in a passion many times, but never in such a state as she now appeared in. Her look fascinated me. She seemed to be trying to read my inmost soul through my eyes, and I remained dumb.

"Oh! Charlie!" she cried, all of a sudden, "tell me it is not true! Oh! why did you do it? Oh! I never thought that my Charlie would have been so-so-so-cruel to me!"

She turned to the table next which she stood, and laying her arms upon it, bent her lovely head down to them and commenced to sob and weep violently without noise.

This was awful. I had never been so tried in all my life before. I jumped up and approaching her sat by her side, not daring to lay a hand upon the girl, whom I felt I did not dare to touch with my polluted fingers.

For fully five minutes we stayed thus, until Fanny, raising her face, all wet with tears, and once more flushed, turned her streaming eyes upon

CHARLES DEVEREAUX

me, and staggering forward fell into my arms. I caught her in them. I kissed that face all lovely still though quivering with the devouring pain she felt, and Fanny let me do so, let me press her to my bosom, let me draw her towards my chair, and let me take her into my lap, where I held her tenderly lying against me, whilst she still weeped and sobbed.

Suddenly she rose into a more upright position, and looking at me, said, "Why don't you speak to me? You are cuing too! What are you crying for?"

"Because, Fanny darling, I can't help it! I can't see you, the girl I love, in such dreadful grief and not feel sorry."

"I am a fool for coming," she said. "Let me go! I'll never, never, never, speak to you again!"

"Stay!" I cried, holding her. "Stay Fannie! You have heard only one side of the story. It is only fair to me to hear mine. I swear to you that I never had the remotest idea of being unfaithful to you, and that it was not until I was actually in Amy's cunt that I knew it was not you whom I was fucking."

Fanny loved me. That is the only explanation of the patience with which she heard me. In her heart, that heart so dreadfully wounded, she wished to find the palliation of my sin. Had her pride only been wounded, she would never, or could, have forgiven me, but love covers a multitude of sins, and Fanny heard my story, not only with patience, but with eagerness.

With passions as strong as mine, with a cunt as susceptible of pleasure as my prick, she could understand me, when I said that the first fuck with Amy over, I felt it impossible to tear myself away from a cunt so fascinating, so blooming as that between Amy's thighs; and as I proceeded and told my story, in such a way as to make it more than evident that, much as I appreciated her sister's cunt, I did not love Amy, whereas my whole soul was bound up in her, she at last threw her arms round my neck and kissed me, and then wept again, but without that violence which was all the more dreadful because subdued, which marked the first outbreak of her passion. For hours we sat thus talking. Fanny quite understood her position. She loved me too much to be able to carry out her passionately expressed threat never to speak to me again, yet it was but too evident that she must consent to share—me with Amy at once, and with Mabel later on. She herself remembered what she had said about concubines and, with a sorrowful smile, she congratulated me on having now three really pretty ladies of my harem. As she grew more cheerful, so did I, and demurring at last on an act, I undid the lace of her bodice and uncovered her lovely breasts, which I once more devoured with my lips, in a manner so full of passion that the poor girl all but fainted from excess of emotion. Snatching the lovely bubbies from my eager lips, she put her mouth to mine and beginning with the top button of my trousers she undid them all, one by one, until, reaching the last, she inserted her little hand and, pulling up my shirt, took possession of my stiff and impudent prick, which looked her boldly and unblushingly in the face.

"Yes," she cried, "it is not my Charlie, but you who are the traitor. Oh! you villain!"

Hard words, but Oh! what soft caresses. I am afraid my prick, like Galileo, paid no attention to her speech, but was too excited for that dearest little cunt, which he had been the first to open. Happy reconciliation. Fanny in a few moments more stood in her naked beauty before me, and in another moment had all but forgotten the agonies of the recent hours in the convulsions of the delirious pleasures I presented.

Sugdaya awoke us. That lovely traitress was delighted to find us naked in bed together. Fanny would have quarreled with her, but she had listened to me and had swallowed Sugdaya with her other inevitable griefs, and our last luscious fuck took place under the eyes of that lovely native girl, and born procuress, who was to be so useful to me in finding me sweet cunts, besides her own, during the next three or four years.

Like Amy, Fanny laughed the cobra to scorn. She saw it in the bottle, but, though she at once believed my story, she only said that the fact of my having killed it, and not of its having killed me, showed that it was intended that I should fuck Amy, otherwise had I been bitten and died, it would have shown that I had been rudely punished. All the same she said it would be better if in future I were to come over to her house, as now, of course, Amy would not be in the way.

Now reader, did you think for one moment that things could have turned out so, did not our beloved Goddess, Venus, stand on my side? I saw her divine and beneficent hand in every turn of our amatory purvey, and never had she a more ardent priest than me. For I did my utmost never to lose a chance of my making her holy alters between my lovely "concubines" thighs smoke with the incense of my offerings.

Oh! those exquisite nights! Those revels when like a God of olden times I sported with my naked nymphs, passing from between the arms of one to between the thighs of the other, the change from one cunt to the second gave me fresh life and greater strength! There was certainly an increase of voluptuous pleasure and delight, but alas! the purity and depth of love which had existed between Fanny and me suffered. We never again were, or could be, to one another what we had been.

And now it remains but for me to show you how, at last I filled up the cup of Mabel's joy, by fucking her, and then I will close the history of my association with those three beautiful and delicious Selwyn cunts.

Neither Fanny nor Amy seemed to be in the least degree anxious that I should fuck Mabel. This was natural enough so far as Fanny was concerned, but Amy, as my dear reader may remember, had made it a sine qui non that Mabel was to have her share of my prick and balls. Experience, however, began to teach her that a whole loaf is better than a half a one, and a half loaf better than the third of one. So I never heard anymore from her of the obligations I was under to fuck Mabel. But it was impossible to prevent Mabel's knowing of my nightly visits to her father's bungalow, and what went on there in consequence, and I have little doubt she often witnessed scenes of joy, in which she burned to play her part, from behind the purdah. Besides, I am certain that Sugdaya, who felt no scruples, incited her to claim her share, and this is how she got it.

One lovely day in December, this is in the delightful cold weather, I was preparing to go out to pay some visits, (among others to our new Padre's wife, Mrs. Paul, of whom much more will be told in my third series), when I saw Mrs. Soubra tie hurrying up from the servants' house. I guessed that the Colonel must have come over for a morning fuck, and, as I wanted to see him, I thought I would wait until he had taken his pleasure, and then I would do so. Although it was an understood thing between us that he was at liberty to fuck Mrs. Soubratie whenever he liked in my house, yet as a rule we did not meet on those occasions, so that unless I actually saw him between her thighs, or saw Mrs. Soubratie pass my door, I rarely knew the exact moment these pleasant meetings were taking place.

I waited therefore seated in my chair. I had not been sitting more than a minute when Mabel appeared, bursting with laughter, which it took all her efforts to prevent exploding out loudly. Coming on tip-toe to me she whispered:

"Oh! Captain Devereaux! Come here! Come here!"

I rose. She took my hand, and leading me into my bed room she took me to the door, in which was a window covered with a thin muslin blind, looking into the room, and on to the bed, on which the Colonel always fucked Mrs. Soubratie. There of course, I saw, as did Mabel, the Colonel about half way through a nice, fat fuck, and Mabel, delighted beyond description, feasted her eyes on her father's splendid prick, passing, in measured cadence, in and out of, up and down, the brown cunt of Mrs. Soubratie. The sight was too voluptuous, especially as Mabel was there, not to effect me greatly, and I unbuttoned my trousers, and put my now burning prick into that delighted girl's burning hand, whilst I raised her petticoats and caressed the little cunt, now well covered with curly locks, which immediately responded to my caresses, with such an overflow that is surprised me. Still attracted powerfully by seeing her father's glistening member disappearing and reappearing, as he fucked Mrs. Soubratie in his solid fashion, and his balls, those huge balls, balancing as they swung backwards and forwards, Mabel quietly moved her hand up and down my prick, until a sudden thrill of pleasure round its collar warned me, that if she continued so doing I should spend, all the more also, because of sympathy, the Colonel being now at the vigorous short digs, would come to the assistance of Mabel's hand. I therefore kept her hand quiet, until the Colonel having finished, and Mrs. Soubratie having made her salaam and left the room, the show had come to an end.

"Well! Mabel!" said I, When the Colonel had walked off with that jaunty side step he always adopted after a good fuck, "You came in the very nick of time to see that!"

"Yes!" said she, looking at my prick, and gently feeling my balls, which she had foraged for and got out, "Sugaday told me I should see something, if I came over here now. I thought she meant this," she continued, looking up at me with a smile, "but I fancy she must have meant that I should see Papa with Mrs. Soubratie."

"She may have meant both, Mabel dear! But take care, child! You will make me spend if you move your hand like that!"

"Oh! What fun that would be! Let me? Do! Captain Devereaux. I should so like to see it!"

"Well!" said I, shivering with pleasure, "all right, dear, but let me take off my trousers first, or they will be spoilt."

I saw that the time had come. This was Mabel's hour and I shut my bedroom door and bolted it.

CHARLES DEVEREAUX

"Now Mabel! Take off your frock, and stays, and stockings, and we will go to bed together."

"Oh no!"

"Oh yes!"

"Oh, how delightful! Oh, you good, good, good Captain Devereaux!" she cried in an ecstasy of joy, "but let us go regularly to bed and take off all our clothes."

"Very well!" said I, laughing, and in another couple of minutes we were both as naked as we were born. Mabel was very pretty. Like Fanny and Amy, she had a very nice, pure, even white skin. Her limbs still required a little more flesh to give them all the roundness that is so desirable, but her little bubbies were really charming, and her plump motte had quite as much hair on it as Fanny's. If her nudity charmed me, my nakedness pleased her immensely, though she had often enough handled my prick and balls, she said this was the first time she had ever really seen them.

Now, it is chilly enough in the cold weather to make one's skin rather want clothing, so I picked up Mabel, laid her on the bed, and, getting in myself, pulled up the bed clothes, well to our chins, and there we lay cuddled together. Mabel had again got hold of my prick, which she was working in such a way that I knew I must spend immediately if she did not leave off.

"Wait! Mabel, you will really make me spend all over you."

"I shall like that!" she cried. "I should like to see what a man's spend is like."

"Very well," said I, laughing, "then see."

I threw down the bedclothes and almost at the same moment let fly a torrent of spend which I could restrain no longer. Mabel shrieked, for the first jet struck her full in the face, the second under the chin, the third splashed against her bubbies, and the remaining jets played on to her belly, and finally to her bush, as I took care so to hold her hand as to give her the benefit of every drop.

"Oh! That was nice!" cried Mabel. "What a lot! How creamy it is! only thicker! but you must have quite emptied your balls!"

"Oh no! There's lots in them Mabel, and when, in a minute or so, I fuck you, they will go on making more for you."

I wiped the streaming lovely body of my bedfellow, as I spoke, and expecting to find a rather obstinate maidenhead, I thought it wise to begin with her as soon now as possible, so that by the time I next spent, she would have had a good fuck.

Judge of my surprise, on taking my position between her open thighs to meet with absolutely no resistance! There was not only not the ghost of a maidenhead, but it was evident to me, that the cunt I was in had been most thoroughly well opened. If Mabel had been already fucked, who had done it? I made no remarks, however, for I was too much amused, and delighted with her expressions of delight and pleasure. Like Fanny and Amy, her cunt was a perfect fountain, easily made to play by the movements of my prick within it, and Mabel made me laugh with her continuous, "There I go again!" but when I came to the short digs, and in my turn inundated her lovely little cunt with a sea of spend, Mabel clutched me with all her force to her convulsed and quivering body, and exclaimed, "Oh! how much better a real prick is than a cucumber!" The cat was out of the bag! A cucumber!

The first fuck over, Mabel told me amidst her rapid kisses and never-ending caresses that Sugdaya had taught her how pleasant a sensation could be produced by a three-quarter ripe banana, with its peel half removed. From a small banana she had progressed to one of larger size, always to the detriment of her maidenhead, until one day, seeing a very nice smooth cucumber, the straightness and size of which struck her as being peculiarly adapted for her experiments, she picked it, went indoors and finished off with a vegetable what, but for that, would have been decided by my prick of flesh! Mabel was a lascivious little girl, a grand poke. Like Lizzie Wilson her mission in life is to fuck. The dear reader will not be surprised to hear that she joined that select number of fair women, who, nominally "kept" by wealthy lovers take delight in relieving the pains of numerous adorers, in which alike the winding path of intrigue, and the voluptuous pleasures to be gathered. like flowers along their shaded ways. If Mabel's present ties were legitimate she would be the Duchess of——. To her was the glory of having the first to give palpable proof of the ecstasies of fucking to no less a personage than one of the Royal Princes.

Neither Fanny nor Amy showed any ill will toward Mabel on account of our mutual participation in the sacrifice, and up to the last night of their stay in Fackabad, these amiable girls were poked by me, sometimes in company, sometimes singly, but always in company unless "illness" prevented.

In March of the following year, just twelve months after I had taken Fanny's maiden-head, the girls went home to England, the Colonel having retired from the service.

Our parting was extremely painful. We made exchanges of locks of hair from our respective bushes, and, so eager were the girls for mementos of mine that it was months before my prick grew out of a forest as thick, or rather as long as it was when first I pressed it against that of Lizzie Wilson at Nowshera.

The End

bookfinity & MINT EDITIONS

Enjoy more of your favorite classics with Bookfinity,
a new search and discovery experience for readers.
With Bookfinity, you can discover more vintage
literature for your collection, find your Reader Type,
track books you've read or want to read,
and add reviews to your favorite books.
Visit www.bookfinity.com, and click on
Take the Quiz to get started.

Don't forget to follow us
@bookfinityofficial and @mint_editions